An author of more than nine ~~~~~~~~~~~
adults with more than sevent, ~~~~~
Janice Kay Johnson writes about love and family and pens books of gripping romantic suspense. A *USA Today* bestselling author and an eight-time finalist for the Romance Writers of America *RITA*® Award, she won a *RITA*® Award in 2008. A former librarian, Janice raised two daughters in a small town north of Seattle, Washington.

A *USA Today* bestselling author of over a hundred novels in twenty languages, **Tara Taylor Quinn** has sold more than seven million copies. Known for her intense emotional fiction, Ms Quinn's novels have received critical acclaim in the UK and most recently from Harvard. She is the recipient of the Readers' Choice Award and has appeared often on local and national TV, including *CBS Sunday Morning*. For TTQ offers, news and contests, visit tarataylorquinn.com

HIGH MOUNTAIN TERROR

JANICE KAY JOHNSON

A FIREFIGHTER'S HIDDEN TRUTH

TARA TAYLOR QUINN

MILLS & BOON

First Published in Great Britain 2023
by Mills & Boon, an imprint of HarperCollins*Publishers* Ltd
1 London Bridge Street, London, SE1 9GF

www.harpercollins.co.uk

HarperCollins*Publishers*
Macken House, 39/40 Mayor Street Upper,
Dublin 1, D01 C9W8, Ireland

High Mountain Terror © 2023 Janice Kay Johnson
A Firefighter's Hidden Truth © 2023 TTQ Books LLC

ISBN: 978-0-263-30739-9

0823

MIX
Paper | Supporting
responsible forestry
FSC™ C007454

This book is produced from independently certified FSC™ paper
to ensure responsible forest management.

For more information visit: www.harpercollins.co.uk/green

Printed and Bound in the UK using 100% Renewable Electricity at
CPI Group (UK) Ltd, Croydon, CR0 4YY

HIGH MOUNTAIN TERROR

JANICE KAY JOHNSON

Chapter One

In her rare glimpses of the sky, Ava Brevick marveled at the stunning blue, made richer by the contrast with snow, ramparts of rock and the deep green of the forest cloaking the North Cascades Mountains.

Picking her way among the infuriating tangle of willow and alder near the river and having to watch for the fallen trees and rocks hidden beneath the snow, Ava hadn't been able to maintain anything close to the pace that was possible on a stretch where snow lay smoothly on top of a trail maintained during the summer. Her snowshoes felt clumsy right now, almost more trouble than they were worth. This was nothing unexpected; even during the kinder time of year, most of the Cascade Mountain wilderness didn't welcome two-legged intruders.

After unsnagging her snowshoe from a whip thin stem that was part of a thicket she thought was alder, she paused for the second time in the past ten minutes to look cautiously behind her.

She'd been alone out here in this snowy expanse for two days now. Trails in the park were closed during winter—and May was still very much winter high in the mountains. A respected wildlife and wilderness photographer, Ava had been dropped by helicopter to work her magic, seeking the extraordinary moment when sun slid through a snow-laden branch or glanced off water dancing between the ice and rocks. She hoped to capture some good photos of the animals that weren't hibernating—or would be emerging from hibernation anytime. Not given to feeling lonely, she loved what most people would say was profound silence, but which to her ears was filled with the crack of a far-off branch, the whisper of wind, the occasionally ominous settling of ice and snow on steep slopes, the high cry of a bird or the scream of a small creature that had just become prey.

She'd already captured enough images she thought would delight the organization that had funded this expedition, but planned to set up another blind this evening in hope more nocturnal animals would wander her way. There were plenty of those deep in the Cascade Mountains, from mountain beavers and porcupines to the red fox, as well as the northern saw-whet owl she had yet to glimpse.

For herself, the only predators to fear in these mountains up by the Canadian border were grizzlies, reintroduced into the Cascades some years back, or an unusually aggressive black bear. She felt pretty confident neither would be emerging from hibernation just yet. Mountain lions could be a threat on rare occasions; she kept a sharp eye above when she passed below a tall rock upon which one might crouch. But a world without other humans was one where she relaxed her usual wariness.

What unnerved her now was the suspicion she *wasn't* alone out here anymore. It was like walking through a dark alley, certain you heard footsteps behind, except they stopped when you did…only, a fraction of a second too late. Someone was behind her, and fleeing would do no good. She couldn't exactly hide, given the conspicuous track she left in the snow, and if she parted from the almost-path following the bank, she wouldn't be able to bull her way through the rampant growth. Unfortunately, the dense vegetation kept her from seeing who might be back there.

She had heard a helicopter yesterday, although she didn't see it and had no reason to think it had landed. When the sound of the rotors had faded until silence reclaimed the wilderness, she'd dismissed any worry. Park rangers might keep an eye on the land they guarded with an occasional flyover.

But if it *had* dropped someone off, it had been a distance away, and how had he—or *they*—gotten close enough behind her that she heard the swish-swish of snowshoes and thought she'd gotten a glimpse of movement? And no, there weren't a lot of alternate choices of paths around here, not with the steep flank leading up to a sharp peak on her one side and the rock-and-ice-strewn river to her other.

If she stopped, would he? If she decided to turn around to go back, would he nod and politely let her pass?

She was being ridiculous; why would anyone want to sneak up on her?

She didn't know whether to be glad or sorry that the trail was parting away from the river now and climbing above a jumble of huge boulders deposited by long-ago slides or avalanches, now surrounded by a clump of evergreens she identified as western red cedar, Sitka spruce and hemlock. Sunlight ahead dazzled her eyes as she emerged into the open.

The way was easier here, and she achieved a smooth stride in her snowshoes even as she continued to gain elevation and evaluated this open bowl of land. Now she had another cause for nerves: avalanche danger was high in this country, and it looked as if the trail led her across a curved, open slope she'd guess slanted at a forty-or forty-five-degree angle. She didn't have an awful lot of experience with winter dangers, but anyone with common sense could see that the long-broken tree trunks poking jaggedly out of the heavy snow weren't a good sign. An avalanche had plunged down this chute in the not so distant past. And yes, the warming conditions—although the day felt damn cold to her—contributed to the danger.

Still, she could see a clear line with the snow lying differently where the summer trail stretched across the way ahead. A single person stepping lightly wouldn't put any significant stress on the weight of snow, ice and rocks higher up.

Except now she felt exposed because of that uneasy feeling that she was being pursued.

A couple of minutes later, Ava couldn't resist stopping and turning. She'd been right. There he was, just emerging from the trees near the frozen river bank, moving fast and with surprising grace, climbing effortlessly to close the distance between them. She saw it was a big man wearing a dark green parka and carrying a huge pack. Only three or four hundred yards separated them.

Foolish instinct said to run, but her attention was abruptly jerked away from him when, out of the corner of her eye, she spotted movement high on the forested ridge across the river from her. To her shock, in an open stretch that had to be the result of a wildfire, a group of men were silhouetted against the blue sky. To her naked eye, they were nothing but small figures that didn't belong there, at least this far north. There was no trail heading down that ridge, summer or winter, Ava was quite sure of that. What's more, they were moving southbound, strung out, picking their way slowly. On snowshoes? She couldn't tell.

Habit had her lifting her camera with the enormous lens that she always had ready hanging around her neck. She snapped off the cap and zeroed in on them, until she saw them as if they were startlingly near, if still very small. They all wore white, including their packs. Or something like white capes draped over the packs? Most had carriers of some kind slung over their shoulders, too, although those were black. Could the group be skiers dropped off by helicopter? She couldn't imagine that kind of commercial venture was permitted within the national park. Besides, they were nowhere near an elevation high enough to be above the tree line. No slope *could* be skied in this vicinity, and she was pretty sure there wasn't one on the other side of the ridge, either.

Suddenly apprehensive, she stared at the sharp image of the man in the lead. Distant as he was, even through her lens, she was shocked to see that he held a rifle, one with a shape that had become all too familiar from constant news reports about mass shootings and war. That had to be something like an AK-47, not a typical hunting rifle—and, anyway, hunting was banned in the national park.

Not even sure why she was doing it, she took photos, moving from one man to the next. A couple of them wore what were probably fleece balaclavas. Several didn't, or had pulled them down. Maybe the sun felt warmer up there, she thought in some distant part of her mind. Those faces she saw clearly, and she photographed them without conscious thought.

Several of them had come to a stop while she studied them. At the same instant, she saw the glint of sun off glass and knew someone up there was looking back at her.

Men carrying automatic weapons, men who shouldn't be where they were, were looking at her.

She hastily let the camera drop and snatched up her poles. Apprehension made her want to turn around and race back toward the trees, nearer if she went back instead of forward, except the stranger was closing in fast on her now.

Go, she thought.

She broke into a near run, wishing futilely that she was on cross country skis instead of the far clumsier and slower snowshoes, but that had never been possible in this difficult terrain.

Go, go, go!

ZACH REEVES HAD spent the past couple of hours speculating on who could be out here in the remote wilderness he'd expected to have to himself. He'd looked forward to cutting his own tracks in the snow.

Call him selfish—he'd *wanted* to be alone. The whole point of this expedition had been to escape the pressures he felt from coworkers, neighbors and crowds at the mall or competing with him for a corner table at the café. After ten years as a spec ops warrior, he wasn't adjusting well to normal life.

Life on the military base between operations had been fine, if not his favorite. He'd always managed during his rare visits home to Minnesota where his sister and brother lived. Now, he almost wished he'd gone to work as a Washington state patrolman or sheriff's deputy who patrolled miles of roads instead of the job he'd taken as a detective for the Whatcom County Sheriff's Department. The work was more interesting, but on patrol he'd have been covering a lot of empty country in the rural county, likely going hours at a time without having to interact with anyone.

This was Zach's vacation, damn it. He'd sought solitude and found a way to achieve it. It was bad enough that he had company, but what in *hell* was a woman doing out here alone?

Given the hefty pack she carried, it had taken him a while to realize the snowshoer ahead of him was female, but he no longer had any doubt. How had she gotten into this remote area, unreachable by road at any season or by trail in what was still winter in the North Cascades? Who did she think would bail her out if she got into trouble? He sure didn't have cell phone service in this deep vee between a high ridge and a higher mountain. He supposed she might carry a satellite radio, as he did.

He evaluated the white slope above before breaking from the trees to climb after her into a bowl carved in the ridge. He knew an avalanche path when he saw one; in July or August, wildflowers and shrubs would dominate in the sunlight, free of the tree cover he'd been traveling through. He'd have avoided this stretch if he could, but a couple of snowshoers were unlikely to tip the balance to bring the icy monster down on them.

Zach raised his head to see that the damn woman had stopped dead, lifted an enormous camera and was staring up at the ridge above the river. Now what? Zach flicked his gaze the way she was looking, and his muscles locked. His radar jumped into the red.

He hadn't heard a helicopter in the past day since his drop-off. Those men almost had to have crossed the Canadian border to get here, and this route wasn't ever an approved border crossing. Right now, with the border patrol stretched thin and on high alert to watch for a known terrorist sneaking into the country, that group had to have slipped in, taking advantage of the remote countryside that couldn't be adequately monitored. They must have expected to stay cloaked in dense, northwest forest, except that a wildfire had burned that cover in the past year or two.

He had razor-sharp vision. Even without lifting his binoculars, he recognized the weapon the guy at the front carried. A flash of light up there had him blinking; the sun must have reflected off the lenses of binoculars. Had they noticed him yet, or were they watching her?

Either way—

A very faint crack that might have been a gunshot came to him. From this distance, that wouldn't have been a concern, but a flash of fire arced across the sky.

A rocket-propelled grenade. He was racing toward the fool woman in front of him even as he evaluated what he'd seen and knew they hadn't fired directly at her.

No, they had a better way to kill a lone traveler who'd seen them.

An explosive burst came from the slope above the two of them on this side of the river. For one instant, nothing changed but for the white puff where the shell had landed. The sound of a second shot came to him. Before he had a chance to react, an enormous crack began to split open in the surface of a thick layer of snow and ice at the top of the slope, at first moving in slow motion in each direction.

Even before Zach saw the increasing speed the crack spread across the slab, he shouted, "Avalanche! Get out of the way!"

She gave a startled look at him, then up.

A loud *whuump* came from the sliding slope.

He wouldn't get to her, he realized in the compartment of his brain that kept him making logical decisions under fire. Couldn't help her, anyway. None of the old-growth trees with their massive boles had survived in this gully to provide shelter. He wouldn't make it out of the path, either. Farther ahead of him, she might reach the edge of the avalanche zone if she put on the burners.

A boulder ahead provided the only hope. It wasn't large

enough to protect him, he knew, but he saw no other possibilities and raced to throw himself behind it.

Then he curled low, braced his pack against the cold rock and waited for one of the most brutal forces of nature to smash into him.

SHE RAN, cursing the need to lift each foot high to clear the snowshoe from the snow. It was as if she were moving in slo-mo even while the monstrous white slab fractured at what seemed a leisurely pace. She knew, *knew*, that appearances were deceptive. Snatching a quick look, she saw in horror that a mass almost as wide as this open bowl of land was gathering speed as it first slid, then thundered into motion down the slope. One last look at the guy behind her. There he was one instant, the next he vanished behind a boulder. Lucky guy. Her thighs burned, her breath whistled. A roar drowned out everything else.

It hit her like a semitruck on the freeway, slamming into her even as it tossed her, flipped her. A last instinct had her wrenching at the handle on the chest strap of her pack. Then her thoughts became nothing coherent. She had the terrifying sense she was upside down as she saw her snowshoes snatched from her feet to disappear in the white tsunami. Her poles were long gone. Winded, Ava flailed for a grip on anything at all, her hands finding nothing. She had to be screaming, but the sound was too puny to be heard even by her own ears. It was like leaping off an Olympic ski jump and not coming down. Weightless, she was flying, but also being buffeted from every side. It hurt, it hurt, it hurt.

THE NEXT THING she knew, she lay still. Astonishingly, when she shook her head, she saw a sliver of light. Had she lost consciousness? She had no idea. Something was choking her, and she gagged. Her legs felt as if they were encased in concrete that she prayed hadn't quite hardened yet, but her arms—yes, she could move them, although it was a struggle. Her groping hand found a flap of nylon, blue rather than the green of her pack. Avalanche airbag. *Oh, thank God, thank God.* She'd remembered to pull the rip cord. It must have inflated immediately, creating a brightly colored pillow that acted to make her more buoyant, lifting her toward the surface.

She broke through the snow and saw sky. The airbag had worked. Fumbling, she discovered her camera had been whipped around her head, and it was the strap throttling her. Awkwardly, she untwisted the camera strap from around her neck. It was a miracle she hadn't lost it. How damaged it was… Not important.

Now she just had to find a way to crawl free from the hardening snow.

She kicked and flung handfuls of snow away, widening the hole around her shoulders and head. One glove was gone, she saw, but she didn't even feel the cold. That wasn't a good sign, but if she couldn't dig herself out, what was a little frostbite?

It couldn't have taken more than a couple of minutes. It felt like forever before she found herself on her hands and knees, facing downhill. Her pack weighed her down, but the fact that it hadn't been torn from her body had saved her life. Would save her life again. She couldn't whip out a phone and call for help. She hadn't even brought an avalanche beacon, because she'd known that, isolated as she'd be in the back country, no one would come in response. With a sleeping bag, tent, food and more clothes, though, she could survive. She could.

She let out a cry. She was alive, but what about *him*? Ava

had quit caring why he was following her; he was a fellow human being. He'd yelled a warning to her, hadn't he?

She staggered to her feet and looked at the devastation around her, frantically trying to orient herself. She'd ridden the avalanche almost to the end, but what about him? He'd started slightly lower than her, but right in the center of the chute. The boulder. Where was the boulder?

It took her a minute, and that was a minute he couldn't afford. In preparing for a trip in Alaska a couple of years ago, she'd read the horrifying statistics: someone who was really buried would start to lose consciousness in only four minutes from breathing their own carbon dioxide. The odds of surviving even after being dug out decreased dramatically as the minutes ticked by.

There! she thought. All she could see was a faint curve of rock surrounded by the tumble of snow and ice, but that had to be it. She didn't remember seeing any other boulders so high above the river.

She scrambled the distance to it on her hands and feet and even knees.

"Can you hear me?" she yelled.

Nothing. No, something stuck out of the snow. Ava tugged it out. A snowshoe. *Oh, my God.* He had to be near, didn't he?

She called out again, waited for an answer, tried over and over as she dropped her pack and unzipped it with fingers too numb to want to cooperate. She'd bought the airbag at the urging of mountain-climbing friends, but otherwise hadn't planned much for an avalanche.

"I'll be careful," she'd told everyone.

Famous last words.

For whatever reason, she'd added a folding probe to her gear. At last she pounced on it. By accident, she spotted her

other gloves and hastily, gratefully changed. Then she unfolded the long probe, stood and began stabbing it into the
snow. The chances of her finding him weren't good. If he'd
been swept too far to the left or right of the boulder, she
could poke the probe into the snow for days and not find
him. If he was buried too deep...

Ava didn't even want to think about that.

She prayed as she'd never prayed before, and stabbed the
probe repeatedly into the avalanche debris.

Chapter Two

Hell of a thing, to die here and now, on vacation, after surviving countless firefights and bombs, silent raids and HALO jumps from aircraft in every war-torn part of the globe.

Zach's struggles slowed. He might as well be in a casket six feet under for all the good kicking and battering with his shoulders and fists had done. It wouldn't take long to burn up all available oxygen.

His mind drifted. He tried to slow his breaths but knew how useless that was. The woman. Was there any chance at all she'd survived? He hoped so. For all his irritation that she was out in this wilderness where he'd wanted to be alone, she'd moved well, as if she knew what she was doing.

Damn, he was cold. He struggled a little more to prevent himself from freezing solid, even if keeping himself from stiffening up wouldn't do a thing to change his fate.

Something poked him. Had to be his imagination, unless...? It poked again. And then he'd swear he heard a voice calling to him, even if he couldn't make out words.

"I'm here!" he bellowed, the effort causing darkness to swim in front of his eyes.

Then all he could do was lie there and wait: for rescue, or for death.

AVA SCRAMBLED BACK to her pack and pulled out the folding shovel. Back at the probe she'd left standing in the snow, she started to dig. The probe might have struck a rock or a solid chunk of ice. It could have been anything. But she gambled. If this was him, she might get to him in time. Otherwise—

No, she had to believe this was her fellow snowshoer.

She flung snow to each side, her muscles burning. Digging as if her life depended on it, only it was *his* life instead.

Dizziness claimed her; she needed to rest, to take some deep breaths, but any pause could condemn him to death. *If it's him.*

The shovel scraped across dark green. Her heart expanded in relief. She threw herself onto her stomach and scooped snow out of the hole with her hands. He wasn't moving, he wasn't moving... Oh, God, which way was his head? If she resumed using the shovel, she might hurt him.

She realized she was talking to him, or maybe pleading with him. *Be alive. Don't leave me alone out here*—even though fifteen minutes ago she hadn't minded being alone at all.

With what had to take massive effort, he wrenched himself upward and gave his head a shake that scattered snow every which way. He gasped for breath.

"Are you all right?" Ava asked. Begged. "Are you all right?"

He turned his head enough so that he could see her. Snow-frosted brown hair, glassy eyes, a day or two's growth of beard on a strong face. Frozen blood in his hair and down his cheekbone and jaw.

"*God.* How did you find me?" Before she could answer, he shook his head again. "I'm stuck. I can't feel my legs."

"I'll keep digging." She calculated. "At an angle so I don't hit you."

He watched with what she guessed was unusual and maybe worrisome passivity.

Something made her look over her shoulder and up to the ridge that reared above the river. If those men had seen the avalanche, they might be scrambling down even now to help. Or…maybe not. Either way, she didn't see anything, and it would surely take them hours to a full day to get this far.

She dug as hard and fast as she could, until he grunted and she realized the blade of the shovel had scraped over his knee. Now that she could see how his body lay imprisoned, she was able to dig with more confidence. She wasn't even aware of the soreness in her shoulders and upper arms anymore, or of the sharper pain shooting down her spine.

The man groaned, planted one hand on the ice to the side of the hole and heaved upward, twisting as he came. Agony flashed across his face. His leg broke free, but it appeared the other one was still trapped.

"You're injured," she said. *Duh*. How could he not be?

"Just get me out," he said from between clenched teeth.

Ava glared at him. "I'm doing my best."

His eyes closed. His voice became grittier. "I know you are."

Okay, foolish to take offense.

Moments later, he was free. He half pushed, half rolled out of the hole. That was the moment when she realized with dismay that *his* pack was nowhere to be seen.

Looking uphill toward the rock, she did see something she'd missed: the other snowshoe, lying on the surface as if he'd casually tossed it aside.

He lay on the uneven surface, his head bare, and shook. As cold as she'd been, now she was sweating, but what she could see of his face was bone white, and he'd clamped his teeth together in a grimace that she felt sure was to keep them from chattering.

"We have to get you warm," she said. Decided. He was way worse off than she was.

She surveyed their surroundings and made herself think. Finding a way to warm him came first, ahead even of assessing his injuries.

Get him off the avalanche path. Pray he was able to walk, even if he had to lean on her to do it. Find a place to set up the tent. Laid out her sleeping bag. Maybe both of them would fit in it. She knew she needed to lie still, evaluate *herself* for injuries, gather herself for whatever needed doing next.

For the moment, she left the probe and shovel both in the snow and pushed herself to her feet. Her pack... There it was. She slung it onto her back again, the weight almost buckling her knees.

"You have to get up," she said. "I'm going to crouch down and help you."

He moved his head in agreement and, with what she guessed took superhuman will, pushed himself to his hands—no, one hand, she saw, his left arm dangled—and knees. She immediately became more aware of his sheer size. It wasn't only that he had to be several inches over six feet tall, but that he was broad. Shoulders, chest, powerful thighs. All of which meant he'd outweigh her by a sizeable amount. Nonetheless, she tucked herself under the crook of his uninjured arm and said, "Okay, let's do it."

They fought their way upright. His weight had her wanting to crumple, but she kept lifting. "That's it," she encouraged. "Upsy daisy."

The man lurched to his feet and his eyes met hers. He

bit out, "Now…what?" before clamping his jaws together again. Shudders rattled his entire body.

"Down, toward those trees. It looks…kind of flat. I have a tent we can set up."

As they staggered, one step at a time, she kept talking without really knowing what she was saying. It hardly mattered; she couldn't imagine he was taking any of it in. The shaking came in waves, receding, then gripping his body again. She tried to time it so they could pause. If he went down, she had to wonder if she'd be able to get him up again.

Finally—*thank you, God, finally!*—they clambered awkwardly off the bottom of the avalanche flow onto snowy ground that was almost flat. Under the protection of evergreens blocking some of the sky, the snow wasn't as deep here as in most places, or they might have foundered.

Ava looked around, her uneasy remembrance of those men on the ridge making her want to find someplace that was out of sight. Yes, there. Low cedar branches hid a shadowy space behind. She steered the man there, pushed aside scratchy branches and finally had to help him lower to a sitting position so she could take off her pack and locate the tent.

When she bought it last winter to replace her old one, she'd almost chosen a bright red one, but now was glad she hadn't. She'd gone with dark green so it didn't stand out in a wild place, where she tried to pass as close to unseen as possible. Seeing that *her* hands were shaking now, too, she still unrolled a tarp and set out the tent. It was the kind that sprang up almost on its own. She also had a pad and sleeping bag that she unzipped.

"We need to take off your boots and some of your clothes," she told the stranger, who nodded jerkily but had to wait until she scooted close enough to untie his boots and

yank them off, hoping she wasn't damaging an already injured knee or something like that. Gloves—they were really
lucky his had stayed on, since he'd never have gotten those
big hands into hers, even assuming she wasn't already wearing her backup ones. The glove had protected a watch, too.
No hat to remove; that was gone. She unzipped his parka,
the same color as her tent, and laid it atop the sleeping bag
for some extra warmth.

Then she eyed the ice clinging to his snow pants and
said, "I think these had better come off, too. I'll put them
between the pad and sleeping bag and maybe they'll warm
up and the ice will melt."

His expression showed no comprehension, but finally he
looked down and nodded. With his one hand he unsnapped
the waist but couldn't handle the zipper. Desperate to get
them both warm—her sweat was making her feel colder by
the second as it dried—Ava had lost all sense of personal
boundaries. She unzipped his pants and, with another effort
on his part, got him onto his one hand and knees again so
she could peel the pants down and urge him to hop/crawl
inside the tiny tent. She shoved the pants under the sleeping
bag and helped him, wearing long underwear and a fleece
top, scoot the rest of the way into the unzipped sleeping bag.

Aching to climb in after him, she listened to the uneasy
voice in her head and made herself find a broken branch,
which she used like a broom to brush away any clear signs
of their trek from the edge of the ice-bound avalanche flow
to their hidden refuge. Since they hadn't been able to go
any distance, finding them wouldn't be hard, but…she'd
done her best.

Only then did she take off her own gloves, boots, stretchy
pants and quilted parka, and remove her fleece hat to pull it

over his head before she lay down beside the big man who seemed worrisomely helpless.

Her parka she bunched to create an initially cold pillow. Zipping up the sleeping bag wasn't easy. She had to practically climb atop him to manage, then found herself pressed tightly against that long, hard, terrifyingly rigid body.

At last, at last, she burrowed her face into the crook between his neck and shoulder, let herself rest for a moment, then slipped her hands up under his fleece top and the waffle weave one that was beneath it. She began to rub his muscled torso with wide, sweeping movements.

"Warm," he mumbled, before he arched in another spasm of the shakes.

Since *she* didn't feel in the least warm, she was even more frightened by how cold he must be.

ZACH HAD BEEN seriously wounded twice in his army career, and he didn't think he'd ever felt as all-around terrible as he did right now. Still, hints of warmth began to penetrate; her heat must have lingered in the hat, and her breath on the bare skin of his neck felt like nirvana.

She was finding a lot of places that hurt as she moved her hands over his torso, but those hands felt deliciously hot, too, and he craved them. Higher, higher, he'd think, then lower. She didn't go quite as low as he really wanted, and he had a moment of wry humor. If he could convince her that was a top-notch way to warm him up... Yeah, probably not.

If he could even imagine getting horny or laughing again, he was probably going to survive, Zach decided.

"You hurt?" he managed to mumble.

Her hands paused. "I...don't really know," she said, sounding perplexed.

He understood. His head felt like a jackhammer had mistaken it for pavement that needed to be broken up. He knew something was very wrong with his shoulder, but other-wise…everything bloody hurt, so how could he identify any particular complaints? Once he was warm again, he decided.

"Your shoulder, or is it your arm…?" the woman said tentatively.

"Shoulder. Dislocated, I think." His damn teeth clattered every time he relaxed his jaw enough to speak. Given the spasms that shook the rest of him, the muscles surrounding his shoulder would be doing the same. Not good.

With a tremor in her voice, she asked, "Do you know how we can put it back into the socket?"

"Hope so, but… I need to get warm first." A vague memory suggested he had the order wrong—there was some reason the reduction should be done immediately—but he couldn't hold on to it.

"Okay." She snuggled closer, if that was possible.

He was able to press his cheek against her head, even though his stubble was probably going to tangle her disor-dered hair. It felt silky, though, and he'd seen some spilling out from beneath her hat when she was digging him out of the ice and snow. *Chestnut*, he thought was the right word. Her driver's license probably described her hair as brown, a lighter shade than his, but mixed in was a hint of something warmer. Red, he thought. It felt thick, warm. He wished he could bury his whole face in that tumble of hair, but sus-pected that wasn't logistically possible.

The movement of her hands slowed. Zach tried to zip his head so he could see her face, but their position made it almost impossible. Her rate of breathing dropped, too. She was falling asleep, he realized. Stress and exhaustion did often lead to a crash. He lifted his good arm enough to wrap it around her, securing her to his side. One of her hands slipped from beneath his shirt and she curled it next to her body, but the other remained splayed on his belly. Warm, comforting. He closed his eyes and wished he could zone out, too, but pain wouldn't allow him to surrender to unconsciousness.

He worried for a few minutes. What if he had internal bleeding? What if *she* did? More than most, he knew people could achieve heroics despite catastrophic injuries. Given how slender she was, the very fact that she'd dug him out quickly enough to save his life was astonishing.

Hell, finding him in the first place was downright miraculous.

Let her sleep, he told himself. *Pay attention in case she starts to struggle to breathe.* He couldn't watch her, not as dim as the light was in the tent, nestled beneath heavy evergreen branches, not to mention how tightly the two of them were squeezed in here. As long as her breathing stayed even, she was okay.

Reality was, he might not be able to do anything to help if she did have a crisis.

Closing his eyes, shutting out the helplessness, he focused on her breathing alone. In, out. The tiny puff of air against his neck. The regularity reassured him, but also freed his mind to wander.

Automatic rifle. Worse, an RPG. Backcountry hikers in the US of A did not carry grenade launchers. He'd blanked both of those memories out since finding himself buried in what could have been an icy grave.

How *could* he have forgotten? Would those bastards be on their way to be sure they had successfully buried the witnesses? Or witness, singular, if they hadn't seen Zach?

Didn't matter; if they made it here, and he guessed anything like a straight line would be impossible, they'd see the huge hole the woman had dug to free him. Had she left any possessions there when she helped him down? Again, did that matter? The hole spoke for itself.

That she'd retained her pack was a miracle itself. Not so much if she'd evaded the avalanche flow in the first place, but he guessed that wasn't the case or she wouldn't have sounded doubtful about whether she was hurt. Did she realize those men had deliberately triggered the avalanche?

Zach wondered, though. He hadn't been all there while she was setting up the tent, but she'd chosen an inconspicuous spot. By chance, because it was a level place she could find? Or because she was trying to tuck them out of sight?

Yeah, his mind wouldn't let up now that worries gathered, and he dealt with the unusual circumstance of not being able to do a damn thing to protect them. He'd curse the fact that he was unarmed because weapons were forbidden in the national park, except his Glock would have been in a pocket in his backpack. The one that could be anywhere beneath the snow and ice.

If at all possible, he needed to go back out onto the avalanche to try to find his pack and snowshoes. He could only hope she'd found her own. They were in trouble if their mobility was that severely limited.

And, hell, did she have enough food in her pack to feed both of them? For how many days? He presumed she at least had a phone that would give them hope of contacting the outside world when or if they emerged from this deep cut between a mountain and a high ridge, but that might be days away. The sat radio he'd carried, on loan from the border patrol, made finding his pack even more essential.

He realized his body had become rigid with tension. Not helping. Focus on her even breathing, the comfort of her supple, female body clasped to his, the lifesaving fact that she did have her pack with a tent, sleeping bag and at least minimal supplies. Without those, he'd be dead, and she wouldn't have had much hope.

Be damn grateful she was so gutsy.

AVA GRADUALLY SURFACED to realize that she must have fallen asleep. That was strange! She never napped, and now to drop off like a baby while she was squeezed into a sleeping bag with a strange man who'd scared her when she first realized he was chasing her down...

Fear tripped down her spine. No, she couldn't have left him to die. That had never been an option. But...now what?

Her body had obviously needed to take a time-out. She extended her senses to feel the entire length of his body, pressed against hers. He hadn't hurt her. He cradled her with one powerful arm. Her hand rested on his bare flesh, beneath his shirt. Right over his heartbeat, she realized, disconcerted. She felt the steady beat along with the tickle of chest hair.

Was *he* asleep? Instinct said no. There was too much tension in that body, and his breathing wasn't slow enough.

Ava cleared her throat. "Are you awake?"

He moved his head. "Yeah. How are you?"

That was a really good question. "Bruised all over," she decided, "and my back hurts, but more like I wrenched it than anything." She wriggled her toes. "Basically okay, I think."

"Good." There was a long pause. "'Upsy daisy'?"

"What?" Were her cheeks heating? "I don't know where I picked that up."

A vibration beneath her hand, breasts and cheek suggested a chuckle.

After a moment, she said, "I feel like I should get up. Except—"

When she broke off, his arm tightened. "We need to talk about what happened, and what we need to do to get out of this alive. We may as well be warm while we do that."

"I need to see your face."

After a pause, his arm relaxed. "Okay."

She squirmed until she could reach the zipper, then pulled it down enough to permit her to escape. Shivering, she took her parka from beneath his head and put it on.

He hadn't moved. Crossing her legs, she looked down at him. Then she swallowed and said, "Who are you? And... why were you following me?"

Chapter Three

"I've been asking myself who the hell *you* are and what you're doing out here on your own," he said with deceptive mildness, "but I don't mind starting. My name is Zach—Zachary—Reeves. I'm on vacation. I had a chance at a helicopter drop so I could enjoy some solitude in the wilderness." He wouldn't tell her yet that his ride had been courtesy of the US Border Patrol. "I was surprised to find out I wasn't alone, after all."

Yeah, that was suspicion in her eyes. Eyes that appeared dark in this light, but he suspected were blue. Bruises discolored one of her cheekbones and her forehead on the same side, but under other circumstances she'd be a beautiful woman, he realized for the first time.

"We must have chosen the same route," he continued. "I came across your tracks yesterday and…" He hesitated, then moved one shoulder. Even that sent a stab of agony through the other, although he was more disturbed by the numbness in his arm. "Was curious, I guess. I was faster than you, so I gained ground."

"Vacation," she said flatly. "Most people go to Honolulu in the winter."

"What are *you* doing here? This backcountry is closed for another couple of months."

"I'm a wildlife photographer. One of the magazines I sell to pulled some strings, and park officials dropped me off and arranged to pick me up again...um, three days from now?" She frowned. "I think. My name is Ava Brevick."

Wasn't familiar to him, but he couldn't remember ever glancing at the photographer's name when he did see photographs of wildlife, however spectacular.

"Well, we have some big problems now," he said bluntly.

Her eyebrows rose. "You think?"

"How did you find your pack?"

"It was still on my back." She reached over to lift at some loose nylon fabric. "I had an airbag, and just long enough before the avalanche hit me to pull on the cord to activate it. It's supposed to help keep you on top, and in this instance it worked."

"What about your snowshoes? Your poles?" He hadn't noticed her camera and asked about that, too.

"My poles and snowshoes are long gone. My camera strap held. In fact, it tried to strangle me." She pulled down her turtleneck to reveal ugly bruises that made it look like she'd been garroted. Carefully covering her neck again, she said, "I did find your snowshoes. They didn't look damaged. I guess I left them out there, but they'll be easy to find."

"Poles?"

Shaken head.

"Maybe if we poke around, we can find my pack."

"We can try," she said doubtfully.

He gave a slight nod to acknowledge her pessimism. Or call it realism. He'd hold off explaining why recovering his pack was so critical.

"You know we didn't set off that avalanche."

She frowned. "You're saying it was just chance that it went while we were in the way?"

"No. Those men you were watching up on the ridge," he said bluntly. "Did you notice the weapons they were carrying?"

"Yes." It was almost a whisper, and she blanched. "I think they saw me. I noticed sun reflecting off glass. It almost had to be the lens of binoculars."

Or the scope on a high-powered rifle. But he didn't say that.

"Probably. They didn't expect to encounter anyone out here. I'm reasonably sure they sneaked across the Canadian border."

The woman—Ava—nodded. "That's what I thought, too. It was so weird seeing anyone up there. A wildfire must have opened up the top of the ridge. Even so, it has to be really difficult terrain."

"They used something like an RPG—a grenade launcher—to set off the avalanche. Whatever they fired was visible crossing the sky. Pretty sure they fired a second one, too, just to be sure. I don't know if they noticed me. Either way, they thought they'd take care of any witnesses."

Ava stared at him for a minute, making him think of an owl blinking in bemusement. "I...almost forgot about them."

"I did, too. We've had more pressing issues."

"Oh, God. You don't think—"

"I don't know," he admitted. "It was smart of you to set up the tent out of sight."

"I was glad it wasn't red."

He tipped his head, but decided not to ask about that.

"And...after you got in the sleeping bag, I went back out and used a broken branch to smooth away our tracks." She made a face. "More or less. So I guess I didn't completely forget them."

"You were smart," he said approvingly. He wished she

hadn't left his snowshoes behind, but did that matter? Little as he liked the idea of either of them spending time in the open, he had to search for his pack.

She gave herself a shake. "You're hurt worse than I am. I should take a look…" In fact, she reached into her pack and pulled out some sterile wipes.

"Like I said, I think my shoulder is dislocated." He hoped that was what was wrong. A dislocation was fixable; shattered bones weren't under the circumstances. Shattered bones might have done nerve damage that would explain the numbness and the weird tingling he felt in his fingertips. If that were so, even if he made it to a hospital, he might have done too much damage for surgical repair to be possible. Even though it was on his weak side, the injury had the potential to end his newfound career.

He held still while she used one of the wipes on his face. Stinging told him there were cuts and scrapes, at the least, but she sat back, looking satisfied. "Anything besides the shoulder?" she asked.

He had one hell of a headache, but why tell her? He'd probably suffered a concussion. There'd been a few moments of double vision, and he was currently nauseated. None of that meant he could afford to lie around waiting to feel better.

"Bruises, like you," he said. "Maybe a cracked rib or two."

"You said you thought we could put your arm back in the socket." The idea clearly made her feel queasy, and he didn't blame her given that she wasn't a medical professional.

The hot coal of pain in his shoulder was making it hard to think, and would surely prevent him doing anything else, though. "I was…a soldier. I've done it for other people a couple of times." And no, he hadn't loved the experience, even though he'd had some medic training. "It works better if you have an assistant, but as it is…"

She took a deep, visible breath and gave a choppy nod. "I'll do whatever I have to do."

His admiration for Ava became something else he didn't let himself examine.

HE ADMITTED THAT they should have done this much sooner, that muscle spasms could prevent the bone from being manipulated back into the socket. He'd *known* that, but in his misery, had pushed the knowledge back.

"On the other hand, I guess you could say we iced it."

Ava gave a small, choked laugh that made his lips twitch.

Hey, he'd have been screwed if he'd been alone, as he'd expected to be.

"Might be easier if I weren't wearing anything, but I'm not about to try to wrestle my shirt off."

"And we can't cut it off, given that none of my clothes would fit you."

"Yeah." He described accomplishing a reduction of a shoulder dislocation as well as he could, keeping it simple. Ideally, he should sit up at about a thirty-degree angle. Maybe they could manage that if she propped her pack behind him. She would have to gently pull, applying traction while also rotating the arm outward until she felt the pop of the ball going back into the socket. It would help if he wasn't screaming. "If there's too much swelling or the muscles object too violently, it might not work."

"Then we'll pack your shoulder with snow and try again later," she said sturdily.

She was quite a woman, he thought again, even as he couldn't help also noticing the delicacy of her bone structure and the firmness of a chin that some would call stubborn. Stubborn was fine by him.

"I wish…" she began, before falling silent.

"You wish?"

"That there was someone else to hold you in place."

That would be ideal, but he'd do what he had to. He blinked against sweat dripping into his eyes. The pain was getting to him. He wanted to get this over with.

"I'm going to bite down on something to keep myself from yelling. Don't want to draw attention."

Her head bobbed. Her eyes were huge as she maneuvered in the small space, inevitably bumping into him a few times and making him wince, to wedge her pack behind him and punch it into a shape that let him half recline.

"Okay?"

"Yeah," he said hoarsely.

Now she half crawled until she was beside him on his bad side, forced to bend over by the curving roof of the small tent.

"One hand here." She gripped his upper arm. "The other on your wrist."

"Yeah. You might want to move down a little so you can pull harder."

She nodded and adjusted her position.

He'd begun to feel like someone waiting for the executioner to do his thing. If this didn't work—if something else altogether was wrong with his shoulder—would he be able to do his part getting them out of this remote country before they starved, froze…or were cornered by men he guessed were terrorists?

Too well armed for mere smugglers, anyway.

I CAN DO THIS.

Ava repeated the few words as if they were a mantra.

Except, wasn't that the concept she already lived by? After years of having next to no control over where she went or how she lived, she'd dedicated herself to changing that. She'd made a success of a career defined by independence. If she could do that, she could do a little thing like this.

She gulped, took a deep breath and began applying pressure, pulling an arm that was easily twice as thick as hers, so muscular that, uninjured, he could probably pick her up with just that arm and toss her over his head.

His back arched. Tendons stood out in his neck, and he bared his teeth around the clean sock she'd offered for him to clench. She didn't dare look into his dark brown eyes, but she knew they'd dilated and never left her face.

Continuing pressure. Rotate outward. You can do this.

It seemed an eternity before she felt and even thought she heard the pop. Ava almost let out a whimper and slumped, but instead followed the remainder of his instructions and gently rotated the arm back toward his body, bent it at the elbow and laid his forearm across his torso.

He shuddered, spit out the sock and swore a few times, creatively.

"Thank God," he finally mumbled.

"It worked." She really hadn't expected it would, Ava was ashamed to realize. Something like that should have been done in a hospital ER, or at the very least by experienced paramedics.

"Yeah." His throat worked. "Pain let up."

"It…can't possibly be fixed that easily."

He grunted. "No. I should wear a sling, but maybe we can figure out how to brace the shoulder. We can't just sit here and wait for rescue."

No. They couldn't.

"You don't have poles, anyway," she pointed out.

"We can make some out of sticks." He frowned, reaching with his good hand to knead the injured shoulder. "If I had my pack, I could jury-rig snowshoes for you. Any chance you carry some cord I could use to tie branches together?"

"I do. It seemed like it might come in handy."

"Good girl." His grin changed a face that had so far seemed grim into one that was both warm and sexy.

"What do you do for a living?" she heard herself ask. Why hadn't it occurred to her to wonder before?

His expression returned to impassive. "I'm a cop."

"A cop." Did she believe him? She wondered again about the chance of him appearing at the same time as those men on the ridge.

"Whatcom County, the northwest corner of the state. Other side of Mount Baker. I'm a detective." He hesitated, watching her. "I got out of the service a year ago. Adjustment to a civilian life isn't as easy as you'd think."

"I've never thought about it." She pushed herself up to an awkward, bent-over position and clambered over his legs. "It's still light. I think I'll go grab everything I left out there. Maybe…maybe I should kind of fill in the hole."

"You're not going alone." He sat up.

"Yes, I am." She hoped he heard the steel in her voice. "If those men show up, they'd just grab you, too. You're not armed." As far as she knew. "If you won't rest *for even a few minutes*—" she leaned hard on that "—you could scout around for some branches that might work to make me snowshoes. I have a pocketknife you can use to cut the branches."

He didn't seem to like her being the one to put herself out there and argued against it, but he had to know she was right. Even if the men who'd triggered the avalanche had continued on their route along the ridge, putting from their mind the two people they'd gone out of their way to bury in snow and ice, Ava and Zach would have a difficult trek out of here with such limited supplies. They had to plan to leave first thing in the morning, and keep moving to the extent of their physical ability. Even fully equipped and in peak condition, they would be looking at a minimum of two to three more nights spent along the way. Now—

They would do the best they could.

"I'm not talking convenience, here," he said, voice clipped. "I have a satellite radio in that pack. We need to be able to call for help, and your phone isn't going to cut it."

He talked some more, although he'd already convinced her. The idea that he might be able to call for help *right this minute*—although she hadn't thought to ask if the thing had any limitations—was compelling.

She did win the argument about who would be going out to search, though. Dressed again, Ava felt like a mouse creeping out of hiding, excruciatingly aware that the cat might be watching her every timid move.

SHE MUST HAVE napped for a surprising length of time as they'd struggled to recover from the avalanche, because the light was already going, and fast. Days were still short in the Pacific Northwest at this time of year, and they were a lot shorter with mountains shadowing the valleys cut deep by rivers formed from glacial runoff.

It didn't take Ava long to return to the gaping hole that could well have been Zach Reeves's grave. Lovely thought. She stood still for a long moment, looking around, listening, but neither saw nor heard any evidence that other human beings were in the vicinity. Apprehension stuck with her, though—crawling up the back of her neck.

She seized the probe first, and began stabbing it into the

much hardened avalanche flow, starting below where she'd found him, then working her way uphill from where he'd ended up. Nothing. She hit hard objects over and over again, but when she uncovered them, all she found were blocks of ice or rocks. Finally, she grabbed his snowshoes, then debated climbing up to see if there was any chance she'd missed seeing her own.

A shiver crawled over her, reminding her how exposed she was, how easily someone from quite a distance away could see her. Say, someone descending the ridge behind her.

Exhaustion already had her shaking. Rested, she could try again in the morning to find his pack. He'd convinced her that radio could be their salvation, and she was scared enough to believe him.

Finally she picked up the shovel and started scraping the snow and chunks of ice she'd dug out of the hole back into it. Her muscles burned and her back protested, but she kept at it until…well, she hadn't one hundred percent disguised the hole, but given how uneven the surface of a fresh avalanche flow was, it probably wasn't visible from very far away.

Zach, she suspected, would have searched longer and harder for his pack, the contents of which would come in really handy above and beyond the radio, but she'd reached her limit. She might have to sit on him to keep him from coming out here to poke and poke in a widening semicircle as darkness fell, but so be it.

She might have to sit on him to keep him from doing it, anyway.

Not that sitting on him would have much effect, she feared; he'd probably just pick her up and set her aside like a toddler who'd gotten in his way. Except that he'd damn well better not try anything like that, given the stomach-turning unpleasantness of…what had he called it? *Reduction of a dislocated shoulder.* That was it. And she did not want to repeat it, even assuming it would work a second time, because he was too foolish to recognize that, however temporarily, he had limitations.

Once again, she found a branch she used to brush away her footprints as well as she could, discarding it once she pushed between the feathery limbs of the cedar tree. Zach sat cross-legged in the doorway of her tent, head up as he watched her approach. His gaze swept over her from head to toe, taking in the few items she carried.

He'd found a way to halfway support his left arm using a cotton turtleneck from her pack. The gloved hand emerging from his minimal sling gripped a long branch he was stripping of smaller offshoots with the blade of her pocketknife. He had a fair pile of similar branches lying in front of him.

"You think that will work?" she asked doubtfully.

"In theory. I take it you didn't find the pack."

"No." She dropped the snowshoes at his side and thrust the shovel into the crusty snow, then folded the probe so she could stow it in her pack again.

He continued to study her with those penetrating dark eyes. "You have to hurt more than you're letting on. And be in shock."

"I'm not—"

Ignoring her protest, he said, "Come closer so I can measure the length of these against you."

After he'd learned whatever it was he needed to know, he muttered, "I hate to start cutting up the cord. If I screw up, we can't tie it back together."

She moved over so she could get into the tent and sat with a groan she hoped he didn't hear. His broad back blocked much of the light as she poked around in her pack.

"I have a stove. I could heat up a meal," she offered.

He turned. "How many meals do you have left?"

Counting was what she'd just been doing. "Um…five." And that only because she'd brought two or three extras, just in case.

"Then I'm going to say no. If you have any snacks, let's stick to those. I had an adequate meal last night, and I'm guessing you did, too."

Ava nodded.

"Worse comes to worst, I can try my hand at trapping rabbits or other small mammals, but that would mean starting a real fire, and until we're sure we're alone, I don't want to do that."

Her head bobbed again. She *wanted* to argue, but couldn't reasonably do so. Her stomach was growling, but she wouldn't starve in the next day. A handful of almonds would suffice.

Zach had already gone back to work, only saying over his shoulder, "See if you can find something that might work as a strap across the front of your boots."

Oh, lord. There had to be something.

"My camera strap," she started to say before changing her mind.

But he turned again, his suddenly intense gaze boring into hers. "You watched those men. Did you get any photos of them?"

She couldn't look away from him. "I…yes. But…what difference does that make? It's not as if either of us would *know* any of them."

"If you got their faces, there's one guy I might recognize. He's on a watch list I just saw."

He'd seen a watch list because he was a cop? Her thoughts took a jump. "You're border patrol."

He shook his head. "No, I told you. I have a friend who is, though. We served together. He's the one who gave me the lift out here. There have been rumors about an assassin whose bomb making is notable, too, available for hire to select fanatic causes, who rumor also says is on his way to the US. You know, the northern border of the US is considered the longest undefended border in the world. It's something like fifty-five hundred miles. Patrols are spread so far apart on the wilderness stretches with no roads, my buddy asked me to keep an eye out, even though the chances of me seeing anything were next to nothing."

"What would he look like, this assassin?"

"He's Russian."

Caucasian, as all the men had appeared to be. Shaken, she fumbled for her camera. "I can show you what I did get."

What if…?

Chapter Four

Zach wouldn't have been surprised if Ava found her camera to be irreparably damaged. The lens showed definite damage. But he held his breath as she lifted the camera and did her thing. An image showed on the screen, although he was too far away to make out more detail than to know he was looking at a snowshoe hare. That didn't mean she'd captured a face clear enough to identify from such a distance, but he couldn't drag his gaze away from the images that continued to whisk by.

Then there was one, a figure clad in white that stood out against the intensely blue sky. A man.

"You mind?" he asked, and when she shook her head, he maneuvered himself closer to her. He ignored the jab of pain trying to persuade him to stay still. Tough. Blocking pain was nothing new to him; he could do it again. He was already ignoring the fact that his skull was splitting open.

Maybe literally fractured? He couldn't let himself think about that.

He studied the digital photo in amazement. There was no visible face; the guy was wearing a balaclava, at a guess, but small as the figure was, the image was still sharp enough he could see quilted pants, heavy boots—and the weapon slung across the man's shoulder.

Ava glanced at Zach, and he nodded. Two pictures later, one of the men had his face uncovered. It was almost in profile. Thin, tanned face. After close study, he shook his head, and she moved on. Two more wearing balaclavas, and then came a man looking directly toward the camera.

Zach hissed in a breath. Ava turned her head and, wide-eyed, stared at him.

"That's him. I'm almost positive. Those cheekbones are unusual. Jaw broader than usual, too. You can't see his widow's peak, but—" He broke off. "Grigor Borisyuk has only been caught by a camera once that the US government knows about. It was a news photographer who took the photo. He was strongly advised to transfer to a domestic beat after that."

"Did he?"

"My friend didn't say. He'd have been foolish not to." Although foreign news correspondents and photographers were known more for guts than common sense.

There was no saying Borisyuk would have bothered hunting down the photographer, of course; once the picture was out there, what was the point? He was known to be ruthless and utterly lacking a conscience, though, according to Reid. Zach didn't imagine Borisyuk as the sort of fellow who'd shrug and say, "Ah, well."

And now a second photographer had recorded his face, with him staring straight at her. He might not have known she held a camera, but someone in their party had seen her through binoculars, which increased the odds that it was Borisyuk who had snapped out an order to kill the observer.

Zach's instinct screamed: pack up *now* and get the hell out of here.

If only it was possible. They weren't going anywhere until he finished the crude snowshoes he was constructing and they found sturdy sticks suitable to serve as poles, by which time it would be dark.

The sky had deepened; the change subtle enough he hadn't noticed. He had to get back to work. They wouldn't want to show a light, that was for sure.

"Straps to hold your boots?" he asked, scooting back to where he'd set down the peculiar bunch of branches. He still had some cord, but less than he'd like.

"Oh, ah…" Looking shaken, Ava didn't move for a minute. Then, "We can cut pieces off the straps on the pack." She twisted and turned her backpack so he could see the tough compression straps used to lessen the bulk of the load, as well as straps dangling after she'd adjusted the fit for her relatively small body.

"Perfect," he declared.

She held out her booted foot for him to measure the lengths he'd need, then watched as he used the pocketknife to cut several lengths. Then, little as he liked it, she left to hunt for straight, solid sticks long enough to serve as poles for both of them.

Her absence split his attention, but he made himself keep working. Right now, she was fitter than he was, smart and capable. A protective instinct had kicked in the minute he saw the avalanche begin its roaring descent toward her, but he had to rein it in. The only way to get out of here was to trust each other.

Turned out she had a small folding saw in her pack, which she took with her. He couldn't believe the crowd from the ridge were near enough to hear even if he and she burst into song, but he was just as glad she didn't have to snap off any branches she found, even if that recognizable cracking sound was common in the backcountry when heavy snow weighted tree limbs down.

She came back sooner than he'd expected, and presented four only slightly curved or crooked sticks that looked sturdy and which she'd stripped of any growth.

"Those look good," he said with a nod.

He saw a flicker of something in her eyes at his approval—humor?—but then she sat down just inside the tent with a sigh. Pulling her pack to her, she rooted around and handed him a small packet of mixed nuts and a box of raisins, the kind his mom had put in his school lunch when he was a kid.

The mother whose face he had trouble recalling, given how long ago she'd died.

Ava produced a water bottle and they both took sips, Zach accepting another couple of ibuprofen. He thought about suggesting she use her stove to boil water, but the bottle was the only one they had, and it was still three-quarters full. Wait until midday or later tomorrow, he decided. They didn't dare let themselves get dehydrated.

Unsure if his unsettled stomach would accept anything he sent its way, he ate the nuts and raisins anyway, before taking another couple of sips of water, as did she. Then they moved out of the tent so she could try the crude snowshoes. He had to make several adjustments and still wasn't convinced the bootstraps would hold.

"Take a few steps," he said. "Better lift your feet higher than usual."

She did and looked down in surprise. "They're heavier than my snowshoes were, but...it works."

"Green wood," he told her. "I hope we don't have to break into a run. This isn't the most solid construction ever, but in theory it should work." He glanced around. "Damn, it's getting dark."

"It happens fast here."

"I know." He shoved himself to his feet. "I need to, ah, use the facilities, then let's try to sleep as soon as possible. I want to go back out there to try to find my pack—" even though the chances lessened as the avalanche flow hardened "—and that'll have to be at first light. We can't afford to take long."

Despite what had to be fear on her fine-boned face, this nod was as sturdy as all her previous agreements had been. He'd prefer to have an army teammate as backup, someone with serious muscle who also happened to have a weapon secreted in his backpack, but—otherwise?—Zach was astonished at how lucky he'd gotten that the woman who had catapulted them into this by taking a few photos was also gutsy, strong and determined.

Now, if only they could escape and contact the people who needed to see that photograph before Grigor Borisyuk succeeded at disappearing into the American population.

"WE'LL NEED TO sleep together," Ava said as matter-of-factly as she could manage. Why she'd felt compelled to say that, she didn't know. What else were they supposed to do? It just…felt like the elephant in the room. Well, the tent. "I hope we *can* sleep so squished together," she added. Although she'd already proved to herself that she could. Ava suspected he hadn't dropped off at all earlier, though.

With the increasingly murky light, she couldn't make out Zach's features any better than he presumably could hers. Lucky, since she suspected she was blushing.

And how ridiculous was that? She hadn't hesitated to wedge herself into that sleeping bag with him when the necessity had been so dire. Well, it still was. To survive, they had to sleep, and they had to share. *So get over it*, she told herself.

"We've had practice," he said drily, his deep voice having more impact after the darkness had shuttered her vision.

She pushed aside the sleeping bag and laid her outer layer of clothing onto the too-thin pad. From rustling sounds, movement and a grunt that was likely pain, Zach was stripping, as well. A moment later, he handed her his garments and she laid them out, too.

Then she shook out the sleeping bag atop the clothing and pad.

"Um...are we more likely to bump your arm if you get in first, or if I do?" she asked.

"I'd better go first. I can't prop myself up very well, and given our respective weights, I should be on the bottom, anyway."

Well, that was true enough, and he'd certainly been tactful. "Respective weights" indeed. He surely out-weighed her by eighty pounds, and perhaps as much as a hundred.

So she waited while he lay down, shifted a few times, then said, "Okay."

Ava zipped up the bag more than halfway before squirming until she was far enough in to rest her head on his chest. Then she groped for the zipper and pulled it up, excruciatingly aware of his contours.

Pretend he's a body pillow, she told herself. *Don't think of him as a man with big bones and powerful muscles.* Especially *don't think of him as the stranger he is.*

The stranger she had no choice but to trust.

She did her very best to lie still, even though one arm was bent awkwardly beneath her and she couldn't quite figure out what to do with the other one.

He shifted and wrapped *his* arm around her. "Try to get comfortable," he ordered.

She rolled her eyes, but wriggled until her position was

the best she could manage. She hoped she hadn't hurt him. Then she sighed.

"I'm not very sleepy," she said after a moment. "It's early, and… I took a nap."

His chest vibrated in what she took as a laugh. "So you did. You needed it."

"Yes. It's just…" How to put into words how shaken she was by all the shocks, slamming one atop another? They tumbled through her head: the anxiety awakened by her awareness that she was no longer alone, was possibly even being pursued; the peculiar and then worrying sight of armed men where they shouldn't have been; the terror of being caught in an avalanche, followed by the possibly greater terror of thinking she wouldn't be able to find and dig out the other person caught in it. Never mind squeezing into the sleeping bag with the stranger who'd scared her, the icky task of manipulating his arm back into the socket—she still shivered, thinking about it—and finally the horrifying discovery that she may have photographed a terrorist sought throughout the free world. A terrorist who could only be sneaking into the US for a purpose that chilled her blood.

"I understand," he said quietly, his breath stirring her hair. His arm tightened slightly around her. "I'm…used to combat, but I don't love the night before I know there'll be action."

She tried to lift her head and failed. "You think there will be tomorrow?"

The pause felt longer than it probably was. "I hope not. I won't lie, though. If that is Borisyuk, he has damn good reason to want to ensure no witnesses are able to report his arrival in this country. That said—" the hand that had been tucked around her torso made a movement that might have been a waggle "—from their perspective, odds are good the avalanche took you out."

"Could they have seen that I pulled myself out?"

"I doubt it. From what you said, you were carried way down the slope. Both of us were. Tree cover is heavy along the creek."

She let herself relax a tiny bit, her mind wandering as she considered how intimate this felt, talking quietly in the night while wrapped in each other's arms. Not something she'd had in a very long time.

"The smartest thing they could do is go on their way," he continued. "Even if you survived, even if they had a glimpse of me, any experience at all would tell them how likely it was that if one or the other of us survived, we'd have been injured, and we'd be hindered by losing some of our equipment. If they got well ahead of us, they can tuck Borisyuk into whatever bolt-hole was planned, and assume we couldn't identify any of them. In fact, even seeing your camera, why would they think you'd have actually gotten a photo of him?"

She appreciated his reassurance, but couldn't take it at face value.

"You think that's what will happen, then? They'll go on?"

Another pause had her stiffening. "I don't know," he admitted. "The guy hasn't been so successful, moving like a ghost until he completes his job, then disappearing again, if he isn't ultracareful. Paranoid."

Her mouth suddenly dry, she swallowed against a swell of panic. "We should be—"

He gave her a little shake. "You know we can't travel in the dark. Even fully equipped, it would be foolish. As it is, a good snag will tear one of your snowshoes apart. I'm confident that they will have as difficult a time dropping down to the river valley, assuming that's what they're thinking of doing."

"They'd have to, at some point."

"Yes, but doesn't a trail drop down off the ridge farther south? It'll be buried under snow, but will still be more navigable than heading out cross-country."

She bobbed her head.

"I'm…not sure I like that option, either, though." He spoke more slowly. "It's fine if they drop down the west side of the ridge, but I don't like the idea of them popping out in front of us."

Don't like the idea. What a splendid euphemism for a squad of terrorists spreading a net to catch Zach and her.

And yet, the two of them had no options at all. They couldn't hunker down where they were and hope their non-appearance convinced the bad guys they were dead and buried under the avalanche, because they didn't have enough food to survive for more than a handful of days, plus they'd need to trek out to where they might have cell service. Her ride had been prearranged…but they'd never make it there in time, not inadequately equipped and injured as they were.

Also…while she had never so much as considered joining the armed forces, she didn't like the idea of she and Zach protecting themselves at the cost of their nation. They *had* to get the word out.

If he'd told her the truth about himself and his background, it occurred to her, he must be utterly determined to do whatever was required to stop an evil man from carrying his war of twisted ideals into their home country. Wasn't that what he'd dedicated his life to?

His concern for her had been evident so far, but however calming his deep voice was in the darkness, however comforting the hot length of his body and the solid shoulder beneath her cheek, saving her had to be second on his list of priorities. And, while she couldn't blame him for that, the realization was…frightening.

What could she say? Nothing came to her, and he remained silent, too, even though she knew that, for the longest time, he was no more asleep than she was.

HE MUST HAVE awakened at least hourly all night. At one point, he'd have gotten up to use the john, but the impracticality of that persuaded him to shove the mere thought to the back of his mind. They had to sleep while they could.

A part of him, sleeping and awake, was listening for any sound that didn't belong. He hated knowing the enemy carried fully automatic weapons while he didn't have so much as a handgun. If only he could get his hands on one of those rifles…

Could he use it, given his present disability? He tightened his fingers into a fist a few times without any noticeable increase in pain. Yeah, he thought he could. Certainly if it was life or death.

He made himself slow his breathing, courting sleep. How long it lasted, he didn't know, but this time when he opened his eyes, he was able to make out the peak of the tent above him. The light, if you could call it that, held barely a hint of gray, but it was enough.

He tipped his head toward Ava's ear. "Up and at 'em."

"Is that sort of like upsy daisy?" she mumbled.

He grinned. "Yeah."

She didn't move right away. "I *ache*."

Now that he thought about it, so did he, and it wasn't just his shoulder and head. Of course they hurt. They'd both been beaten within an inch of their lives yesterday. When he said so, she groaned.

"I haven't forgotten. Ugh."

"You can stay cozy for a little longer while I go poke around for my pack," he suggested.

She rolled her eyes. "Don't be silly. Just…give me a minute."

Her minute was brief enough, so he didn't have to push. She sighed and wriggled her way against his body until she was free of the warm sleeping bag. Zach couldn't help thinking he'd be aching in a different way if they didn't both hurt, and their situation wasn't so urgent.

"Brr!" she exclaimed. "Roll over!"

He obliged, and she snatched up first his clothes, thrusting them at him, before grabbing her own and scrambling into them.

His shoulder and arm had stiffened up during the night, not surprisingly, and getting his quarter-zip fleece top on was a challenge. By the time he succeeded, Ava had shoved her feet into her boots and was separating the flaps of the tent.

"Wait!" he said sharply.

"We're still alone." She slipped out, and he heard a hint of a footfall and then nothing.

Damn it! She probably had to pee—now that he'd thought about it, he was near to desperation himself—but he didn't like her taking the lead.

As if he could have protected her if a terrorist materialized in front of them, Zach thought, disgruntled at his own weakness and frustrated anew at being unarmed. He used his left hand to help him get his boots on, then half crawled, half hopped out of the tent before rising to his feet. Ava pushed aside a feathery, low-hanging cedar branch and stepped into sight.

"I'll dig out something for us to eat."

"Thanks." He went the same direction she had, relieved

himself, then detoured for a glimpse at the avalanche flow. The light was brighter up above the peak; down here in the vee of the valley, details were still elusive. He wondered how firmly the ice and snow had set, whether it would even be possible to dig a hole in it now. Damn, he hoped the hole Ava Brevick *had* dug wasn't visible to eyes looking for just that.

She'd already rolled the sleeping bag when he returned but left the pad open for them to sit on as they quickly ate more nuts and some dried apricots. His queasiness lingered, but if he had to expel this small amount of food, it wouldn't take more than a minute, and he could hope to do it without her noticing. He chased the bites with a few swallows of extremely cold water. Worse came to worst, he reminded himself, they could drink from the river where it appeared between sheets of ice and snow. Becoming infected with a possible bacteria wouldn't kill them in the near future, although odds were good she carried tablets to purify water.

He was left feeling useless as he watched her roll the pad and dismantle the tent, stow the tent in her pack and finally strap the roll and sleeping bag together where they'd rest on her lower back.

"I'll carry that," he said.

She yanked it toward herself, her expression indignant. "Don't be ridiculous! You're *injured*."

Ready to argue, Zach opened his mouth, but she added, "Besides, I'd rather have you able to keep watch and…and respond or at least make decisions if you see or hear anything."

He glared at her, then let his head fall forward. Fine, but he had no weapon. How was he supposed to "respond"?

The very question pulled him back from the frustration that served no purpose. She was right—and he needed to start thinking about what he *could* turn into a weapon, or how, if the opportunity arose, he could take out one man—

and acquire ample food, weapons and equipment for him *and* Ava.

"We'll talk about it again once we really get started," he said roughly. "Okay. You all set?"

There was the nod that caused a squeezing sensation under his breastbone every time he saw it. He thrust his feet into the snowshoe bindings, saw her do the same with her makeshift ones, and they both gripped their sturdy sticks.

He stepped out from the shelter provided by the cedar tree, took a good look around and started out over really difficult ground. This would be a test of her snowshoes.

It didn't take them five minutes to reach the foot of the avalanche flow, which he really took in for the first time. A hundred and fifty yards wide or more, he estimated, stunned. The sheer amount of material flung down the slope was frightening. It was a miracle they'd survived—particularly that she'd found him. Good God, what made him think there was a chance in hell of stumbling on his pack in the vastness of this avalanche field?

He had to try.

They tried, at the stubborn woman's insistence, but he weakened fast. A couple of times dizziness brought him to his knees. He waved off her concern, pretending he thought he'd spotted something.

It was a relief when the hour he'd given them for the search was up. Premature relief, given the day facing them. A short rest was all he allowed them. Increasing awareness of the sun rising and the enemy that might be in pursuit drove him to ignore his physical limitations.

Once they were on their feet, on their way, he just hoped Ava's snowshoes held up until they reached the trail they'd both traversed yesterday, where the way would become somewhat easier. Trail or no, though, they wouldn't be able to move fast enough to stay ahead of any serious pursuit.

Chapter Five

Ava fell down twice in the first twenty yards or so. The
first time, she failed to notice a rock lurking just beneath
the snow and crashed down with an *uumph*.

Zach swung around in alarm, but fortunately she'd come
out of the snowshoes, which didn't appear damaged. She
made a face at him, ignored what was sure to be a new and
painful bruise on her hip, and levered herself back up with
the help of her pole. Booted toes back under the straps, she
started out again behind him.

The second time, a springy whip of alder or something
equally bedeviling snagged her. Now, a couple of the more
fragile crosspieces in one of the snowshoes snapped, but
after Zach crouched and examined it, he said, "I think it's
still solid enough."

He was kind enough not to add, *If you don't put too much
stress on it.* But she'd known, as well as he must, that this
stretch where there never had been a trail cut, never mind
maintained, would be the hardest going. Next to impossible,
if not for the snow cover that buried some of the rocks and
teeming growth the river valleys in this temperate rainforest were known for.

Their pace felt, and undoubtedly was, glacially slow. He'd
have been able to go way faster if he wasn't stuck with her,

she thought, but then it wasn't her fault that her snowshoes had been lost in the avalanche. She more than made up for that handicap with the supplies in her pack she *had* held on to.

Between each stride, she held her breath, however fleetingly, so that she could listen for the sounds of anyone else moving behind them. Zach must have been doing the same.

Despite her own struggles, she became aware that he wasn't moving with the smooth efficiency she'd seen when she spotted the man gaining ground on her yesterday. Of course he wasn't! What if his arm popped out of the socket again?

She took a couple of hurried steps and said, "Are you all right?"

He stopped and turned at the waist to look at her. "What?"

"Your shoulder. What if you reinjure it?"

For a long moment, his expression didn't change. Then he grimaced, deepening lines she'd already seen on his face. Yes, he hurt.

"I'm wondering if we can strap my upper arm to my torso so that only my lower arm is free."

He must've hated having to keep admitting to any vulnerabilities, but he was doing it, anyway.

"It'll be hard for you to use your pole effectively, but… I don't see why not. Why don't you look for someplace we can at least set the pack down and maybe sit?"

"How are you doing?" he asked, his gaze holding hers.

What her body needed right this minute was a spa with hot bubbling water loosening painful muscles, but he must feel worse.

"Fresh as a daisy."

His grin took her breath away. "Like daisies, do you?"

"As a matter of fact, I do."

She soaked in the power of that smile and the glint of warmth and humor in his eyes until he inevitably turned away and started out again.

Two steps later, her right stick plunged into a hole. Leaning on it as she was, she stumbled, barely saving herself from falling to her knees.

Although she regained her balance, despair grabbed her. Even aside from possible pursuit—or an ambush set in front of them—how could they hope to cover enough miles with her walking sloppily on a bunch of small branches, and falling every ten minutes?

Zach must not have noticed her latest mishap, because twenty feet opened between them before she braced herself and resumed the clumsy, knees-high marching steps. What was she going to do? Drum her heels and whine, *I can't do this*? They had no choice at all. This was life and death, and not only for them.

I'm stronger than this, she told herself, and fixed her gaze on the man leading the way despite his own pain.

FOR THE NEXT ten or fifteen minutes, it was all Zach could do not to turn his head constantly to check on Ava. He didn't like the fact that she was both the one to have to struggle with the jury-rigged snowshoes and to carry a heavy pack while he strode ahead unhindered.

He'd have suggested he try to convert his snowshoes to fit her smaller feet so they could switch, except his greater weight on the flimsy snowshoes she wore would ensure his progress was even more difficult than she found it. And... he needed to be able to move fast should something catch his eye.

Move fast to do what?

And…how was he going to do it with a splitting headache and a tendency to get dizzy if he turned too fast?

Finally spotting a downed log covered by a six-inch coverlet of snow, he stopped. He'd have liked to feel relief, but the truth was, he felt as if his shoulder had been pinned together with a rusty spike.

Ava wasn't as far behind him as he'd feared. She lifted each foot in an exaggerated move and strode forward without hesitation, her concentration intense enough she was only a few feet away when she noticed he'd stopped and did the same.

She shuffled forward, planted her improvised poles and shrugged the pack off her back. Zach grabbed it with his good arm and lowered it to the log.

"We should see our tracks from yesterday anytime," he said.

She grimaced. "That'll have to be an improvement."

"Yeah." He sat down carefully, and she did the same. "I wish it would snow."

"Not likely this late in the season, but—" She tipped her head back and gazed at the sky. Seeing the same thing he had, she said, "I didn't pay any attention this morning, but that cloud cover does have a certain look to it."

Glad she'd confirmed his instincts, he said, "A few inches would hide our tracks."

"Not just behind us, but ahead, too."

"Right. If we can keep going even if it's coming down hard…"

"They might conceivably think we were buried in the avalanche. Except…"

She'd seen the fatal flaw.

"We're taking the logical route out of the mountains. They'll be behind us, and able to move faster."

"Unless they kept going along the ridge."

He hoped she couldn't hear the deep apprehension in his voice. "And are maybe waiting ahead for us. Yeah."

Zach hated being the walnut that would be crushed by the nutcracker. The situation was familiar to him, but this time he was as vulnerable as any civilian, and needing to protect Ava besides.

"You holding up okay?" he finally asked. They'd been on their way a ridiculously short length of time and shouldn't have stopped, but, damn, he hurt, and she was having to work at least twice as hard as usual to make any progress.

"Fine. And it so happens…" She raised her eyebrows. "I carry ace bandages."

Zach found a grin for her. "Mary Poppins."

Ava's laugh lit her face. Damn, she was beautiful, bruises and all. He couldn't look away. He wasn't sure what she saw on his face, but wariness stole her amusement. She proceeded to dig in her pack, finally producing a red canvas bag with the classic Red Cross symbol on it.

He pressed his upper arm to his side. "Do your worst."

That earned him a distracted smile as she unrolled the first stretchy bandage. "I think I'll need to use both. These are designed for a knee or some such. Your chest and arm together are wide, especially when you're wearing the parka."

Zach held still as she stretched the bandage over his arm just above the elbow, then across his back and chest. There wasn't much overlap, but she fastened it securely, then duplicated her effort with the second bandage.

"I'm not sure it'll hold if you yank against it," she said doubtfully.

"I'll try to be good."

"You inspire me with confidence."

Hearing her teasing, he smiled again. "I have my moments."

Her chuckle warmed him. "Wait—I think there's some cord left that's about the right length."

She was right. He just hoped they could untie the sturdier cord when they needed to.

With his movements even more hindered, Zach was irritated to discover how little help he could give her, even with something as simple as lifting her pack and slipping her arms through the straps.

She didn't say anything when he set out again, figuring he should pick out a path given his vastly lighter and stronger snowshoes. Plucky as she was, she stayed close behind, although she had at least a couple of mishaps in the next few minutes, judging from her under-her-breath grumbling. He probably swore a couple of times himself as he adjusted to the even more limited range of motion, as well as moments of double vision.

He'd been right, fortunately; maybe ten minutes later, he saw their tracks veer up gradually to cross the formerly open bowl of land. Those tracks ended abruptly at the edge of the now impassable mass of snow, rocks and ice.

Which would slow their pursuers down considerably if they came this way.

Zach would have said that he and Ava had been unbelievably lucky, except their survival wasn't all due to chance. Contrary to his original incredulity at the sight of a lone woman traveling in these mountains, Ava had planned well. She'd escaped the avalanche because she'd made the smart choice to prepare, and had had the presence of mind to trigger her airbag. *He'd* survived because of her determination—and because she'd brought the probe and folding shovel she'd needed to find and dig him out.

He liked everything that told him about her.

Zach gave a last, frustrated look back, wishing there'd

been some way he could have held on to that damned pack, and told himself to give it up.

With the going becoming easier, he waved her ahead of him. This way he didn't have to constantly look back to judge her pace and see whether she was struggling. She was unlikely to notice his brief stops to clear the dizziness.

Initially glad they both wore parkas and pants in shades of green and gray that blended with the foliage, he began to wish they wore white, like the men on the ridge had. Zach had seen a documentary about the Tenth Mountain Division fighting in World War II. They'd been mobile in conditions not so different from this on Nordic skis and wearing white from head to boot. They would have moved through a blizzard like ghosts. He wondered if the terrorists—or only one terrorist and a pack of mercenaries to escort him—had gotten the idea from those mountain troops, but doubted it. All you had to do was study photos of this daunting country, glaciated and snow swathed, to see you'd blend in the best clothed in white.

Unfortunately, Ava hadn't had the least warning of any danger, and even Zach hadn't taken very seriously his buddy's suggestion he watch for anyone looking like they'd gone cross country over the Canadian border. What were the odds?

He was still stunned. There had to be hundreds, thousands, of easier places to slip across the border. Short of taking the same risks in the Rocky Mountains around Glacier National Park, this had to be one of the more challenging routes.

Which also made it one of the least patrolled, of course, especially at this time of year with the backcountry closed.

Even as he watched Ava struggle ahead of him and tried to block out his own pain, Zach did his best to frame a plan that might allow them to survive. The options were few, and shaky, unless Borisyuk and company used their heads and ran for it.

Unfortunately, his gut said that was unlikely.

PICK UP MY FOOT. *Now the other one. Left. Right.*

Ava focused her entire concentration on each step. It reminded her of swimming laps, when she counted how many she'd done. It worked like meditation, she'd always thought: *ten, ten, ten*—flip turn—*eleven, eleven, eleven.* No room for stress.

Left. Right.

At least now she had tracks to follow.

She had no idea how much time had passed when Zach spoke to her back. "Let's take a quick break to talk."

Surprised, she came close to stumbling but managed to right herself. There wasn't any place to sit down here; the vegetation was thick. Ava laboriously turned herself to see him looking grimmer than she liked. She hoped the expression was a result of the pain getting to him versus him having heard or seen something—

"I've been thinking."

Her heartbeat quickened.

"I'm betting they split up. Possibly the main group moved on, but sent two or three men to make sure no one survived the avalanche."

She could only stare at him.

"Those men might have started descending the ridge, but it would have been extremely difficult going. Impossible in the dark, even if they have headlamps. Either they somehow set up camp partway down—and it couldn't have been very comfortable—or they used their heads and didn't begin the descent until first light. Which means they'll be well behind us even though we didn't set off until this morning. They'll take some time to try to find evidence of anyone surviving."

"Which they will immediately."

He nodded. "Our tracks. I thought about trying to wipe them out, but it would have been painfully slow. And once the men reached the trail on their way to rejoin their group, they'd have seen that two people are moving ahead of them. They'll be able to move one hell of a lot faster than we can, too."

"But...why wouldn't they have all gone on?" She was begging, but couldn't help herself.

Muscles bunched in his jaw. "As I said before, I really doubt Grigor Borisyuk would be willing to leave a witness alive. On top of that, as a group, they were counting on going unseen. They may not have known there are stretches burned in recent forest fires where they'd be exposed. Why would they, unless they'd looked at Google images? As it is, suddenly they realized that not only had they been noticed, but the person watching them wasn't just seeing small figures from a great distance. She had the kind of lens that meant she *really* saw them. Put yourself in their shoes. They'd be desperate to get under cover. What if she—and that's assuming they realized you're a woman— was in radio contact with someone? If a spotting plane or helicopter passed over, they'd be dead ducks or else have to take actions—say, shoot down a helicopter—that would bring even more attention to them. I believe they scuttled for tree cover, then decided to descend from the ridge to make sure the avalanche took care of you."

Ava didn't know what to say. She'd led a more adventurous life than most people, but none of that had involved human beings out to kill her. Or people who were capable of shooting down a helicopter. Thank God Zach had been close enough behind her yesterday! Otherwise, she'd be alone, unaware that the men up on the ridge had triggered the avalanche, never mind that one of them was a terrorist hunted throughout the free world. She might have figured out an even more primitive snowshoe design and set out to head back down the valley, but when those strange men caught up with her, she'd have no idea that they intended to kill her.

A shudder rattled her, one Zach saw. His eyes narrowed. "Ava?"

"You don't think they saw you."

"I doubt it." He hesitated. "Once they spot our tracks, though…"

They'd know there were two of them.

She nodded numbly. "It still looks like it might snow." But it hadn't. She let that go. "You're saying we need to really hurry."

He was watching her intently as he hesitated. "Yes, for now. If we keep moving, I doubt they can catch up with us today. The closer we can get to being able to call for help, the better."

She was torturously slow. It was like the turtle and the hare. No, a bicyclist on the freeway being chased by a sports car that didn't even have to exceed the speed limit to go sixty miles in an hour to the cyclist's…what? Five miles? Ten?

Zach had to know how far they really were from being able to call anyone at all. But that had to be their goal. If they could reach a point where the vee of the valley widened and a few alternate trails separated from the main one, she wouldn't feel quite so trapped.

"Then…then you think we can hide?" she asked.

"I hope I can find someplace off the trail to set up camp for the night."

And then what?

His expression hardened. "After that, at some point my goal will be to hide *you*. If I can take down even one of those men, I'll be armed. I may be able to arm you. That changes the odds."

Horrified, she opened her mouth, then closed it. Those odds sounded *abysmal* to her. She decided not to bother pointing out that she'd never in her life fired a gun, and she wouldn't remind him that he was already injured. So he'd been a soldier; how much combat experience did Zach actually have?

"I hate that idea," she said, straight out, "but I don't have any alternative to suggest."

A nerve twitched in his cheek and his eyes softened. "I'm not wild about it, either, but I think our only chance is to go on the offensive."

She lifted her chin. "Right now, we'd better get moving."

"Afraid so."

Ava shuffled back around so that she was pointing south, more or less, and picked up her right foot. Then left.

Trying to run would be a mistake, she felt sure, but she was in good physical condition. She'd increase her pace.

Right foot. Left. Right.

HE'D SEEN HOW she blanched at his plan, but clearly, crumbling in fear wasn't in Ava Brevick's nature. He should have asked whether she'd done any target shooting, but he could do that later. It was safe to say that a wildlife photographer didn't hunt wildlife as a hobby, which meant any experience she had handling guns was extremely limited.

That didn't mean she wouldn't pull a trigger if she had to.

Don't get ahead of yourself, he reminded himself. *Keep a sharp eye out, both ahead and behind. Think about how an unarmed man could set up an ambush.* Once he had her in hiding, he'd have her remove the ace bandages and cords strapping his arm to his body. It would be bad if the arm left the shoulder socket again because he hadn't given it time to heal, but sometimes you just had to gamble.

He couldn't help second-guessing himself. If they could have stayed completely hidden at the foot of the avalanche, maybe the group would have been satisfied and gone on their way. Sure, he and Ava would have been short on food, but humans could go on for a long time with nothing to eat.

Only—what if they'd made a single mistake? Say, missed a track one or the other of them had made below the foot of the avalanche? Dropped something from Ava's pack?

We'd be dead.

If the terrorists hadn't headed south on the ridge as fast as they could go, which was the smart thing to do, he reminded himself.

Ava fell in front of him. Zach helped her up and crouched to examine her snowshoe, pulling off his gloves to tighten the strap designed to hold her boot in place. Straightening, he said, "I wish..." but made himself break off.

His father would have growled, *Wishes are horses, boy, and you don't know how to ride. Life's hard. You need to be hard, too.*

He shook his head slightly. *Thanks, Dad.* No, his father had never, in Zach's memory, been anything Zach would call loving, kind, supportive. He hadn't ditched the kids he didn't seem to have any use for, though, and maybe the toughness he'd taught had been useful, in the end. Someday Zach would have to ask his brother and sister what they thought about it.

"You wish?" Ava prompted softly.

"Nothing helpful, I'm afraid."

She offered him a twisted smile. "I wish, too." Then she set out again, giving no indication she'd twisted a knee or ankle during any of these falls, or was suffering from the massive bruising she must have acquired courtesy of being flung down a long, steep slope by a behemoth of snow and ice.

Chapter Six

Every hour or two, he insisted they stop. She moved steadily, but he watched for tiny falters and would call a break. He chafed at their speed, but wasn't sure he'd have done that much better on his own without full use of his upper body. Twice he took more ibuprofen, too, for what good it did—especially since it exacerbated his nausea—and insisted she swallow some, too. He was grateful for all her preparations, especially the fact that she'd tossed a full bottle of pain reliever into her pack.

At what he deemed to be lunchtime, he spotted a decent place for them to sit down.

"We'd better have a bite to eat," he said.

"I'm...not really hungry."

If she was lying because she worried about them running out of food, that was one thing. If she really *wasn't* hungry, that was cause to worry given their extreme energy expenditure. What if she, too, had suffered a head injury she hadn't mentioned?

He was the one to dig in her pack for the individual packets of nuts and dried fruits. He opened one of each for her and poured them into her gloved hand. She stared down incomprehensibly for a minute, then to his relief started to eat.

He followed suit, chasing down a couple of bites with a drink of water before handing her the bottle.

For a moment, he only listened to the silence. The sky felt heavier, almost oppressive, but not a single flake of snow had yet fallen.

"You travel a good part of the year?" he asked, going for conversational in part to hide his intense curiosity.

"Oh…more like three or four months out of the year. Choosing and editing the photos I want to use is time-consuming, and I have to market myself, too."

"Where do you live?"

"Right now, Colorado." Her shoulders moved. "I spend some time with…a friend in Maine." Her pause was almost infinitesimal. "Whales have become something of a specialty of mine. Oh, and my roommate from college is in Florida."

Was the friend in Maine a man? Ridiculous to dislike the idea so intensely.

All he let himself say was, "So when you need a little sunshine…?"

Her expression had become livelier. "Exactly. Plus…lots of wildlife in Florida."

He groaned and stretched. "I hate to say it—"

"No, you're right." She hastily zipped up her pack, eased herself into it and stood. "We shouldn't have stopped."

"I'm the one who insisted," he said mildly.

"I know, but… You'd be faster without me. Don't deny it. I'm fine, though. I can keep going as long as we need to."

"Yeah." He was already talking to her back as she took a first step, lifting her foot in that crude snowshoe high. He even believed her.

HER ENTIRE BODY HURT. Every bruise, every wrenched joint, every insulted muscle made themselves felt. Ava tried to remember the fluid stride that carried her along before. She capitalized the word: *Before*. It was as if she was a different woman now, in the After. Desperately fleeing for her life.

Right foot. Left. Right.

Trusting a man. A stranger.

No choice.

Her chest burned, her every breath seared until it froze as she released it. Her shoulders... She didn't even want to think about her shoulders. Half the time, the pole sank too deep, making her lurch; she stabbed each one forward, preparing for the next stride, with growing trepidation.

Her thighs and even her butt burned, too. Her feet and ankles hurt, which was new; having to lift the makeshift snowshoes higher than usual wasn't part of her practiced stride, the one that worked for snowshoeing as well as it did for running.

Right foot. Left. Right. Left.

She clung to the mantra, using it to—mostly—drown out the pain. The fear, too. Because this was all she *could* do: keep going, as fast as possible without breaking one of the snowshoes and slowing them down for as long as it would take Zach to make a new one.

She kept her teeth clenched, too, to hold back the faintest of whimpers. He was certainly stronger than her, but the shoulder injury trumped all her relatively minor aches and pains. And he had those, too, Ava didn't doubt. Maybe more than that. A couple of times, she'd thought his eyes looked as dazed as they had when she first dug him out of the snow. He did some odd blinking, too. Whatever was bothering him, she hadn't heard a single groan or bout of muffled swearing coming from back there.

"It's snowing."

Right. Left. Right.

She picked up her left foot, then had to think before she set it down. Her rhythm was broken. What had he just said?

She blinked a few times. A big, fat snowflake drifted down toward her nose. Going cross-eyed, she watched it continue on its way until it settled on her parka, remaining visible for a long moment.

Ava raised her face to the sky and saw not just a few stray flakes of snow descending, but enough to muffle the impact of the green of the trees surrounding them.

She twisted in place, so she didn't have to bother laboriously shifting her snowshoes. "It's snowing!"

His grin blazed at her. "Didn't believe me, huh?"

"Oh, my God! I *can't* believe it."

He shuffled forward until he was almost stepping on the back of her snowshoes, reached a big, gloved hand around her nape and planted an exuberant quick, kiss on her mouth. "Someone is on our side."

Shaking off the effect of his cold lips, warm breath and the smile that made her heart jump, Ava said, "I hope it keeps on and buries our tracks."

"But doesn't drop two or three feet and bury *us*."

She wrinkled her nose.

Zach nodded ahead. "I hate to say it—"

She hated it every time he said that, but nodded. They had to keep moving, take advantage of being able to follow their own track as long as possible, because if the snow continued to fall, eventually they'd lose it. After that, finding the trail at all would be as hard as it had been when she traversed it days ago. Harder, if the snow kept falling, reducing visibility.

As she took the first step and then the second—*right, left, right again*—she wished vengefully that the men who might or might not be pursuing them weren't used to traveling on foot in a snowy, mountainous landscape.

Although… Russia had plenty of that, didn't it? Why couldn't this group have come from a sunbaked part of the world where the biggest challenge from nature was sandstorms?

THEY KEPT MOVING as long as Zach thought they dared. Longer. Not only couldn't he see any hint of a track ahead now, the quality of light was changing. He found it harder to make out the falling snow against the deepening sky.

The entire way, he searched their surroundings for a possible open spot well off the trail that wouldn't be painfully obvious to a passerby. A couple of times, he made some effort to give the impression they might have turned off, if only to briefly slow down any pursuers. He had no trouble catching up with Ava, and he wasn't even sure she'd noticed what he was doing.

They had crossed a stretch that was more open than he liked—a long-ago remnant of another avalanche or wildfire—then plunged back into the more typical, tangled vegetation he was really growing to detest. At the moment, he couldn't see or hear the river, although it lay off to their right.

He still hadn't picked up anything from behind them, but Ava was noticeably flagging when he finally saw what he'd been looking for.

"Hold up," he said.

She stopped so fast, he almost stepped on the tails of her snowshoes.

"Let me check this out." He stepped cautiously toward the river, able to slide between a thick growth of willows and alders and heaven knows what else. He bet this was, or had been, a game trail. Not obvious, but passable. If he could find a flat place large enough for them to set up the tent...

Ten minutes within what felt like a frozen jungle, he saw what he sought. He poked with his crude poles. No, this wasn't flat ground perfect for a campsite; there seemed to be a snarl of dormant growth below the snow, but he wasn't feeling real picky about where he laid his—their—sleeping bag right now, and he bet Ava would agree. Some nice, low branches of the cedar he'd just circled would veil them from anyone more than a few feet away, just as they'd been in last night's campsite.

He tipped his head, picking up the murmur of running water. A distant *crack* was easily identifiable, too: a branch breaking beneath a heavy load of wet snow. They'd hear that sound all night. Speaking of—

He took out the knife he'd pilfered from her pack and cut off a couple of stiff cedar branches.

Carrying them, remaining careful with each step, he made his way back to Ava.

"I found a place to set up camp for the night. I'd like to not break any of the vegetation—" he gripped some shrubby alder in his gloved hands "—if we can help it. I could carry you—"

She set her jaw. "Don't be silly."

"Okay. Follow my track."

She did, every movement exaggerated, gingerly. Satisfied, he turned to go backward, following her and using his branches to obliterate the tracks they were laying. Bending over, a couple of times he felt close to passing out. Had to be done. At the rate the snow still fell, he felt sure that within half an hour, their passage would no longer be visible.

By the time he caught up with her, satisfied, she'd slipped her feet from the snowshoes, set them against a nearby branch, removed her pack and taken out a tarp to lay across the snow. Tent next. She didn't argue when he helped her erect the thing, although it was easier than any tent he'd ever slept in. She half crawled in and unrolled the thin foam pad. Despite everything, he admired her taut butt in tight-fitting pants as it waggled before she turned for the sleeping bag. He set his snowshoes right next to hers and, one-handed, hauled the pack inside the tent.

Darkness had been falling with astonishing speed. Already he had trouble making out her features with any clarity. Last night, he'd had too much on his mind to be as aware of how cramped the quarters were. He couldn't shrink himself, but he suspected she wouldn't have cared if they'd had half the space.

He sat his butt down on the foot of the sleeping bag, letting her take the top. "Now if we just had a Jacuzzi."

"Room service."

He grimaced. "I'd settle for a hot shower." Yeah, he felt sure he didn't smell sweet right now. He'd worry more, except she'd been at least as long away from a last shower or bath as he was.

For what had to be a couple of minutes, neither of them moved or spoke. He felt as if they were inside a room designed and built to be soundproof. His eardrums felt odd.

"I'm starved," Ava said. "Do you think we can use the stove?"

"Yeah. We can set it up right at the opening here. We could both use an actual meal. We need—" He broke off. He didn't have to tell her that they needed to be strong tomorrow. For the moment, they could revel in the release in tension.

Assuming that was possible when stopping made him aware of every aching muscle, as well as the deep throbbing in his abused shoulder. At least his head was grateful for his stillness.

"Can you help me unwrap my arm?" he asked.

"Oh! Sure. It actually held all day."

He smiled crookedly at her. "It did. Solid construction." Her laugh made him feel triumphant.

She scooted close to him, peeled off her gloves and picked apart the cord and then unfastened the two ace bandages. Then she very carefully rolled them up again before setting them aside.

He might let her put them back on in the morning—he thought he'd had some relief from the limited range of motion—but he couldn't hamper himself when he went on the offensive, so maybe it wasn't worth wearing them for what, if they were lucky, might be only a few hours.

Zach had no doubt that tomorrow was the day.

Unless, of course, he reminded himself for the umpteenth time, the whole party had stayed along the ridge and either continued on their merry way, or set up in wait for the survivor(s) of the avalanche. In that case, he guessed he and Ava would meet up with Borisyuk and company the day after tomorrow.

He needed to prepare for either possibility, but his gut said somebody was tracking them already.

ZACH RELUCTANTLY GAVE her permission to do the cooking. Ava hid rolled eyes from him. Sensing how intensely protective he felt for her, she wouldn't wish herself in this situation with a different kind of man. Or alone, God forbid. On the other hand, she wondered how controlling Zach would be on a day-to-day basis in normal life. Did he ever let up?

Well, she'd never find out. This intense closeness was temporary. It wasn't as if they had any kind of relationship that would go anywhere. They'd part ways; him back to western Washington, her to Colorado. Home, only it didn't quite feel that way.

All of this was assuming they both survived the next several days, of course.

She didn't even ask him for his meal preference, given how limited options were. She freeze-dried the meals for trips herself, and was rather proud of how good she'd gotten at it. Tonight, they were having teriyaki chicken with brown rice.

Zach thanked her when she handed him her one dish and a fork, leaving her to eat out of the pan using a spoon. He took a bite and looked up.

"Damn, this is good. Doesn't taste much like the MREs I'm used to."

"I'm assuming that's the military version of my meals?"

"Yeah." He took a couple more bites, obviously savoring each one. "In theory, they're better than they used to be. In practice... I'd usually prefer just about anything else."

"What kind of soldier were you?" she asked. "Or...no, I suppose you'd have said sailor if you'd been navy."

"Or airman if I'd served in the air force," he agreed. "I was an army ranger in the regiment that does special operations."

Her lips formed the words "spec ops."

"Yeah, constant action. We were...inserted in some pretty dangerous places. Rescued hostages, accomplished raids, gathered intel. I...lost a few too many friends, came back from a final injury—" he rotated his right arm—the good one—in remembrance "—and decided it was time to get out."

She just watched him.

"Which is easier said than done. They warn you, but you shrug it off."

Why was he being so open with her? Because he suspected they wouldn't live, and wanted to connect with her, the last person he could spend time with?

If that was so…she understood. Even felt the same impulse. Why hide anything from this man? Maybe…it would be freeing, to talk about some of the bad stuff. Part of her wished she could see his face, but that would mean he could see hers, and maybe talking was easier in the dark.

"Why the military?" she asked.

"My mother died when I was eight years old. Dad was career military. A colonel." Wryness sounded in his voice. "When I was being rebellious, I talked about college. He sneered at eggheads. Useless. The first to go down if violence erupted."

"Except that they invented most products he used, including weaponry," she pointed out.

"Try telling my father that."

"He's alive?"

"Yeah. We don't see much of each other. I do stay in touch with my brother and sister."

He fell quiet, leaving her to fill in the blanks, of which there were many.

After a minute, she said, "I think I'll just use snow to wipe these dishes out. We should try to refill the bottle in the morning." When he asked, she agreed that she had some purifier tablets.

Naturally, she rejected his offer to clean up, and he conceded, letting her crawl past him and do the task. Out of the corner of his eye, she saw him lift his newly injured arm and rotate it. He caught her eye, and said, "I have a better range of motion than I would have expected. Binding my arm today was the right thing to do. With a little luck, by morning the soreness will be reduced."

She and Zach took turns to find some privacy outside before each, in turn, scrambled back into the tent. The snow still fell, although she thought more slowly now. The temperature had definitely dropped with nightfall, though. What was spring down below sure as hell wasn't here.

When he started peeling off clothes, she pretended she didn't notice. They'd slept together last night. Why she felt nervous tonight, she had no idea.

Because he'd kissed her?

Maybe, although she didn't think he'd intended it in a sexual way. She *had* seen him watching her in a way that definitely was sexual and made her tingle, though, so she shouldn't discount the kiss.

They had absolutely no choice but to sleep together. Listening to the rustles as he slid into the bag, she undressed, too. He rolled over to let her lay her clothes atop his, then rolled back over, holding the bag invitingly open.

She slithered in, squirming until she was *almost* comfortable. He was able to zip up the sleeping bag tonight, after which he adjusted her position to suit him. She'd have complained, except she was definitely comfier.

Warmer, too. His big body radiated heat in a way hers didn't.

"Okay?" he murmured.

"Mmm-hmm."

As tired as she was, she couldn't imagine falling asleep immediately. She'd never been so aware of a man's body stretched out against hers, even on the few occasions she'd let anyone get that close. Of course, she wanted to move, to rub against him, to—

She told herself to knock it off. This was nothing but a

reaction to the possibility that they might both die tomorrow. *Have some pride.*

Anyway, *he* wasn't doing a thing but lying there, his breathing completely even. He was no closer to sleep than she was.

"Tell me about you," he said after a moment. "Is this friend in Maine a guy?"

Talking. What could be a better distraction?

"No. Eileen is—" Oh, why not just tell him? "We went through two foster homes together. Aged out of the system and graduated from high school together, too. We've… stayed close."

"How long were you in the foster care system?" The low rumble of his voice, felt as well as heard, was more comforting than she would ever have expected.

"From the time I was a feral seven-year-old on. Nobody considered me adoptable, and I was difficult enough, so I got moved over and over."

She couldn't miss the sudden tension in the muscles supporting and enclosing her. "Feral?"

Ava had never, as an adult, told anyone this.

"My mother had drug problems. She just didn't come back one day. I…waited for a long time, then finally went looking for her. I was on my own for a while. Maybe as much as a year. No one, including me, knows. Turns out everyone assumed she and I had taken off, so nobody was looking for me. The house was vacant, after all. I was…too scared to look for help, I think. The stuff we left behind, well, no one would want it, anyway. Mom had never enrolled me in school. I didn't know any adults who weren't addicts. A cop pounced on me one day. I kept the picture they took of me when he hauled me in. I was skin and bones and filthy, and had this wild bush of hair. I hardly looked human."

After a long, fraught silence, Zach said in a constrained voice, "I've seen kids like that. In other parts of the world."

She bobbed her head, knowing he'd feel that. "Well, I got cleaned up, tutored so I caught up in school. Humanized. You know. Still, Eileen was the first person I really bonded with, and we were both fourteen by then. She'd been abused. I guess…we understood each other. That foster home wasn't so great, but a social worker rescued us, and we spent our last three years with a really great older couple. It gave me an idea what home might feel like."

"You still in touch with them?"

"Yes." John and Alice still treated the two of them like daughters, just way younger than their biological ones. They meant a lot to Ava, had maybe been her salvation.

"And the photography?"

"That was actually from an earlier foster home. The wife was a news photographer for a local paper. She saw how interested I was and gave me my first camera. I was hooked. At the time, it was way better than phone cameras. I never looked back."

It was true. She still thought about Jennifer long after most of her foster parents' faces and names had blurred. Someday, she should get in touch with her to say thanks, even if Jennifer and her husband had dumped Ava, too, at the first hint of problems.

"I want to hurt somebody for you," Zach said, in a voice that wasn't quite as expressionless as he probably intended, "but it's way too late, isn't it?"

"Yes. I'm…okay."

"Are you?" he asked softly, but not as if he expected an answer.

She didn't give him one.

Chapter Seven

Zach tipped his head back to look up at the sky. A few snowflakes still drifted down. Any and all tracks had been obscured the evening before, which was both good news and bad. His and Ava's pace was even slower this morning. He'd taken the lead instead of letting her risk her flimsy, primitive snowshoes.

Yes, anyone behind them would be moving slowly, too, but they were better equipped. He bet every single man they'd seen on that ridgetop was in excellent physical condition, prepared for winter travel in the backcountry. Unless somebody had taken a fall, none were injured, either.

He'd hoped the effects of what had to have been a concussion would have relented by this morning, but no such luck. There wasn't a damn thing he could do about it besides take the ibuprofen. That, and try to block out knowledge of his headache, a dull backdrop to the sharper shoulder pain. He consoled himself with the fact that the nausea hadn't recurred since yesterday afternoon.

He and Ava forged on for one hour, two, three. He kept an eye on his watch, glad he'd worn one. Sometime during the second hour he'd begun to feel an unpleasant but all-too-familiar itch crawling up his spine to his neck. He wanted to blame his imagination, but couldn't. He'd relied on this same feeling countless times over his years in dangerous parts of the world. It had saved his butt, and the lives of others in his unit, because he didn't let himself brush it off.

He felt like crap, but it was still time to set his plan into motion, he decided. Like yesterday, he kept a sharp eye out for anyplace he could stash Ava.

Fifteen minutes later, he thought he'd found it.

He said quietly, "Hold up," and made sure she'd stopped and sagged forward with her weight on the poles to rest. She must've guessed what he was going to do.

As he had last night, he left the trail, doing his best to stay on top of all the low-growing, tangled growth beneath the snow that wanted to snag his snowshoes, while pushing through the ubiquitous willows and alder and branches of smaller evergreens. Once again, he moved with extra care so as not to break a branch that would catch the eye of anyone looking for signs of human passage. An enormous log, the tree a real old-timer, had fallen about twenty feet from the trail. Given that it hadn't yet rotted enough to start service as a nurse log for countless seedling trees, he'd been lucky to notice it. What he was hoping...

Where the roots would once have been torn from the earth, he started probing with one of his poles. It immediately plunged deep. *Yes.* He couldn't feel any shrubbery filling in the hole yet, either. Probably it had come down as recently as this winter.

He turned and realized he could barely see Ava where she waited. The trick would be wiping out any trace of her passage—and his both going and coming. He hoped she wasn't given to flashbacks, since he'd have to leave her sunken in a well filled with snow, but he had faith in her resilience.

"This will do," he said aloud.

"Should I...?"

He'd carry her, he decided. He suspected her snowshoes wouldn't hold up to easing through such thick growth. They couldn't afford for her to fall and break branches off.

"Wait for me," he called, and began gingerly edging his way back to her.

It probably wasn't even noon yet, he realized. Maybe they could go on farther...but if he were Borisyuk, he wouldn't tolerate less than his own zeal in his underlings. Once again, Zach had deemed it futile to try to erase the tracks he and Ava had made.

The tracks between the trail where she waited and where he planned to stow her—those, he thought he could make less noticeable. Once he set out on his own, all he had to do was shuffle a little here and there to make it appear as if there were still two of them.

Or, he'd turn around and go back. He'd seen a couple of places that he thought would lend themselves to the ambush he had in mind.

Any way you looked at it, this was a long shot. His only real chance was if they'd sent a scout on ahead, knowing how much noise a group their size would make.

One man he could take out. Seven or eight at the same time, no.

The fact that there was only one path they could have taken made him and Ava incredibly vulnerable. On the other hand, short of continuing on the ridge, the bad guys had the same limitation.

He was gambling that he had guessed right, and Borisyuk had sent only two or three men down to check out the avalanche while the rest of them proceeded on the planned route. It made sense. Delivering Borisyuk safely into the US was the primary goal, chasing what might turn out to be shadows secondary.

He still suspected that the main group would be waiting at the foot of the river valley. But Zach had enough confidence to believe that, if he could whittle the numbers down and, by so doing, arm and provision the two of them, he and Ava would have a good chance. How much actual combat experience would a group of mercenaries have? If they had any, it might have been gained invading Ukraine, and that wasn't the kind of warfare that would serve them here.

Right now…he had to go with his gut, and he had to give Ava the best chance to live if he couldn't return to her.

So FOCUSED ON plodding forward—*left, right, left*—Ava had almost forgotten Zach's intentions until he'd ordered her to stop. When he emerged from the entangled growth to tell her he would be leaving her here, terror choked her.

"But—"

The expression in his dark eyes was both kind and implacable. "We talked about this. There are not a lot of choices here."

"But…they could kill you."

"People have tried before. Now, come on."

He insisted on carrying first the pack then her through that vicious, scratchy growth. No man had ever slung her up in his arms like this. She wanted to struggle, knowing he couldn't feel much better than she did, but only held on tight to limit how much of her weight he had to support with his left arm. She kept her eyes fixed on his throat and stubbled jaw, which were generally not revealing. Once he set her back on her feet, she couldn't see what he had in mind.

"There's a big hole here." He stabbed his pole in a few times to demonstrate. "See that root bole there? It was torn out of the ground. This hole could be six or eight feet deep, maybe more. We're going to dig out enough for you to make a nest, then I'll build a wall of snow and try to make it look natural. If they're not familiar with old-growth forests, they won't know what they're looking at."

"And... I just *wait*? I don't understand how you think you can overcome even one heavily armed man, never mind several!" Did that sound hysterical? She didn't care. "You're hurt. I can tell."

"I know what I'm doing. Trust me."

Ava didn't argue for long. She grasped the shovel and began to dig out a mountain of soft snow, trying to envision the hole as an igloo.

"Let me look through your pack," he said absently, as if he might find—what?—a 9mm handgun she'd forgotten to mention? All she saw him pocket were the remaining pieces of line, a couple of stretchy bungee cords, the telescoped probe and, once he was satisfied at the depth of the hole, the shovel. Then, rising to his feet, he looked at her.

"Spread the tarp as a bottom layer. Wrap yourself in the sleeping bag. Use extra clothes if you have to. Staying warm will be your biggest challenge." His gaze was intense. "Nibble on food. Be quiet, whether you hear anything that worries you or not. Got it?"

"Yes, but—"

"I'll come back for you."

She had to ask, her voice on the verge of cracking. "What if you can't? How long do I wait?"

His mouth tightened. "At least today. Better through tomorrow. By that time, my guess is they'll have given up looking for you."

"Then why don't both of us—"

He shook his head. "They know by now that *someone* is ahead of them. If they get their hands on me, they may decide they weren't following two people after all. How could they ever find you?"

"But—"

"We need weapons if we're going to make it."

Hearing no give at all, Ava gritted her teeth to keep them from chattering. This was the worst thing he could have asked her to do, but he was right. She'd be a hindrance rather than a help when it came to trying to take down an armed combatant. He'd be so worried about her, he wouldn't be able to concentrate on what he needed to do.

"Yes. Okay."

He took her hand, presumably intending to help lower her into the pit, but went very still.

"Ava."

The intensity in his eyes was still there, but now he was utterly focused on her face. His gaze flicked to her lips. He bent slowly.

She suddenly wanted nothing so much in the world as for him to kiss her. Grabbing his parka with both hands, she pushed up on tiptoe. She met his mouth clumsily, but didn't care. Despite the cold, and the fact that he wore heavy gloves, he cupped her jaw and tipped her head to an angle that let him warm her lips, taste them, part them. She welcomed his tongue, tried to block out everything but this moment.

Which worked until he groaned, took his mouth from hers and leaned his forehead on hers instead.

"Ava." His chest rose and fell fast, hard. "We have to do this."

Her eyes burned, and she averted her face. "I know." As an excuse to avoid looking at him, she slid down into the hole, pulled the tarp from her pack and spread it, then sat down.

He already had the shovel in his hand, and in mere moments had shaped the pile of snow from the hole into a long, smooth rampart that even from her perspective could have been new-fallen snow atop a log.

He looked down at her, and it was all she could do not to let him see her fear.

"Be careful," she whispered.

He nodded, said, "I'll be back," and disappeared.

She heard him for a few minutes, brushing the snow so that no one could detect the path back out to the main trail.

And then she was alone in a hole that could have been dug out for a coffin.

ZACH DECIDED TO go back the way they'd come. When the first guy he intended to take on saw the returning track, he'd guess the person, or two people, he was pursuing had hit an impassable obstacle and were seeking another route. Since the actual trail was buried under snow, it would be easy to wander off it.

Except that those opportunities were few and far between, given the rampant growth in a river valley deep in a temperate rainforest. But one thing Zach felt sure of: these guys weren't from around here.

He hesitated briefly at the first spot he'd seen to believably turn off. Part of him wanted to go on, to set up this confrontation as far as possible from Ava, but he couldn't risk suddenly coming face-to-face with one of these guys. Plus, he needed to hoard his strength as much as he could.

The way was initially easy enough; he guessed it was a kind of spur off the main trail. Could be an animal trail, or ground worn by the feet of hikers deciding to take a break and have a bite to eat at a particularly pretty place beside the small, tumbling river.

He walked as far as the river bank, then circled around to set up by a particularly bushy group of small trees to serve as a blind. His chosen location was out of sight of the main trail—its other primary benefit.

Once he set out on the hunt, he became the soldier he'd once been, emotions buried, his mind occupied with imagining every possible outcome to every choice he made. In the end, he was left with his original plan.

He constructed his snare out of a couple of whips of willows, pulled across the way and knotted to the base of other wiry growth. Just in case his prey didn't fall for the first trap—he'd have to lift his snowshoes extra high at that particular spot—Zach crouched a couple of feet farther on to lay a second snare with one of the bungee cords he'd taken from Ava's pack. Then he stood to shake a couple of strategically placed evergreen boughs so that snow tumbled over the snares. Just enough to hide them. Natural seeming. If he or Ava had come this way, they could easily have brushed those branches. A deer could have done the same.

Then he chose where to wait, ready to spring. When the moment came, he couldn't hesitate. A single shot taken would alert all of those *other* heavily armed men, up and down the valley.

Zach was going to do his hunting as silently as was humanly possible.

IF YOU LEARNED one thing in special ops, it was patience. Hide or disguise yourself, and wait. The bursts of violence or hurry-up-and-go were scattered between long periods of waiting. He hadn't felt the humming tension in a long time, but it was familiar.

Eyes and ears sharp, he allowed his mind to drift, mainly to Ava but also to Borisyuk's agenda. Was he here for a single assassination, a death that would throw government and politics into disarray, or a high-ranking military officer whose insights and influence had become inconvenient for whomever had hired an assassin? Or had he been brought here for his bomb-making skills, the intended targets more plentiful?

Zach did wonder, and not for the first time, whether he could have imagined seeing the sought-after terrorist in that photo. If he hadn't just been shown the one-and-only previous photo of the guy and been asked to watch for him, would he have taken such a wild leap?

Since he had plenty of time, he ran through the same logic, the same arguments, that had convinced him in the first place. An especially distinctive face. The weaponry those men carried. That they'd fired an RPG to take out an innocent backcountry snowshoer who was no threat to them.

Because Ava's camera with the huge lens *was* a threat more significant than an automatic rifle.

Even if Zach had leaped to a conclusion about the one ugly face with singular features, why *did* those men sneak across the Canadian border into the US? What did they plan to do with more armaments than a typical army ranger unit carried? Why had they determined to set off an avalanche to take out one person who should have been too far away to disturb them? An innocent, at that?

It didn't add up to anything good.

If nobody showed up in pursuit, he might reshuffle his logic. He'd still believe somebody would be waiting for them where they emerged from the valley. And if that wasn't true—well, he'd call his buddy to show him Ava's photo.

His thoughts slipped, as they did every few minutes, to Ava. He had hated walking away from her. If he got back to find her dead because someone had stumbled on her... He wasn't sure he could live with that. This woman had gotten to him with stunning speed. She'd become a trusted teammate. But Ava was more because she was also a beautiful woman who had unhesitatingly shared the warmth of her body with him to save his life. She blushed when he betrayed his desire for her, which suggested she was having those same thoughts.

And last night, she'd decoded the mysteries of her personality for him, clawing him up inside. If she never showed him the photograph of the feral, hopeless child she'd been, it didn't matter. He could see it, blue eyes wild in the face of any of those skin-and-bone children clinging to life in war-torn parts of the globe.

He hadn't had to ask why she photographed nature and animals instead of humans. Or why photography, he thought now, defined her life.

He still didn't hear voices, however soft, or the shush-shush of snowshoes. He and Ava could have gone on for another hour or two—but if they had, he might not have found as perfect a place to hide her.

If I'm wrong… But the twang between his shoulder blades hadn't relented.

AVA HAD NEVER listened harder in her life. But then, what else could she do? Stare up at the sky, where she once saw the impossibly distant contrail of a jet, another time a bald eagle sweeping against the pale gray backdrop? Imagine the now scattered snowflakes coming more frequently? Envisioning herself, literally buried in snow, completed the horror she felt as she waited.

Would a gunshot be the first unnatural sound she heard? Careless voices as some of those men tramped past on the trail, oblivious to her presence? Or would it be her name, in Zach's velvet-deep voice?

Please let that be it.

Obedient because he was right, she made herself nibble occasionally on peanuts and dried fruit. Sip the water that tasted of the tablet that had purified it. Keep her joints limber with small movements. Shiver and readjust so she could unroll the pad to lift her butt farther off the snow. Huddle, wrapped in the sleeping bag, and not let herself even *think* about climbing out of the hole and going looking for him.

After all, she knew how well *that* worked. She'd never uncovered so much as a trace of what had happened to her mother, not as a child, not as an adult.

But…*could* she make herself stay right here, alone, the rest of the day, and then the night, and then another day?

Ava didn't know.

Crack.

She tensed, even as she knew that wasn't a gunshot, only another tree limb giving way beneath the weight of snow. Head back, she glanced warily around, but didn't see any that would drop on her.

She heard a woodpecker at work, saw what she thought was a peregrine falcon soar overhead. A gray jay and a raven took turns sitting on a branch to study her, heads tipping first one way and then the other. Thank goodness a vulture didn't arrive to contemplate how much lifespan she had left. *Were* there any vultures in the North Cascades? She was pretty sure not, which made sense; in these perpetually damp woods, bodies decomposed quickly without help.

At that point, she descended into the kind of morose thoughts she abhorred. Still, it was probably inevitable to ask herself, who would even notice if she disappeared, never to be seen again?

Eventually Eileen, of course, but Eileen knew Ava was on assignment, off in some remote location without cell phone coverage. Post-trip she often plunged into editing her film, too, and forgot to even check voice mail. It would be a couple of months before Eileen would really worry.

Laura would wonder, of course; almost every winter Ava spent a couple of weeks with her in Florida, but they went long stretches without communicating the rest of the year. Plus, since Ava's last visit in January, Laura's boyfriend had moved in with her, which had made Ava wonder if staying with her for more than a night or two at a time wouldn't be awkward now.

John and Alice, but she'd spent Christmas with them so recently, and they, too, were used to long silences.

Some of the editors Ava worked with—except for Richard Vickers, who'd set up the funding for this trip and would be puzzled and irritated and possibly even litigious if she didn't submit the promised photos—would give her passing thought and start buying work from other photographers.

What a sad list that was. And really, did she care if a bunch of people out there wailed and beat their breasts at the word that she was presumed dead?

She gazed up at the sky, blinked away a snowflake and thought, *No.* She just wished there was one person who was more to her than an occasional phone call or visit, who would know *immediately* if something was wrong. Who truly loved her.

That wish feeling like a fist in her chest, she knew she had to try harder to open herself to relationships once she got out of here. No, there weren't a lot of men like Zach Reeves around, but maybe she could find one of them.

And then she growled, not quite silently. Oh, for gracious sake! She didn't do self-pity and wasn't going to start now.

Of course she'd make it home! If she had to, she could wait as long as she needed to.

A greater truth crept into her consciousness: She had faith Zach *would* come back for her. Maybe that was foolish, when she'd known him such a short time, but this certainty felt bone deep.

Right now, the best thing she could do was hold on to it.

Chapter Eight

Zach moved often enough to keep from stiffening up. He rolled his shoulders, evaluating his pain level and dismissing it. He snacked a couple of times on dried fruit rather than the nuts he'd left with Ava; the fruit wouldn't crunch under his teeth. He hoped she was following his instructions.

One side of his mouth crooked up. "Advice" was a better word. In general, he doubted Ava was a woman who'd appreciate being given orders.

Despite himself, restlessness grew. Maybe he wasn't as patient as he used to be. Probably lucky he'd retired—

Swish, swish, swish.

He stiffened. The sound was subtle, not close. Rhythmic, though—and exactly what he'd been listening for.

Swish, swish, swish.

He turned his head, peering through branches toward the main trail. There were no voices, not so much as a grunt. That sounded like a single snowshoer, although he might be mistaken. Would the man see the turnoff at all, or be too focused on what was directly ahead? If he did, Zach was still undecided about his course.

No, the guy couldn't be that foolish.

Swish, swish, swish. Getting closer.

Slower, too. Hesitating.

Zach rolled his shoulders, flexed his fingers a few more times and crouched.

Silence.

Then a few tentative sounds. The obvious track of one or maybe two snowshoers that Zach had laid was proving irresistible.

The swishing sound resumed, but quieter, as if the man was stepping carefully. He couldn't tiptoe, but he was doing his best. Ah, there he was, appearing around the bend. Clad in white, head to toe—yes, including the hood and cape that covered his backpack—but for the black automatic rifle slung to one side that clashed. Zach eyed the poles greedily. Those would be a big improvement.

No hint that the guy had company. If he did, they must be spread out.

Zach had already divested himself of his snowshoes. Now he peeled off his gloves and let them drop to the ground.

With a nice straight stretch ahead, the tracks leading out of sight ahead, nothing visible, the guy gained confidence and sped up.

That's it, Zach urged him on. Nice path, no reason to think about the snow that had obviously fallen from branches ahead. His prey passed him, head not turning. One snowshoe passed over the first snare, but he was sloppy lifting the back foot.

It caught, sending the man stumbling forward. He swore sharply, but not in English. Russian wasn't one of Zach's languages, but he knew the profanities from it.

He launched himself before the white-clad man could regain his balance, hitting him hard. A guttural cry escaped the man as they crashed down, Zach's weight forcing the other man to the ground. Zach had the advantage from the beginning, since the man's feet were tangled with the snow-shoes and he had to release the poles to free his hands.

He twisted frantically. Zach was ready, slamming a fist into that face. Despite the fleece covering, blood spouted from the nose hole. Zach kept hammering him. The guy was groping for something beneath his parka—a gun? a knife?—but Zach drove his knee onto that arm, hearing a snap, followed by a strangled scream that gurgled from the blood that must be filling his throat.

Zach locked his arm around the Russian's neck, wrenching back to gain complete control. Instead of submitting, the man fought viciously to dislodge Zach, making him think of a hooked trout flopping on the bank. He tightened the vee of his arm just as the man bucked with his entire body. Zach heard another snap. No, felt it.

Oh, damn, he thought, sickened. Not immediately releasing the hold, he bent to let the suddenly limp body sag onto the snow to one side of the trail. He stayed cautious, pressing his fingers to where the carotid artery in the neck should be pulsing and finding nothing.

Zach rose to his knees and stared down at a man he hadn't intended to kill if he could help it. He yanked up the balaclava, seeing the face of a stranger.

He'd really have liked to question this guy. Whatever his native language, he surely wouldn't have been chosen for this trek unless he spoke English with reasonable fluency.

Also…aware of a level of discomfort, Zach realized he had acclimated more to civilian society than he'd realized. He had started thinking like a cop, not a soldier fighting terrorists in lawless parts of the world. No, he couldn't have arrested this guy. He had no cuffs, no jurisdiction, but he could have tied him up, left him with whatever he needed to stay warm and sent the border patrol back to pick him up.

That wasn't happening.

An urgent voice in Zach's head said, *Get him out of sight. He can't be alone.*

He heeded it, setting aside the rifle and removing the pack from the man's back, then putting on his own snowshoes before dragging the dead man around the back of the cedar tree, well out of sight of the trail.

Then, feeling angry and unsettled, he hefted the rifle and pack behind the tree and did the same for the snowshoes and poles. They were intact, he was glad to see. He'd expected the bindings on the snowshoe, at least, to be damaged. The man had much larger feet than Ava did, but Zach was confident he could adapt these.

He returned to the trail and found a couple of new long growths of willow or alder, flexible enough to be bent to lie level with the ground, and secured them in place. He used the shovel to do his best to erase any sign that a struggle had taken place. After brushing snow over the top of the new snare, he took a few strategic steps in his own snowshoes, making it less obvious that one set of tracks had ended rather abruptly. Finally, he backed around the tree, erasing his own tracks as he went.

No, he didn't believe for a minute that this guy had been entirely on his own. More likely one had lagged, maybe because he'd investigated an animal track. Zach hoped the companion or companions hadn't been close enough to hear that scream.

He searched the body for weapons, appropriating a wicked knife and sheath, but found nothing else of interest. Then, pausing every thirty seconds or so to listen, he employed the shovel to dig a shallow grave in the snow, roll the body into it and cover it. A predator could dig it out with no effort, but at least it wasn't immediately obvious.

Zach knelt beside the bulging pack but paused for a moment to scan himself for new and old pain. Yeah, he'd felt the hard blow to his thigh, but it wasn't anything to worry about. His shoulder...wasn't happy. He swung his arm in a full circle. It was functional; all he could ask. His head throbbed, but his vision hadn't been impacted.

Then he started his search of the pack with the outside pockets. That's where he would stow additional weapons. Worse came to worst, he *was* armed now, but what he needed to employ was guerrilla warfare, which tended to be silent. Pulling the trigger of an automatic rifle amounted to jumping up and down and waving his arms.

Here I am! Come and get me!

The first and most accessible pocket held goggles and dark glasses. Both potentially useful.

He recognized the shape of what was inside the matching pocket on the other side even before he touched it. A handgun was noisy, too, but...

He lifted it out, a grin splitting his face. Zach was glad Ava couldn't see him right now; he probably looked more like a winter-starved wolf about to bring down a caribou than the kind of man she'd ever known.

But hot damn! This was an American-made pistol with a suppressor screwed onto the barrel. It was all his Christmases wrapped into one—a nearly silent, effective way to fight their way out of the trap this deep-cut valley increasingly felt like.

He could just shoot the next SOB who came down the trail.

The breath he let out scraped in his throat. No. He couldn't do that. He'd keep it handy, though, in case his catch and—not release—hold wasn't going to work. Or if he faced *two* opponents.

He had time to take a look inside the pack, pushing aside changes of clothes to see packets of freeze-dried meals—descriptions in English, all presumably purchased at a Canadian store that equipped hikers, climbers and skiers—and lots of loose candy bars. Matches, a stove—

Swish, swish, swish.

Body aching now, Zach wished he could just arrest the next creep, haul him to lockup and go home to a hot shower, a bowl of something comforting like chicken noodle soup and the chance to lie down on a comfortable mattress in the dark until he felt better.

Instead, he crouched again in his blind, let his gloves fall to the snow at his feet and waited.

AT SOME POINT during the afternoon, Ava had lay down on her side and curled up, still clutching the sleeping bag around her, staring at the snow wall in front of her. Sitting up, keeping watch, wouldn't do her a speck of good, would it? What was she going to do, scrape her way out of this pit to attack one of those monsters with her bare hands?

Except they weren't bare, so she couldn't even use her fingernails. Which wouldn't be much use, anyway, because long, beautifully tended fingernails weren't compatible with her lifestyle.

She hadn't heard a single gunshot or voice. A snowshoe hare had hopped by, startling at the sight of her. More birds paused in branches high overhead. Once she did hear a piercing cry, as some small creature became prey. It sent a shock through her, because she felt as small, inconsequential and vulnerable as the mice and squirrels and chipmunks and hares that fed the larger predators.

The light was going, she began to realize, with a new chill

of fear. Zach wouldn't wait until dark to return, would he? How would he find her?

Maybe he couldn't.

Would he dare call her name if he thought he was near?

God, she felt pathetic. She never, never wanted to be in this position again. It threw her back to that terrible time in her life when there'd been no safety anywhere for her, when *she* was the smallest, the most vulnerable.

She clenched her jaw. Zach said to wait, so that's what she'd do.

That was when she heard the swishing sound of someone approaching.

Ava strained, trying to decide which direction the person was approaching from, unable to be sure.

Whoever it was started coming directly *toward* her. Then Zach said softly, "Ava? Tell me you're here."

She let out an undignified whimper she prayed he didn't hear, and sat up. In an equally low voice that she thought came out remarkably calm, she said, "Where would I go? The mall?"

She heard his chuckle before she saw him, tall at the foot of the hole.

"We'll stay here tonight." He tossed a pair of snowshoes down and knelt to heave off a big pack. Two sets of poles followed the snowshoes, and then he lowered the pack, followed by—*gulp*—an automatic rifle.

That's when she really looked at him and saw his eyes. There was a wildness in them that made her shiver. He might sound completely self-possessed, but inside, he wasn't.

"You killed someone," she whispered.

The eyes flicked up and met hers. "Yes."

She swallowed and nodded, unable to chew him out, or not, or... What *could* she say?

Nothing.

"Let me wipe out my trail," he said, in that same, conversational tone. "Probably not necessary, but…" He vanished, and she transferred her gaze to his gleanings.

It finally registered that he had *two* sets of poles. Only one pack, but he couldn't carry more than one.

Unable to really even hear what he was doing, Ava just sat there until he reappeared, took off his snowshoes and jumped down into her hole.

"Are you okay? I was gone longer than I expected to be—"

She shook her head. "I'm—" Not bored. She hardly knew how to describe what she felt. "All right." Now she was.

He nodded and took a rolled sleeping bag from beneath stretchy bands at the top of the pack. A pad had been rolled up with it, she saw.

"You have two sets of poles." Ava hadn't even known she was going to say that.

"Yeah," he said gruffly. "I waited a long time to find out if anyone else would come along, but it appears only the two were sent on cleanup duty."

"Are they—"

"Both dead?" His eyes still didn't look right. "No. I… incapacitated the second man and left him tucked into his sleeping bag and tied up to a tree. We'll send someone back for him."

How did you "tuck" an unwilling man into a sleeping bag and then tie him up? Oh, duh—he must have been unconscious.

"I acquired quite a bit of food," he added. "Freeze-dried dinners and some desserts, too."

"Really?"

He smiled, and seemed to settle a little. "Our Russian terrorist had a sweet tooth."

Had. So he was the dead one.

"Are we really staying here for the night?"

"Where better?"

"I kept thinking—"

His eyebrows climbed.

"Well, that this looks an awful lot like a grave waiting for a coffin."

His head turned and he swore. "I'm sorry. That didn't occur to me."

At last, she could smile. "No, I shouldn't have said that. I had too long to think, that's all. Really, what could be co-zier?"

Maybe he intended that sound to be a laugh.

"Shall I start dinner?"

"Yeah. I think we're safe here for the night. We probably don't want to break out in song, but I can't carry a tune, anyway, so that's just as well."

"Really?"

"Really. You?"

"I love to sing."

Now he openly grinned. "I love to listen."

Then they were a match made in heaven. Ava cringed, hoping he didn't read her thought.

She sat cross-legged and busied herself with her small cookstove. "These are my last dinners," she told him. "Pasta primavera. If you saw something better in there…" She nodded at the pack.

"I'm…not really hungry. Pick whatever you want."

She narrowed her eyes. "Why aren't you hungry?"

He opened his mouth, hesitated and then closed it.

Thought better of lying to her? "I've…had a headache. Some nausea, too. Turns out extreme activity stirs it up."

"A concussion."

"Probably." He sounded amazingly unconcerned.

Mad, she said, "You didn't think to tell me this?"

Those eyes, not as expressionless as he probably imagined, met hers. "What could you have done?"

"We could have slowed down. Looked for a place to rest sooner! I could have—"

"No, Ava," he said, his voice both rough and gentle. "I'm not in that bad a shape. We have to follow the plan."

Frustrated, she wanted to keep arguing, but "should have" was pointless now, and she couldn't have set a snare, as he described it, bringing down the two armed men tracking them. He'd produced real snowshoes for her, food to sustain them and weapons she prayed she didn't have to use.

Her admiration for Zach swung higher, but she knew he didn't want to hear about it, and would shut down any attempt on her part to thank him.

Instead, she said, "Will you try to eat?"

One side of his mouth tipped up. "Okay. But make it pasta primavera. The ones I, er, acquired are store-bought. Which are better than MREs, but—"

She smiled, as he'd intended. Waiting for water to boil, she finally said, "Do you want to tell me about it?"

He seemed to be concentrating on the small flame. "Maybe after we eat."

HOW LITTLE COULD he get away with telling her?

Watching her as she prepared their meal, just as she had the previous night, he reconsidered his instinct to tell half-truths. No, she wasn't a soldier, but given her childhood, he suspected she wouldn't shock easily. They were in this together. He owed her the respect he'd have given any other teammate. What's more, the blunter he was, the more ready she'd be to pull that trigger if she had to.

He just hoped to God it didn't come down to that.

"You have a memory card in that camera?" he asked, nodding toward her pack.

"Yes, of course. Two different kinds. I've filled some."

"I want you to take out the most recent cards. We'll each carry one."

"Oh." She bent her head so he couldn't read her face well. "Yes, of course."

"Smells good," he offered. It did, and suddenly he was starved, too, but damn, what he craved most was stretching out in the sleeping bag and not moving for eight hours or more.

As they ate, they talked quietly. He told her a little about his current job as a detective for a rural county. "I like working independently," he said. "Using my head, figuring things out."

"Versus action?"

He grimaced. "Yeah. They wanted me on the SWAT team, but I said no. I used the excuse of my injury, but the truth is, I'm done with that."

"Except you're not."

"No." It was a minute before he added, "Lucky I haven't had time to get fat and lazy."

Ava laughed. "I just can't picture that."

He grinned. "You never know." The scrape of the spoon told him he'd eaten his entire serving. His stomach felt better enough, and he wondered if he'd mostly been hungry.

She talked about some of the outlets where she sold her work, telling him she had an agent, which was a good thing since she didn't have the right personality to do all the marketing herself. "Super outgoing and engaging isn't me. Of course," she said with a sigh, "I have to do a certain amount of it, anyway."

"You envision doing this forever?"

She set down the aluminum pan. "I know I can't. Once my knees go, you know…" When he smiled, she shrugged. "There are other types of jobs in the field. Sports, newspapers… I could sell prints of my work from an eBay shop."

If they stayed in touch—if they started something together—he was going to hate waving goodbye when she set off into the African bush or the jungles of Thailand or wherever the hell else she went to do her job. Except he guessed some of the time, maybe most of the time, she wouldn't be on her own. She'd have a guide, at least.

Okay, he could live with that. Except…what he'd really like was to go with her. Carry, fetch, cook, watch her back.

And he was getting more than a little ahead of himself here.

He handed her his own dish and then dug in the pack he'd appropriated, producing a handful of candy bars. She pounced on a Twix; he went for Almond Joy and resisted having seconds when she did. Better be cautious.

Finally, watching her wiping out the dirty dishes with snow and stowing them away, he said, "I found passports."

Chapter Nine

Her head came up. "Real ones?" Her nose wrinkled. "You know what I mean."

"One was Russian, the other from Kazakhstan. The men flew into Montreal on different dates, close to two weeks ago. Both passports showed some previous travel, nothing likely to catch anyone's attention. Do I think those are their real names? No. When we get out of here, I'll give the passports to the border patrol."

"Do you think the man you left alive will survive until we make it out?"

He tried to keep his expression impassive. "Let's hope it doesn't take too long."

Her nod hid a lot, and he understood.

He talked more about the snares he'd set, and how well they'd worked on both occasions. "It helped that I had some height and weight on both of the men. That won't always be the case. I was also lucky because neither had a weapon in hand."

"Hard to use a pole if you're also clutching a gun."

He inclined his head. That would be a problem for him, too.

"There were eight men on that ridge?"

"No, I think seven. I can check for sure."

She twisted to take her camera out of her pack. What had to be a really expensive lens was obviously toast, but the camera itself came on for her. That had to be a super battery.

She brought up the photos again. She was right. Seven men. He took the camera from her and studied the three faces that she'd captured. None of those matched the two members of the group he'd taken down today.

"Five to go," he murmured. "And Borisyuk is one of them."

She didn't ask the obvious: Would the prime target expend his men before he got his own hands dirty, or would he enjoy killing two inconvenient Americans?

It was getting hard to see Ava's face, which Zach regretted. Even as tense as they both were right now, he liked seeing every flicker of her expressions.

"You brought your own sleeping bag," she said.

"You don't know how close I was to dumping it." He saw her startle. "I liked sleeping with you," he said wryly. "I'm afraid if I'm not, I'll wake up constantly, groping around to be sure you're there."

"We won't be far apart."

"I guess there's only so much space," he admitted, acknowledging the limited width of their hole.

She hadn't moved. He waited out her silence.

"We could…zip the sleeping bags together," she said softly.

WITH HER CHEEKS BURNING, Ava was grateful for the oncoming darkness. She also hoped he didn't take her invitation for more than she'd intended it to be. Sex wasn't casual for her. Truth be told, she'd never been able to relax enough, give enough of herself, for sex to be all that great—or, really, worth bothering with. She'd felt more intimacy sleep-

ing in Zach's arms last night than she ever had when naked
with any other man.

Maybe...

No. Don't even think it.

"I can go for that," he said calmly. "Shall we set up?"

"Yes." Woman of the world, that was her. "Then I suppose
I'd better crawl out of here and, um, find some privacy."

"Ditto. Wait. You haven't stayed stuck in this hole all
day?" He was obviously frowning at her. "I didn't think..."

Could her face get any hotter? "No, I, um, used a plastic
bag. Which I'll dump while I'm behind that tree."

He bent his head matter-of-factly. They took turns, Zach
leaving the job of zipping the two sleeping bags together to
what he described as her more nimble fingers.

He'd looked better over dinner than he had when he first
appeared, but whatever good the meal had done him was
already gone. His shoulders sagged. She caught him rubbing his temples when he didn't think she'd see. What bothered her most was seeing how...*still* he held himself. For a
man who crackled with intensity, he seemed to have wound
down.

She could not imagine that sex was on his mind.

Finally, in complete darkness he climbed into the sleeping bag, lay on his back with his head on a balled-up parka
and waited while Ava slid in beside him.

She reached for his hand, which clasped hers firmly. "Are
you okay?" she asked.

Long pause. "Been better," he admitted. "A night's sleep
will do wonders."

She hoped so. If he looked this bad in the morning, she'd
try to talk him into staying put where they were now that
they wouldn't run out of food. She'd be even more strongly
in favor of that if not for his injuries—the ones he'd told her

about, and the ones he didn't want to admit to. He needed a hospital.

Also…would the terrorists, if that's what they were, really continue on their way minus their two compatriots? Or would they take the time to come looking for them—and for the problem they clearly hadn't solved?

Ava had a sick feeling that's exactly what they would do.

She'd have thought Zach had fallen asleep, except the hand holding hers hadn't relaxed. So she wasn't surprised when he spoke from the darkness.

"How are you?"

"Scared," she admitted. "Grateful."

He shifted. Turned his head to look at her? "For?"

"You," she said honestly. "I wouldn't have had a prayer alone. No, not just alone—even if I'd brought someone along on this trip. I've never met anyone like you."

"You must know some former soldiers."

"Yes, but…" They weren't warriors, but she wasn't sure he'd like that description. "You have different instincts, skills. How many people would know how to make snowshoes from some tree branches and a few cords? Would have the strength to go on when they were injured as badly as you were?"

"I'm okay—"

"You're not!" she said fiercely. "Don't lie to me!"

"Hey." His voice a gentle rumble, he rolled toward her enough to gather her up into his arms and settle her against his side. "I told you. I'm used to functioning with some pain. I'll bet you're a mass of bruises yourself, and you kept moving as long as you had to."

"It's not the same," she mumbled against his chest.

He seemed to be rubbing his cheek or jaw against her head. "Under the circumstances, my background has come in handy. You're right about that. I've faced worse odds and come out alive."

"But have you had to protect someone else?"

"Sure." He sounded surprised. "Locals in a bad spot, and my teammates, always. You…"

What felt like a hesitation drew out.

"Me what?"

"I…care about you. I'm not expecting anything from you, but if we'd met differently…" He huffed out a breath. "I need to keep you safe."

Her eyes stung. For an instant she listened to his heartbeat. "I want *you* safe, too. I *hated* it when you left today, or thinking you'd sacrifice yourself."

His arms tightened. "I have faith you're capable of fighting if you have to."

Was he right? Ava tried to imagine how she could have brought down either of the men he'd surprised today, and knew she couldn't have done that. But could she pull the trigger of a gun to save his life, or hers? A hot coal of anger said, *Yes.*

"I just…want to say thank you. For being here."

"Which I wouldn't be if you hadn't dug me out of a snowy grave." That had to be a smile in his voice.

She sniffed, hoping he wouldn't hear, but something inside her relaxed, too. He was right. This partnership wasn't one-sided. She wasn't useless by any means.

"I got your arm back in the socket, too," she reminded him.

His chest vibrated with what had to be a laugh. "Yes, you did."

"Okay. Part of me wants to talk about tomorrow…"

"Let's wait until morning. I have some ideas, but I'll need to look at a map. Assuming you carried one?"

She bobbed her head. What she thought qualified as a hug followed. Really grateful she'd suggested they double up the sleeping bags, Ava concentrated on his warmth along her body, his heartbeat, his slow, deep breaths…and fell asleep.

ZACH'S EYES SNAPPED OPEN. Had he just shouted? His skin felt electrified, and he was desperate to jump to his feet, to be ready—

Taking in the silence but for the soft, rhythmic sound of Ava breathing, he made himself lie still. Damn, the nightmare had been a bad one; one of the worst. He'd been doing better, sleeping more peacefully.

Nothing like going to war again, killing, to stir up the muddy depths of a man's psyche.

He muttered a few foul words under his breath. Weirdly, except for the nightmare, he felt as if he were waking from a coma, no sense of time having passed. He'd been out until he was flung into an ugly moment of the past, and was now wide awake.

He became conscious that the night was exceptionally dark. Either cloud cover was heavy enough to hide the moon entirely, or the surrounding trees and high ridges did the same. After a long period of stillness, he didn't hear anything alarming. The wake-up call had been in his own head.

In fact, as he forced himself to relax, muscle by muscle, he realized that he was amazingly comfortable with Ava cuddled up to him. Her head still rested in the hollow of his shoulder beneath the collar bone, and their legs had come to be tangled.

He hadn't spent the night with a woman in so long, he could barely remember the last time. Since retiring, he hadn't even wanted sex enough to play the games required with a new partner. Apparently, he thought wryly, he was ready—except Ava wasn't the game-playing kind.

Because it was necessary, Zach ran the usual checklist: shoulder, not too bad, head still ached. How would he know if he was dizzy?

He slowly lifted his right arm and, without disturbing Ava, was able to punch the button on his watch to see that it was 3:00 a.m. Thank God his bladder didn't demand attention. He still had no desire to move. Lying here with an armful of woman suited him just fine. In the absence of another nightmare, he could get two or three more hours of sleep before dawn lightened the sky.

Not that they could get the same early start they had the past two mornings, he reminded himself. He'd have to tinker with the straps on the snowshoes to make them fit Ava's smaller feet. Then the two of them had to have a serious discussion about how they might evade Borisyuk and company.

His mind circled, not coming to any conclusions, until Ava mumbled something.

He bent his head. "Did you say something?"

"Quit worrying," she said drowsily. "I can hear you. Feel you. Something."

He smiled and pressed his lips to the top of her head. "Yes, ma'am."

She seemed to sink back to sleep immediately, and the exchange freed him to do the same.

Ava squirming to get out of the sleeping bag woke him come morning. In the gray light, he said, "What?"

"Have to pee."

"Oh." He lay back and enjoyed watching her wriggle into multiple layers of clothing, even though that meant she wouldn't be coming back to bed.

She grabbed something from her pack and scrambled

up the bank, vanishing from his sight. With a groan, Zach pushed himself to sit up.

Damn. He felt even more battered than he had yesterday morning. His conditioning was sufficient for the traveling, but he hadn't needed two brutally physical fights, given his injuries. Curious, he lifted his fleece quarter-zip, along with the cotton tee beneath, and saw a motley collection of bruises that were a different color than the ones that lay beneath them. When he probed experimentally, he had to wonder if he didn't have a cracked rib or two, as well.

It wouldn't be the first time. He shrugged and winced. Good thing Ava hadn't seen that. He needed her to believe in him.

By the time she reappeared, he'd gotten dressed, too, not without wishing either of the men he'd tackled had been closer in size to him. He'd sure like a change of clothes. Standing, he groaned, wishing he'd had a chance to alleviate his stiffness.

"Oatmeal?" she asked.

"Sounds good." Boots on, he followed her path to the woods, and while he was there, he forced himself through some easy exercises to limber up his tight, aching muscles. The shoulder was improved today, he thought, despite what he'd put it through yesterday. The headache might have relented, too.

Neither talked much over breakfast. Ava kept sneaking looks at him he pretended not to notice. He suspected she was assessing his condition. He did the same in return, thinking that she'd visibly lost weight. They hadn't been eating enough, and both were probably getting dehydrated, too. The additional food and the second water bowl he'd acquired should help. He'd encourage her to drink more.

As she washed up the dishes and boiled water for what coffee she had left, he asked about her experience with firearms.

"I...did a little target shooting with a .22 rifle when I was a kid. It was fun, and I had a good eye, but that was a really long time ago. The target wasn't moving, and, well, it wasn't alive."

"No, you wouldn't have hunted," he acknowledged. She might be grateful right now for his capacity for violence, even the knowledge that he'd killed, but later, that might bother her. They weren't an obvious pairing.

He shook off more premature thoughts.

"I'm going to have you carry a handgun from here on out. I'll show you how to use it in principle, but even though the one I'm going to keep has a suppressor—a silencer— I'd just as soon not risk firing either gun."

"No! Oh, no."

He took out the Colt 9mm he'd lifted off his second victim, then showed her where the safety was and how to release it. He'd already verified that it was ready to fire, and that the magazine was full.

It was heavy for a woman's smaller hands, but she held it steadily, listening to his advice.

"Aim low. It'll kick up." He doubted the men hunting them wore any body armor. They were armed to the teeth, but hadn't really anticipated encountering anyone in the wilderness. If a helicopter had spotted them, they had come with the capability of shooting it down, which was different.

They must be cursing the chance that had led to them being spotted, and frustrated at not being positive the avalanche had taken the witnesses out. They couldn't realistically have expected the two scouts to rejoin them yet, not when they'd been ordered to take a lengthy detour. That said... Zach and Ava had lost most of a day after the avalanche hit, and then another full day when he went back to deal with the pair of hunters.

The question now was whether the main body of the group would simply wait there, or whether they'd proceed north again to pick up the two missing members, and potentially any survivors of the avalanche.

Before he started on the snowshoes, he asked for any maps she had, and they pored over the one she produced.

"Where were you dropped?" he asked.

She tapped a marked campsite.

His finger traced the length of the trail to roughly where the avalanche had caught them. "I was set down farther upriver, since I intended the trip to last no more than a week."

Ava looked rueful. "I was about to turn back. Just think, if I had before I set eyes on those men..."

"If you'd snowshoed downriver with no detours, you might have met up with them there."

She made a face. "I wonder what would have happened if I'd been able to call for a national park helicopter and they'd heard it coming."

Rather than reacting to that, he frowned at her. "Why *didn't* you turn back, if it was already on your mind?"

"I'm embarrassed to say it was because I suddenly realized someone was behind me."

"So you were running away from me." In other words, her involvement was his fault, one hundred percent. If she'd turned back that morning, he'd probably have exchanged a few polite words with her, then continued northward—and likely been alone when he saw the heavily armed group above. The binoculars he'd carried were fine, but he doubted he would have been able to pick out Borisyuk's face.

"I...suppose so. Except, it had long since become obvious

you were gaining ground on me." She looked perturbed. "I don't really know what I was thinking."

If not for the camera, would the terrorists have bothered to try to bury Zach under an avalanche? He didn't know, but if they had, at least Ava would have been safely going on her way, unaware of what she'd missed.

And he'd be dead, assuming he was in the same place at the same time.

Which was unlikely. Chances were better he'd have been deep in tree cover and unable to see the ridgetop on one side or the mountains on the other. He'd have enjoyed his trip, maybe wondered about the beautiful woman snowshoeing on her own out here—and Borisyuk would be passing unobserved through the wilderness, close to a planned pickup point.

He shouldn't regret anything, if there was the slightest chance they could stop that bastard. And yet, he did. He'd give damn near anything, including his life, to know that Ava was safe, even if that meant he had never had a chance to sleep with her pressed against him, her head on his shoulder.

Damn it.

Chapter Ten

"There are several trails turning off when we get closer to the end of this one," he said, tapping them with his finger.

"Yes, but one is where hikers on the ridge will emerge from—"

He conceded that with a nod.

"And this trail dead-ends at a lake." Her fingertip almost touched his. "I'm assuming they have this map, or a comparable one." Too bad the men weren't traveling aimlessly, but they were too well equipped not to have a compass and maps.

Zach told Ava what he was thinking. "There are a couple of possible alternatives. One is that, if we see tracks descending the ridge trail, we head up it." Assuming he and she made it that far.

She looked at him in surprise. "They'll just let us stroll by?"

He grimaced. "Not unless I can eliminate whoever was left on guard there. If they plan well, the rest of them will be spread out across all the possibilities."

Emotion flared in her eyes. "I hate it when you say things like that."

"Eliminate?"

"Yes!"

"We're now either victims or victors," he said bluntly. "I don't know about you, but I want to be able to—" *Go home.* That's what he'd almost said. A picture crossed his mind of the small rambler on an acre he was currently renting while he decided whether to stay in the Bellingham area or not. Home? No, it was a place to lay down his head, no different than base housing. Funny time to realize what he *wanted* was a real home that included a family.

She was staring at him. Waiting for him to finish.

"I want to be able to get *you* home safely," he concluded.

"Home," Ava echoed, in an odd tone. Then she sighed. "Okay, what looks like the best bet to you?"

"We either head out cross-country—there are a couple of possible creeks—or think about the trail that climbs over this pass." He touched his fingertip to the map. "The zig-zag line suggests it's steep, but it has to be doable. I wonder if the snow isn't year-round up there. Hikers and mountain climbers obviously navigate it. And once we get high enough, we'll have a better chance of cell phone coverage."

Her gaze met his again. "They'll surely be watching that route."

"Yeah. But all of them?"

Divided they fall. And he *was* armed now.

"There's not really a choice, is there?"

"No. Unless—keep checking your cell phone."

"Did either of them carry phones?"

"Both, but they're the cheap ones you pick up at the pharmacy. Who's your carrier?" When she told him, he nodded. "I'm betting you have better coverage."

"Okay."

Fortunately, one of the many smart decisions she'd made was to bring a couple of portable chargers. Her phone wouldn't run out of juice.

Except for a few necessary words, neither said anything else while she packed up and he worked on the bindings of her newly appropriated snowshoes.

Once he had her try them on, she offered him a crooked smile. "I deeply appreciate the expertise that allowed you to make my existing snowshoes. Really. But I'll still be thrilled to toss them into the woods."

Zach laughed. What he didn't say was that they wouldn't have dared take on what had to be a difficult climb to the pass if he hadn't been able to provide a replacement for the flimsy snowshoes that were already breaking apart.

Just before they set out, he changed into a white parka, even though it was a tighter fit than he liked, and utilized the white tarp to fling over the heavy pack. Ava looked alarmed, but only nodded when he said, "It'll give them pause at first sight."

As they beat their way back to the trail, Zach adjusting again to the weight of the pack, he couldn't prevent himself from running his own calculations, over and over. If the five remaining men continued on the ridge trail until its natural end, down at some other creek—if memory served—how long would it take them to head back up the valley, realize the two men sent on a separate errand should have appeared, and then figure out where he and Ava had gone?

What would he do if they came around a curve and found themselves face-to-face with any or all of the men?

Reaching the trail, completely untracked as it continued southward, Ava said unexpectedly, "We can worry ourselves in circles without helping."

How did this woman read his mind? "You're right," he said shortly, but planted a pole to free his hand long enough to pat the pistol he carried in the pocket of the parka, then reached back to estimate how long it would take him to get the automatic rifle in position to spray bullets.

ZACH INSISTED ON taking the lead, she presumed because of what he wore. The sight of that familiar parka and fur-lined hood might provide a critical couple of seconds before they realized he was a stranger.

Please.

It took her a few minutes to adjust to wearing the less cumbersome, modern snowshoes again, as well as having real poles, but after that she marveled at how fast they were now able to move. If Zach was being hindered by his shoulder injury or headache, she couldn't tell. A couple of times he opened enough of a lead on her that he paused after glancing over his shoulder so she could catch up. She didn't let herself feel chagrined. He was bigger, stronger and longer legged. After all, he'd gained fast on her even that first day. Still, Ava felt confident she wasn't holding him up much.

There weren't a lot of distinctive landmarks along this stretch. One small creek—mostly ice choked—crossed the trail. She poked with the tip of her pole at some ice and was surprised when it didn't so much break up as disintegrate. That was the moment when she became aware that she was too warm.

"Hold up," she called in a low voice.

Zach stopped and deftly turned his snowshoes so he could raise his eyebrows at her.

"It's warming up," she said.

He frowned, taking in the many snow-laden branches to each side of the trail. "Snow's not melting yet."

"No, but almost."

He pushed back the hood, as if testing the temperature. "That could be good or bad," he said thoughtfully.

Ava knew what he meant. A sudden melt would turn the trail into a slushy mess and expose whatever growth had happened since park personnel or volunteers had cut it back. Probably a brief warming wouldn't extend long; the park wouldn't really open to hikers until July. But she and Zach were at a relatively low elevation here, at the bottom of the valley.

"I'm going to take my parka off." She stripped off her gloves and unzipped, aware Zach was evaluating what she wore beneath. No, her next layer, a fleece quarter-zip, was not bright red, so she ignored his scrutiny but saw that he wasn't following suit. Of course not; that white parka with the hood was a disguise. Once she stashed her parka beneath an elastic strap, she pulled on her gloves again and said, "I'm ready."

His eyes lingered on her for a moment that felt…personal. Even warm. But abruptly he turned and set off again, Ava falling in behind him.

If we get out of this, I'll probably never see him again, she reminded herself, but discovered that she didn't actually believe that. Given what he'd said, would he let her go that easily? Would she go without making some effort to find out whether he might be interested in—

What? Spending a couple of nights together?

Ava was disconcerted to realize she'd take even that. She wanted to keep sleeping with him, and more.

The sound of something thrashing through the thick vegetation snapped her back to the present, and she came to a stop behind Zach, who'd raised one hand to signal her. A deer stepped out into the open in front of them, saw them, and took a giant leap into the tangled growth on the other side of the trail, going toward the river.

"She didn't expect us," he murmured, and resumed his long, easy stride.

An hour later, they had another unexpected encounter with wildlife. Zach stopped and said quietly, "Look."

A wolf stood so still beneath the branches of a cedar, his golden eyes on them, they might almost have passed without seeing him at all. Ava longed for her camera, packed away with the damaged lens. Reclusive creatures, gray wolves didn't show themselves any more often than did the lynx she'd hoped to see. She'd heard howling, but in the far distance. Now he evaluated them, then melted out of sight without making a sound.

"Suggests he hasn't met any other people recently," Zach said softly.

That was a heartening thought.

They made swift progress, finally stopping for a bite to eat beneath an old cedar tree much like the one the wolf had used for cover.

Ava was glad to shrug out of the pack for a few minutes. She felt stronger today, though, and it wasn't just the new-and-improved snowshoes. The avalanche had been...she had to think. Three days ago? Yes. Three nights had intervened. Her aches and pains were fading. She hadn't been able to see her face, but guessed the visible bruises were, too.

As Zach spilled some raisins into the palm of his bare hand, she studied him. His face was thinner, she felt sure, maybe even gaunt, although with the brown scruff that was swiftly becoming a short beard, it was hard to be sure. She'd noticed earlier without paying attention that he had dark bruises beneath both eyes. Not quite black eyes, but close. Now the almost purple color was muddied by some yellow. The lines carving his forehead seemed deeper, too, if she wasn't mistaken.

He'd moved today with the strength, grace and certainty that she'd seen when he first appeared behind her, but that had to be deceptive. He seemed determined to hide his pain, which might have offended her, except she guessed soldiers in the kind of unit he'd belonged to were always reluctant to show weakness. The fact that she was a woman might have nothing to do with his determination to disguise any vulnerability.

Or maybe he wasn't thinking about it at all; maybe he was utterly focused on what lay ahead of them. What he still had to do.

Yes, she thought. That's the kind of man he was.

He was looking right back at her, she suddenly realized, one of his unusually mobile eyebrows quirked. "Deep thoughts?"

"No, just thinking you look leaner. I suppose I've lost weight, too."

"Easily regained," he said lightly. "You ready to get going again?"

"Of course." Turning her face from his, she tucked the remnants of her snack—or was this lunch?—back into a pocket of her pack. While she was thinking about it, she took out her phone.

At his raised brows, she had to shake her head.

Shortly after they set out again, Ava realized the trail was climbing slightly to proceed higher above the level of the river. It now cut across a side hill. Although much of the undergrowth—the salal and gooseberry, the Oregon grape and lower clumps of devil's club—were mostly buried under snow, the trail here squeezed between a heavy growth of trees, the ubiquitous cedar, hemlock and spruce mixed with more deciduous ones than she'd noticed farther up the valley. She thought she recognized maples, even without any hint of budding leaves. She seemed to remember that dog-wood was common, too, as well as aspen and the every-present alder and willow.

Zach had slowed down somewhat, although she didn't see any awkwardness in his stride or the way he planted his poles. He might be watching more carefully. He wouldn't like not being able to see far ahead, she knew, given the density of the forest, as well as the curve of the trail. She tried harder to listen, too, but was afraid she wouldn't hear an approaching snowshoer over the *swish-swish* of their own steps.

"I think I see a sign sticking out of the snow," he told her over his shoulder, voice barely audible.

She hadn't come from this far south, but of course national park employees would mark trails.

"Wait," Zach said sharply, but still quietly. "There are tracks on it."

Oh, God. Ava froze between one step and the next.

Then a voice called what sounded like an inquiry…in a harsh language she didn't recognize.

ZACH HAD REHEARSED for this moment since they started out this morning. With his hands encased in thick winter gloves, he couldn't get his index finger in to squeeze the trigger on the handgun he carried in the pocket at his hip. Given the warming temperatures, he considered leaving off his right glove, but the day still hovered around freezing, and he didn't dare let his fingers get numb or stiff. So he'd practiced, over and over.

Yank hand from the glove, leave it hanging from his pole. Reach the short distance, take gun from the pocket.

He'd left the safety off to eliminate the one step.

He had run through it over and over in his mind, and

practiced ditching the glove and reaching for the butt of the gun a dozen times. Either Ava was concentrating intensely on maintaining her pace, or giving what attention she had left over to watching and listening for company, but she showed no indication she'd noticed what he was doing or why.

Now, when the white-clad snowshoer appeared not fifteen yards ahead, Zach pulled the gun within three to four seconds.

The greeting, initially friendly sounding, gave him the time he needed. With five or six days' worth of scruff covering half his face and sunglasses over his eyes, Zach couldn't look that different at first glance from this guy's compatriots.

But when Zach didn't respond immediately, there was a gradual shift in body language and expression. The gaze slid past Zach, took in Ava.

This enemy's hand moved swiftly to the firing mechanism of the sniper-type rifle he carried slung over his shoulder, barrel pointing forward. Toward Zach and Ava.

Zach dropped his poles and braced his own gun in a two-handed firing position. With the suppressor screwed to the barrel, it was more awkward than what he was used to, but from this distance—

"I'm an American police officer," he said loudly, clearly. "Put down your weapons. *Now!*"

The man lifted the rifle, and Zach swore he was pointing it at Ava.

Zach fired, even as the man facing him did the same. Behind him, Ava cried out and either went down or flung herself to one side. He couldn't afford to turn.

He pulled the trigger three times, stopping only as he saw the white-clad figure folding in on itself, tumbling to the snowy ground. Zach had seen death take enough people to recognize it on this man's face. Still, he raced forward, yanked the rifle away from his adversary, and then spun clumsily and scrambled back to Ava.

Who, thank God, was picking herself back up. "He tried to shoot me," she whispered. "I think he *did* shoot me."

"What?"

"My arm stings, that's all, and—" She reached up to finger a tear in her parka on her upper arm.

"God." He fell to his knees beside her. "You scared me."

"*I* scared you?"

"*He* scared me." Zach had a bad feeling he was shaking, but he couldn't let himself yank her into his arms. The seasoned soldier he was had begun scanning for any indication of company before he'd even pulled the trigger. He wished he hadn't felt obligated to give a warning. He'd been desperate to prevent the other man from firing.

His brain was already turning that over when Ava said, "I didn't hear his gun go off. Or yours. Well, except for a few pops."

"You're really all right?" he demanded to know.

Her eyes were wide, shocked, but as always, determined. "Yes."

"Let me see," he insisted.

Wincing, she eased her arm out of the parka, and he was able to push aside the torn fabric of her fleece top and the turtleneck she wore beneath it to see a graze. Blood seeped, but treating it could wait. An inch or two to the left, and they'd be dealing with a real wound. Conceivably a shattered bone.

Heart racing from the close call, his thoughts jumped back to her comment about hearing only a few pops.

Galvanized by his realization, Zach pushed himself to

his feet and returned to the rifle that lay where he'd tossed it, sunken in snow. He picked it up, astonished. Yes, it, too, had been fitted to fire silently. The AK-47s the other two had carried hadn't been; he wasn't even sure they *could* be. The shooter had to practice to achieve accuracy with the addition to any of the military's various sniper rifles, but they could be and sometimes were fitted with suppressors. There were moments when you had to go in quiet.

Zach couldn't believe his luck. He hadn't been primarily a sniper, but he'd gone through training at Fort Bennett and had utilized his skills plenty of times. He might still have qualms about picking off the remaining members of the terrorist group like ducks in a shooting gallery, but the fact that this man's first instinct on seeing Zach and Ava had been to gun them down sent a strong message.

"He's…dead?" she asked from behind him.

"Yeah. It was him or us."

"I saw." She'd stayed on the trail but advanced to within a few feet of the man. "What do we do with him? And which way do we go?"

God, he could love this woman, tough enough to pass through terror into practicality and grit within a minute or two.

Maybe he already did.

This wasn't the time to become mired in the sinkhole created by emotions.

He still didn't hear any indication of other people nearby. They had to have spread out, the way he'd both feared and hoped.

That didn't mean he and Ava could afford to waste a minute.

He slung the rifle over his shoulder, straightened and looked around. "Get him out of sight, for starters." He evaluated the tracks. "Don't know how far he went up this trail before he decided we couldn't possibly be ahead of him and turned to come back. Maybe all he was doing was rejoining the main trail, but he might have been ordered to hang back out of sight, to lie in wait for us. Somehow, we surprised him."

"He certainly surprised *me*," she said dryly.

Zach spared a glance at her face, to see that for all her outward gutsiness, it was pinched. This was likely the only violent death she'd ever seen—unless at some point during that year while she'd tried as a seven-year-old to survive on the streets, she'd seen someone stabbed or shot. It was all too possible. He'd have to ask her what city she'd been in.

"Okay," he said. "You're going to stand guard while I carry his body back to the main trail and look for a good place to dump him. Then I'll get rid of his pack and snow-shoes, too."

"Rifle?"

"That, we're keeping. In fact—"

To her obvious consternation, he gave her a one minute short course in firing a McMillan TAC-50, a sniper rifle used by Canadian military as well as by other countries. Zach had never personally fired one, but it made sense these guys had been able to get their hands on one on the black market.

Fortunately, for these purposes, she could ignore the scope. All she needed to do was point and fire. She wouldn't be shooting anyone from more than twenty, twenty-five yards, tops.

Ava did not look thrilled, but finally nodded, her teeth sinking into her lower lip. "Just…hurry, okay?"

Hanging around here at the junction of two trails was dangerous. "Yeah."

It took only a matter of minutes for him to drop his own pack, strip off the dead man's and heave the body over his right shoulder. Feeling the strain and the pain on the injured side of his body, he grunted. The guy was no lightweight, and Zach hoped he wouldn't have to go far to find the right spot.

He turned back the way he and Ava had come, and hadn't gone thirty feet before he noticed a particularly thick tangle of vegetation. He strode as close to it as he could, trying not to break branches, and did his best to fling a body that had to weigh 180 pounds or so. To his gratification, it disappeared.

He hustled back, seeing that Ava appeared frozen in place but still held the rifle in firing position, and crouched to conduct a cursory search of the pack. Another passport, this one from Uzbekistan. He pocketed that. Otherwise, the only thing worth holding on to was a handgun with a suppressor. He switched it out for the 9mm he'd given Ava earlier, then hauled the pack down the trail and threw it next to the body.

He took a few minutes to try to erase tracks, grimacing at his mixed success, and then smoothed over signs of the violent confrontation as best he could.

Finally, since no one else had appeared and he didn't hear any indication of someone close by, he gently took the rifle back from Ava and pulled her into his arms.

Chapter Eleven

Ava didn't know why she felt so traumatized now, after all the horrifying events of the last four days, but heaven help her, she might as well be a quaking aspen in a stiff breeze. She did a lot more than lean on Zach; she wrapped her arms around his torso, buried her face in his parka-clad shoulder and hung on for all she was worth. And shook.

He was talking, or only growling things under his breath. She couldn't make out a word he said. It had to be a couple of minutes before she realized she wasn't the only one shaking. The cold, bare hand that smoothed hair from her face definitely had a tremor. She rubbed her cheek against it, hard, and wished they were done, that this was the end and they could just stand here in each other's arms for the next half an hour or so.

But fear still squeezed her heart, and at last she lifted her head to look up at him. Eyes espresso dark met hers, and he said something else, still imperceptible. Then he wrapped her jaw with one hand, lifted her chin and kissed her.

This was like the other time, but more. He demonstrated with his mouth and teeth and tongue how desperate he felt, how hungry. Scared, too, she thought. *Like me.*

He all but devoured her, except she responded with equal

ferocity. She *needed* this. Him. Her mind blurred, until she quit thinking, only wanted.

But then, with a gut-wrenching groan, he tore his mouth from hers. His eyes burned into hers. "Damn, Ava. You have no idea—" He bit off the rest, as if she couldn't guess what he hadn't said. His hand still shook, if for another reason now, when he stroked her face, as if that touch was precious.

Only, he straightened after that, and she had to loosen her grip on him and do the same.

"We have to get moving," he said gruffly.

She swallowed and squared her shoulders. "I know. I just—"

"This trail leads to the lake. I think we have to take it and then set out cross-country. I hope to God that's even possible."

She couldn't think, not without looking away from his intensity. "There's only the one track leading this way," she heard herself say.

"Yeah."

"But if he's already made it here, the others…"

"Must have divvied up the alternatives."

"Except, he thought you were one of his buddies."

"Momentarily, yeah. Maybe he assumed a teammate had cut back to report a sighting. Still, they wouldn't have split up and started investigating alternate routes the way it appears they've done if they'd hadn't started to worry. Even so, they're probably still pretty confident. For good reason. You and I haven't moved very fast, between the twenty hours or so before we were able to set off at all, and the slow pace because of your primitive snowshoes." He grimaced. "And my condition."

"So the rest of them have been expecting the two sent off

to make sure no witnesses survived to zip along by now, or at least any minute, and say, 'No problem.'"

His mouth quirked. "Probably in another language, but yeah." His grimness returned. "Three down, four to go."

Her stomach rolled. "If they gang up on us—"

"We're still in deep trouble," he agreed. "I'd like to avoid that happening. And unfortunately—" he lifted his arm and checked his watch "—we've lost a lot of this day. If you're up to it, we should still keep going for a few hours, but that won't get us much past the lake, if at all."

"If only we'd searched harder for your pack. I'm sorry."

How many times had they had this discussion? The satellite radio he'd carried would have brought help within hours. If only *she'd* been smart enough to carry one, too—

"Knock it off," he said roughly. "We searched as long as we dared. It was miracle enough that you found *me*."

What more was there to say? Ava only nodded, taking in the sight of a man who looked as battered as she felt, yet also dangerous and still strong. His lips were a little swollen and had cracked. Averting her face, she licked her own and tasted blood.

Oh.

She felt his gaze on her face, and there was a discernible pause before he stepped away. He slung his pack on his back again, and the rifle over his shoulder. She saw him pat the right pocket of his parka where he carried the handgun, pull on his gloves and grip his poles.

"You lead," he said, moving aside.

Well, at least someone had broken the trail for her already. She set off briskly.

THE TRACKS THEY followed ended fifteen minutes later, where the latest dead man had turned around to go back.

The unbroken snow slowed them down a little, since it wasn't always clear what was trail beneath the snow and what wasn't. They were left to flounder a few times before backing up and trying again.

Their next break, Zach and Ava studied the contour map again. That itch aggravated his spine constantly now, but however much he'd have preferred an alternative, it still looked like their best bet of cutting over to the ridge trail was from the lake, nestled in a high bowl. A fold of land lay between the two trails—not a high ridge, but steep on this side and forested. To his regret, with the sky high and blue, there was no possibility of another convenient, late-spring snowstorm to help them disappear.

That probably would have been asking for too much.

He turned so frequently to watch behind them, he'd have whiplash by the time they stopped for the night. He didn't dare miss anything, though. Any faint sign of a pursuer, he'd send Ava on ahead and set up himself with the rifle. He didn't need a snare this time; he could kill long-distance.

Not for the first time, he wondered how law enforcement would judge his choices, but he was damned if he'd second-guess them. Everything that mattered to him was on the line here: bringing Ava, an innocent civilian and a woman he could love, to safety; stopping a threat to the nation he'd spent ten years of his life fighting to protect; and, probably in last place but still meaningful, his own survival. He'd hoped never to kill again, but he intended to do whatever proved necessary to protect what mattered to him.

He paused where he had a decent sight line to the trail behind him between tall trees and scanned with binoculars. Still nothing. Where were the others? In the next hour or two, they'd know for sure that they had a major problem on their hands. Zach had to circle back to wondering what

Borisyuk was thinking. Shouldn't his mission be at the fore-front? He'd lost some men; Zach doubted this cold-blooded terrorist gave a damn. He was still in a position to get the hell out of this wilderness and on his way to the job await-ing him. Why *wouldn't* that be his choice?

He could have gone on with only, say, one of the men, leaving the others to clean up behind him. If that was the case, he might still be able to wreak havoc that could be devastating for this country. But he also risked having one or more of those men captured and, potentially, talking.

Zach hummed in his throat. If these were all dedicated terrorists, Borisyuk might believe he was safe from betrayal no matter what. If they were mercenaries hired to get him across the border, though…that was different. Did those men even know who he was?

When he wasn't snatching looks over his shoulder, Zach rarely took his eyes off Ava, which was distracting in its own way. Hard not to let his gaze linger on her long, strong legs and taut butt outlined in stretchy fabric. To picture her face, and aching at the memory of her passionate response to his kiss.

That wasn't what he should be thinking about now, though. Protecting *her* was too much of what mattered. In a way, she represented all the other Americans who would suffer if a terrorist accomplished his goal.

The psychology of his opponents, and particularly their leader, played in Zach's mind as he climbed the trail rising above the deepest cut of the river, following a creek that murmured in the background of his consciousness, but only made a sparkling appearance from snow cover and ice to tumble in mini waterfalls on occasion.

What Zach thought was that Borisyuk had an ego prob-lem. Maybe he'd set out on his deadly path years ago with complete dedication to a twisted ideal, but he'd been too successful. He'd become a legend, and he *couldn't* let himself run like a frightened rabbit. He would not, could not, let himself believe he could be outmaneuvered, refused to believe anyone was smarter or more capable than him. Maybe it wasn't even the possibility of a photograph that still drove him. Once he realized three of his men had failed to stop whoever had survived the avalanche, his determination would harden. One or two people, mere backcountry travelers? Inconceivable!

At this moment, he probably still felt smug. One of his men would show up with evidence of the death of any Americans foolish enough to get in his way. But that smugness would wane as time passed. Eventually, he'd send someone to venture back up the trail, where the snowshoe tracks would initially be confusing, but eventually make clear that three people had met up—and only two of them had gone on.

No, Borisyuk wouldn't be prepared to quit, to say, "A photograph of me? What does that matter?"

Of course Zach couldn't be certain, but he thought he was right. And *that* was both good and bad. Good because it meant he and Ava still had a chance to kill or capture an infamous terrorist. Bad because they were still in great danger.

The trail broke into the open, and Zach paused to lift binoculars to his eyes and scrutinize the land below him. Still nothing, but that might only be because the dense Northwest rainforest hid so much.

Another hour passed, and the two of them paused for a drink and a handful of nuts. At Ava's worried look, he shook his head. They didn't talk at all, only went on. Two hours, three. The sun was dropping in the sky. In another couple of hours, it would go behind the mountains, and they'd lose light fast. They needed to take refuge soon. Not generally an optimist, he thought maybe he'd been expecting pursuit sooner than it could reasonably occur. The lake couldn't be far—not that it offered any safety.

His eye was caught by multiple deer tracks diverting from the trail. He'd seen them off and on all day, sometimes going off into the forest. This was different. It looked like a favorite route for the four-footed residents of these mountains. And, damn—that almost had to be a track left by a bear. Or Bigfoot.

"You seeing deer tracks up there?" he called.

Ava stopped and looked back. "Yes. I can see the lake, too. The ice is breaking up."

"Come here and tell me what you think."

She lifted her snowshoes in a quick turn and returned to his side.

He pointed with his pole. "Animal trail."

"Going the way we want to go."

"That's what I'm thinking."

"I say we take a chance." Her eyes widened. "Is that a bear track?"

"Has to be." His mouth quirked. "Probably just woke up. Can't be in a good mood."

Ava made a face at him. "Thank you for that. Do you want me to go ahead again?"

"Yeah, I'm going to try to muddy the tracks a little."

She nodded and set off. Looked like they'd face a steeper climb now.

Zach tramped all the way to the lake, made a mess in the snow then turned back. He went a little past the animal trail, snapped off a branch, swung around again and started swiping behind him as he moved backward. He did the same for ten yards or so onto the alternate trail, but going backward uphill was a strain, so he abandoned the effort. His best hope was that a few more animals would travel this way as the day waned—and maybe some nocturnal creatures, too. Someone hunting humans might not pay attention to the deer, rabbit and raccoon tracks that they'd been seeing everywhere.

Zach didn't relax his watchfulness any as he turned and sped after Ava.

AVA'S THIGHS BURNED. The trail meandered in a way one cleared and leveled by humans didn't. It turned out deer didn't think a thing of bounding straight upward, too. She had to pause every ten minutes or so, breathe deeply and wait for her muscles to relax. It was like doing sprints in training, she consoled herself; short, fast sprints divided by brief rests.

She hated that, when she caught a glimpse of Zach behind her, she couldn't read his expression at all, beyond obvious grimness. It was as if he'd pulled inside somewhere. His gaze didn't meet hers; his eyes were dark and curiously flat. He moved steadily but for his regular stops to search the landscape behind them. His head would tilt, and she had a suspicion he had better hearing than she did.

She hoped he did; she was depending entirely on him right now.

She didn't descend into the kind of exhaustion she had in previous days, when she couldn't think about anything but which foot to move next. *Gee, I've gained some conditioning*, she thought. But really, it was more the shock and fear of the earlier encounter sending her adrenaline into overdrive, and she still felt it circulating in her blood.

The speed with which the incident had erupted stunned her. Very few words exchanged, a gun barrel swinging toward her, the weird, compressed sound of silenced guns and the sting as a bullet creased her arm. The body collapsing, the *look* in his eyes—

Ignoring the momentary queasiness, she reminded herself to wash and bandage the still stinging place on her upper arm. She felt sure Zach wouldn't have forgotten.

The track curved to level out briefly, although they hadn't reached the top of the ridge. Just as it curved back and began to climb again, bear tracks continued straight. She had bigger things to worry about, but still exhaled with relief. She'd be just as glad not to stumble on an irritable, hungry bear.

Maybe he had a cave up here, it occurred to her. He might be like the famous groundhog; he or she had emerged to decide whether winter was past, and thought, *Nah. I'm going back to bed.*

A strange sound came to her ears. She froze between one stride and the next, trying to identify it. Zach exploded into action, catching up to her with shocking speed.

"That's somebody behind us. Don't know if there are two of them, or whether he stumbled, cracked his shin and swore, but that was a voice."

She clenched her teeth to be sure they couldn't chatter. When she was confident she wouldn't give away her panic, she asked, "What do we do?"

"Go on until we find a place I can set up," he said tersely. For the first time in the past couple of hours, she felt as if he was seeing *her*, and his expression was raw. "If I can hide you and my pack, I may climb a tree."

She bobbed her head. "You go ahead, then. You know what you're looking for."

Without another word, he passed her and set off fast, despite the crosshatch technique needed to climb in snowshoes. She did her best to keep up. The worst part was that she didn't hear so much as a whisper of sound behind her. It made her picture a little red dot centered on the back of her head. One pull of the trigger—

Go, go, go.

"Here," Zach said suddenly.

They weren't at a high enough elevation for the trees to be stunted yet. He seemed to have his eye on a cluster of big hemlock or Douglas fir, she wasn't sure, probably spruce and certainly cedar. The snow cover thinned to almost nothing beneath the spreading branches.

He pointed. "Get under cover, well back. Hunker down. Have your handgun ready to fire. Do you understand?"

"Yes. Yes."

He didn't move until she took a couple of steps, then removed her snowshoes and kept going on the side hill, a foot slipping here and there, but she caught herself with a hand on the branches and rough trunks.

When she glanced back, she couldn't see Zach anymore. That scared her, but she had to trust that he knew what he was doing. Of course he did.

Finally, she crawled beneath a cedar tree. The feathery branches brushed the ground. Ava had to push them aside. With shuddering relief, she dropped the poles and snowshoes, eased off her pack and dug the gun she didn't even like to handle out of the outside pocket.

Then she crawled to a position where she could just see traces of her own tracks between the thankfully lush branches that she hoped would still hide her. She decided to sit up; a lot of positions would be hard to sustain for long. Then she took off her right glove, as Zach had taught her, pushed the tiny button to turn off the safety and listened to herself breathe. She just couldn't let herself get so scared that she accidentally shot Zach.

No. I have to wait to make sure.

MUCH LIKE HE'D done setting up the previous ambushes, Zach continued on ten yards until the trail curved enough that a pursuer was unlikely to notice that one of the two people ahead had peeled off. He'd see only tracks heading on.

Then Zach stepped carefully off the trail and circled back to his chosen trees. He stashed his pack and equipment out of sight and, with the rifle slung over his shoulder, started to climb.

This was an old enough cedar to have branches he hoped would hold his weight. If he could get high enough, he'd be able to step over to a spruce that would give him a better sight line down the trail. He'd kept his gloves on to give himself a good grip. If a branch broke and he fell, they were screwed.

Each scramble upward was made gingerly. He tested some of his weight on a branch, then all of it, but kept an arm around the trunk or a hand gripping the limb above to keep himself from plummeting.

He still didn't hear anybody approaching, but knew he couldn't be mistaken.

At last, maybe twenty-five feet off the ground, he found a perch that felt secure and gave him a hell of a view.

He was planning to kill in cold blood. He couldn't issue a warning, not when this SOB was likely carrying a fully automatic weapon that could spray bullets to cut him down along with half of this stretch of forest, too.

The shot wouldn't be long, which was just as well since he hadn't practiced at the range at more than two hundred yards since he got out of the service. The old skills were probably there, but he was just as glad not to have to test them. If all went well, this shot wouldn't even be a hundred yards.

Nothing to it.

He rolled his shoulders. Stuck both his gloves in parka pockets and worked at slowing his breathing. How many times had he done this?

More than he wanted to remember.

He rested the barrel of the rifle on another branch, needing to compensate for the extra and unfamiliar weight of the suppressor. Then he zeroed the scope. Details sprang out in what had been a faraway scene. The length of a football field. Now, he could almost reach out and touch.

Slow and easy. Breathe in, breathe out. Wait for the natural rest.

Ten or fifteen minutes passed. Longer. Then suddenly a white-clad man appeared without Zach having heard him. Despite the warming day, he wore the hood up so that the fur almost obscured his face. He blended in remarkably well, only his boots gray or brown instead of white. The AK-47 stood out, of course.

Zach could have fired, but waited. *Closer, closer.*

Some instinct had his opponent sliding the rifle off his shoulder to ease it into firing position.

Can't let that happen.

Zach set the gun sights over the chest, safer than a head shot now that he knew the others hadn't worn Kevlar vests.

He let out a breath and gently pulled the trigger.

Dead on.

He'd have new nightmares, but refused to feel guilty. These bastards were hunting him and Ava relentlessly, as if planning to mount their heads on a wall.

He'd done what he had to do.

Chapter Twelve

With no way to tell the time, Ava could only guess. Each minute probably felt like fifteen. She strained her ears and eyes. It already felt like forever when she thought she heard…something. A *pop* that made her feel queasy. Then she decided she must have imagined it, because nothing else happened. Zach didn't appear, or call out to her to emerge from hiding.

She rested the gun on her thigh, holding it with her left hand every so often so she could flex the fingers on her right hand. How *could* it be so quiet? Why couldn't she even hear a bird call? It was as if nature held its breath. Maybe these old mountains and this forest resented the violence that invaded an ancient landscape meant to be a refuge. Except, these mountains also were home to several of nature's top-of-the-line predators.

What if she had heard a gunshot, only it was *Zach* who'd been shot? The thought sickened her, but after some deep breathing, Ava convinced herself she didn't believe that was possible, not for a minute. Zach had brought down *two* men when he was hurting and unarmed but for a folding knife. The next one, heavily armed, had come face-to-face with them, and Zach had outgunned him.

Who knew she'd ever be able to think so matter-of-factly about stuff that was so horrific.

No matter what, she kept her guard up. She flexed her fingers again, peered in every direction and strained for any sound at all.

IT HAD TO be an hour or more before the low call came to her. "Ava? Where are you?"

"Here." Her voice croaked. Her next effort was better. "Here!" She tried to stand but found her knees had pretty much locked. Still, she sent the closest cedar branches waving, and within a minute she saw him turning his head as he came into sight.

She staggered to her feet just in time. "Oh, thank God!"

He gave a weak grin. "Now, now. You need to have faith."

"I do," she said quietly, almost hoping he didn't hear her. From the way his gaze sharpened, she thought he had. "What happened?"

Carrying the rifle, he ducked into her shelter. "There was only one man on our trail. I went down almost as far as the river to be sure there wasn't a second one." He rested the rifle, butt down, against the tree trunk.

"He's dead?"

In the act of lowering his pack to the ground, he gave a clipped nod as he glanced quickly at her before looking away.

"Did you, well, learn anything?"

"No." With a groan, he sat down a couple of feet from her, leaning against the tree trunk. If she'd thought she had seen him tired before, it was nothing in comparison. He pulled off a glove and scrubbed his hand over his face and dug his fingers into his hair beneath the fleece hat. "Damn."

On instinct, she reached to lay a hand on the forearm he had braced on his knees. "I'm sorry. I wish I could do more."

The turbulence was back in his brown eyes. "Like kill people?"

The sharp edge in his voice shocked her. She snatched back her hand. "I should have said, I wish you didn't have to kill people."

"I'm the one who's sorry," Zach said heavily. "I hated doing it, but there wasn't any option except raising our hands and saying, 'Here we are, execute us.'" His mouth twisted. "*I'm* the executioner instead."

Feeling tentative, she said, "You said yourself that this is war. We *can't* let that monster loose on our country! Isn't this every bit as critical as whatever you had to do in, I don't know, Afghanistan or the other places you were sent?"

His eyes met hers. He didn't so much as blink for a minute before he finally dipped his head. "You're right. I know you are. I guess I've been getting mushy in my retirement."

She snorted, and one side of his mouth curled up.

"Okay. I'll quit with the self-doubt."

"Thank you. You saved both of our lives today. *Twice.*"

"Yeah, I guess so. Damn, I'm beat." His head turned again, as if he was evaluating her hidey-hole. "I'm thinking this is as good a place as any to spend the night. Maybe we can set up a little deeper in this stand of woods."

"Okay. Do you want to rest for a few minutes first?"

"Maybe." He tipped his head back and closed his eyes, thick dark lashes fanned on tanned, still discolored skin.

Ava let him brood, if that's what he was doing. If he fell asleep...well, she'd find them a campsite and set up, then come back for him.

"This was another Russian," he said unexpectedly. "I'm betting ex-military. Probably all of them are. Were."

"That makes sense," she said softly.

"The odds are almost even now, except…" He broke off. "I wish I could keep you out of this."

"So far, you mostly have."

"If we could just get our hands on Borisyuk himself."

"Wouldn't it make sense for him to run for it?" She was practically begging for the answer she both wanted to hear and didn't, but also… There was no *logic* in a man whose goal was to disrupt this nation in some significant way wasting time to hunt down two snowshoers who, for all he knew, hadn't even had a good look at him.

Zach told her some of what he'd apparently been thinking about today, and she had to agree it was logical. And no, she didn't want Grigor Borisyuk to go on his way. Despite the struggles in her life, she'd never felt vengeful until now. She wanted that man to die next—or, better yet, for Zach to capture him and be able to hand him over to authorities.

THE END OF an operation was when you evaluated every decision, every pause, every command. Every hiccup. It wasn't Zach's habit to second-guess himself constantly mid-op, but he couldn't seem to help himself this time.

He did get himself moving so that he and Ava could find a secluded campsite even farther from the trail, but when she insisted on setting up the tent and rolling out the sleeping bags—and zipping them together again, his ears told him—he let her. He felt as if he'd been pounded.

He always had hated his rare sniper missions. He didn't know how the guys who did it day after day, month after month, came home even semisane. The combination of looking into someone's face so clearly, it was as if you could touch them, while they had no idea they were going to die, always sickened him. In modern warfare, it was necessary. He got that. But he'd rather any day be involved in a shoot-out across the street in some red-brown, dusty town, a straight-out battle where everyone involved knew what was at stake. Or having a hand-to-hand fight, as with the first two guys he'd brought down, even if he'd given himself the advantage from the beginning with the element of surprise.

Get it out of your mind, he told himself.

Which was fine, but then he devolved into thinking that, tired or not, he and Ava should have gone on, opened more distance between themselves and any pursuers.

Yeah, except it was likely one or two of these guys had also advanced up the ridge trail and would therefore be lying in wait for them. Better to face them after a good night's sleep. As good as he'd have, when he'd be keeping an ear out all night for any faint noise that didn't belong.

Ava broke into his brooding. "Any preferences for dinner?"

"Food."

She chuckled. "On our way out, maybe the helicopter would drop us in the parking lot at a pizza parlor."

"That sounds good to me." Now he was *really* hungry. He also liked that she pictured them together sharing a pizza. "I should have taken a turn cooking tonight. No reason for you to wait on me."

"An enlightened man," she teased. Then her voice and expression turned serious. "You're the soldier. I'm the one who has to wait. Of course I should contribute any way I can."

He frowned. "I'd be dead if it weren't for you, remember?"

"Yes, except if not for me, there probably wouldn't have *been* an avalanche."

"You're in a mood, aren't you?"

She closed her eyes for a moment, and her shoulders

seemed to relax. When she opened her eyes, she fixed her gaze on his face. "I guess so. I *hate* waiting, not knowing what's happening to you. The last thing I should do is whine after you come back safe."

"Ava."

Her lashes fluttered a couple of times.

"You may be the bravest woman I've ever met. This has been a monumentally bad few days, and you've endured it all without any whining. You had to have passed the point of complete exhaustion and continued on for hours without a word at least a couple of those days." He smiled ruefully. "You cuddled with a complete stranger to warm him up. You popped his arm back into the socket. You let him leave you for *hours* in a hole that looked like an open grave. So let up on yourself."

Her mouth curved. "I will if you will."

He stiffened. "What are you talking about?"

"I know brooding when I see it."

Zach grimaced. "Set me up, did you?"

Wrinkled nose. "Kind of. I do feel useless, but I am smart enough to stay out of your way and help where I can. So let's eat, and go to bed the second it's dark enough to sleep."

He glanced around. "It's getting there fast."

"I know."

Dinner was a stew that he wolfed down, even though it wasn't very good. Ava had given him a much bigger portion than she ate. He saw that she'd opened three packets tonight instead of just two. Thanks to his scrounging, they had more than enough food.

See? There's a positive.

The candy bar was another positive, as was the cup of coffee. And knowing he'd be sleeping with Ava in his arms.

Tonight she boiled some water, and they took turns using

a thin bar of soap, a washcloth and a towel. Each found privacy to scrub what they could. He imagined she was fantasizing about a hot shower as much as he was. He smelled his underarm dubiously before and after washing it, and couldn't decide whether there was any real improvement. Probably irrelevant, since he had no clean clothes. He hadn't felt he could afford the time, but he still regretted not ransacking the packs of the two men he'd shot in hopes one had been close enough to his size. But really, in the grand scheme of things, what difference did it make? On operations, he'd gone a lot longer than this without a shower.

None of this would have crossed his mind if it weren't for Ava.

He had reluctantly helped himself to a toothbrush from the first pack he searched, did his best to wash it clean of any germs and then used it. He wasn't going to subject Ava to his bad breath because he was squeamish about sharing spit with a Russian terrorist.

His outer layer of clothes went between the pad and the double sleeping bag. Lying down made him aware of every sore place in his body, yet was also such a relief that he groaned aloud. Ava, soon to join him, laughed, and he grinned at her. Her pencil flashlight lit up the interior of the tent enough to allow him to watch as she stripped off clothes, as well. Just not enough of them. As was their routine, he rolled, she spread them out with his, he rolled back onto the now double pad, and she turned off the flashlight before slithering in beside him.

Also as usual, she lay stiff for the first minute or two, until he reached out his right arm and pulled her into him. In no time, her head rested on his shoulder, her body pressed against his side and her hand lay splayed on his chest. He felt her fingers flex a little, and his body stirred. Making a move on her wasn't on the table, though, even if he thought she was attracted to him, too. He didn't like the idea she'd have sex with him because she was grateful, or how awkward it might be if she said hell no. A first for him, he might hate almost as much them making love only because she was thinking they could both die tomorrow and was grabbing for life with both hands.

Yeah, damn it, but what if they did die tomorrow, and had never—

He cut that train of thought right off. He wanted…something entirely new to him, and hadn't a clue whether she felt anything similar.

The remaining tension in her slowly eased. Eventually, she'd throw a leg over his. He also knew she wasn't asleep yet. Her breathing would change.

An owl hooted softly, not far away. He heard a squeak. Nothing to worry about, though. Letting himself relax toward sleep, he spoke without thinking.

"I feel as if I've held you like this every night for a lot longer than we've really known each other." He'd almost said, *For all my life*. Good catch, even if he shouldn't have said as much as he did. And, damn, suddenly he regretted every night he *hadn't* spent with her.

The ones to come, he couldn't let himself think about yet.

There was a minute tightening in her muscles before she whispered, "I…know what you mean. I've never been so comfortable before, or slept as well as I do with you, despite everything."

"I guess we fit together," he murmured.

"We do."

That sounded sad, which worried him, but he didn't know what he could do or say to make any of this better.

One more day, he told himself.

ZACH FELL ASLEEP before she did. Not that he snored, but... she could just tell. He was right. What would it be like in the imaginary future when she was able to go back to her life, crawling into a bed alone, shifting around, trying to find a place to rest her head that felt *right*? She'd never known before that she really needed, well, a body pillow to wrap herself around, too. Except, that body pillow wouldn't have a heartbeat; it wouldn't rise and fall in a gentle rhythm. It wouldn't be warm. And there'd be no strong arm around her, either.

She was grieving already.

I don't really know him, Ava tried to convince herself, but knew that was wrong. It was true they hadn't shared the trivial stuff people might on first dates: tastes in movies, music, books, favorite color, first celebrity or real crush. But none of that mattered. He'd told her things about himself that cut much deeper, giving her a glimpse of a complex man who probably suffered a degree of PTSD from his service. A man who, in an often-selfish world, was capable of enormous self-sacrifice. A man skilled at killing, who still showed kindness and an ability to understand what drove her, after knowing her less than a week.

She'd told him more about herself, and so quickly, than she had anyone else, too.

She was falling in love with him, Ava realized with less shock than she should feel. What to do about it...? Well, that wasn't obvious. Nor whether he felt anything similar for her. For heaven's sake, she hadn't even thought to ask whether he had someone waiting at home, a girlfriend or even a wife, although she believed he wouldn't have kissed her the way he did if that was so.

Worry about tomorrow, she lectured herself, and at last felt sleep claiming her.

Darkness was complete the next time she surfaced. Aware she'd half climbed on top of Zach, she puzzled over the big hand clasped over her butt cheek, while the other had found its way under her knit shirt to have a firm grip on her waist. First time that had happened. In her current state, she didn't mind. In fact, a hold so proprietary gave her a warm feeling of security. It let her slip back to sleep.

Some tension in the big body beneath her awoke her the next time. Was he holding his breath? Maybe he'd lifted his head slightly. She'd know, since she had tucked her face against his neck.

He was listening, she decided.

"Do you hear something?" she whispered.

After a long moment, he said, his voice low, "No. Probably came out of a dream."

He'd have plenty of nightmares to draw on, it occurred to her. As she herself did; frighteningly often, she reverted to being the hungry, desperate little girl who didn't dare trust anyone, who tried to be a ghost while stealing what food she could get her hands on and carrying it back to whatever nook she'd found that provided even minimal shelter.

She patted Zach's chest. A faint rumble rose beneath her hand.

"Comfortable?" he asked. And yes, that had to be a trace of amusement in the quiet question.

"Um..." She was suddenly unsure of herself. Okay, she'd been asleep, but she had taken an awful lot of liberties with his body. "Yes," she admitted.

"I like it." He squeezed her butt and rubbed his cheek against her head, catching hair on his short beard.

The position of her thigh, sprawled across him, had become a little less comfortable due to what felt like a bar on a sleeper sofa, but which she knew quite well was his erection. Arousal washed over her, tightening in her belly, melting down lower. Her nipples had to have hardened.

He'd notice.

Except…he was the one who'd started this.

"Ava?" he asked huskily.

She made a sound that might have been a whimper. When he wrapped both hands around her waist and lifted her, she went eagerly. Their mouths met clumsily in the dark. He had to pull back to swipe a long hank of her hair out of the way, but then they kissed with urgency like nothing she'd ever felt before. This contact was more important than anything in the world. His tongue thrust into her mouth, and she sucked on it, tangled her tongue around his, followed it back into the depths of his mouth. She tasted blood but didn't care.

She'd come to be straddling him, and even as they kissed, he gripped her hips and worked her up and down on his hard length.

"Swore I wouldn't—" he mumbled once, but she didn't let him finish. She didn't want to hear his qualms, or consider her own.

If she had any.

He found his way under her shirt to her breast. Ava had never been more grateful that she had stripped off her bra every night for comfort. He cupped her completely, squeezed and rubbed gently, and oh, she wanted his mouth where his hand was, but even more she wanted—

"Let me," she said in a strangled whisper, and climbed off him enough to push her stretch pants and panties down. If only this was as simple as taking off a pair of jeans. Beside her, he had to be pushing his pants off, too, or did they zip or button open? Ava had no idea. At last, she contorted herself to grip the hem at her ankle and yank the wretched pants off that leg.

His fingers slipped between her thighs and her hips rocked.

"You feel so damn good," he said, in the voice like gravel. "I need you. Are you sure, Ava?"

"Yes." She'd given up getting the pants all the way off and flung her leg back over him.

"I don't have any—"

"I'm on birth control." A moment of sanity had her asking, "If you're—?"

"Yeah," he said hoarsely, even as he used his greater strength to position her, opening her.

As desperately ready as she was, he stretched her, filling her beyond capacity...except, after the first shock, she knew his size was just right.

We fit, he'd said, and they still did.

On her knees, she rode him even as he guided her, sometimes hurried her, slammed her up and down as she'd swear his entire body bowed up to meet her.

What hit her felt like the avalanche, a natural cataclysm, except being spun around and around was like flying, and she never wanted to come back to earth.

The pulsing inside her set her off again, something that had never happened before. She loved the raw sound he made that vibrated against her breasts as she collapsed against him.

In the sweaty, breathless, shaky aftermath, it would have been so easy to say, *I love you.* Instead, she made herself wait to hear what *he* would say.

It came after a minute, a ragged, "I never knew."

She'd never known, either. Scared as she was of making herself too vulnerable, Ava couldn't be a coward.

"Me, either," she whispered, closing her eyes to savor the way he stroked her, kneading occasionally, never stopping. *She* didn't move, because she didn't want him to slip out of her.

Turned out, she didn't have to worry, because faster than she would have thought possible, he was swelling inside her again, moving slowly, nudging her, until these impossible feelings rose in an inexorable tide, and they made love again.

Chapter Thirteen

Ava awakened to strong hands kneading her—butt, back, shoulders. It felt amazing.

"Morning," a gritty voice murmured in her ear.

She pried open her eyelids. "Not morning."

"Close enough. We want an early start."

She'd had such sensational dreams, and now came the hard clunk back to reality.

Not dreams. Oh, God. They'd made love *three* times, and each had been as good as the last. A quiver deep in her belly let her know that a fourth time would be absolutely fine with her, except… She let out a whimper. Or was it a whine?

"Sorry."

A last squeeze had her sighing before she squirmed her way out of the cozy, warm sleeping bag into frigid air.

He rolled the sleeping bags and pads with quick efficiency while she fired up the stove. Not fifteen minutes later, they were eating oatmeal with raisins in it and sipping coffee. Neither of them said a word about last night. She didn't know what to say, while he… Oh, he was a man. She'd been there, and why would they bother talking about it?

Ava suppressed a sigh.

Craggy and scruffy, his face came into focus as the sun rose. Ava was sure the lines beside his eyes hadn't been that deep the first time she'd climbed into a sleeping bag with him. His lips were even more cracked, as she could tell hers were. She grimaced, knowing she must look like something the cat had dragged in, as her last foster father had said. They'd both lost weight, despite the supplement to their diet. Think of the calories they were burning!

It didn't take her a minute to clean and repack the stove, pan and dishes, and not that much later she slid her booted feet into the bindings on her snowshoes.

"This is going to be rough," Zach warned.

She leveled a look at him that made him grin. Which lightened her heart, at least briefly.

He'd been right, she thought. Why bother getting into sticky emotions, assuming she wasn't the only one feeling them, when today might be the day they'd die?

The climb was a struggle. Occasionally, they had to remove their snowshoes to scramble up bare rock that tilted steeply upward. The rest of the time, they wound between stands of trees that became more stunted the higher they went. Obstacles lurked everywhere beneath the snow, some forming lumps, others dips: rocks, fallen trees, stumps, clumps of what might be huckleberry bushes or the like. Both kept having to untangle their snowshoes from whatever had seized them. Twice in the first hour, she went down and began to resent Zach's greater muscle mass that allowed him to stay upright even when he was tripped up.

He paused every twenty feet or so to scrutinize their surroundings. Ava appreciated the breather, but always felt her heart rate accelerate when his gaze paused on something or another and his eyes narrowed. She quit asking what he'd seen.

She was concentrating on where she put her feet when he said quietly, "There's the trail."

Lifting her head, she stepped on the back of one of his snowshoes and grabbed his parka for balance.

Crossing their current path, there were undeniable tracks on a level path covered in formerly smooth snow, but following those tracks with her eyes, she saw how the trail zigzagged to continue to climb steeply.

"Are they ahead of us?"

He leaned forward on his poles, studying what wasn't a clear-cut print. "Up and back, I think," he said at last. "This wasn't one man."

She absorbed that. "Do we dare—"

"Check your phone."

Ava lowered her pack to the ground, fumbled to open a pocket and removed her glove to touch the phone. She didn't have much hope, given that the trail had just started the steepest part of its climb, and if she turned in place she could see the surrounding Cascade peaks with dominating elevation. Still she stared at the phone in frustration. "Nothing."

"You've charged it?"

"You saw me!"

Ava stayed quiet and let him take out binoculars and scan, lowering them and frowning without saying anything. He was thinking.

Out of the corner of her left eye, she caught movement, or maybe the sun reflecting off something. Her adrenaline spiked.

"Zach?" she whispered. "Off to the left."

He whipped the binoculars in that direction just as she saw a flash of blue.

"Blue jay," she said in relief.

Zach studied the stunted trees growing amidst rock protruding from the snow for another minute. "Might have been scared into taking off."

She held her breath until, satisfied or temporarily dismissing any possible threat from that quarter, he turned the binoculars down the ridge again.

"Birds don't just hang out on branches all day, you know."

He didn't smile. She wished he would have.

"We have company coming," he said tightly. "Quite a ways down, but heading our way."

"They're afraid we went cross-country."

"That's my take."

"One, or the whole party?"

"I see only one man."

His eyes met hers. They were almost expressionless; this was the spec ops warrior looking at her. He'd quashed his emotions in favor of clinical decision-making and action. She would ache for the loss, but this part of him was the reason they were both alive.

"I need to stash you again," he said.

Somehow, she wasn't at all surprised by his pronouncement.

KEEP IN MIND how fast two people heading toward each other will meet up, Zach reminded himself as he strode as fast as the damn snowshoes allowed. *Set up an ambush, or gun him down.*

Zach didn't feel so much as a stir from his conscience this time. He no longer had the slightest doubt that this was life or death for him and Ava. Seeing the grenade launcher slung over this slug's back was the clincher. He had knowingly fired the shots to try to kill an innocent woman.

Never mind everything that had happened since.

Zach's mind seemed to have a split screen: his current surroundings and what he had to do, and Ava.

He didn't love the most recent hiding spot where he'd left

her. The scattered clumps of stunted trees provided scant coverage because of the higher elevation. The best he could do was tuck her at the foot of a small drop-off along with both their packs. She couldn't be seen from the trail, but that didn't mean he felt comfortable with the choice.

She was armed, he reminded himself, but he lacked confidence she'd be able to pull a trigger to kill a man—at least, without hesitating too long.

Hell.

He'd done all he could. When he left, she'd had the handgun in a pocket of her parka where, worse came to worst, she could access it easily. At his last sight of her, Ava's bare hand had been buried in that pocket.

Concentrate on the war of attrition he was conducting, he ordered himself. Four down, three to go. He couldn't afford a moment of carelessness.

His pace slowed. He'd rather set up, wait for the enemy to come to him. The idea of being too far from Ava ate at him. He hadn't liked the other times he'd left her, but this…

He traversed another switchback, finally spotting a small cluster of trees on top of a rock ledge that should allow him to see anyone coming up the trail before they saw him. Clothed in white, he should be hidden by the twisty group of mountain hemlock and subalpine fir.

He'd decided against setting any kind of snare. Lying in the snow, rifle set on a bipod, he might as well be in a shooting gallery. *Pop, pop*, done.

Zach used the binoculars sparingly under the theory that his target would be pausing regularly to use *his*. Best not to give him any warning.

He wasn't feeling real patient, though, and with every passing minute, his nerves stretched tighter. Could he have imagined seeing someone?

No.

Could the guy have halted before the pair of new tracks appeared on the trail and turned around to rejoin whatever compatriots he still had? Zach didn't believe that; any scout would have gone considerably farther before giving up. He wouldn't dare return too soon; Borisyuk would expect his minions to go to the last extreme.

Still, Zach detected no movement at all below him.

Disquiet had him feeling edgy and thinking hard. That peculiar, not-quite-itch crawled between his shoulder blades and up his neck.

What if the jay *had* been startled by humans? What if danger had been up the ridge, and the man Zach had seen was a decoy? What if that man had showed himself deliberately with no intention of advancing up the trail?

Without even knowing he'd made a decision, Zach was moving. Backing away from the edge, locking the bipod in place, hitching the rifle over his shoulder as he shoved his feet into the snowshoe bindings.

He was perilously close to panic. What if he was too late?

AVA WASN'T SURE she'd ever have the capability to wait patiently again, whether in line at the grocery store or to check in at the airport. This was torture, plain and simple. It had been all she could do not to beg Zach not to leave her. Only pride let her follow his instructions and do no more than whisper, "Stay safe," before he left.

Weird, when she thought about it, because her career was all about patience. She could lie for hours, impervious to stiff muscles or hunger, watching the entrance to a fox's den for a pup to emerge, or crawl into some absurd position in a tree where she could see the nest of a peregrine falcon. She'd been lucky enough that time to catch extraordinary photos of tiny beaks cracking open the shells, of the emergence of the babies and their first meal.

She'd like to think she could summon that kind of patience again, but right this second she wanted to scream.

He had a watch, but she didn't. Although, being able to see the seconds pass, wait for a minute to go by, then another, might make this worse. *A watched pot never boils*, right?

He'd asked her several times to have faith in him, and she did. Really. But he was one man against a terrorist sought by a good percentage of the governments in the world, and that terrorist had a squad backing him. Zach was still outnumbered three to one, and that was assuming their count from the photos she'd taken of the group on the ridge was accurate. There was no saying a couple more men hadn't been trailing well behind for some reason, or had gone ahead and already disappeared behind tree cover. What if there'd been a dozen more men?

For heaven's sake, she was talking herself into hysteria. Ava made herself take a few slow, deep breaths. So far, unless Zach had lied to her, he had hardly been challenged as he eliminated one opponent after another. There was no reason to think this would be any different.

Except she felt very, very alone.

A soft sound came to her. Her head turned sharply. Was Zach already back? Or—

A white-clad man reared above her on that rocky ledge. Her brain said, *Shoot him!* Her body tried to collect itself to move, but she was too slow. He sprang down, slamming her into the snow. Something cracked and pain shot through her. His gloved hand closed over her face, covering her mouth and nose. She couldn't breathe, couldn't scream. He'd broken her arm, Ava knew, which didn't prevent her fighting as viciously as she could to get out from under him.

She managed to get her mouth open and bit hard on what was probably mostly glove, but the man holding her down with sheer weight snarled something harsh.

He must have risen to his knees, because he wrenched her up, still stifling her ability to scream. She twisted and fought with everything in her. The next time she managed a bite, that big hand mashed so hard on her face she couldn't part her lips. Blood filled her mouth.

A calm voice behind her said something in that other language she assumed was Russian, and her captor turned her to face a second man who pointed a black handgun at her in a negligent way. If she hadn't already been terrified, the sight of him would have done it.

He was strange looking—not ugly, exactly, but as Zach had said, so distinctive no one would ever mistake that face. Cheekbones that, along with an exceptionally wide jaw, made the lower two-thirds of his face a square. As she stared at him, he pushed back his hood, and she saw the sharp widow's peak. The eyes that stared back at her were... No, cold didn't even describe them. Reptilian was closer to it.

Grigor Borisyuk himself. Ava knew this man would torture her to get what he wanted, and kill her with no more thought than most people gave to an ant on a sidewalk they'd accidentally stepped on.

It might almost be better if she was nothing to him but a problem he could solve with a snap of his finger. As it was, she and Zach had frustrated and inconvenienced him, and Ava suspected that wasn't a common experience for this monster in human form.

"You took pictures," he said, his English heavily accented. "I want your camera." He nodded at the other man, who loosened his grip on her mouth.

Could she talk without her teeth chattering? Her whole body wanted to tremble, but she made herself stiffen.

"My camera was damaged in the avalanche."

"You should have died." His eyes bored into hers.

"I was lucky." So lucky, she almost wished she *had* died, instead of being tormented by discovering hope and meeting a man she could—probably did—love.

"Give me the camera."

Scream? Ava knew she no longer dared. There was nothing to stop them from shooting her now and rooting through the packs on their own. She nodded as well as she could.

Another jerk of the head and the man holding her from behind spun her to face the packs. His rough handling must have grated the bones in her upper arm, because the pain that had been buried beneath shock and fear had her crying out.

She tried to reach out for the pack with both hands, but couldn't lift her left arm. She'd have to do everything with her right hand.

She'd still be able to shoot, she realized in a part of her brain that must be walled off from the emotional distress and pain. The man she'd fought, the one whose face she *hadn't* seen, must not have noticed the shape of what she had in her pocket.

She could dip her hand in that pocket right now.

No. She'd be dead before she could pull the gun out.

Wait.

With her right hand, she began fumbling with the zipper that opened her pack.

Was there any chance at all Zach would come in time?

SWEAT RAN DOWN Zach's face. It might be freezing, but he neither knew nor cared. Despite the steep climb, he was all-out running. His gut told him Ava was in trouble, that he'd been lured away from her. He'd felt a twinge of unease when that blue jay shot into the air. He'd have sworn if he could have spared the breath. He knew better than to ignore his own instincts.

At least one of the two remaining men had waited up above. Maybe both were there. If they'd seen where he rejoined the trail when he started down—they could go straight to Ava.

God. He needed to be more aware, not get himself shot because he was too single-minded, too afraid for her to care if he was the target instead.

He stopped, scanned. Continued, did the same. He didn't see any sign of life higher on the ridge.

That's because they weren't there anymore; he was terribly afraid they already had Ava.

Going up was slower than down, however hard he pushed himself. Sweat stung his eyes. He gasped for breath.

Soon, he had to get off the trail. Approach her position from an unexpected direction. Remember that he might still have one man coming up behind him.

Now, he decided, stepping gingerly onto a rock slab because he couldn't risk damaging his snowshoes. He took them off. Had to be quiet, too. Let Borisyuk and company think he was still down the ridge, fooled into thinking they had the upper hand.

AVA FUMBLED AS slowly as she could, which wasn't really pretense. The camera had settled down toward the bottom. First she pulled out the damaged lens, showing it, then dropping it on the snow when the Russian only sneered. She had to pull out packets of freeze-dried meals, rolled-up socks and wadded-up clothing, and let them fall, too. Finally she came to the camera and worked it out.

Borisyuk snatched it from her. The guy behind her tore off her hat and grabbed her braid, tugging her head back as if he enjoyed making her uncomfortable.

Of course he did.

Borisyuk brought the camera to life and began scrolling through photos. It took him time, but she knew the exact moment when he found his own face because he went completely still, not even blinking as he stared down at the screen.

His eyes scared her even more when he lifted them to her this time. "You have a…card. Or did you send this photo…?" He waved upward.

"I have a card."

"Do not play games with me. Show me."

Would he notice that there was a second slot for a different sized memory card?

Who was she kidding? Of course he would.

She indicated an empty slot.

"Where is it?"

"I—" Where had she put it? Her brain didn't seem to be working at top speed.

He backhanded her. Now her cheek hurt along with her neck. The man behind her laughed.

Borisyuk's cold gaze lifted, and he snapped out what sounded like a series of orders. The other man replied—argued?—and Borisyuk's face took on a cruel cast. He said a few more words that might have been ice pellets, but also raised the handgun to level it at her chest.

Her braid was suddenly released, and she bent her head forward in temporary relief as she sensed the second man rising to his feet. Finally, sidelong, she saw his back as he clambered back up the drop-off to where they'd presumably left their packs and snowshoes.

New fear squeezed Ava's chest painfully. He had been sent to watch for Zach—or even to join the hunt for him.

"Where is it?" Borisyuk asked again, and before she could open her mouth, the back of his hand connected with her cheekbone again.

Stunned, she had to blink a few times. If he knocked her out, he wouldn't get an answer...but maybe he didn't care. He could search her body and her belongings without any help from her. In fact, she wondered why he hadn't killed her yet.

"Where—"

"I have it," she interrupted, only her words didn't come out quite right. Her mouth must be swollen. She swallowed blood. She reached out again for her pack. She remembered slipping the card into a small, flat pocket near the top, probably designed for passports or driver's licenses or the like. It would have been easy to overlook, but refusing to produce the card would get her killed. Now, instead of later.

If he wasn't satisfied—no, she didn't *want* him to be, because then he'd be done with her.

She held it out, and he switched the gun to his other hand as he took the memory card from her. She dropped her own hand to her side and began inching it toward her pocket.

"There should be another one," he declared. "Give it to me."

Wham.

Her vision blurred. She wasn't sure she was seeing out of her right eye at all anymore. That meant *he* was right-handed, the way he was hitting her. Ava didn't know why that made any difference, but knew it did.

"My friend," she mumbled. "The man I'm traveling with. He has the other one."

She had never seen anything approaching the rage that built on Grigor Borisyuk's ugly face. His next blow knocked her over. She lay helpless on the snow as he glared down at her, the one memory card fisted in his hand, the gun pointing at her.

So much for her gamble. Why wouldn't he pull the trigger right now?

Chapter Fourteen

He heard voices and then a cry of pain, but also movement to his right. Zach threw himself flat onto the snowy ground, only slowly lifting his head. It was one of the men, but he passed out of sight before Zach could ready for a rifle or even pistol shot.

And did he dare do either? He gritted his teeth. Suppressors did just that, limiting the cracking sound everyone knew as gunfire. But they weren't true silencers by any means. Anyone with Ava was close enough to hear and recognize the peculiar *pop* if he fired now.

He wished he could be sure whether the guy had gone uphill or down. Or cut across the side hill to report back to Borisyuk, if that's who was with Ava.

Keep moving, he decided and rose. After taking a couple of steps that resulted in him sinking deep into the snow and leaving what looked like postholes, he awkwardly put the snowshoes back on. Soft as the snow was, he still sank, but at this point, tracks had ceased to matter.

Fear came close to clouding his ability to envision a scene and make a judgment. Ava cried out at nearly exact intervals, and each cry felt like a lightning bolt burning through his entire body.

Picturing the place where he'd left her, he realized he

couldn't approach from below. Under the wide ledge, he'd be too low to effectively launch an attack, and too visible. Get back to the path he and she had used in the first place? That made him uneasy. There'd been a small bluff above her, which would have been the ideal way for someone to sneak up on her.

The cluster of trees didn't provide the kind of cover he'd like—they were too scrawny, too thin—but that still might be the best option.

Suddenly, two men were speaking what he thought was Russian. Ava was silent.

THE SECOND MAN came back twice to report to Borisyuk. Ava would have given almost anything to be able to understand what they were saying. Had he killed Zach and was now receiving congratulations? A growl in Borisyuk's voice suggested displeasure.

Where was Zach?

Through her daze of pain and with her blurred vision, she realized Borisyuk's attention was back on her. She was still on her knees, curled forward despite her best attempt at dignity.

"Why did you take my picture?" he asked.

"I—" She swallowed a mouthful of blood. "Whenever I'm looking at something, I click the shutter. I'm a wildlife photographer. That's why I'm here."

"You took—" he kicked her camera "—eight, nine pictures. Why?"

"Because…" She hesitated.

His hand blurred, coming at her so fast. Pain exploded. She could only mumble.

"What? I cannot hear you."

"I was curious." She tried to form the words to his satisfaction. "Nobody should have been up on that ridge. I thought you must have crossed the border from Canada. There are no border checkpoints anywhere near."

The nearest she could come to describing his expression was displeasure.

"I saw the assault rifles some of the men carried. That... scared me. I thought I should report what I'd seen."

"Did you?"

Knuckles slammed into her face again, and she rocked in place.

Would he believe her if she lied? Would her answer, either way, make any difference?

No.

She swallowed more blood. Her tongue instinctively tried to find out whether he'd knocked out any teeth.

"No," she whispered. "Not yet."

"Your...*friend*?"

"I...don't know," she lied.

Wham.

This time she toppled sideways to the snow, landing on her broken arm. She'd thought it was almost numb, but now learned better. Had to keep her right arm free, though. Sooner or later, Borisyuk would get careless and she'd have her chance. Maybe the next time his teammate—no, his mercenary—returned.

"Do you know why I didn't kill you yet?" he asked in a tone of mild curiosity.

"No."

"You might be some use." He studied her. "You have a name?"

Nope, not me.

"Ava," she mumbled.

"Eva?"

"Ava. A-V-A."

He grunted, frowned and looked in the direction his man had disappeared.

She tensed, but before she could so much as stick her hand in her pocket to retrieve the gun, the Russian again turned that emotionless gaze on her.

She had to ask. "What use?"

"To, how do Americans say it? Ah. *Take care* of your friend."

Trap Zach. Persuade him to lay down his weapon with only the faintest hope they'd release her.

Don't do it, Zach, she pleaded. *They'll lie, then kill me, anyway.*

She was in enough pain right now, death didn't seem as frightening as it had.

Borisyuk bent and yanked her to her feet, his hand gripping her right upper arm with punishing force. "Stand." He pushed her a foot away from him. "You can stand," he said brusquely.

She could and did, but found it hard to keep her eyes open. Well, her left eye—she thought the right one was swollen shut. But she couldn't let herself sink into the dark abyss that beckoned, not while there was the slightest chance that Zach would save her—or that she could save herself. Or even him.

Borisyuk began to appear bored, if she wasn't imagining things. *Yes, do think about your plans, your deadline, these irritating delays. Anything but me.*

He looked the same direction again. She squinted. No sign of that creep. Had Zach gotten to him?

But…was that movement, off to her left? The Russian hadn't noticed. She might be imagining that his boredom and indifference was shifting very slowly into tension.

She mustn't react at all. All she could do was wait.

Out of the corner of her only good eye, she could see a sliver of a man not quite hidden behind a wind-twisted tree. White arm, white hood framing his face, just as all those men wore. But it had to be Zach. What was he doing? Slowly, so slowly lifting a rifle into firing position.

Borisyuk was mostly behind her, so that she inadvertently blocked any shot. Would Zach risk it, anyway? That might be their only chance. Except, her captor thought she was helpless, and she wasn't.

If only Zach could draw his attention. The terrorist didn't seem to notice her hand creeping toward her right pocket. She couldn't pull the gun out unless he was distracted, but she could—her thumb found the tiny button that allowed her to turn off the safety.

With what felt like her last reserves, she ignored the useless left arm, all the pain, and poised on the balls of her feet to move faster than she'd ever moved in her life. She'd either shoot, or dive for the ground so Zach had no reason to hesitate. If Borisyuk heard anything and grabbed her, he could use her more effectively as a shield, and she couldn't let that happen.

She envisioned every action she had to take. Pull the gun out so smoothly it didn't get tangled with fabric. Or kick and dive.

"Grigor?" Zach called.

Borisyuk spun on instinct toward Zach. She yanked the gun out, leveled it, and just as the Russian thought to turn enough to grab her, she pulled the trigger, then pulled it again and again.

His gaze held hers as his own weapon fell from his hand, and then in eerie slow motion, he collapsed. It was like watching a puppet, animated one minute, losing all semblance of life when the strings were cut. He was dead before he hit the snowy ground. She could tell.

She backed up a step, then another, and finally dropped to her own knees to purge her stomach.

"Sweetheart." Zach was there, crouched beside her, hand on her back. "You're amazing. You'll be okay."

He kept his voice low, she thought in puzzlement. Didn't he know the monster really was dead?

And then she remembered there were still two more men, armed, alive and a threat.

SITTING ON HIS HAUNCHES, Zach wanted to haul her into his arms but knew he couldn't. Depending on her injuries, he'd hurt her, not give her comfort.

Deeper inside, he knew in horror how close he'd come to firing, despite the risk of hitting Ava. Thank God he hadn't. Thank God.

From the minute Ava looked up at him, rage joined the adrenaline-fueled emotions already so tangled he couldn't separate them. She looked bad, and would look worse once the bruises gained more color. Her right eye was too swollen to allow her to open it. She could have a broken cheekbone or jaw, or have had teeth knocked loose or out altogether. He'd seen pictures of women brutally damaged in horrific domestic violence episodes who looked better than she did.

Around the lump in his throat, he asked, "Where are you hurt?"

"My arm is broken." As swollen as her mouth was, the words were barely understandable. She touched her left upper arm in a tentative way that spoke for itself.

"I need to move you." He'd never hated saying anything more. "I assume that guy will come back—"

"Yah." Ava turned her head slowly, as if searching for her pack.

"No, for the moment, just you." He grabbed both handguns from where they'd fallen in the snow, switched on safeties and shoved them in pockets. He'd take Ava back the way he'd come, he decided. He had to pick up the rifle he'd dropped once Borisyuk went down, anyway, and he just needed to get her out of sight. "Can you stand?"

With his help, she rose shakily and showed no sign of collapsing. At his instruction, she put her right arm around his neck, and he scooped her up. Zach winced at the small cry that escaped her, but strode toward the tree cover, scanty as it was.

His thoughts scattered like a flock of pigeons at a clap of sound. He hoped there were still painkillers in that bottle she'd brought, or in one of the other packs. Borisyuk's and the other man's had to be nearby. What could he use for a splint? He could pack some snow on her face and the break—at least there was plenty of that. How quickly would the second man return—and what if the third one had joined him by now?

Zach wanted to get his and her packs out of there before reinforcements arrived. They wouldn't know how badly she'd been hurt, or how far away she could be. But he also needed—

"Is your camera working?" he asked.

She peered dazedly up at him. "Um…yah, if I can get… 'nother lens on it."

"Photos with your phone would do," he realized.

A mumble answered him.

"Okay, I'm going to set you down here," he said, having seen a long crest in the snow that had to be a fallen log. Moving slowly to limit how much he jarred her arm or any other injuries, he bent and lowered her to a sitting position. "I need to grab our packs," he said. "I'll only be gone for a couple of minutes, but I want you to have protection."

That wasn't enthusiasm he saw on her face—truthfully, expressions on a face as battered as hers were next to impossible to read—but Ava accepted the handgun, flicked off the safety again and nodded at him. Her bare hand was probably freezing, but she didn't complain.

This was a woman who would never quit. The knowledge had his knees buckling with gladness that he'd met her, even as he wished she hadn't had to endure any of this.

Then he moved as fast as he could. He hurried to stuff her scattered possessions back into her pack before slinging it over one shoulder, his own over the other while carrying her poles and snowshoes. Now nothing remained in the vicinity except the body.

No—he frowned and scanned the trampled snow again. She'd have taken off the one glove to be able to shoot. But there was no sign of it.

He hustled back to where he'd left her, grateful to see her still upright and gripping the gun. He dropped everything in front of her and unzipped the pocket where he knew she stowed her phone.

She traded the gun for the phone and opened it for him, then they traded again.

As hard as he was listening, he wished he could swivel his ears like a rabbit, but no such luck.

Back to the clearing. As if he were a forensic photographer approaching a crime scene, he snapped pictures from a distance and then closer and closer before he rolled the body to get some clear ones of Grigor Borisyuk's dead face. Finally, he took a few more as he stepped back before dropping the phone in his pocket.

He broke off a couple of low limbs from an evergreen and used them to try to mitigate his tracks from going and coming repeatedly. At best he blurred them, but had to hope that was good enough.

Once he was beside her again, he gently removed the gun from her hand and laid it atop his pack where he could easily reach it. The magazine had been full, and she'd only shot three or four times, he thought.

He dug in the jumble he'd made of her pack until he found some plastic bags, dumping out the contents—dirty clothes, he thought—and filling them with snow before wrapping each in some of those same dirty clothes. "Where's your glove?" he asked.

"Pocket." Or that was his best guess for what she'd said.

He found it, held it for her to insert her hand in. "I'm going to put this on the right side of your face. Can you hold it while I get a look at your arm?"

Ava nodded. Once he'd positioned the first ice pack against her face to cover her cheekbone, brow, eye and jaw, she raised her right arm and replaced his hand with hers.

Under almost any other circumstances, he'd have cut off her parka to avoid hurting her, but he was painfully aware of how swamped she'd be in one borrowed from any of the men. None of them were small. Continuing to wear her own would be best. They still had to get to where they could make a cell phone call. If he had to leave her, the inactivity would make her especially vulnerable to cold.

So he carefully removed the glove on her left hand, said, "This is going to hurt," and started easing the arm of the parka off. She couldn't entirely stifle a few whimpers and cries, and he apologized nonstop, grimacing the entire while.

He couldn't put either of them through this again. The fleece quarter-zip and turtleneck she wore beneath were replaceable, so he used the wicked knife he'd taken from one of the packs he'd rifled and cut the fabric at her shoulder. If only he had scissors—

Since he didn't, he sliced the sleeves from the top down to her wrist until they fell off.

It wasn't hard to see the break.

Still holding the ice pack to her face, Ava craned her neck to peer down at her upper arm. "I hab…" She licked some blood from her lips. "First aid kit."

The reminder was good. He hoped she hadn't used up most of what the kit held treating him. Once he dug it out, he marveled again at how prepared she'd been when setting out on her trek, knowing she'd be beyond help if she injured herself. He found a foam splint, and, though it wouldn't match a cast, it would help until they reached a hospital.

First, though, he pressed the other bag full of snow against the grotesque swelling.

Her slit of an eye fixed on him. "Otter mun?"

O… Other. Other man.

Zach shook his head. "I set up not far down the trail and waited for him, but when he didn't appear I got worried that he was a decoy."

"Was."

"Yeah. I hauled ass back to you, but I heard voices before I reached you."

She bobbed her head. "Knew you'd come."

He had to be getting better at understanding her thickened mumbles. He wished he could put an ice pack in her mouth, which was bloody. Had she bitten her tongue? Lost teeth? God. "I almost didn't." He was tortured with the knowledge of how close he'd come to being too late. The vicious ache felt as if a blow had cracked his sternum.

"Did."

Zach closed his eyes and bent to press his lips very softly to the cheek on the—mostly—uninjured side of her face.

Her worries now almost had to echo his.

"I could go out to the trail and shoot anyone who shows up, but that would mean leaving you alone." Vulnerable. "Not doing that again."

A tear had leaked from one corner of her eye.

"I wish I knew what they'll do when they find Borisyuk dead." Go for revenge? Or run for their lives? The answer depended, again, on whether they were hired muscle or dedicated zealots.

And where was the guy who'd left just as Zach arrived? Lying in wait along the trail, thinking he could pick Zach off? Meeting up with his buddy?

Zach wished he could be a hundred percent sure there *were* only two men remaining. He hadn't said anything to Ava, but he knew the group they'd seen up on the ridge could have been strung out far enough that they hadn't all been visible silhouetted against the sky. If so, they might be spread out watching other trails, per orders.

A faint, alien whisper of sound reached him, and he stiffened. Obviously watching him, Ava did the same. She set down the snow pack and picked up the handgun.

Zach cocked his head, waiting.

It came again, not quite a *swish-swish*, but walking in deeper snow was a lot harder work than striding along a trail. One man, he thought. He rose to his feet, careful not to make a sound, and lifted the rifle from where he'd propped it against his pack.

That someone moved past them, higher up the ridge than where they'd holed up. Angling in to rejoin Borisyuk? Damn, Zach wished he and Ava had been able to move farther away. If this guy chose to use his fully automatic rifle to spray bullets in a circle, he could mow them down.

Zach held out a flattened hand to indicate that she should lie down. Without a word or so much as a cry of pain, she slid to her knees, then half rolled over the log where she'd been sitting so she would be behind it.

He eased behind the largest tree in this small clump, even knowing it was inadequate cover. Better than nothing.

Then he fitted the butt of the rifle to his shoulder, rested the barrel on a branch and focused through the scope. Through it, he clearly saw the one guy, who had seemingly left his snowshoes up above but jumped down and rushed to Borisyuk. The very clarity offered temptation. Had this man been guilty of injuring Ava? Zach's finger tightened slightly on the trigger, but he waited. Despite everything, he found himself thinking again like a cop instead of the soldier he'd been. That didn't mean, if this bastard made one wrong move—

But he didn't. Shock appearing, he made a hoarse exclamation, looked around in panic and then turned to scramble back up the steep rise. He made a lot more noise retreating than he had arriving.

Zach swung around and moved quietly in turn toward the trail, feeling Ava watching as he passed her.

A pack slung over his back now, the visitor was hustling down the ridge. Running. For help, or with the intention of fleeing?

Lowering the rifle, Zach wished on one level he'd killed the SOB, diminishing the count by one. Fine time to be hit again by how much he disliked killing, seeing death on those men's faces.

After a minute, he returned to Ava, who in turn lowered

the handgun down. "I think we have time," he said. "Let me help you up."

Time, at least, to splint her arm to the best of his basic medic ability, get some painkillers and something to eat in her, and figure out whether she was capable of striking out for the ridgetop.

Chapter Fifteen

Zach had kept wincing as Ava tried to eat the snacks he poured into her hand. The raisins weren't too bad, but her jaw hurt too much when she tried crunching on almonds or even peanuts. Eventually, he'd conceded that she had done the best she could, and the super dose of ibuprofen he'd convinced her to swallow didn't seem to be upsetting her stomach. Not that she was sure she'd notice, given how much she hurt. No, not true—she distinctly remembered puking after she'd shot and killed a man, so close up she'd never be able to block what she'd seen from her memory.

Her arm felt marginally better after Zach set it—he claimed it was a clean break—splinted it and then constructed a sling from a turtleneck shirt he ripped and re-shaped.

"It's getting later than I'd like," he said finally. "I'd hoped we could make it up high enough for cell service today, but I don't see how that can happen. We can't stay here, either, though, not without knowing whether the two remaining men will come gunning for us."

"Why would they?" she tried to say.

Seemingly understanding her, he shrugged. "Because they're enraged? I don't know what they'll do, and I don't like that. We can't forget they're out there."

She was in no danger of forgetting.

"I think we should combine whatever we think we really need into one pack now. My suggestion is that we go up the trail and watch for someplace we can camp for the night that isn't quite so close to, er…"

The body. The man she'd shot dead.

The farther the better, in her opinion. She felt weird, but also steadier than she had. Yes, she hurt, but Zach must have hurt as much after the dislocated joint and head injury, and he'd been able to cover miles. *His* head had been slammed by a wall of snow and blocks of ice. Borisyuk had wanted to hurt and scare her, but she doubted the force he'd applied had been remotely comparable. If Zach could go on after that, so could she.

"Head?" she asked, tapping his temple with a gloved finger.

His alarm was obvious. "Your head worse?"

"No. *Your* head."

He gave a bark of laughter. "You're worrying about *me* after you've been beaten to a pulp? Today's been eventful enough, I've kind of forgotten about my headache. I think it's mostly gone, though. No more dizziness or double vision."

She scowled at him, then wished she hadn't. "Didn't tell me—"

"I didn't want to worry you."

Ava would have rolled her eyes if she could have. Any woman would have had the sense to tell her partner that she was having worrisome symptoms so she'd have someone to watch out for her. Superman here hadn't wanted to worry her.

He'd also saved her life several times over, she reminded herself.

"Can go on," she managed to say.

After a sharp look at her, he turned his attention to inspecting the contents of both packs, discarding a good-sized pile, then repacking with an occasional addition or subtraction made by her. She was secretly glad he hadn't fetched Borisyuk's pack. She didn't want anything out of it.

As if their minds were in tandem, though, Zach sighed. "I need to find Borisyuk's pack. See if there's anything I should take from it."

"Don't want—" she protested, but he shook his head.

"He might have carried something that will tell us who his target was, the contact info for whomever he was meeting up with, that kind of thing. In case the pack isn't here anymore when the border patrol comes for the body."

"Oh." That made sense.

He left her with his usual precautions, and she listened hard until he returned fifteen or twenty minutes later, moving so quietly she didn't hear him until he was close enough to startle her. His grim expression didn't surprise her, but she didn't ask what if anything he'd found. There'd be time for that; she had to believe that, after all this, they'd make it.

He attached one of her poles to the pack before helping her into her snowshoes and to her feet. Eyes keen on her face, he was obviously watching for any hint she was about to collapse. Even though she didn't want to take a step, Ava was careful to hide how awful she really felt.

So, okay, she did understand why he'd done the same thing when they'd absolutely had to keep moving those first couple of days.

Progress was painfully slow as they slogged toward the trail, sinking into deep snow, tripping over the usual hidden obstructions. Seeing how desperately he wished he didn't have to put her through this kept Ava strong. The one time he had to pick her up and she tried to give him a reassuring smile, though, she saw immediately that the attempted smile had had the opposite effect. Not one of her best, apparently.

Once they neared the ridge trail, he left her again to reconnoiter. Returning, he said tersely, "Don't see anyone."

She nodded and followed him.

I can do this, she told herself fiercely, and kept repeating it.

The way was easier on the actual trail, especially because of the other tracks going both up and back on it. At least it had been maintained well enough through the autumn; it was mostly free of fallen limbs and rocks. What's more, at this elevation, they were leaving behind the tree line. She could tell Zach didn't like being so exposed, but he'd have been on edge no matter what their surroundings. The enemy was still out there, and he had to protect her.

She quit keeping tabs on him and bent all her concentration on the next step. Every movement hurt her arm and head. Even reverting to thinking, *Left foot, right, left*, was beyond her. She plodded and focused on the tracks right in front of her, blocking out everything else.

She could and was doing this.

ZACH HAD SEEN teammates injured and going on with that same intense focus, but watching Ava moved him beyond anything he'd felt before. A couple of hours ago, she'd had her arm snapped and then been beaten; she could only use one pole, and he knew damn well the dose of ibuprofen he'd given her hadn't done more than slightly mute the pain. Yet there she was, marching on up the switchbacks of a precipitous climb.

If he asked her, he knew she'd say she could keep going as long as necessary, but unlike her, he'd been keeping an eye on the sinking sun. He was desperate to reach the top, prayed the phone could make contact from there to a cell tower, but no matter what, they didn't dare continue once the light started to fail.

What worried him was that she'd feel worse in the morning than she did now.

He bared his teeth in a grimace that she, thank God, couldn't see. No, that was one of a long list of worries. At the top was staying aware that Borisyuk's two or more remaining men could be hunting them. He stopped frequently to use binoculars to scan behind them. Unfortunately, not even high-quality binoculars could penetrate the dense woods low in the valley. All he could do was be sure no one could sneak up behind them.

Remembering the grenade launcher kept that irritating prickle crawling along his spine. They were out of range now, he was confident—unless someone else awaited them at the top of the ridge.

At last he spotted what he'd been looking for—a small cluster of subalpine hemlocks, able to survive where other trees couldn't because of their slender profile and down-sweeping branches that shed heavy snow. Below them was a sharp drop-off, so no one could approach from that direction. He hoped there was a level spot that would allow two people to stretch out, but even if they had to sit huddled against each other, this was the best they were going to find.

"Ava. Wait."

She stopped but didn't even look back. Just stood there, confirming his belief she was at the end of her rope.

He came up next to her and pointed with his pole. "We'll spend the night there."

Still without looking, she nodded.

"Wait until I make sure it's accessible." Without pausing for a response, he left the trail, every movement cautious. He quickly discovered he was clambering along a rocky ledge. A fall wouldn't be great, and likely would ensure broken bones or heads. With each step, he stamped his foot a couple of times to bare the rock as much as he could. There'd be no hiding the trail he and Ava would make—but he already knew he didn't dare sleep tonight.

As he'd hoped, the trees had been able to take root because of a deposit of soil, however thin and rocky, left in a small dip on the mountainside. Zach poked around and found a clear place large enough to set up the tent, although he didn't plan to do that. He wanted a 360 degree view around them.

He set the pack down and went back for Ava. A dull gaze lifted to him when he appeared in front of her.

He'd rather carry her, but when he offered, she said, "I can keep going." Of course she did.

"Okay. Follow my tracks. The rock isn't far beneath the snow. I'll be right behind you."

With that same absolute concentration, she trod in the path he'd laid, one cautious step after another. Behind her, he stayed poised to lunge forward and catch her if he had to—but she reached his pack and stopped.

He laid out pads before he gently helped her step out of her snowshoes and sit down. Even with his arm around her, lowering herself to the ground clearly hurt like hell. Zach discovered how much he hated seeing her suffering, but all he could do was try to make her as comfortable as possible.

He wrapped the sleeping bag around her shoulders, then encouraged her to sip water. Without complaint, she held another snow pack to her face while he got out their stove, fired it up and peered into a couple of packets of freeze-dried meals before finding what he wanted—one that would probably taste more or less like the stew it purported to be, but didn't appear to have much texture.

In fact, heated, it looked a lot like canned dog food, but didn't smell bad.

To his dismay, Ava looked vaguely surprised when he held the pan in front of her. Had she not noticed that he was cooking? How bad was her concussion?

But then she mumbled what he thought was "Thank you" and took the spoon from him. He stayed close to wipe her face when she didn't quite get every spoonful in her swollen mouth, and to take over after her hand started to shake.

Most of it went down, though, and when he took the pan away she met his eyes.

"D'ank you."

She was all there. Thank God. He smiled. "You're welcome. This isn't as good as the meals you brought, but…"

She lifted fingertips to her lips.

"Easier to eat," he finished, and she nodded.

Zach wolfed down his own portion, wishing it was a greasy burger with cheese and an extra-large serving of French fries, although pizza would have been fine, too, or real stew with tender chunks of meat and potatoes.

He'd have liked to think, *Soon*, and believe it, but couldn't quite. There was no guarantee they'd find cell phone service even at the top of the ridge. As for their next step… He hit a wall. Yeah, he was tired, but he would figure it out when he had to.

After cleaning up, he readjusted the sleeping bag so he was under it with Ava, and settled for cuddling her. She lay her head on his shoulder and just…rested. The unfamiliar warmth in his chest felt like happiness, despite their perilous circumstances.

It had to be fifteen minutes before she mumbled, "Missed pickup."

"Yeah." He'd had other preoccupations, but now that she'd reminded him… "I never heard a helicopter."

She shook her head, he assumed to say that she hadn't, either.

"When you didn't show, they should have mounted a search."

"Maybe just think I'm late?"

"Alone out here? They're irresponsible if they don't ask the park service to start looking for you." That would have cheered him more if he'd heard any helicopter however far away, but still, at the top of the ridge, he and Ava would be highly visible. Too bad there'd be no wood, dry or otherwise, to build a fire that would draw attention.

Against his upper arm, she tried to say something. He had to pull back and raise his brows.

"Wish we had…"

She was back to dwelling on that damn satellite radio. He shook his head. "None of that. We've made it this far. We'll make it the rest of the way."

Given her swollen face, he couldn't be positive, but he thought Ava was peering deep into him, seeing… Who knew? His confidence?

Or was it pretense she saw?

He said, "Why don't you lie down? You can use me as a pillow."

Not easy to arrange, but it worked.

BECAUSE OF THEIR increased elevation, darkness came a tiny bit later. Between mountains, Ava even saw a lingering, gradual deepening of the sky rather than the sudden plunge into night to which she'd become accustomed.

She held on until twilight made it hard to see at all, and despite the pain that tried to consume her, she fell asleep. Or lost consciousness. Rousing several times to darkness, shifting in futile attempts to find a more comfortable position, she knew Zach never slept. Each time, his hands were there, reassuring, helping her settle, his touch tender, his voice husky and words comforting. She couldn't have said whether she'd been in a coma or truly asleep. If there were dreams, they didn't linger.

This time when she opened her eyes, the sky had lightened enough she could see Zach's face above her. She lay on her side, she realized, arm propped on the pack, head on his thigh. He seemed to be staring contemplatively down at the intersecting valleys now far below them, until he must have become aware she was awake—she'd tensed, or her breathing had changed. Who knew?

"Hey, sunshine." He smiled, peeled off a glove and cupped the less painful side of her face with a big, warm hand.

She nestled into it.

"Don't suppose you're feeling your best," he murmured.

Ava thought about it. "Yesterday, I didn't think I'd live to see this morning," she pointed out. And, wow, her speech sounded clearer, didn't it? Had her swelling gone down?

His dark eyes never wavered. "Think you can sit up?"

Think about, maybe. Actually doing it...not so much. But...she had to, didn't she?

"Yes?"

He laughed at her. "Heartfelt positivity."

She'd have wrinkled her nose, but had a bad feeling it was broken. Maybe her cheekbone, too. Teeth... She ran her tongue over them. Thank goodness, they were all there, although a couple felt like they might be loose.

Just as well she hadn't brought a mirror.

He helped her as she raised herself an inch at a time, groaning. Zach supported her lower arm with one hand until she was upright, then tied her makeshift sling back into place. The water in the bottle was almost too cold to drink, but she washed several ibuprofen down with it, anyway, then waited eagerly for the pills to take effect.

If they did, the effect wasn't all that noticeable, but she was able to eat the oatmeal he prepared, and savored every drop of her cup of tea, even if he'd overloaded it with sugar.

Drinking his own, he scratched his jaw irritably.

"Itch?"

"Like crazy."

She'd almost forgotten what he looked like without the scruff that had now become a shaggy beard. At least it helped keep his face warm.

At last, reluctantly, she asked, "What's the plan?"

Regret in his eyes, he said, "I think we need to find out whether you *can* go on. I hate the idea of leaving you, armed or not. These guys can shoot from such a distance, you might not even know they're coming."

She shivered.

"Damn." He leaned forward. "I'm sorry. I shouldn't have said that."

"No. Should. Need a motivational talk."

He glowered at her. "Are you making fun of me?"

"Maybe?"

Zach grunted, but one corner of his mouth lifted.

"Not that far."

"No. Maybe a couple of hours should see us at the top. We'll have wide visibility there, which'll give us an advantage if anyone is behind us. Otherwise…"

She patted the pocket of her pack holding her phone.

"Yeah." He cleared his throat. "Might be worth a prayer or two."

THE WORST PART was getting started. Every joint creaked, every muscle hurt as if she'd wrenched it. Her head felt as if it had blown up to twice its size and her neck wasn't adequate to keep it upright. It throbbed. Her dark glasses didn't seem to block the glare; she kept wanting to close her eyes—okay, eye—but fought not to succumb. For Zach's sake.

But gradually, as she warmed up, she found she was moving more easily, the lift and stride in the snowshoes natural. She'd have given a lot to be able to use both poles, but considering the alternative—say, getting shot, her body abandoned like trash in the snow—this wasn't so bad.

To Zach, her pace undoubtedly felt like slow motion, but he never forgot about her long enough to let any significant space open between them. She knew he was pausing frequently to watch her, but she didn't let herself meet his eyes. Better to empty her mind as much as possible and just keep going.

He did insist they stop once, making her eat a handful of raisins and drink some water, but kept it brief. He must've been afraid her body would stiffen.

More than it already had.

For a while, she counted legs in the switchback, but really that didn't help, since she had no idea how many remained ahead of them. Her concentration waned. She kept moving, but wasn't thinking at all. Just step, swing pole, step. Once warmed up, her legs didn't feel bad, but her head and arm coalesced into blazing agony. The last coherent thought she had was, *How had Zach done this?* And for days?

"Sweetheart."

She liked him calling her that, but didn't let herself break stride. If she stopped now, Ava wasn't sure she could start again.

She collided with him, teetered, and let him catch her in his arms.

"We're here. You made it, Ava."

Here? After blinking a couple of times, she turned her head and saw that the trail had leveled off, and a dazzling panorama surrounded them. Even so, with her mind working sluggishly, it took her several minutes to understand. They'd reached their goal. He was right: she *had* made it. Only...

He said it for her. "Now's the moment of truth."

Chapter Sixteen

Ava's phone produced a single, flickering bar, and that was after Zach tromped knee-deep in snow in circles for a good ten minutes, pointing the damn thing every which direction. When he saw that small flicker, he froze.

"Got it." And if he so much as twitched, he'd lose it.

"Oh, thank God." Ava didn't try to get up from where she sat with the pack.

Trying to hold the phone completely steady, he tapped in his friend's phone number. Then he held his breath…to no avail. The call could not be completed.

Unsurprised, he thought some foul words.

"Text," Ava said from behind him.

Yeah, they sometimes went through when a call wouldn't. Naturally, he lost the bar while he wrote a short message saying, basically, Borisyuk dead, need pickup for two, the ridge identified. It took Zach two or three minutes to find the perfect spot again to recover that fragile, single bar. He pressed the arrow to send the text on its way, and held his breath again. He didn't so much as blink while he stared at the phone.

Was there any way to know if a message reached its goal? He had no idea. What if it had gone through fine but Reid was busy, didn't check his phone for five minutes or five hours? Zach wouldn't get any response unless he stayed as still as a statue—or found this exact spot again. Damn, he should start thinking about plan B—

A message popped up with startling speed.

What the???? Your ride on the way as fast as I can find a pilot and get the chopper in the air.

Blown away, Zach tried to take it in. He could only imagine the confusion, consternation, hope that his few words would have aroused on the other end.

He sent back a thumbs-up, pocketed the phone and turned to Ava.

"They're coming," he said simply.

Her mouth trembled and a couple of tears leaked from her open eye. She hadn't believed this would work.

He felt like whooping, picking her up and swinging her around, kissing her until they both forgot where they were... but of course he couldn't do any of that. Who knew how far an exuberant yell would carry in the vast quiet?

So all he did was sit next to her, gently kiss her cold cheek and dig in the pack for something to eat and for the water bottle.

He couldn't find any raisins. The dried apricots and other fruits would take some serious chewing. He offered her peanuts again, and she stared at them with an expression of loathing before taking the small packet from him.

"French fries. *Salty* French fries."

He laughed, joy welling up from deep within him. "Hate to tell you this, but you'd be sorry if you ate anything salty with your mouth in that condition."

Her sound of frustration made him laugh again. For a few minutes, he let himself savor being able to sit beside her, his arm around her back, her head tipped against his upper arm. Along with a tangle of other emotions, he felt an unfamiliar sense of peace.

Of course, it couldn't last, since he wasn't foolish enough to forget their potential pursuers. He and Ava would have quite a wait...and they were more exposed up here than he liked.

He downed a good-sized handful of raw almonds, swallowed some water and made himself get back to his feet. The binoculars still hung around his neck, and the rifle leaned against the pack, ready for him to grab.

"DAMN." ZACH'S FRIEND Reid had to shout to be heard in the noisy helicopter. "That's really him." He hadn't torn his gaze from the screen of her phone. He sounded incredulous, for which Ava didn't blame him. Really, what were the odds that a noted terrorist had crossed the border here, in Washington State, and that in this vast wilderness, his retired army friend out for some winter camping had happened to stumble upon him?

Ava watched from her seat, *not* designed for comfort, and tried to keep her teeth from chattering from the vibration. She didn't mind flying—although she definitely preferred a big jet to a small plane—but really didn't enjoy helicopters. She'd had no choice but to take one to drop her in the midst of the park. This time, though... Well, it had appeared like an angel from on high. She hadn't fully believed she and Zach had survived until she saw that helicopter swooping toward them. She was afraid she'd actually cried at that moment, although she'd wiped away any tears before the copter gently settled onto the snowy top of the ridge.

Zach had wanted her to be conveyed straight to a hospital, while Reid argued for them to first retrieve the terrorist's body and pack. Ava had shaken her head to silence Zach's protests. The border patrol agents and maybe somebody like the National Guard would undoubtedly swarm through this segment of the park once they heard the whole story, but that would take time to organize, and she understood their priority. She wasn't dying. What difference would another hour or two make?

Only to herself did she admit that the detour also gave her a little longer to watch Zach and to revel in his frequent, searching glances. He hadn't put her out of his mind the second that rescue had arrived. Once this helicopter did land on a hospital helipad, she knew she'd be whisked away while he involved himself in the hunt for the remaining terrorists and the maybe rescue of the one he'd left trussed up, to use his words.

Ava had no doubt she'd see him again. They'd become close enough that she believed he would come to see her, verify that she had arrangements in place to go home, and to say goodbye.

It was the goodbye part that she dreaded.

She'd lost track of how many days and nights they'd spent together since she had started across the avalanche slope with the uneasy awareness that a man was behind her, maybe even chasing her, and gaining ground by the minute. It had to be less than a week...but one of heightened emotions, physical exertion like she'd never imagined and a reliance that went both ways with an extraordinary man. The before felt...pallid, in comparison. Or maybe not even real. Her future was a blank.

It was silly to mourn the loss of a man she knew in one way, and not at all in others. There'd never been any chance that—what?—he'd throw over his life to follow her to Colorado? That he'd want to have her waiting patiently for him at home every day, once he could get away from his real life investigating crimes? That didn't sound like him, or her.

But for the first time in her life, she knew she'd make sacrifices to be able to stay with him.

Ava pushed at even that acknowledgment. The intensity of what they'd shared would fade. What felt most real now no longer would as the days passed, as she downloaded her photos and became absorbed in editing, settled into her usual routine.

She turned her head to see him watching her again, lines furrowing his forehead, concern in his dark eyes. She tried for a weak smile that failed to smooth those deep lines at all or lessen the intensity in his expression.

Habit, she tried to tell herself. The bond they'd formed would take time to thin and eventually disappear. Given his many deployments and the losses in combat, this experience was probably familiar to him. One minute, the people around you meant everything, the next, you said your goodbyes and flew back to a base where you had to reconnect with friends and family you'd left there.

Ugh. Knock it off.

Things became tense—snapped orders, cold washing in the open door of the helicopter as it hovered above the snow-covered ledge where she and Zach had left the body of the man she'd shot and killed.

Something else not to think about.

Apparently the body was still there. The pack, too, she saw, when Zach was winched up carrying it on his back. The body… Ava looked away at that point. The two men deposited it somewhere behind her.

Then, as the helicopter rose into the air again, Zach came to sit beside her.

"Hadn't been touched," he shouted. "The two survivors must be on the run."

"What about...?"

His eyebrows climbed. "The guy I left alive?"

She nodded.

"He's our next stop, if I can pinpoint the place from the air. Although—" now he sounded bleak "—I doubt he could hold out this long."

Of course he hadn't forgotten the one man he'd been able to leave alive. She reached over and squeezed his hand, rewarded by the way their eyes met and held.

She did know him. She did.

To Zach's astonishment, Jarek Krasnitskiy—or so his passport claimed him to be—was alive. In bad shape, but bundled for warmth, given oxygen and fluids, he would soon be in the hospital along with Ava.

Zach had known he wouldn't be able to stay with Ava until everything he knew, had done and had thought since he first saw those men silhouetted atop the ridge had been sucked out of him. He had no doubt agents would pounce on her, too, once doctors gave them the go-ahead.

After watching her get placed on a gurney and rushed into the hospital, he went to the local border patrol headquarters and submitted to the interrogation. He did his best to put Xs on the detailed topographic map, showing where he and Ava had first spotted the men—and where the other bodies could be found. Somebody, somewhere, would have to decide whether he was justified in shooting and killing, but his conscience felt clear. He and Ava wouldn't be alive if he hadn't had the skills he'd brought home from his service in dangerous parts of the world.

When they were done with him, at least temporarily, he

called a taxi to take him to the hospital. A receptionist directed him to Ava's room. The door marked with the right number stood half-open. As he pushed it fully open and started into the room, a nurse hurried toward him.

"I'm sorry. Visitors aren't—"

"We're friends," he said. "I was with her when she was hurt."

Her lips compressed, but she nodded. "Please keep your visit short. Authorities are eager to talk to her, but Dr. Chavez has refused them access."

Zach smiled at her. "Good."

His first sight of Ava in the hospital bed took him aback. Her face looked even more discolored and swollen against the white pillowcase. Her eyes were closed and her body appeared slight beneath the sheet and thin blanket. He couldn't see the vibrant woman who had dug him out of the grave made from snow, ice and rock, who had warmed him with her own body…until her eyes suddenly opened.

One was still a slit, but the deep blue color was apparent. "Zach. Is everything all right?"

Despite appearances, the swelling was definitely decreasing, giving her speech improved clarity.

"Yeah." He cleared his throat. "Let me find a chair."

He pulled one from under the window to her bedside, then sat down and reached out without thought for her hand that lay on top of the covers. Their fingers twined together, the action so fluid they might have held hands through years instead of days.

"I see you got a cast."

"Yes, and it helps." Her nose crinkled. "Whatever they're pumping into me through the IV helps even more, I suspect."

He grinned. "I have no doubt. You had to be dehydrated besides. I'll bet you've lost a lot of weight."

Her gaze seemed to drink in his face. "You, too. You've had something to eat?"

He cleared his throat. "Ah…"

"A cheeseburger. And fries?"

Had she caught a whiff of his breath? "Afraid so."

Ava made a sound that expressed indignation.

"Maybe I can sneak something in. I assume they're keeping you tonight?"

"Yes. They think I had a concussion."

No kidding.

She frowned. "You should get looked at, too."

"I'm feeling fine." Exhausted, relieved, grateful and scared about how she'd respond when he talked to her about the future, but the headaches were gone, and his shoulder… He rotated his arm experimentally. "Shoulder is good as new."

This time she snorted.

He laughed. "Really. And no, I haven't forgotten that it will be more susceptible to a dislocation if I get hammered by an avalanche again, but I'm hoping to avoid that."

"Me, too," she said quietly. It was a minute before she asked about Krasnitskiy, although she didn't remember the name.

No, Zach realized, he'd never told her any of the names, only the nationality claimed by the passports they carried.

"He's not up to talking yet, but it looks like he'll make it. He'll even keep his fingers and toes."

"You bundled him up well."

"Yeah." Uncomfortable with the implication that he was a good man, Zach cleared his throat again.

Behind him, someone else did the same even as the curtain rings rattled. It was the nurse, he saw, who looked sternly at him.

"Ms. Brevik needs to sleep. I'm afraid you'll have to leave now."

He didn't move. "I'm not going anywhere. I'll spend the night right here."

She frowned. "That's against—"

Ava said, "Please. I...feel safe with him here."

To her credit, the nurse backed down, but insisted on turning out the light after taking Ava's temperature and pulse, and then reminded her that she could push the button at any time if she required assistance.

The darkness wasn't all that complete, light from the hall seeping around the curtains, but Zach felt himself relax.

"She's right," he murmured. "You need to sleep."

"You, too," she whispered.

"I will. I can sleep anywhere."

If anything, her fingers tightened around his hand. "Do you think...?" She hesitated.

Zach leaned forward. "Do I think?"

"You could lie down with me?" She sounded tentative, and vulnerable. "I'd...sleep better."

Heart squeezing like a fist, he answered in a low voice, "I haven't showered yet."

"I don't care," she whispered.

"Your guard dog will probably kick me out when she sees us, but...yeah. I'd sleep better, too."

While he kicked off his boots and pulled his quarter-zip over his head, Ava shifted herself sideways on the narrow bed. He carefully climbed on, stretched out beside her and helped her find the position they knew worked best—her cast lying across his chest and belly, her head nestled in the hollow beneath his shoulder.

He wanted to sleep like this every night for the rest of his life—minus the cast.

She sighed, squirmed a little and murmured, "Sleep tight."

Smiling, he closed his eyes, refused to let himself think about tomorrow and stayed awake only until he knew from the slowness of her breaths that she was asleep.

AVA AWAKENED WITH vague snippets of memory telling her the nurse had checked on her a number of times, making her answer questions and expressing her disapproval of Zach sharing the hospital bed, but she must have given up and left them each time. He was gone now, although Ava was sure he'd stayed through the night. Her heart sank when she saw the empty chair.

"Breakfast will be here in just a minute," a new nurse told her cheerily. "Do you need to get up first?"

Oh, heavens—she did. That chore completed, she climbed back into bed laboriously, feeling as if she were old and arthritic.

He'll be back, she told herself. That he'd wanted to stay the night meant everything. Today, though, she'd be released from the hospital.

"Do you know where my friend went?" she asked.

"I'm afraid I didn't see him. Nobody was here when I came on."

Ava could only nod. She actually was hungry, and the breakfast looked surprisingly good to her. Scrambled eggs and oatmeal, easy to eat, a slice of whole wheat bread, and tea and orange juice. Her jaw felt better, she decided as she ate. She started to think about practicalities.

Where was her pack? Obviously not here. None of the clothing in it was clean, but what she'd been wearing—and she had no idea what had become of that—had to be indescribably filthy. Besides, she'd need her wallet, keys, phone. What day was today? Had she missed her return flight home? Probably. Ugh—replacing the ticket would be costly.

Just as she pushed away the tray, Zach appeared around the curtain. A new Zach—clean and freshly shaven, wearing cargos she didn't remember seeing and a long-sleeve, navy blue T-shirt. And he carried her pack slung over his shoulder.

"Oh, thank goodness!" she exclaimed. "I had no idea what happened to my stuff."

She'd almost forgotten how handsome he was beneath the shaggy growth of beard. Hadn't cared. What had mattered was *who* he was.

"Reid's wife offered to wash your clothes." He glanced down at himself. "He and I are close enough in size. He loaned me something to wear."

"I have clean clothes?" What a thing to get stuck on!

His broad grin sent her pulse into double time. "Best thing that's ever happened to you."

She laughed. "Well, not quite."

On a sharp pant, she knew: the best thing that had ever happened to her was meeting him. The time they'd had together, however fraught with fear and danger it had been.

"So." He set down the pack and sat in the chair. "Do you have a plan?"

"I haven't gotten that far. I just finished breakfast."

He eyed her empty plate, expression dubious, but didn't comment. The silence felt uncomfortable.

Zach rolled his shoulders, which she'd learned was something of a giveaway for him. He had something to say he didn't want to. Was this the *Goodbye, I have to be back at work, you take care of yourself?*

"Will you come home with me?" he asked. "Heal up for another few days? My place isn't fancy, but—"

"I'd love that," she said in a rush. A reprieve. She was ready to seize that with both hands.

"Good." His relaxation was noticeable. "Maybe I should say this first, though. It could be awkward if you're not thinking anything the same."

The leap of hope plummeted like a stone thrown high in the air. She could only nod.

"We haven't known each other very long, but... I don't want to say goodbye to you." His voice was gruff. "You're the most extraordinary woman I've ever met. My life isn't all that exciting anymore compared to yours, but..." He appeared momentarily lost for words. "I've been falling for you. Hoping you might have room in your life for me. So we can figure out—"

His face blurred. To her horror, Ava realized she was crying. No, sobbing. She snatched up a corner of the sheet and tried to quell the flood, but failed. Salty tears stung as they found raw places.

On an exclamation, Zach moved to sit on the bed and gently lift her until he could wrap her in his arms and it was his shirt front she was soaking. His *clean* shirt.

"I'm sorry," he murmured. "Damn, I didn't mean to upset you. God, Ava. Please quit crying. Please."

"They're happy tears!" she wailed, but he probably couldn't make out a single word she said.

Only...he started to laugh. Rocking her, rubbing his cheek against her head. "It's okay, sweetheart. Damn. You scared me. I thought—"

She straightened, pulling back enough to gaze at him through even puffier eyes, knowing perfectly well how pathetic *she* must look. "I kept telling myself what I felt wasn't real, but it was. It is! I was terrified of having to saying goodbye."

He grabbed a handful of tissues from her bedside table and mopped up her face as tenderly as if she were a baby.

Tossing the tissues, he agreed roughly, "Yeah. Same. I'm…in love with you, Ava. I'll move to Colorado if that's what you want. I can get a job anywhere. I'll hate waving goodbye when you head out on expeditions, but I hope most of them aren't as dangerous as this one. And…maybe sometimes I can go with you."

"We can live here, you know. There's a lot of spectacular country around here. The Puget Sound, the Gulf Islands, mountains everywhere, the rainforest. I didn't leave anything important behind in Colorado. It's just…a place. I don't mind moving."

He absorbed that. "Then, once they let you go, I'll take you home with me. It's, uh, just a rental, but we can buy something we like together. I can afford it. I didn't want to commit when I first took the job."

"Yes." Oh, it hurt to smile, but she felt as if she must be glowing from some inner light. A niggling thought surfaced, though. "You're not in trouble, are you?"

Zach shook his head. "I have an official offer from the border patrol to join."

"Will you?"

He shook his head. "Too close to what I did the last ten years. I never want to go to war again. Regular policing, that's different."

"I wish you could kiss me."

He bent forward and rested his forehead against hers. "You have no idea how much I wish the same. Soon. And… we have time."

"We have time," Ava echoed, her emotions indescribable. She'd never expected to believe in something like forever with a man, but she had already given Zach her trust, and would keep giving it. He wasn't a man who'd ever let her down. "I can hardly wait."

* * * * *

A FIREFIGHTER'S
HIDDEN TRUTH

TARA TAYLOR QUINN

To all of the many teams of hotshot firefighters in Arizona and across the US who risk so much and spend so much time away from loved ones for not nearly enough pay. You are known and so very much appreciated.

Chapter One

It had been almost five years since he'd had sex with her, paid her off and walked out of her life. Like she'd been nothing more than a prostitute instead of the partner in a whirlwind, weeklong romance she'd dreamed up in her head. An overactive imagination—while professionally lucrative—had its downfalls.

There was nothing imaginary about the man's face. Even with an oxygen tube, hair that needed a wash, a blank gaze in those unforgettable vivid blue eyes and his head on the pillow of his bed, she knew him.

"His name is Luke Dennison." Shelby turned to walk out of the hospital room, leaving the police to deal with their problem.

"You know me?" The voice—the timbre of it sending an unwanted wash of desire over her—stopped her in her tracks. As angry as she still was nearly five years later, there was something else going on inside her, something she wouldn't allow herself to explore. Something to do with the fact that the man's four-year-old son was currently at home with his babysitter.

And the hotshot firefighter sounded so…needy. As though he'd start begging if she didn't turn around.

She'd heard her father beg after breaking her mother's heart. Too many times to count.

"Yes, unfortunately, I know you," she said, turning back around but stepping no closer. The door was her immediate destination.

The man in the bed frowned as though he was in pain. And maybe he was. He'd been found out in the desert, would have died in the fire he'd seemingly been attempting to contain on his own when he'd slid, falling backward. The police had surmised—based on the crime scene and the location of the rock that had slammed into the back of his head, rendering him unconscious—that he was only alive because the wind had shifted, changing the course of the blaze. "I'm sorry, have I done something to upset you?" He looked truly perplexed.

Which pissed her off.

And she'd learned long ago that it was more to her advantage not to let that show.

"Come on, Luke, why would I be upset with you?" The question was pure sarcasm. Her smile and tone of voice made that obvious.

"I'm guessing if you weren't before, you're going to be now," he said then, shaking his head. "Because I have to ask, who are you?"

If he'd been in his right mind, the irony would have been too much to bear. Shelby took a deep breath, giving herself time to determine her next course of action. Did she walk out the door and thankfully bid good riddance to the man once and for all?

Or did she listen to the softer part of herself, the one who looked for the human-interest stories a lot of reporters didn't bother to find, and give the man another chance?

Why don't I have a daddy like Jason does? A replay of

Carter's tear-filled, heartbreaking question flashed through her mind. From when Carter's little friend Jason got to go fishing for the weekend.

And immediate answers became clear. She had to buy herself time. "I'm a reporter," she told the man, the only part of their truth she was willing to let him know. The police had said his memory loss was complete. Meaning he wouldn't remember that she'd gone to his home to tell him that she was pregnant.

And wouldn't remember the way he'd accused her of lying, telling her the kid couldn't possibly be his.

Dare she hope, for Carter's sake, that he'd matured in the past five years?

That the great, self-sacrificing part of the man she'd interviewed back then had gained the upper hand over the womanizing snake in him?

"I did a human-interest story on you five years ago," she said, walking closer to the bed as the detective who'd brought her to the room for identification stood by. "For a digital forestry publication." She'd moved up in the world dramatically since then.

Made enough per story, freelancing to top digital venues, to be able to pick and choose what, where and when she worked.

Not that she'd tell him, but the story she'd done on him had been what had jump-started her career. The managing editor of *The Custodian*, one of the largest digital news publishers in the world, had read that story. And had offered her one chance to prove herself.

Pregnant and alone aside from her mother, who was also alone and on a fixed income, she'd given her all to that opportunity.

And had succeeded.

Luke Dennison's eyes opened wider, showing a true interest. And perhaps a bit of desperation as well. That's what her intuitive eye saw, anyway. Not that, in her current situation, she was open to trusting that special gift of hers.

It had almost ruined her life the first time she'd met the man.

Except that she'd persevered. Had wanted her baby even if he hadn't.

"Would you mind…if… Do you have the time…to sit with me a few minutes? To fill me in?" He glanced toward the detective, who shrugged and left it to Shelby to answer the victim.

She wished she hadn't insisted on driving separately from the law enforcement investigator who'd walked her in. She had wanted an immediate escape route. It was turning into a trap.

"I can stay for a few minutes," she heard herself say, even over the loud internal groan in her head.

Detective Johnson nodded, excused himself and left.

The warmth, the gratitude in Luke's gaze as he kept his eyes glued in her direction—even when she moved— touched her empathy nerve.

And she knew she'd made a big mistake.

ONLY ONE PERSON in the world seemed to know who he was, and she was clearly not fond of him. Didn't bode well.

What had he done before he'd been found nearly dead by the local fire department?

Did he really want to know?

She'd written an article for a digital forestry publication? On him?

The great-looking mystery woman didn't sit. She stood there in her black-and-white sundress and black flip-flops, with her wavy, long blond hair almost a shield around her, and seemed about ready to bolt.

"How old am I?" Not as ancient as he felt, although his hair wasn't gray.

But how many years had he screwed up? How many decades left to fix it all?

Or... God forbid, what if he found out he couldn't fix it all? What if he found out that he'd done things he needed to forget?

"You're thirty-two." Her answer took a while to arrive. Leaving questions in its wake.

Did she really know?

"Why are you so hesitant to talk to me?" he asked, figuring it was what he needed to know most. But with the meds keeping his aching head from exploding, he wasn't sure he could trust his own judgment.

Having your memory check out on you did that to a guy.

"When I did that story on you almost five years ago, our association ended rudely."

That was it? He'd been rude?

Sheesh.

Still didn't explain why he'd been in the hospital for two days and no one had reported him missing or come forth to claim him.

What had he done to make no one want him? Was he on the run?

Didn't feel right, him a runner.

But nearly dying in a small desert fire didn't sit right with him, either.

"Why did you do a story on me?"

"Because of what you do for a living." She came a little closer, sat on the edge of a plastic chair along the wall several feet to the side of his bed. "I'd read about the Bodell fire. Everyone was writing about the hotshot-crew lives that were lost, and there you were, the one lifesaver, with only a brief mention—and not only a trained hotshot but a smoke jumper with EMT certification as well…"

"Wait." He sat up straight, nearly pulling off the oxygen tube he no longer needed. "You're telling me I'm a hotshot firefighter?"

He knew what that was. Did everyone?

She nodded.

"And an EMT?" He definitely knew what that was.

Another nod. Holy hell!

He was a good guy.

"Am I married? Do I have family? What about parents? Where was I born?" Suddenly, he couldn't get enough. Kept lobbing questions even as she shook her head.

"Detective Johnson said the doctor told him that it's likely you'll start remembering things fairly soon."

Yeah, he'd been given the same information. He could expect the return to take a couple of weeks at most. But if something she told him could trigger even a slight peek…

Seeming to have made a decision, the woman nodded, opened her mouth to speak, but he blurted out, "What's your name?"

"Shelby Harrington."

He searched his massive blank spaces. Found not even the slightest recognition of her.

"I have no idea if you're married. You told me back when I interviewed you that your schedule precluded any kind of partnership or relationship. You said a lot of guys make it work, but you didn't want to put a woman through constant, unexpected absences for sometimes weeks on end, with the risk that you might not ever come back. Your mother died when you were a teenager, and her loss had something to do with your decision."

"I told you that?" Didn't seem like something he'd say.

"No, I asked if that was the case, and, after thinking about it, you acknowledged that it was. That's it—you just said yes."

Had she asked for personal or professional reasons? The question intrigued him. A lot. But considering how little he had rattling around in his brain, her small details pretty much had the place to themselves.

His mother was dead. The knowledge brought sadness.

Because he remembered her? Even a little?

Or just because it was a sad thing?

He looked for any flashes of a funeral. Of a smile. Or a reprimand.

Came up blank.

"What about my father?"

When she glanced down at her hands, his gut sank.

"He died last year in a car accident."

Luke jerked. His entire body stiffened. And then…nothing.

"Now that you know who you are, you can look all this up."

"If I knew what to look up," he said, still feeling the shock of his father's passing. Feeling it for real?

He was pretty sure he was. And he had a flash of a watch. His watch that had survived the fire. Had his father given it to him?

"My guess would be that your hotshot team will know more than anyone else. You probably want to contact them when you can," she said, and he stared at her. Why hadn't he thought of that?

He had a team?

"Detective Johnson said they were called to a fire in

northern Arizona the afternoon you were brought in. It's zero percent contained, so they might be there awhile. He said as soon as I made the formal ID this morning, he'd be getting in touch with the forestry department…"

Zero containment. He knew what that meant. Nearby population had to be assessed, evacuation orders established, containment lines determined. But when he tried to stay with the orders in his head, to see more, he ran into nothingness.

Still, adrenaline coursed through him. For a second there, he'd felt like someone who knew exactly how to fight a wildfire.

He had a team!

And a reason no one had come to identify him. A few short minutes, and two days of frustration and growing anxiety were easing dramatically.

There'd been nothing to indicate that his memory loss was permanent. To the contrary. He just had to be patient…

Patience didn't feel like a familiar companion to him.

Was he remembering that, too? Or was he just highly impatient with his current situation?

"Where do I live?"

"I've had nothing to do with you for nearly five years."

Funny how easily he recognized a prevarication. "Did you know where I lived then?" Made sense. The interview could have been in his home.

"You were working out of the San Diego area, and you had a temporary apartment there. You owned a cabin here in Arizona. North of Phoenix."

An apartment. Didn't resonate. The cabin sounded right, though.

Shelby stood up, and he sat up straight again. "Don't go." She was his lifeline…

"I have to go," she told him. She didn't elaborate.

"Will you come back?"

"Anything I'd have to tell you is in the article I wrote. Just google both our names, and it will come up." She was walking to the door as she spoke.

Clearly done with him. Eager to get away.

Which didn't sit well, for more than just his selfish need to be with someone who knew things about him.

"I'm sorry."

"For what?"

"Whatever I did that was rude."

Nearly at the door, she shrugged. Didn't even turn back.

"What was it?" he blurted out before she could reach for the handle to let herself out.

She stopped. Stood there, her back to him.

"Probably best if you get your memory back before we go there," she finally said, glancing at him over her shoulder.

"Does that mean I'll see you again? When my head's back in shape?"

She shrugged once more.

"I guess that's up to you. I'm easy to find. Always have been."

And yet...

He'd apparently never gone looking.

Luke wanted to know why.

What had he done to her?

As he sat there alone, watching the closed door she'd left behind, he had a lot of questions. But none that he wanted answered more than that one.

Chapter Two

Shelby's brisk walk from the hospital took effort. She wanted to run. To get away from the man who'd rocked her more than any other, in so many ways.

Because, just as strongly as her urge to run, she'd felt compelled to pull that damned hard-plastic chair up to his bed and spend the day doing what she could to help him.

She'd admired the heck out of him even before she met him. All the research she'd done on his team, on the forestry-technician hotshot crews in general, had left her mostly in awe. She'd been prepared to be at least a little disappointed in the real thing. He was, after all, just a human being like everyone else in the world. Instead, she'd been mesmerized. He'd been decent to the core. And had a sixth sense about him: seeing things in people or situations that others might miss. She'd always been that way—looking at people and seeing what wasn't being shown, hearing what wasn't being said. Luke Dennison had been the first person she'd ever met who could inhabit that world with her. She'd only known him a week and actually thought she'd met her soul mate.

And then she'd woken alone the morning after they'd made the most incredible love, and had picked up the envelope he'd had delivered with the breakfast he'd ordered for her. She'd opened it and found a thousand dollars in the thank-you card...

She'd seen him one other time. She'd looked up his address and had driven up to his cabin in Payson to tell him that she was pregnant, figuring she'd leave him a note if he was—as she'd hoped—out at a fire. Or still in San Diego. Not that she'd wanted a fire anywhere; she'd just hoped he would be gone for a few days.

So she could have more time to get over her own shock and figure out a new plan for her life.

He'd been home. Had come outside to speak with her, pulling the door closed quickly behind him, but she'd still heard the woman inside, calling out to him to come back to bed. And when she told him that the baby was his, he'd said she was lying. Had firmly denied the possibility since they'd used a condom, and then stepped back inside and shut the door in her face.

And then, nearly five years later, she saw his picture on the local Phoenix news, depicting a guy who'd been pulled unconscious from the desert just north of the city and had awoken without knowledge of who he was. At first, she'd turned away. Waited for someone else to tell authorities who he was. But by the second day, with the fact that his father had died nagging in the back of her mind, that he had no other family to her knowledge, he didn't live in Phoenix, and his hotshot team could likely be out on a fire, she'd called the police. And had reluctantly agreed to see the man to positively identify him.

She'd told herself she was doing her duty as a good citizen, but that part of her brain that she tried not to listen to when it came to adult men in her life—the part that loved the good in them even when she knew full well that the bad outweighed the good—had perked up, too.

Three times Carter had come to her, asking why he didn't have a daddy.

And she didn't even have a grandpa or an uncle to give him.

So what if, like her own father, Luke turned out to be a good dad—while sucking at being a faithful or trustworthy romantic partner?

And what if, when the man regained his memory, he turned out to be as awful at fatherhood as he'd been at even considering the possibility that he might be a father?

She'd planned a full day's work after leaving the hospital, stopping by various places, including a dance cooperative, looking for her next story. An entire file of potentials hung out on her computer; she read all the requests but only in case something in them triggered her nerve.

Otherwise, she kept her eyes, heart and ears open and pursued anything that spoke to her.

Nothing was going to speak to her that Wednesday morning. And there was only one place she wanted to be. One person with whom she wanted to be—Carter. Turning toward the home she'd purchased the previous year, she couldn't stop her mind from going right back to where it had been. Grinding out thoughts, the same ones over and over, faster than she could process them.

She was in a quandary, unable to land on whether or not she was going to attempt to see Luke again while knowing that, for Carter, she couldn't just walk away.

Not if there was even a slight possibility that the man would be a good dad.

But no way was she exposing Carter to him until she knew more.

That's where she was.

For the first time in years, she actually toyed with the idea of trying to find herself a husband. After Luke, who wasn't her first disastrous romantic relationship, she'd figured she was one of those women who were attracted to men like their fathers, and she had made a very clear, rational and contented choice to be done.

With a baby on the way, she just hadn't been able to risk being her mother.

Couldn't take any chances that a child of hers would grow up like she had.

Still, there were a lot of great guys out there. She turned down dates as often as many people mowed their grass—partially because, with her job, she was always meeting new people.

Maybe trying to find a good man would be the lesser of two evils. Instead of giving Luke Dennison even one more thought, maybe she should try to find a father for her son…

The fact that the hotshot firefighter's face had shown up twice on her television set, just as she happened to be watching, didn't have to be an omen. It could have been a coincidence.

Some people said there were no coincidences, but the word existed for a reason, right?

Turning the corner into her neighborhood, she slowed down to take the dirt-and-rock shoulder she was being forced onto due to road-widening construction, hating that she had to put her pretty new blue SUV through the abuse every time she came and went. Knowing that most people just powered right on over the shoulder at normal speed, she checked her rearview mirror to make certain that there wasn't someone barreling down on top of her.

She saw the delivery truck approaching quickly just as there was a bump, a loud noise, and her car jerked hard to the left, like someone had taken control of her steering wheel. She didn't let go. She saw the truck about to rear-end her again and pulled so hard to the right a muscle in her upper arm popped, throwing the vehicle over a slight incline and then down into a ditch.

After being smacked in the face by her airbag, Shelby had no idea what had just happened, and with shaking hands and few wits about her, found her phone and dialed 911.

LUKE HADN'T EXPECTED to see Detective Johnson again. He was just an amnesia patient now, no longer a missing person. Figuring the guy was just being nice when he knocked on Luke's hospital-room door and stuck his head in, asking if he could talk to Luke for a second, Luke readily waved him in.

He'd never imagined how quickly a guy could go stir crazy with so little in his brain. Watching television was boring to him. He couldn't relate because he had no memories to pull from to make anything personal. He'd found out he had a cabin in Payson, an hour and a half northish of East Valley, so he would have a place to go when he was released from the hospital. His phone had burned up in the fire, he'd been wearing an old watch that had survived, and Johnson had already called late that morning to let him know he had bank accounts and credit cards in his name.

He'd readily given the detective permission to access any and all information, including expenditures, to help him start to put his pieces back together and had discovered that his finances were being handled by a personal banker, Gerard Michaels.

A call to Mr. Michaels had filled in many blanks in his life details, like the fact that he was quite well-off, having earned his own money by taking dangerous side jobs when he wasn't out fighting fires; he had a trust fund left by his mother; and he'd also inherited a sizable chunk when his father had died the year before.

The man had also told him, when he'd asked, that his old watch had been his father's. He'd known.

That meant a lot.

He'd requested a laptop and new phone ASAP, and both had been delivered earlier that afternoon. He could look himself up.

And look up Shelby Harrington, too.

Which he'd done first. And had only just started clicking on links when Johnson showed up.

"I wanted to let you know a couple of things," the detective said, pulling up the chair that Shelby had left by the wall that morning. "But first—you're feeling okay?"

Luke, sitting up in bed with a T-shirt on, figured that one was obvious—no way a guy who couldn't remember anything about himself was feeling okay—but nodded anyway. "Smoke inhalation can be a problem in the days to come, but for now, I'm clear. Breathing is fine. I'm not hoarse. The burns were all superficial—nothing I can't handle. And if tomorrow's tests on my head come back okay, I'll be released. Doctors say I'm one lucky son of... Well, you get the point." He didn't feel lucky.

He felt...angry.

And then some. If he was some hotshot firefighter, putting out blazes that covered hundreds or thousands of acres, and climbing up mountains that reached the clouds, how in the hell had a forty-acre desert fire gotten the better of him?

A first-year rookie in the Phoenix fire department could have handled that one.

And how did he know that?

"Glad to hear it," Johnson said, but the man didn't look glad. His frown could have been due to fatigue or borne from some personal problem, but watching him, Luke didn't think so. The man seemed...perplexed.

Concerned.

And he was staring straight at Luke.

"What?" he asked. Had the good detective found out something else about him? Something not so good?

Like what heinous thing he'd supposedly done to make Shelby Harrington uneasy even being in the same room with him?

"A couple of things," Johnson said.

And clearly, they weren't just wishing him well and having a good life type stuff.

"First, there's clear evidence that the fire you were found near was human caused."

"A four-wheeler sparks in that dry brush and..."

How did he know that? He wasn't even finished with his internal wondering before Johnson shook his head.

"It was set deliberately. There was a trail of gasoline leading right up to where we found you. If the wind hadn't changed course, you—and all evidence of how the fire started—would have burned."

Staring in horror, Luke felt completely helpless. Someone had set a fire and, what? Had dared him to put it out on his own? Who would do that to him?

And how in the hell would anyone even put together a suspect list if he couldn't come up with anyone who knew him? Or anyone, other than Shelby, that he'd pissed off?

"There's more."

With dread in his gut, he waited.

"The bash to the back of your head... It happened before the fire started. Forensics came back on the rock. Your blood was on it prior to the smoke."

"I didn't fall and hit my head?"

"From what Forensics tells me, the rock hit your head from a different angle, clearly knocking you out, and then was placed under your head. Blood splatter and blood pooling were pretty clear on that one."

So not only would he be dead, if not for the grace of fate, but also whoever wanted him that way had taken extreme measures to make certain it happened.

And he couldn't remember a damned thing to help himself.

The detective wasn't asking what Luke assumed would have been the usual questions: Did he know of anyone who had a beef with him? Anyone he'd angered? Someone, maybe, whose woman he'd slept with?

Or stolen something else from?

"I'm not in debt," he said.

Johnson nodded. "I know."

Of course he did. Luke had given the man access to his own financials. Johnson had seen them first.

"I've never been married," he said, laying out another fact Johnson had told him. No ex-spouse wanting him dead for his money. Or nearly ex.

But that didn't rule out a girlfriend.

He had to get up to Payson. Ask around about himself. Talk to someone in the hotshot crew he'd been told he was part of.

"There's one other thing," Johnson said then, and Luke stared, chin jutted forward. Would the guy just please get it all said so Luke could at least figure out what he couldn't figure out?

"Shelby Harrington…"

He sat up straighter. Ready. He needed to know what he'd done to the woman,

"After she left here, she was in an accident…"

The detective's frown touched Luke's nerve endings, putting every one of them on alert.

"Shelby's hurt?"

The shrug was better than a shake.

"She's bruised. And shaken but okay," Johnson said. "Thing is, she had a tire blow on a brand-new vehicle..."

"Tires don't blow on new vehicles," Luke said. "Even if you run over something, you get a slow leak..."

So he knew about tires.

"On rare occasions, there could be a manufacturer defect."

Right. Possible. But about as likely as winning the lottery.

"But that's not what happened here. The sidewall had been cut, a thin line that didn't go all the way through. Just far enough that when she hit a big bump, or bumpy patch, the tire would blow."

"You're saying someone deliberately tried to kill her, too?"

Because of what he'd done to her?

"I'm not saying that. At all." Johnson's head shake wasn't as convincing as his words. "I do think that it's strange that someone wants you dead, and the person who comes forward to identify you ends up in life-threatening trouble right after being here, where you are."

Right. Made a hell of a lot more sense than a very brief five-year-old connection.

"Shelby says that there was a delivery truck coming up fast behind her when her tire blew. If she hadn't been able to wrench the SUV over an incline and into a ditch, she'd be dead."

Growing cold and angrier, frustrated and confused, Luke shook his head. "Did you find the driver of the delivery truck?"

"No. And she's certain which company the truck was from, and they had no deliveries in the area this afternoon."

"Someone could have paid an off-duty driver..."

"There are protocols, but sometimes trucks do go places other than their assigned routes... For enough money, I imagine someone with knowhow could dismantle any Global Positioning System or tracking the company puts on their trucks to make a little side trip."

Okay, but...wait...

"How could that person have known right when her tire would have blown?"

Johnson's nod, that worried look on his face, snatched any of the relief Luke might have felt before he even had a chance to get to it.

"The road right outside her neighborhood is under construction." Everyone who was familiar with Phoenix knew about the never-ending road construction.

Great. He had useless tidbits but nothing that could save a life?

"Cars are forced onto a rocky shoulder. Anyone knowing where she lived would know that it would be as sure a tire blow as you could get. All he'd have had to do was follow her and bump her as she hit the rough patch. Tire blow, fender bender, and off she goes."

"But...how would anyone know she'd been coming here?"

"That's what we have to figure out." Johnson stood, then added, "And maybe the two incidents aren't related at all."

But the man didn't sound convinced of that.

And neither was Luke.

If Shelby Harrington felt that she had reason to hate him for what happened in the past, this turn of events sure as hell wasn't going to change her mind.

Chapter Three

The first thing Shelby did once she had driven herself home in a rental car after being checked out at the hospital was hug her son. The second was pay the babysitter, see her off and then dead bolt herself and Carter inside the home she'd made for them.

And then, while her son played in the family room set up like a kid's haven, she called her mom, packed a bag for Carter and drove her little boy down to Tucson, an hour and a half away from the near-death experience she'd just had.

If Carter had been in the car with her...

Sylvia Harrington begged Shelby to stay the night. The only reason she did so was because Carter was tired and had asked her if she could please not leave for work until breakfast time. Her son was used to having days at his grandmother's. He never complained. Sylvia adored him, doted on him, and Shelby always felt guilty leaving him there. Every time.

Except that one.

As she left her mother's home the next morning, she was comforted by the fact that Carter would be safe there until she could figure out what in the hell was going on.

Detective Johnson and his team were investigating, of

course, but she knew enough to realize that cases like her crash could go unsolved for eternity.

Their only real lead was what, to her, seemed an absolute obvious link, not just a suspicion: Luke Dennison.

Which was why she typed the address to the hospital into her map app before she even pulled out of her mother's driveway.

The man already had so much to answer for. Knowing him for one week had changed her entire life, shaped her future, forever. And he'd sent her off to deal with it all alone. No way he was going to skate on this one.

Her knocking on his hospital room door was more of an announcement that she was entering than a request to come in. So much so that the power of her knock caused the slightly ajar door to swing inward, revealing a man standing in a pair of tan shorts, pulling a short-sleeved white shirt over his head.

Her gaze went straight to the chest. After five years, she'd been certain she'd embellished her memories. With a displeased gulp, she realized that she hadn't.

How could the mere sight of a chest she'd kissed all over—she recalled the feeling of his moans vibrating against her lips—melt her insides?

"Luke…" she said, starting right in, ready to tell the man he had no right to implode her life, when he stuck his head out of the collar of his shirt and stared.

"Shelby! Thank God. Seriously. I've been trying to reach you. Johnson wouldn't give me your number, and it's not listed on any internet people-finder, either."

She was a mother with a vulnerable young son to protect. And a very public job. "I'm on the national registry to keep my number private."

Detective Johnson had asked for her permission to share

her information with Luke at Luke's request. She'd declined. And hadn't explained herself to Luke, either.

Nor did any of that make sense with her telling him, at the end of their first meeting, that if he wanted to find her, he could.

"First, regardless of Johnson's need to keep an open mind while he looks at all the evidence, I'm taking full responsibility for your car crash yesterday. Johnson said the vehicle was new, and I'm going to see that you get another, brand-new one, rather than having yours fixed."

She opened her mouth to protest. Because her independence gave her strength... But then he said, "A car with an accident report on it loses value."

He was right.

And really, when you looked at four years' worth of child support... Yeah, he could buy her a car. But... "I didn't own it free and clear," she told him. "I'd settle for whatever the difference is from the insurance payoff or trade-in to what I owe. I hadn't even made my first payment."

She wasn't out to make him finance more than his share. She needed to know if he'd be a good father, and then she'd have to find out if he'd consider changing his mind about having a son.

All of which had to wait until he got his memory back. He could hardly explain what he didn't remember.

"Okay, on to the tough stuff," he said then, standing there with his hands on his hips, facing her like he had complete control of his world.

Something she recognized from the past. One of the many things she'd admired about him—his ability to just take on whatever was before him—until he'd thought he could pay her off and then shut the door in her face.

"I've hired a firm I've done some work for from time to

time," he told her. "Sierra's Web—they're out of Phoenix. You know of them?"

She did. Had actually covered a couple of cases the nationally renowned firm had taken on. After the fact. But... "The private firm that provides experts in pretty much any field, yes. I didn't know you worked for them." She was shocked. Felt betrayed.

And recognized she was being asinine.

His shrug was a bit embarrassed, but his composure and confidence didn't seem to suffer much as he said, "I actually didn't know, either, until last evening." Throwing up a hand, he told her how he'd followed his own financials, seen that the firm had paid him, and looked them up and given them a call. "I'm trained for many different kinds of dangerous, emergent situations, and apparently the firm was involved with child-trauma management during a fire I commanded three years ago. We hooked up from there."

She wanted to close her heart to his words. Knew her and Carter's well-being depended on her ability to maintain objectivity. And yet the part of her that had sought Luke out five years before to tell his story recognized the selflessness of his work life.

And admired him all over again.

Just like she'd always been drawn to the good qualities in men with major ethical failures.

"Here's what I'd like to see happen," he said. "Hear me out first, and then see what you think."

Did he remember that she waited to reserve judgment until she'd heard the whole story? Remember part of her?

Would she get her answers sooner rather than later and be able to walk away?

While her mind fought its usual battles when it came to men, she nodded.

"One of the big immediate questions is how someone knew, before you were here at the hospital yesterday, that you were coming. Your tire had to have been slashed in the parking lot here because Johnson said you drove here straight from home, and you had to drive over that bumpy stretch of shoulder to do that."

Having her tire slashed at the hospital was the most likely conclusion. She'd already reached it herself the night before.

"So how did someone know you were coming? And why?"

Was he actually standing there and accusing her of putting herself in danger by telling someone about her mission the morning before?

"I didn't say a word to anyone," she told him, not even blinking as she looked him straight in the eye. "Only my babysitter knew I was gone, and she thought I was doing research for a couple of potential stories, which I had also planned to do."

His nod seemed appreciative. She warmed to it.

Stop it.

"It's more likely that someone here at the hospital or within the police department had been approached when I turned up alive, and that person was subsequently paid off. Johnson has had a crew outside my door since yesterday afternoon."

She'd seen the uniforms five or six feet on either side of his door. Had nodded at them.

"That being said, the plan is for Sierra's Web to get us safely into hiding. We'll have bodyguards at all times, and no one but the firm, and Johnson, will know where we are. All expenses will be paid through the firm, and I'll reimburse them…"

No way was she going into hiding with him.

"...a team of experts is already being pulled together to work on every aspect of my life. I've apparently worked with the IT guy before. Then there's finance, a medical expert and a PI looking into my private life. There will be overlap, but we need this done as quickly as possible."

She was not going into hiding with him.

"As far as our safety is concerned, we can have two separate and distant places. That is not advised, however, as you and I need to be able to converse, and we won't be able to do so if we aren't together. We both have to cease use of all electronics and cell phones. At least until we get a better handle on what we're dealing with."

"I can't be without my cell phone." Carter. Done deal.

"If we're looking at someone with police connections being paid to make sure I don't escape again, the second you use a phone, you're putting a target on your head."

Wow. No intuitive understanding there.

Or maybe there had been.

He didn't know...

"I have a child," she said.

"You're married?"

Yeah, right, uh-huh. The father of her baby wanted to be her husband.

"When it became clear to me that I had no desire to ever marry, I chose to have a baby and raise him on my own."

Eyes narrowing, he homed in on her. "How old is this kid?"

Heart pounding, mouth dry, she knew she had to be more careful. No way could she let him know yet.

If ever.

She needed his answers first.

Ones he didn't yet have.

But he had a firm of experts who would most probably find out.

Because she'd become one of his targets.

Damn. Why was it that any time the man showed up, she had to suffer?

"He's four." But his birth certificate, his exact birth date, was private. She'd call Johnson and make sure it stayed that way. Even if it meant telling the detective why.

Luke's glance intensified. She prepared herself for the truth to fly out long before it was supposed to. Before she was anywhere near ready to deal with his response.

No matter what it was.

"And you interviewed me five years ago."

The article was dated. He'd surely already looked it up. From what she remembered about him, he probably had the whole damned thing memorized.

She nodded.

His shoulders dropped. His entire countenance diminished as his gaze fell to the floor. When he raised his head, his expression was filled with regret.

Which didn't mean a whole lot when he didn't know the facts—didn't remember slamming the door in her face when she'd brought him the news of Carter's conception.

She hadn't told him where Carter was. Could put in a call to her mother to take Carter and leave the state until further notice. Just the mention of the possibility of Carter's father's advent into their lives would ensure that she'd keep the boy safe. If there was one thing Sylvia had perfected, it was keeping kids from their snake fathers.

If anyone knew about Carter's parentage, if they wanted to get at Luke, they'd...

Her breath caught. Surely, Luke would see that it was best if...

"It was me, wasn't it?"

Feeling the blood drain from her face, she just stared.

"Whatever it is I did to you, it's the reason you decided you never wanted to marry. I drove you into a life of single motherhood."

Relief making her almost giddy, she maintained her stance.

Unable to believe her luck.

Wow. He couldn't have walked into that one any better.

She told him the absolute truth: "Yes, you did drive me into single motherhood."

Looking him straight, belligerently, in the eye.

"Tell me what I did."

She shook her head. "No way. You don't get to start building up different justifications in your head to cloud real memories with fiction."

His brows raised, he studied her another second or two. Nodded. "Fair enough."

She thought they were done. Until he said, "But it was so bad that you were pregnant within three months?"

More truth burst out of her in an attempt to hide the one thing he couldn't know—for Carter's own safety, she now realized.

"It wasn't just you." She'd already made her choice to never marry before she'd interviewed Luke. Which was why her consequent behavior had been such a shock to her. Had opened her eyes to her complete inability to discern male character when she got involved with them. "I won't bore you with details, but I'm drawn to men who have great qualities but who make immoral choices in their personal lives. A therapist I saw suggested that it leads back to my father. After getting hurt three different times, I decided to be kind to myself and stop."

"So it wasn't me?"

For a second there, she wanted to keep the hope that she saw in his eyes alive. She could almost feel how desperately he needed to be able to cling to that hope.

"Oh, it was most definitely you," she said. He'd been her fall off her own addictive wagon. The one that had straightened her up for life. "You just weren't solely responsible."

He nodded again. Shrugged. "If it means anything at all, I'm sorry about it now."

"If you remembered the way it went down and said that, it would mean something." Her response wasn't kind. Not to him. She was being kind to herself.

So why didn't she feel good about it?

The response came to her—because she wasn't like him. And that did ring true. A major moment. A reminder.

She would not become bitter like her mother. While Sylvia was fabulous with Carter, there was no man involved in his life.

At some point, Carter was going to be a man. And would need one as an example.

"I'm done."

Shaking her head, shrugging, she looked at Luke. Done with her? With talking about her past?

"I asked you to hear me out. You've done so."

He was waiting for her response. "I want two separate bedrooms," she said.

"Two rooms? You plan to bring your child?"

Oh Lord. Of course not.

"Why on earth would I put him in danger like that? Someone only wants me because I can identify you, and while I have no idea why that matters, I'm confident that my son is of no use to them."

Unless as a way to get to her? "But," she went on, "if you

wouldn't mind getting a bodyguard to an address I don't wish to specify to you, I would very much appreciate it."

"Done."

Good. At times, he was a really decent man. Times when others' lives were at stake. He'd risked his own countless times to save someone else.

That mattered.

"I meant two bedrooms, at the very least, in the safe house."

Eyes pointing intently at her, he said, "You're agreeing to one safe house."

"I am. But I need a burner phone or some way to communicate with my son."

"If you're in agreement, I'd like to leave those details up to Sierra's Web."

She was. She nodded.

And she soon found herself being whisked away, down into the bowels of the hospital, through a bunker of sorts and out another way, with Luke hurrying right behind her.

Watching her back.

Chapter Four

They set up shop in a hotel suite. As though his existence wasn't surreal enough at the moment, they'd been transported in the back of a windowless van, on side seats, like prisoners. Luke had had no idea what Shelby was thinking about it all. She sat, mostly expressionless, watching out the front window as they drove.

Taking stock of where they were going, he figured.

He didn't ask. Didn't want to push his luck with her.

Bruce, one of their two bodyguards, had been concerned that they were being followed for several minutes there.

If they'd had a tail, he never got close enough for a description of the driver, and Bruce, with some quick turns and doubling back, had lost him. There'd been no front license plate—it wasn't law in Arizona—but Bruce had called in a description of the vehicle to Johnson.

The suite—in a luxury hotel in the middle of a ritzy part of Phoenix—was spacious. The open living and conference area was easily the size of his entire cabin.

A flash hit.

Home.

Dropping to the sofa he'd walked past on the way to his room, he closed his eyes. Clinging to the image. With all his might, he tried to hold on, but it slid away, leaving emptiness as though that's all there had ever been.

But he'd seen something in his mind's eye. He remembered having the memory.

Bruce and Lorraine, the female bodyguard assigned to Shelby, were plugging in electronics at the conference table, their noise bringing him back when he didn't want to be there.

His cabin. Not big.

Hand on his forehead, he pushed.

Come on, damn it.

And...there... Another flash.

He took a mental picture that time.

Brown corduroy couch. Ceramic-tile floors.

Tile didn't burn like wood did.

The cabin had had solid wood floors when he'd purchased it...

When had that been?

He pushed. Looked.

And saw gray again.

"Is your head hurting?" Shelby's voice was close. Jerking his hand down from his head and opening his eyes, Luke saw her standing, still in the shorts and tank top she'd had on when she showed up in his hospital room that morning, just a couple of feet away.

Her frown of concern, while kind, left him feeling weak. Not in any good sense. Weak as in helpless. Not strong.

A bit warmed, too, and not in a bad way. Which was bad.

Glancing over at the bodyguards and an IT expert, who'd be working from the suite, setting up across the huge room, he kept his voice low.

"No," he told her, sitting back with a sigh of resignation.

His condition, the memory block that was taking his life from him, was absolutely no fault of hers.

"The gash, the stitches…" She was keeping their conversation between the two of them, too. A small thing to notice. And not of any import. Except that when you were drawing mostly blanks, small things could take up a lot of space.

And look bigger.

"It felt like my head was going to bust open the first day or so," he admitted.

He hadn't actually seen the back of his head but knew that some of his hair had been shaved for the fifteen stitches that were due to come out in another three days. Bruce had received instruction on wound care, but Shelby had been standing by at the time and would have heard it all, too.

"I don't even notice the stitches," he told her. "Until I'm lying on them. That's not pleasant and something I try to avoid." Small talk. He wasn't good at it. Not a memory—just something he seemed to know. "I need one of those cushions with a hole in the middle for my head at night," he said, making matters worse. The only such cushion coming to mind was one used for sitting after hemorrhoid surgery.

He was trying to make light of the untenable situation he'd unknowingly pulled this woman into. Had to get to work—to do, not just sit—and find a way to solve the problem.

She wasn't smiling. And he noticed the tablet she held in her hand and glanced at it pointedly. She said, "I was just coming out to show you this."

She handed him the ten-inch white device.

He read, growing colder with each word. A daily online report for a small-town police department said that police had been called by a neighbor to a home on Willoughby Lake at noon on a Sunday dated not quite four years before.

The private rental vacation residence had been the site of a weekend party and was trashed. The person who'd rented the home and thrown the party was Luke Dennison. Mr. Dennison had made full and immediate restitution, and no charges were filed.

"I have no memory of this." He said the words like they held some weight. Like the fact that he didn't remember actually held credibility. But…

"I know my cabin has tile floors because wood burns too easily," he told her, handing back the tablet, as if that somehow mattered. "And that I'm not good at small talk. I'm gaining back a sense of who I am, and this doesn't compute. At all."

He heard himself trying to convince her, trying to gain credibility for his words, and from the outside in, he even failed to convince himself.

"You should share that information with the team," he said then.

"I already did."

Right, of course she had. Sent his information to strangers before giving him a heads-up. He was looking to get his life back and be alive to live it. She just wanted safely out of there.

And then it occurred to him… They'd just arrived at the suite. The tablet was brand new. As were the clothes and incidentals that had been waiting in their individual rooms for them. How had she happened to access that small snippet from years ago so quickly? And had already had time to pass it on?

Concerned now for their safety, he asked, "You aren't accessing any of your professional investigative databases, are you? Depending on how good this guy is, he could already have a trace on your personal log-ins." More particularly, if their mole was in the police department.

Hugging her tablet to her, she shook her head. "I'd already sent the file to Sierra's Web from the hospital."

And the firm was somehow routing things over a series of networks to a room several floors down and then using a private mobile network within the firm to transfer information back and forth from their suite upstairs. He was an emergency guy, not a techie.

But…

"You already sent the file?"

She nodded.

"You just happened to find a completely innocuous police report overnight?" And what else might she have found to turn her against him further?

All activities of which he knew nothing and so could therefore not only not defend himself but couldn't anticipate, either.

No way to prepare himself.

And why in the hell, with all that he was facing, did he give a damn what she thought about him?

He needed her safe.

And then they'd go their separate ways.

She hadn't answered him. Glancing up at her, he was surprised to see Shelby looking somewhat uncomfortable. As though she'd actually done something less than perfect. For once.

"I didn't mean just the police file," she told him. And then stood there in front of him, still holding her tablet with both arms to her stomach, and admitted, "After you were…rude to me… I'd already written the article, had been writing it over a course of a few days' worth of interviews, and before I saw who you really were, I'd sold the article and had turned it in. I'd already queried the publication, and they'd agreed to buy it if they liked the finished product."

What her dissertation had to do with the police file, he had no idea, but he found himself listening like a dehydrated man crawling toward a pond.

Significant pieces fell into line in his head. The interview had taken place over a few days. They'd met more than once.

He hadn't done whatever he'd done until later.

How much later?

"Anyway, after...everything... I started to worry that the article was going to hurt my professional reputation because I'd originally seen you as a really good guy, and I depicted you that way..."

He'd read the article earlier that day. Though he hadn't remembered anything included therein, he'd felt as though he aligned with it.

Had been holding on to hope that the man she'd seen, the man about whom she'd written so eloquently, was who he really was.

But he also wasn't perfect, and he'd somehow managed to offend her. He did tend to say things up front to get right to the point.

In his line of business, there wasn't time for nuance. Most often, his mind was busy assessing. People, danger, weather, wind strength and direction, height of blaze, natural accelerants, distance to communities, in which directions, predictions of speed of blaze travel, crews, personalities, needs...

The information was just there. Pouring through him. He let it settle over him. *In* him.

And was surprised at first when she said, "So I did periodic searches, intending to fix what I'd written earlier if need be. I couldn't have my article be something that was used to make you look better than you were to cover up who you were."

Just that fast, he was back with her. Right smack in the middle of his private hell. He knew, without remembering a damned thing, that he'd rather be out fighting a Level 5 fire than be sitting in that suite right then.

Level 5. The highest level of wildfire.

He was coming back. Just as the doctor had predicted. But how in the hell could he speed up this process? Get what he needed rather than bits and pieces that didn't help at all? Tile floor wasn't going to find a potential killer.

"And you kept a file of everything you found," he said, finally catching up with her.

She nodded.

"I'd like to see it."

Lifting her tablet, she tapped and slid her finger along the screen and then turned it to him.

As badly as Luke needed to see what she'd collected, he dreaded looking just as much. Chances were good—based on Shelby's continued and obvious low opinion of him—he wasn't going to like what he saw.

SHE'D INTENDED TO give him the tablet and head back to her room. To let the various professionals do all their digging and pray that they solved the case that day. To be available for any and all conversation pursuant to her.

To try to clear her mind and find a way to be objective about Luke Dennison. Because even when they caught who-ever was trying to kill him—and her, too, apparently, for identifying him—she still had a real dilemma staring her in the face.

The questions consuming her.

Could the man be a good father to her son?

To his son?

But before she'd turned to head back to her room, Luke said, "Would you mind staying?"

Yeah. She was looking for a polite way to express the response when he added, "Sit, please? Whatever is in this file, you have background on. A frame of reference as to where something took place or what other events were going on at the time, things I won't have."

His request was fair. The research was hers. She knew how she'd come about every piece of information.

And the man had no memory.

Helping him rediscover his past might help him remember...everything.

And he could try and explain to her why he'd done what he'd done. Depending on that answer, she could start making better decisions of her own.

He'd only been reading a minute or two when something else occurred to her.

"Don't you find it odd that someone tried to kill me after I'd already identified you? It wasn't like if I were dead, authorities would suddenly forget who you were. Once they had your name, the rest would be kind of by the book."

She'd been wondering the same since the night before... peripherally. Mostly, she'd been rattled by her near-death experience and afraid that someone would try again.

That Carter would be hurt.

"From what Johnson said, it's possible someone thought my identity would still be in question for some reason. Or thought that authorities wouldn't be able to identify me conclusively and would need to rely on you in case of a battle for my estate."

Johnson hadn't bothered sharing that tidbit with her.

"I don't have fingerprints on file in the system," Luke said. "No family."

"So who gets your estate?"

He shrugged. "No one has found a will on file for me. Gerard, my personal banker, isn't aware of one. Or aware of any bills paid to an estate attorney."

For all Shelby knew, there could be an ex-wife in the picture. She hadn't gone as far as keeping track of marriage and divorce records. His choice to take a partner didn't reflect poorly on what she'd written. And as far as Carter went...

Maybe she hadn't wanted to know.

Maybe he had other children.

Her stomach tightened. Children who knew him as a father, while Carter cried because he didn't have one?

"Think about it," he said. "Everyone who's confirmed my existence is just doing so based on your confirmation and then showing my driver's license photo from that identification to others. For all we really know, I'm not Luke Dennison. Maybe I'm just someone who looks a lot like him."

He sounded so lost...so powerless...her heart lurched. The man she'd known, even in creep mode, exuded strength. Confidence.

She'd just been starting out, and his high levels of energy had spilled over to her, giving her confidence in herself. That man had believed there was nothing he couldn't do to save a life.

And had run into fires over and over again, willing to die trying to save them.

"Dorian, the Sierra's Web medical expert, will have medical records soon."

"Unless I've got some artificial joint with a serial number on it or a scar I don't see that proves some surgery, the only things those records are going to do in terms of proving identity is confirm my picture or social security number, which is what she's using to access them."

True. She knew that. Just...

Wasn't thinking as clearly as she needed to be.

Mostly was thinking that she had a way to prove his identity with a simple DNA test—Luke's compared to her son's.

Unless something happened to suddenly question the validity of his identity, she was absolutely not going to offer that source.

No one was questioning who he was except for Luke.

Because he was playing without a memory bank. She sympathized. But no way was she going to sacrifice her son just to give Luke Dennison peace of mind.

As much as her heart yearned to help him.

Chapter Five

The second he got up off the couch, Luke called Bruce into his room and asked him to get an urgent message to someone to get up to his supposed cabin in Payson and find out what kind of floors it had.

His lack of memory was making him vulnerable to everyone.

And he had a killer after him.

The next thing he did was look through the flash drive of financials Johnson had brought him, going specifically to the date on the police report Shelby had shown him.

And there it was. A large, stupidly wasteful payment to a private vacation-rental broker.

He didn't feel like a partier. He felt like the guy who'd rather live in a cabin in Payson than have a place in Phoenix. Or any other big city.

But what did he know?

There'd been other things in the file Shelby had given him. Fires he'd fought, lots and lots of them. As though she'd been gathering information to support her article, too, in case there was future backlash based on his lesser self. Not just looking for reasons to possibly write an addendum to her article, acknowledging that while he did some heroic acts, she didn't support his other life choices. Because that's where she'd really been going with all that.

But the worst thing she'd found...

He'd read it once. Had almost lost the contents of his stomach. A report of disturbance in a hotel room. Loud noise. Possibly someone hurt.

The police had been called, but it turned out to be a happy threesome, role-playing. While there'd been alcohol present, no one was drunk. And all had acted responsibly when speaking with members of the hotel staff. There'd been no damage to the hotel, and the threesome chose to leave then and there, of their own accord.

Nothing illegal about it.

He wasn't even sure how Shelby had managed to get hold of that report. Didn't seem like something that would show up on a public police activity log, but the "how" of the situation hardly mattered. She was a damned good investigative reporter. Fine. He got that.

But the rest of it...

If someone asked him right then, right there, if he'd ever even thought about taking part in a threesome, he'd have adamantly denied it. He liked his women focused solely on him and liked to focus solely on them as well.

As in, one at a time.

Not as in, one woman—the only woman—all the time.

Or he thought he did. Apparently not.

So was anything that was coming to him real? The doctor had said his memory could come back in flashes or all at once. The fire-assessment flashback he'd had earlier... he'd known...could feel himself running through the mental process... That had to have been real, right?

Unless he had a strangely vivid imagination, and the

things that had come to him weren't legitimate parts of the process?

He went for his new tablet to look up training for the forestry technician hotshot crew and...

Had no internet access. Of course.

Sticking his head out the door, he made another request to the team at the dining table and had the information on his screen within minutes.

He perused information that was like taking a shower; it was that much a part of him. He'd taught the stuff...

Oh.

He'd been an instructor, too?

Please let that one be real.

Leaving his room, he strode across the space to Shelby's, knocked briefly and opened the door, intent on his mission—and realized, too late, that he should have waited for a "come in," as he read her shocked expression.

She was fully dressed, if you called shorts that showed off those gorgeous legs and a tank top that showed him more shape than it concealed fully dressed. She was sitting at the table for two just down from her dresser, in the corner of her room opposite the couch and coffee-table conversation area. The room was identical to his. He knew its layout.

But concentrating on such inane details reeled in the thoughts he most definitely should not have been having. That moment was critically not the time to get his libido back.

Or to be sexually aware of a woman who kept a report about his threesome and his partying, and who already apparently had personal reasons to disrespect him.

"I apologize," he said, bowing his head. Then: "May I come in?"

"Yeah."

Breathing relief at her non-defensive tone, he stepped just inside the door.

"I just had a memory of teaching a hotshot class. Am I an instructor? It didn't say so in the article you wrote, and I didn't see anything about it in the follow-up collection." Thinking of the threesome—horrified that she knew that about him—he stood there looking for some kind of redemption.

Not wholly for the man he'd been; there was good there. But for some of the things that man had done.

Not that teaching made up for being offensive.

Or offending Shelby Harrington, at any rate.

"I don't know," she said, giving him the dissatisfying answer. "You didn't mention it during our talks. And nothing about it came up in article searches."

She'd been searching the internet for dirt on him.

Whatever he'd done had stuck with her. Didn't bode well for him finding out whether he could live with it.

He needed to go. Had obtained the answer for which he'd come.

She wasn't asking him to leave. Instead, she was looking at him like she expected more conversation.

Or needed more from him?

She could join the club on that one, getting in line behind him. Once he had his answers, he'd give her absolutely everything he had.

She'd risked whatever ill he'd done to her—something bad enough to solidify her decision to be off men for life—to come identify him.

Really, that was all he needed to know about her.

But he wanted more. So much more.

He was looking at her. She was looking right back. Someone had to say something. Or he had to go.

"How did you find out about the threesome?" The words fell out. He cringed. And felt as though he'd done so countless times before. He wanted to know what she'd accessed for information that wouldn't have been in an article. And the last thing he wanted on her mind was that damned hotel fiasco.

"Police records are public in Arizona."

She'd gone that far. She hadn't just happened on the party-house police log through an internet search. Whatever he'd done had made her fear he'd be in trouble with the law?

Wishing he didn't feel so drawn to her that he didn't want to stay and talk, he pulled the door closed.

Praying that his acute attraction to her had only to do with the fact that she was the one person around who could give him personal insights into the life he didn't remember.

"LUKE?" SHELBY CALLED out to the closed door more loudly than she meant. She'd been looking for a way to tell him what she'd just found. Feeling like she needed to talk it over with him, as next of kin, before saying anything to anyone else.

As a courtesy—nothing more.

"Yeah?" The door opened immediately and there he was, attentive and all hers.

For the moment, she reminded herself.

One of the things she remembered most about Luke Dennison was the mesmerizing way he could make a woman feel like she was the only person in the world he wanted to be with. She'd been younger then. Still falling for stupid—her own brand of stupid, that is.

She'd seen what she'd wanted to see. Or rather, hadn't seen what she hadn't wanted to see.

Because while she'd been what he wanted, and he'd been

all in with her the one night they'd spent together, he'd made it very clear afterward that she was nothing at all in his life after that night.

He'd told her—in the interview, when he'd talked about his unmarried status—she just hadn't listened.

"You did just call out to me, didn't you?" he asked then, frowning, and looked as though he might retreat.

"I did." They had to find a way to be together without tripping over every word. Just while they were sharing bodyguards, at the very least. She nodded toward the other chair at the table where she sat.

And warmed inside when he took the chair as though he owned it. Another thing that had drawn her to the man: the way he owned his space.

Even without conscious memory of who he was, he walked with confidence. As though he was certain he could handle whatever came next.

She wasn't so sure.

"I've been doing some research of my own," she said, hearing words spill out much more haphazardly than she'd heard them in her head. "I know you've hired the best, and I'm not purporting to be anywhere near their standards. It's just that… I look for the story behind the story, within the story—the story that no one else sees in a situation… That's my brand…and…"

She was pretty sure he didn't give a damn about her digital publishing brand.

"I started thinking about everything that's happened, and one thing that came up a couple of times was your father's car accident."

His brows raised in clear surprise. Like he'd been preparing himself to hear something else entirely.

Because heretofore, in his memory of knowing her, she'd

been nothing but the bearer of bad news. Once she'd gotten past the part of giving him back his identity.

"I've been following you for so long. You were my first big story, and your father dying... Something about it just spoke to me. So last night, I asked Johnson to send me the police report for the accident, which he did. I just opened it a little bit ago."

His jaw clenched. She knew that meant he was emotionally moved. Hated that she still seemed to remember every nuance about the man. And then, keeping her gaze away from him—as though she could shield herself from his reaction—she said, "I'm not sure it was an accident. Actually, I'm fairly certain it wasn't."

She turned her tablet around, showing him the report.

"I've purposely stayed away from looking up the accident," he told her, drawing in her gaze despite her decision to remain distanced. "I wanted to wait until I remembered my father before reading about his death."

So he wasn't going to look?

He didn't have to. She was ready to show her findings to the team out in the dining room and let them either investigate for themselves or get the information to Johnson.

After looking her in the eye for what seemed like forever, Luke lowered his gaze to the tablet.

And then, eyes wide, stared at her again. This time with the intensity she'd noticed in the past. "The accident was put down to a faulty tire."

Yep. He'd seen the same thing she had. Circumstances of the two crashes were different, of course. There was another car involved with his father's.

Her theory might be wrong.

"This can't be a coincidence," Luke said.

Which gave her the impetus to tell him what else she was

thinking. "They haven't found the delivery vehicle I saw in my rearview mirror, but if this is some version of the same stunt—and it might not be, with the fact that your father hit the other car... But if it's the same, we know the car and the owner of that one."

"We might have our first real lead to the killer," Luke said, standing and heading toward the door with her tablet.

Just like that.

He'd been with her, and then—taking her possession with him without even acknowledging her presence or participation in the situation—he was gone.

HE'D WANTED TO hug her. Luke couldn't believe the temptation he'd felt. Overwhelming to the point of not recognizing himself.

And he caught the irony in that thought with absolutely no sense of humor.

It had to be that he was identifying so strongly with her because she'd identified him. Because she'd known him. He kept telling himself, reassuring himself. But as Sierra's Web investigators got to work on his father's car accident, partnering with Johnson, he holed himself up in his room, where he wouldn't chance a run-in with the far-too-sexy reporter.

He spent the time poring over hundreds of pages of his own financials, hoping that something would spark a memory and, in the meantime, learning more about his life.

Still on his first pass through it all, continuing where he'd left off the day before—when he'd been interrupted with the news of Shelby's accident—he was only skimming accounts, payees, amounts, looking for anything that jumped out at him, but he intended to go back and check the items line by line. It wasn't like he had anything else to do.

And he had to keep his thoughts focused so they didn't

slide back over to Shelby. If he just knew what he'd done to offend her, maybe then he could get past her.

He wanted to think so.

There was a knock on his door, and his head jerked guiltily toward the sound. As though just thoughts of her had conjured her up.

Having her in his room, her scent lingering behind, wasn't a good idea. Whatever they had to discuss could happen in the living room, he determined as he strode over and pulled open the door.

Bruce stood there, with the rest of the Sierra's Web team behind him, still seated at the table. But all five experts were watching him intently.

Like he was a donkey getting its tail pinned again and again.

"What?"

Was he some kind of criminal? Going to be arrested in moments?

Hudson Warner spoke. "We just heard from the off-duty officer we hired to drive up and check out what type of floor you had in your cabin."

Okay, so they all thought he was making less-than-stellar choices by paying to have someone drive an hour and a half to look at his floor. He'd apparently done much worse.

"Was it tile?" he asked, needing a nod in the worst way. Needing to trust the little bits and pieces that were coming to him.

"The place burned down, Luke," Bruce said, his tone man-to-man but with a definite hint of compassion, too.

He suddenly understood all the looks.

He didn't want anyone's damned sympathy.

But…

Come again?

He had no idea what he'd lost…

He finally found a way to inject himself back into the conversation. "When?"

"The day you were found in the desert."

Feeling the blood drain from his face, he stepped out into the great room. Sat in one of the three vacant chairs at the table. Next to Hudson Warner, the IT partner at the firm, who was also running the team of experts on his case.

"I don't get it. The same day?" he asked the table in general.

"The fire in Payson was set after the desert fire," Hudson told him. "The authorities in Payson tried to reach you, but your phone just went to voice mail."

"This guy doesn't just want me dead—he wants all traces of me to disappear." Even for a man with no past to lose, the thought was too much to comprehend.

What atrocious thing had he done to make someone hate him that much?

With no answers, he homed in on the first question he'd had.

"Was the floor tile?" So it wouldn't burn. No humor there, either.

"It was," Bruce said.

And Luke almost wept.

Chapter Six

With her door open, Shelby could hear the drone of conversation taking place at the conference table in the suite's large living area.

Other than their bodyguards, the rest of the Sierra's Web team were only there for the day. They'd each be returning to their homes, or the firm's headquarters, or wherever else they did their actual work after this initial first meeting.

Which would, feasibly, leave her time to be alone with Luke. Time to talk to him, to try to figure out her own next moves. Once the killer was caught.

She'd thought she would have to wait until he had his memory back, could explain his earlier actions to her, but maybe she was missing the opportunity she had right in front of her. Wouldn't his current state more likely reveal the real man inside Luke Dennison, the motives and heart that drove him, more clearly than when those same traits were muddied with memories and outside perceptions?

After Luke left with her tablet, she'd gone through and put away the new clothes and essentials that were waiting in her bedroom when she first arrived at the suite. Without her tablet, she had little else to do.

The trauma of the accident the morning before—the soreness, meeting with Johnson, driving to Tucson, sitting up and watching her son sleep, the early-morning drive back, and then being whisked off to protective custody—had caught up to her. Closing her door, she tried to use the time to rest, dozed on and off for a bit, but eventually gave up.

Watching television didn't appeal.

Starting to feel trapped, she opened her door again.

She wasn't going to be able to handle too much of the current situation. There were three changes of clothes in the shopping bags she'd emptied. Three days of being cooped up in a room?

As opposed to, say…being dead?

Luke's voice joined the conversation, and she was envious. Because he had something to do other than sit?

Because the Sierra's Web team got to spend time with him?

Had the accident rattled her brain more than anyone had thought?

The conversation outside her room seemed to get a bit louder all of a sudden, and she tensed.

Had they found something?

More bad news about Luke's past?

Something current?

When she heard the word *fire*, she stood, went to the door. She was just walking out when she caught the tail end of Hudson, the team leader, saying, "The cabin fire is clearly a sign that someone wants all evidence of Luke gone. Why? We need to know *why* to better find out *who*."

What cabin fire?

When?

Luke's back was to her. No one else seemed to care that she'd ventured out, and she sat on the couch, listening to the ensuing discussion.

"What if I had something stored there?" Luke's distinctive voice reached her. "Some kind of evidence of something?"

"Or some contraband," the investigator, Will, said.

Shelby's heart lurched. Painfully.

Wait.

Cabin.

Luke's home was a cabin.

Oh, God. Had the man's entire life burned down without him even knowing what he'd lost?

Tears filled her eyes. She quickly blinked them away, feeling ridiculous and young and not at all herself.

Yeah, the man was in a horrible situation at this moment, and he'd made some pretty horrendous choices in life, too.

But criminal ones?

Why else would someone attempt to kill him and then burn down his home?

"Maybe to make certain that no will could be found."

She said the words aloud, turning her head to look toward the table. All eyes were trained on her.

"What if someone believes he or she is an heir to Luke's estate?" She'd asked him earlier about a will. Not because she wanted anything for her son. At all.

But maybe someone else did.

Another "her" out there. Someone else he'd impregnated and shut the door on...

She'd been burning up for a second there as she considered telling the team the truth about herself, telling them about Carter. She needed them all to turn back around. To leave her alone.

They'd have to put her on the suspect list.

She should have kept her mouth shut.

Always the nosy one, feeling around for what's not being said in a situation.

Except she wouldn't have tried to kill herself.

As conversation started up again beside her and she started to breathe once more, Shelby realized that there was no way anyone would think she'd identify Luke and try to kill herself if she wanted him dead.

And beyond that, she had no reason to tell a soul about Carter. No one, absolutely no one, knew that Carter was Luke's son except herself.

And Luke, if he'd chosen to store that in the memory bank that was yet to open.

Not her doctor, not her mother, not one single person knew who'd fathered her son. Which meant Carter being Luke's son couldn't possibly be an issue in the case.

But...if he'd denied her pregnancy, Luke could most certainly have done the same to someone else.

"She has a point," Hudson was saying. "We got nothing on a marriage-or-divorce-record check, but we need to get to someone on his team and have someone up in Payson ask around, find out who Luke's seen in the past ten years, if you can get back that far. Check birth records for Arizona and California, see if his name pops up..."

She turned toward the sound of Hudson's voice, saw the back of his head; then she saw Luke stand, his back ramrod straight, and leave the table.

He couldn't refute the theory that he'd fathered children who could legally attach to his estate if he were gone.

Though he didn't know it, she could give proof to the validity of that very real possibility.

UNLESS SOMEONE DIED because of him, Luke was pretty sure the day couldn't get any worse. It was horrifying enough to wake up without a life—but to doubt whether or not you ever wanted it back, to fear what you were going to hear about yourself next, was worse.

The fact that Shelby Harrington was present to hear it all, that the reporter who'd spent a whole bunch of time researching his life was actually coming up with viable theories about who could be after them, was horrifying him.

For no good reason.

What did he care what she thought about him?

She'd identified him. He wasn't even sure anymore if that had been a favor or a curse—and yet he yearned for her good opinion.

When had he ever cared what someone thought about him?

Other than his parents and himself, of course.

Oh.

Something new.

He'd cared what his parents thought of him.

Which meant…he must have grieved his father's death. And maybe the incredible sadness and untenable weight of responsibility he'd been experiencing in waves since finding out his father's accident looked suspicious were borne out of emotional memory.

Starting with the watch. He'd put it on as soon as it was given back to him at the hospital. There was nothing fancy about it. It did nothing but tell time, and not even digitally— but at the moment, it was worth more than gold to him.

His bond with his father had mattered to him.

That piece of information, he'd take.

And be grateful for.

To know that he'd cared deeply for someone other than himself…

He'd been back in his room, desperately searching for

himself in his spending habits for about an hour when Hudson knocked on his door, asked him back to the table.

He looked for Shelby first as he exited his space, saw her on the couch, pursuing something on the tablet Hudson must have returned to her. Only one night had passed since she'd identified him, and yet he felt drawn to her as though he'd known her for years.

He *had* known her for years.

And wanted to know her a whole lot better. In very detailed ways a decent man wouldn't think about a woman who'd never given him a signal that she shared his desire.

Who'd never told him yes to a request for...

"We've got something you need to know about," Hudson started in, and Luke's gut sank even lower. He'd already seen those looks around the table too many times that day.

He sat in his chair next to Hudson, determined to take it on—whatever *it* was.

Amazing, really, that one guy could have so many possibilities for people wanting him dead and still be alive.

Should he count himself lucky?

"There's this charity account," Hudson said, and Luke glanced across the table to Jeremy, the finance professional handpicked by the firm's financial expert, Winchester.

"I know. I've seen the regular deposits to it," Luke said, glad to have a reason for some enthusiasm in his tone for once. He'd been called to the table for good news after all.

Glad, then, that Shelby was listening behind him, he continued, "Bodell Charitable Society. More than ten percent of my income goes there."

The 10 percent was significant. Somewhere in his brain, he had the idea that 10 percent was a decent charitable contribution.

He did good stuff.

A lot of it.

There was proof.

Jeremy's nod did not contain any sort of matching enthusiasm. And when Luke glanced at Hudson beside him, the team lead's expression was equally grim.

"The Bodell fire is…"

"I know it," he interrupted. When all eyes he could see grew wide, he shook his head. And heard movement behind him.

"It's how I first met Luke," Shelby said, taking an empty seat directly across from him. She was there for her own safety but also as someone who knew him personally and who knew a lot about him prior to the day before.

"I read the article she wrote about my part in that fire," Luke finished, holding Shelby's gaze.

Regardless of what she might think, and what he might wish he thought, he was extremely glad she was there.

Beyond just being grateful.

Strangely enough, considering her low opinion of him, Shelby's presence gave him the one brief light of hope he could see at the moment.

"I looked up any and all charities associated with the fire," Jeremy said then, drawing Luke's gaze and attention back to what was really happening around him. "I was hoping to find someone who knew you, thinking you give them so much money that maybe you do more, make appearances at fundraisers or something…"

Yeah. Good. He'd like it if he'd done that.

"Turns out, Bodell Charitable Society is not a charity that provides any monies to any known fund or program assisting with anything to do with the aftermath of the Bodell fire. No family members who lost hotshot firefighters that day have ever heard of it. None of the rebuilding funds have ever heard of it…"

He got the idea. "What's that mean?" he asked, getting to the point and focusing only on the man with the information at the moment.

"It means it made me suspicious enough to ask our finance partner to dig deeper, and he found out that there is no such registered charity in the United States—not national, not state. In fact, the Bodell Charitable Society is the name of a shell company attached to an asset that is housed in the Cayman Islands."

Good God.

Just when he'd thought it couldn't get any worse.

What in the hell had he done?

"What am I involved in?" he asked, pretty sure he'd reached the lowest point in his life. Wondering why he'd fought hard enough to survive to get back to face this moment.

Jeremy's shrug was almost too much. Luke sat there, every muscle and nerve clenched, and waited for the moment to pass.

Hudson took over. "Winchester has been in touch with Gerard."

His personal banker. Good.

"The first concern—to a finance mind, anyway—was whether or not you'd be charged with tax fraud," the man continued. "I guess fake charities are a means to avoid paying income tax…"

Luke felt himself freeze, from the inside out.

"Pay whatever is owed. Now."

Hudson shook his head. "You didn't take the tax cut."

Luke's gaze shot over to Shelby then, the first time he'd looked her way since hearing the latest bad news on his record. Her expression changed as soon as she caught him looking... But for a second there, he'd seen warmth.

Compassion.

No sympathy. Just...like she understood what he was going through. Like she...knew.

Like he wasn't stranded out in the middle of nowhere, sinking in black turbulent waters, all alone.

Being alone in danger, getting out of it alone, was his thing.

No, wait. He had a team.

"According to Gerard, you opened the account shortly after the Marnell fire."

Shelby's gasp drew his attention back to her. He made a quick mental check through all he'd read and learned in the past thirty-some hours and remembered...the Marnell fire had happened right after she interviewed him.

And, he was presuming, right after he'd done whatever atrocious thing he'd done to her.

Please, God, knock me dead now if I laid a wrong hand on that woman. If I so much as tried to kiss those lips without permission...

She was no longer meeting his gaze.

He tuned back in to hear most of what Hudson was telling him. "...said you just gave him the account number, told him how much money to put into it, and when asked about using it for a charitable contribution, you told him to pay whatever taxes were called for."

"So how do we trace an account in the Cayman Islands?" Luke asked.

"That's just it. We can't. But Gerard said that this month's automatic deposit was returned due to account closure."

"The account's been closed?"

Nods from the partners were all he saw.

"I closed it?" Had he hidden the money in his cabin? Had someone trashed the place, found it and then burned it down?

"Or someone you were involved with—someone who wants you dead, for instance—did so."

"So where's the money?"

No one had any answers to that one.

Chapter Seven

The man who'd spent the majority of his time risking his life to save others was in agony. He sat alone in the suite's living area, at a room service table set for two, holding a fork and staring at the chicken fricassee he had yet to taste.

Shelby's own plate of Asian chicken salad in hand, she turned away from her bedroom door and made her way to the far-back corner of the room—in front of a window overlooking the Phoenix valley—and put her dish down on the white linen tablecloth.

The Sierra's Web team was dining together at the conference table; some working, some in quiet conversation. Once the experts left that night, she likely wouldn't see them again.

If they solved their case, she wouldn't have reason to see Luke again, either. Her son needed her to spend time with the man while she could. She'd already sent messages, via Lorraine, to her mother and heard back that Carter was doing fine. And that they'd been assigned a bodyguard, a Charlie Dresden, as well.

That news was a big reason she was back at the table.

Luke was looking at her, watched her pull the metal lid off her plate, saying nothing.

"Thank you for arranging protection for my son."

He shook his head. "Wasn't my idea. The Sierra's Web team and Johnson were all concerned that it would be easy for the killer to find out about him and then use him to get to you."

Because of Luke.

It all came back to that. Every time.

Good and bad.

"All I did was pay for it, and that's a no-brainer," he said. He picked up his glass and finally took a sip of wine, followed by a bite of chicken.

He wasn't eating because of her, but it kind of felt like it, and she was gratified. Tried to tell herself it was for Carter's sake. That Luke having an emotional core that could be reached was a good thing. As long as Carter reached it.

Or something...

It just felt good sitting across the table from him again. Facing him. Feeling like he was glad she was there.

And it shouldn't.

Because she knew—with Luke, with any man who attracted her—where it would lead.

But *oh*. He'd been the one. Physically, for sure, but much more than that, too. For those few good days...

He was eating like he was really hungry but was also watching her over his glass as he sipped. And she knew that he had something to tell her even before he opened his mouth to speak to her.

"I've been remembering some things." Fork midair, he swallowed, his look was intent.

And it hooked her. Just as it had five years before.

As though they were speaking without words. They both were able to assess and see what others missed...

She couldn't fall back...

She couldn't turn away, either.

"Like what?" she asked. That his cabin had had tile floor, apparently.

More of the same?

"I feel like I've kissed you before."

Her fork slipped. She caught it before it banged against the china and set it down. Glanced across to the far end of the room, where the team was working and talking, engrossed in their own business.

Not watching Luke and Shelby.

A definite separation of employee and employer.

Or so it felt to her.

"I haven't told anyone else," he added, as though her glance across the room had denoted worry that others knew.

If only *he* knew.

Their kisses were the least of her worries where he was concerned. She needed him to remember past that.

To the money he'd paid her.

And the door he'd slammed in her face.

But…she didn't feel ready for that, either. She needed to know more about the man's personal life than the fact that he was a snake with women.

She needed to know if the Sierra's Web team's search had come up with other women, children, who'd want a part of him.

See how he reacted to them.

She licked her lips. Had a split-second thought about a quickie while in isolation, no hearts involved, and gave herself a strong mental shake.

"I can do the math," he said then. While she'd been having a meltdown, he'd resumed his dinner.

Jerking as he delivered his statement, right as she'd been reaching for her wineglass, she'd have toppled the rose liquid if not for his fingers on the stem as well. Steadying her.

His warmth…

It was like they were naked again, and his hand was sliding over her stomach on its way to…

She stared at him.

The math?

What exactly had he remembered?

"I'm the last man. The one who tipped you over the edge. You're off men because of me," he said. "At least, I'm the solidifier in a stew that was already boiling," he added. "That means that whatever I did to offend you was on a personal man-to-woman level. And while I could theorize that you'd come on to me and I rudely turned you down—thus humiliating you, which would be offensive…that's not what happened, was it?"

She didn't break eye contact.

Or move any other muscle in her body, either. He was theorizing.

He didn't remember anything but a sense of having kissed her.

Pulling her wineglass free from his grasp, she lifted it to her lips. And an orneriness she didn't know she had pushed her to lick her lips once more when she lowered the goblet.

Not in a sexy come-on way.

She wouldn't be that bold.

But she was human enough to take a moment of satisfaction when she saw him glance at her lips. And then get back to his food.

Suddenly hungry herself, she dove into her own dinner with a lot more gusto. Enjoying the bursts of taste with every bite. Feeling more alive than she had all day.

"I remember the feeling of needing to kiss you."

She glanced up again. He was frowning.

Serious.

Not at all trying to give her a hard time.

Probably hadn't been since he'd started the conversation. She was the one who was all over the place. But then, she had a lot more ground to cover when traveling back over their past than he did.

"I wanted it. Intensely. In a way I'd never wanted another woman."

What in the hell was the man playing at? Anger spiked up in her, and she set her fork down in the middle of her plate, preparing to take it—and her wine—to her room, as originally planned.

She should have known better than to let any softer feelings she'd experienced toward Luke take center stage.

Even for a meal while he appeared to be struggling.

"Shelby."

The one word, the serious tone, gave her pause and brought her gaze up to his.

"Please don't go. I'm not trying to make you uncomfortable."

Her hands still on the sides of her plate, she sat there, staring at him. Hard. He was going to have to do better than that.

"I'm trying to let you know that whatever awful thing I did in the end, it didn't start out that way. You weren't just another woman to me."

God, she wanted to believe that.

So, so, so badly.

Even with the way it had ended, if she could at least know that the night her son was conceived had meant something special...

"Think about it," he said, leaning in as he spoke, his voice low and yet burning with energy, too. "What have I got to gain from you? You've already identified me. You're here, helping us find my killer... I already did whatever I did—you aren't going to forget it even if I never remember. And even I'm not jerk enough to hit on you under our current circumstances..."

Relaxing back in her seat, she let her hands drop to her lap as she held his gaze.

And then she nodded.

She had to.

It felt completely right.

As did the gift he'd just given her.

The week they'd shared that had resulted in her son... She hadn't imagined the power in it.

HE'D HAD TO tell her. It seemed wrong to walk around with the feelings these brief snatches of memory of her gave him, without her knowledge.

She'd feasibly been attracted to him at one point. Or else how could anything he'd done hurt her?

Unless he'd forced himself on her.

Not likely that she would have bothered to come forward to identify him without saying so, if that were the case.

He could have hit on her, though. And taken her rejection badly?

"This whole thing—you, me, the past you know and I don't—it's driving me nuts."

There. It was out.

Pressure eased in his chest.

Even as his gut clenched, ready for her to actually vacate the table that time. He'd managed to keep her with him once. And had to go and push harder.

Obviously, he was a danger-zone junkie.

"I'm not trying to be mean by withholding what happened," she said, surprising him with the warmth in her tone, the compassion he read in her gaze. "I just don't want to have you dreaming up possible reasons to justify your actions before you actually remember the real ones."

Made sense. Though why any justification mattered to her at this point, he didn't know. Still, he owed her...over and over.

"But I also know that you're struggling to know if what's occurring to you is real or just imagination... And I know how desperate you are to have signs that you're getting your memory back and to be able to trust what you're getting..."

Something inside rejected her hitting him so on target. "You got all that from me saying I feel like we kissed?"

"No, I got it from your reaction to finding out that you had tile floors in your cabin."

Oh.

Right.

He eyed her with what felt like new respect—admiration, even. She could see what others overlooked...

Did he know that now? Or from back then?

Was that why he'd done the interview with her?

Wanting to be interviewed didn't really seem like him.

"We did kiss," she told him then.

And he had to ask, "Did I force it in any way?" And held his breath.

"No."

His sigh was so loud he was sure it could be heard across the room. No one looked over, so it probably hadn't been that loud, but...

"Thank God."

She was watching him, assessing him.

He smiled.

She smiled back.

And he wanted to kiss her again. Right then. Right there.

Strangely enough, he was pretty sure she wanted it, too.

"More wine?" he asked, lifting the bottle from the iced decanter beside him, half expecting her to shake her head. Half thinking she should, too.

"Thank you." She held out her glass, no longer smiling or looking at him but...still there.

There was more between them. More she remembered and he didn't—besides his fall from grace. It sat there on the table between them. Lingered in the air they were breathing.

And thrummed through his body.

Was it beating in hers, too?

"You want to know if we did more than kiss," she said, glancing down, up at him, at her wineglass, back at him.

"I'd rather be prepared than suddenly be sitting at the conference table and be hit with an image of how gorgeous your breasts look naked in the moonlight."

Lightning crackled. Tingled his skin.

His damned mouth.

Eyes wide, horrified, he stared at her.

And she watched him.

As though waiting.

"That was a memory, wasn't it?" he asked. "I told you your breasts look gorgeous in the moonlight."

Lips pursed—in a jut, not a sexual tease—she nodded.

"They were naked at the time." *God, bring that visual back to me.*

No. Don't. It would be torture.

But what sweet torture...

"Yes."

"You've seen me that way as well."

"Yes."

Had he been as hard as he was growing right there in that chair, his lack of restraint free for her to see rather than as it was now, hidden by the table and its expensive cloth covering?

"Was it good?"

What in the hell was he doing?

More importantly, why was he doing it? He didn't feel like fun and games. Or a night of casual sexual innuendo.

Truth was, he didn't feel like casual anything with her.

She didn't blush. Flinch. Or smile, either.

"For me, it was." She could have been talking about a movie she'd watched or a song she'd heard, for all the emotion in her response.

Something had gone wrong.

They'd already established she wasn't going to tell him what.

But... "I told you it wasn't good for me?"

Being blunt, that sounded like him. But not enjoying sex with her? No way in hell could he see that one. Not with the way he was feeling, without a single memory of the act to spur him on.

"No."

"Then why did you say it like that?"

"I can only speak for myself." She leaned forward. "I'm not going to feed you my impression of what you felt," she said. "Nor am I going to repeat what you said. Either of which could taint your perception of what really happened."

Damn.

She was right.

Didn't make him any less frustrated.

"I'm guessing this isn't what you want—me sitting here, having flashes of intimate memory, with more back there, waiting in line to show itself to me."

She shrugged.

"I keep trying to distract myself from the feelings… They're not making it easy."

"You want me to stay in my room?"

If he thought it would help…

"I'm getting them while alone in my room, too, not just out here with you…"

Her chin jutted that time as she nodded. And took a rather large swallow of wine. Maybe he should snag another bottle from the refrigerator behind the wet bar.

But…considering that alcohol had a tendency to enhance libido…maybe not.

"Look, don't worry about me," she told him, meeting his gaze, but the intensity he'd read earlier was gone.

Banked, at least.

Well banked.

Before he could come up with a response to that, she continued, "The second I chose to make those memories with you, I was giving up any right I had to keep them from you…"

Sitting back, Luke stared at her, impressed all over again.

The woman had a way of looking at life, at the world, that cut right to the quick of the matter.

As his words had a tendency to do.

"So that just leaves me with one more question on the subject," he said. One question he was willing to ask, at any rate.

"What's that?"

"Do you want to know?"

"Know what? The question?"

"Do you want to know what I remember, when I remember?"

She blinked. Sipped.

Took a deep breath.

Studied him.

And said, "Yes."

Chapter Eight

She had to know. Which meant she wanted to know.

But oh, she so did not want to know that Luke was having flashes of her bare breasts. When she thought about the other things they'd done that incredible night they'd spent together...

They were painful enough, arousing enough, as distant memory. But for him, they'd be brand new.

In the moment.

And without her step back of pain to unsweeten them. He hadn't been hurt. Humiliated. Devastated.

He'd been the hurter. Not the hurtee.

Things had ended at his bidding. Just as he'd wanted them to.

As she relived those moments with him, she had to remember all of it. Not just how it had begun but also how it had ended.

She had to keep her mind on her own course.

They'd finished dinner, but neither left the table. They sipped their wine. She couldn't say why he didn't walk away.

"Have you remembered a lot of things today?" she asked. She knew about the tile. And now her breasts. How much more was there? At what rate were things coming back to him?

Not that one day was anything to go by. He could wake in the morning with full memory.

Or never get it all back, though doctors had thought that unlikely.

When he shrugged, there she was, noticing the shoulders again. Reacting to the timbre in his voice. "I'm getting things constantly, I think, but mostly impressions of things I know or who I am."

"Who you are?" That's all she needed. *Just tell me who you really are.*

Or which part of you is most dominant.

In her father, the untrustworthy philanderer had been a fifty-fifty thing. If he had shown up as he'd said he would, he would have been the perfect dad.

And if he wasn't in hot pursuit of some new woman, he'd almost always shown up.

"I'm not good at conversational nuances."

"No. You were blunt. But from what I could determine, you're honest, and that matters more. At least someone knows where they stand with you."

In the moment. Problem is, you had no warning when the moment was going to change.

"I know what I know, and I think I expect others to listen and follow."

She almost smiled at that one. "True. But it's because you do know what you know. You're an expert in your field. And lives are saved when your orders are followed."

"What about in my personal life? Do I order people around?" His look intensified. "Did I order you around?"

"No." She had to give him that. "You were quite respectful." Until...

"You never tried to sway or direct my interview, or anything else about me," she continued, trying not to let her own prejudice interfere with the truth.

"And if we had differing views?" he prodded, giving her the suspicion that he was trying, in a roundabout way, to find out what he'd done wrong with her.

"You didn't try to change my mind. You just spoke your own truth and left it at that."

He studied her. Sipped his wine. And said, "For what it's worth, I'm sorry."

She could only shrug at that.

"You don't believe me."

"How can you be sorry for something you don't remember?"

"I'm sorry that I did something to hurt you."

Didn't matter.

"You don't believe me."

He wasn't working at full speed. "I believe the part of you you're in touch with right now means what you're saying. The rest of whatever lives inside you that prompts other reactions isn't here right now."

But he'd be back. As the Sierra's Web team pushed their dirty dishes to the end of the table and seemed to be convening, she glanced back at Luke. There was more she needed.

"Do you get the sense that you and your father were close?" He'd said he had a plethora of impressions. She needed them.

"Yeah. I know we were. I can't remember any specific conversations—or even, for sure, what he looked like—but I know I trusted him with my life. And stayed in touch with him. Crazy, huh? Why do I know that but couldn't tell you what he looked like?"

"Maybe you're remembering what matters most to you first?"

She froze as soon as those words were out of her mouth.

Was she implying that her naked breasts held one of the top honors?

She knew for a fact they hadn't. He'd paid for the use of them...

"Hold it!" The abrupt command came loudly from the other side of the room; Shelby's gaze jerked quickly in the direction from which it came.

Bruce stood, his moving glance taking in every person in the room. "Pack up, we're moving out," he said. "Now."

Before the words were even completed, Lorraine was by Shelby's side, ushering her to her room, while Bruce took charge of Luke. There was a brief sense of commotion as the Sierra's Web team gathered everything off the table, and then her door was shut and she and her bodyguard were closed off from the rest of the suite. Five minutes later, after dumping her brand-new possessions—other than the completely offline tablet she was holding—down a trash chute, Shelby kept her head lowered and let Lorraine lead her down a flight of stairs.

Heart thudding in her chest, she prayed that Luke was okay.

And that she would make it home to her son.

THEY'D HAD AN exit plan from the time they arrived. Luke learned of it when Bruce told him to gather up everything in his room in preparation for trashing it. His bodyguard then led him up a flight of stairs reserved for staff, through a ceiling panel and down a ladder-like thing in the walls— built as a means to service the cargo elevator, he presumed.

He didn't ask.

They weren't talking.

He thrived on the physical exertion, was working with Bruce to determine their quickest route to the ground. If it hadn't been for the knowledge that Shelby was somewhere near, possibly in life-threatening danger, he'd have been in his element.

Fighting the physical environment to save lives was his thing.

Fighting it to save his own life, while someone else remained in danger...was not.

He didn't breathe easy again until he exited into a basement, where he was hustled into the back of a different van—smaller, red instead of white—and saw Shelby already there.

Was that worry he'd seen in her eyes when the door opened? Followed by relief when she saw him?

He took the seat directly beside her, strapped himself in as the van pulled up a ramp and out into the now-darkened night.

That morning, he'd been seated across from her. She'd never looked at him. Turning his head now, he expected to see her staring out the front window.

She was looking right at him.

And when she didn't turn away, Luke held on—his gaze and hers. Touching.

"The dessert tray had arrived outside our door. Bruce pulled up the feed on the hotel security camera for our floor and saw a glass of milk instead of a sealed carton, which had been established protocol. He put us in motion then. Lorraine has since received confirmation—because it all happened so swiftly and employees were still all on shift—that a member of the staff was paid a thousand dollars to switch out the carton for the glass. They're assuming the milk was laced with something but won't know until it goes through Forensics," he told her.

They'd been made. In less than twenty-four hours, in the

middle of a huge city and buried in one of many mammoth luxury hotels. Whether the milk itself had been tainted or it was only a test, no one paid a thousand bucks to switch a glass for a carton just for kicks.

"Sierra's Web is good," Shelby said, still watching him.

"They're the best." He wanted to take her hands. They lay in her lap, her thumbs worrying back and forth across each other. "I'm doing everything in my power to keep you safe," he told her instead.

She nodded. "I know."

Everything in his power, and then he'd left her alone with someone who wasn't him, who might not have his extreme level of tolerance for danger when he was saving a life. Memory or no memory, that trek he'd just taken with Bruce—climbing through plumbing and hanging from rafters... He'd seen each step before the next.

Hadn't hesitated a single second.

Shelby deserved that level of dedication. Of adrenaline.

"You have a son waiting for your return," he told her. "I swear to you, I will be by your side, fighting whatever comes our way, until I can get you back to him."

The words were said in almost a whisper, and when he heard them, he figured they sounded almost laughable.

And yet...

She wasn't laughing.

Her eyes were moist as she stared at him.

A long time.

And then, with a tremulous smile, she nodded.

WHAT WAS SHE DOING?

Breaking eye contact with Luke, Shelby couldn't quite make herself move away from him. Or quit absorbing his energy.

He was right: he was the guy you wanted around when you were in danger.

And he'd just promised to get her home to Carter.

He'd put her son front and center.

Something a parent would do.

They ended up in a shack off a dirt road out in the middle of a barren desert—someplace up north, she guessed, based on the temperature gauge on the dash. It had dropped from a typical hundred-and-five to eighty-two degrees.

They approached with the headlights off. She and Luke were told to stay down when the vehicle stopped, which Luke did not do. She saw him keeping watch as Bruce jumped out, and then, minutes later, Lorraine gave the direction to head inside. Shaking, completely sure she didn't want to exit the van, Shelby climbed down as she was told, but she caught up to Luke before they'd even entered the place.

"I'm not staying here."

"It's just for the night," Bruce said from in front of them. "We're on a private ranch. The owner owed me one, and I'd already arranged this in the event we had to move quickly."

After shoving them inside, he left, closing the door behind him. She heard the van start up almost immediately and drive off.

"There's a bunker close by where he's hiding the van," Lorraine said, as though someone had asked. She'd already lowered the room-darkening shade in spite of the shutters that were down over the outside of the one window.

"You think someone followed us out here?" Shelby asked, shivering. Luke, looking focused, was busy opening every cupboard, checking under the one bed, then up, beneath the mattress, and on to the couch cushions across the small space. The plastic-topped table and two chairs were the only furniture he left untouched.

"It's our job to prepare for every eventuality," the female bodyguard said, standing at attention by the door. "We believed the hotel was secure..."

Right.

You never knew.

Hands on her shoulders, Shelby just stood there. Feeling useless. And afraid. Two things she'd promised herself, after Carter's birth, she'd never feel again.

She wasn't a prisoner. She was free to go.

To walk out, demand a ride back to the city, and take on any and all possibilities that whoever was after Luke, whoever had tried to kill her, was no longer interested in her.

To take him on by herself—if he did indeed still want her dead.

He *or* she... If some woman had been pushed too far and was after Luke's money to support the child he'd had with her...

"What can I do to help?" she asked.

And Luke, apparently satisfied with the furnishings, moved over to the table. "Come sit with me," he said.

"We've got a briefing for you as soon as Bruce gets back," Lorraine told them both. "He and I will be trading off sleeping on a cot out in a lean-to at the side of the shack, and standing guard tonight."

"You don't have to sleep outside," Shelby blurted out because... Well... It seemed... One bed...the couch...the small room...her... Luke.

"We're outside so that we're the first to know if we've been compromised," the bodyguard clarified. And pointed out the door Luke had already opened and shut, leading into a space only large enough to hold the toilet and sink that jutted right next to it. "You hide in there if you hear anything," Lorraine said. "There are two dead bolt locks on the inside."

"This place is built for security," Luke said. "The walls are reinforced steel."

"Yeah."

"Who is this guy? Who's the owner?"

"I have no idea."

Shelby wasn't sure Luke believed the bodyguard, but Shelby did. Lorraine was doing her job. Doing it well and with composure.

Still, Shelby had a feeling that the woman was uneasy.

Which made her want to crawl in and cram herself beside the toilet, under the sink, and just stay there.

With Lorraine and Bruce outside and Luke guarding the door. She was a human-interest reporter. Not an adrenaline seeker.

A mother. A daughter.

Luke reached for her hand. She let him hold on to it.

A woman who most definitely fell for the wrong kind of man…

"I promised you," he said softly, holding her gaze.

And the panic inside her settled back down to lie in wait.

Chapter Nine

The place was built to withstand fire—gunfire included. It was the closest thing he'd seen to an underground bunker that was above ground.

Luke's thoughts stalled as yet another fact revealed itself to him; he had no way of knowing if it had come from his own knowledgebase or was just something that his bored brain had put together from his imagination.

Had he been in an underground bunker at some point?

No confirmation presented.

Bruce came in, his face all business beneath the light of the one overhead bulb. Feeling Shelby's foot bump against his as she jumped, Luke would have liked to have kept hold of her hand, and almost grabbed it again as Lorraine slid out the door before Bruce closed it behind her.

"I've got the team's rundown to distribute," the six-foot-two, two-hundred-and-twenty-pounder said, maintaining his post by the door. "I'll have radio connection tonight, and we'll regroup in the morning. The team's planning to have people on this all night and are hoping to have the identity of the killer by morning. No guarantees on that one, of course."

Luke nodded. Sierra's Web employees were experts; they weren't superhuman. "I appreciate everything all of you are doing," he said, antsy to get the report and know what else he had to deal with. What else Shelby was going to know about him that he had no means to explain.

Again, why her opinion mattered so much rankled him. Why didn't he care what Bruce or Lorraine thought of him?

If he could remember other women in his life, would Shelby still matter as much?

All questions added to the other million for which he had no answers.

"Financial report. They're looking more closely at your personal banker. The Cayman Islands account is a concern, and Gerard Michaels's explanation fell short. Detective Johnson is getting a warrant to look into Michaels's financials," Bruce said, looking directly at Luke, reciting from memory. The man was impressive. Someone he'd want on his team. If Bruce had fire training...

With a blink, Luke brought his thoughts back in focus.

"IT has found the same screen name on a few adult sites, all paid for by the Cayman account. And they're following up on some apparent associations established on common social media sites with the same screen name."

"I don't do social media. And I don't do porn." There was no arguing that one with him.

But what credibility did he—a man without a memory—have to offer?

Jaw tight, he couldn't look at Shelby. And was glad he was no longer holding her hand. Saved him from having to feel it slide away.

"If Michaels is somehow involved in this, it could be him using the screen name, sir," Bruce said, then shook his head as though he'd been speaking out of turn.

Right. Good.

Well, not good that the man he'd trusted with his entire financial life might be screwing him over and wanting him dead. But at least there was a possibility that Luke wasn't a slimeball he didn't want to remember.

Although he *was* something of one. He knew that.

Shelby's initial reaction to him, her continued distrust of him, was proof of that fact.

"Sierra's Web investigators have spoken to a member of your hotshot team, Randy Miles, who relayed that they were devastated to hear about your near death but glad to know why you hadn't shown up at work. Apparently, that was a first. Randy would like to speak with you."

The name meant nothing to him. "I'd like someone to get word to him, and the rest of the team, that I'll be in touch as soon as I can."

Bruce nodded. Luke felt confident that the message was as good as sent.

"Our investigators—there are two experts on your payroll as of now—are also looking into any other relationships you've had. They're using financials to trace where you might have entertained. There is a list of names of women, if you want it, but none of them that have so far been approached seem to have any beef with you. Mostly, they wish you well."

"Are there any with kids?" Shelby piped up, and Luke was cut by the edge in her tone. The woman's low opinion of him was getting more difficult to digest.

He had to make amends.

But how do you fix what you don't know?

"Not that I've been told." Bruce looked at Shelby as he spoke. The bodyguard didn't seem to notice anything amiss, and Luke swallowed his frustration as the report continued.

"Johnson has reported that the department has reopened your father's death, looking at it as suspicious rather than accidental. Based on photos, the tire of your father's vehicle was slit in exactly the same way as the one on Ms. Harrington's SUV."

"Shelby. Please." Shelby's voice was surprisingly strong, drawing Luke's gaze to her. Her attention, of course, was focused all on the bodyguard, but Luke saw renewed strength in her expression.

"Shelby." Bruce nodded, then said, "In reconstructing the photos from the accident, they were able to determine that the tire blew, causing your father's car to ram into the vehicle in front of him. They suspect that the vehicle was stopped, positioned to block him from going forward when he hit the bumps and forcing him to hit the cement embankment…"

"Made to look like an accident." Shelby nodded as she spoke.

"You were right," Luke told her, impressed. And grateful.

The glance she sent his way was more a "let's get on with things" than any kind of self-aggrandizement. "Let's just hope it leads us someplace."

She wanted to get out of there. Had a life waiting.

The reminder was important.

He was living in a no-man's-land. He wanted her around.

She didn't want to be there.

"Also pursuant to investigative work," Bruce continued, his tone unchanged, "police got a description of the guy who paid a thousand dollars to switch out the carton of milk for the glass. He was six feet tall, white, was wearing a blue hoodie…"

"A hoodie in one-hundred-five-degree heat?" Shelby blurted out.

Bruce's shrug seemed to concur with her questioning the man's choice—or rather, why others hadn't noticed it. But maybe they had.

"He had tattoos on his face," Bruce continued. "Leaves

scrolling down one side, a snake on the other. They're looking for any gang or other affiliations there might be to them."

"I'm guessing he was also on someone's payroll," Luke said. His father's death, getting away with it, setting two fires, causing Shelby's accident and not getting caught or even noticed...probably not looking at a perp with ink scrolling his face.

"They're scouring cameras, both inside the hotel and out," Bruce added.

Luke asked the question that mattered most to him at the moment: "And no one has any idea how we got made?"

"None. IT has been over our secure server, looked at the network we had set up, and nothing was hacked."

"So we were followed this morning like you first thought?"

Had it only been that morning? Seemed to Luke like they'd been in that hotel suite for days. They hadn't spent one night there.

Bruce, shaking his head, looked to Shelby. "That's the obvious conclusion, but I find it highly doubtful. Both Lorraine and I are trained to know when we're being followed. We're certain we lost the one vehicle that made us both uncomfortable, and there was nothing else suspicious..."

And yet, as the bodyguard had pointed out, it was the obvious conclusion.

Just like figuring he watched porn, threw wild parties, had fake charity accounts tied to the Cayman Islands, had a threesome in a hotel room and had seen Shelby naked, after which he'd offended her so horrendously she'd sworn off men forever.

Of all of it, the only thing that rang true was seeing Shelby naked.

She'd even confirmed his impression to be correct.

But he didn't get to choose which parts of himself he wanted to claim. Whatever he'd done, he'd done. Including offending Shelby, which she'd also stated as fact.

He had to live with his past.

Could only make better choices in the future.

"And the medical report," Bruce said, pausing as he glanced from Luke to Shelby. "We can do this privately, if you prefer."

Luke shook his head. "Go ahead."

She had some reason not to trust him, but he trusted her. And figured—considering the circumstances her good deed on his behalf had put her in—she had a right to any and all information at the moment.

"Aside from everything you heard when you left the hospital this morning, something potentially important has come up. You were injured in a fire five years ago, the Marnell fire—"

Shelby's gasp came right in line with his own recognition. He looked at her, saw her glance at him and then away.

Did he dare hope that he hadn't meant to offend her? That maybe it was all a big misunderstanding? He glanced back at Bruce. "Hurt how?"

"A head injury," Bruce said. "You lost your memory then, too, briefly."

"'Briefly?'" How brief was *brief*?

"A couple of days," Bruce said. "The pertinent thing here is that your current memory loss could be related to that one. Or could have been triggered by it. Your doctor will want to do another series of tests as soon as we determine you're out of danger here…"

Fine. Whatever. His gaze was glued to Shelby. Had the

news made a difference to her? Could he hope that he hadn't knowingly hurt the woman as badly as she'd thought?

Health laws wouldn't have let his medical information go any further than his care team...

She wasn't looking at him. As Bruce gave them instructions for getting his or Lorraine's attention, reiterating what Lorraine had already told them about protocols for the night, Shelby stood, facing the bodyguard, her back to Luke.

He stood, too, because it seemed the decent thing to do, wanted Bruce to hurry up and get out of there, and prayed that when Shelby turned back around, he'd find forgiveness in her gaze.

SHE COULDN'T LOOK at Luke. She needed time to assimilate. There'd been no report of injuries during the Marnell fire. Not that she'd seen.

Didn't mean there hadn't been one. Medical records rarely lied. Just meant the injury didn't make it to a fire-incident report. The memory loss would have come after Luke was no longer servicing the fire. Maybe the supervisor thought he'd had a minor concussion and was fine...

Which, ultimately—in just days—he had been.

She clung to factual thoughts as long as she could to distract herself from the importance of the news of earlier memory loss.

If any.

Bruce had said that, after the injury, Luke had lost his memory, which would have included the week before the fire. If he hadn't remembered having sex with her, one could possibly understand why he'd accused her of lying. He'd gained memory back right away, he'd thought, but who'd have known if memories of her were still missing? No one knew about them but Luke and her.

But…to just shut the door in her face. Most particularly if he'd suffered from memory loss. He'd have known that there could be a chance she was telling the truth, and he hadn't even engaged in conversation.

And the Marnell-fire memory loss had no bearing on the fact that he'd paid her off. He'd done that before he'd left to go to the fire that morning.

Before he'd been hurt.

What he'd done to her was reprehensible.

Still.

Staring at the door Bruce had closed, she felt trapped. Had nowhere to go that didn't also contain Luke Dennison.

And that was kind of as it had been for the past five years. Every time she looked into her son's blue eyes, she knew that Luke was there. Part of her and Carter.

Even as determined and single-minded as he was, he couldn't wipe out his biology.

And apparently, even a woman as in the know and fore-warned and devastated as she was couldn't stem the flow of awareness, of compassion, of…bonding she felt with the man who'd treated her so heartlessly.

Because she felt his heart.

In the actions he'd performed over and over again, running headfirst into danger to save lives. In the way he'd seemed to listen to her feelings as well as her words during the week they'd spent together.

In the way he was giving everything he had to keep her out of danger.

Taking responsibility for a past he didn't remember.

And caring about a future he couldn't yet see.

Luke didn't seem angry or entitled. He was clearly eating himself up inside with regret for things he didn't remember doing.

Disliking the man he'd been when he'd done them.

But what happened when he remembered...

"You going to stand there staring at the door all night?"

She'd been there a long time. Way too long. And still didn't turn around to face him. The room was too small.

Her emotions too huge. And raw.

She'd had to tell her son good night, to tell him that she loved him, via prerecorded video before dinner, to be taken by the team back to Sierra's Web headquarters when they'd left the hotel that evening.

Prior to the whole bugout thing.

She was used to being gone overnight. Carter was used to having her gone. But she always told him good night and heard his "I love you, too, Mama."

Every night.

"Do you believe a person can change?"

Luke's question, clearly loaded, shot through her. They were going to be sharing the small space until daylight. She couldn't stand frozen, staring at the door until then.

Turning, she saw him seated where he'd been earlier, on one side of the small table. Her empty chair seemed glaring in the little vignette.

It called to her.

Better that than the couch.

And most definitely not the bed. If they slept at all, he could do it there.

She would not lie down on another mattress with him in the room.

A flash of her on the bed, with Luke waking up and joining her—quietly, tenderly—sent liquid fire through her veins of such a magnitude that she had to move.

Or melt.

She put her butt in the chair and, as though they were

strangers discussing philosophy, said, "I think that we all change, all the time. We learn by experience and by the accumulation of knowledge, both conscious and unconscious, and the collective then shapes our perceptions and choices."

He was watching her. The hint of...something pleasant in his expression unhinged her a bit. Made her blurt out, "But I also think that we have certain character traits that will be with us our entire lives." Her father just couldn't stop himself from liking women. Different kinds, different shapes, but always in the plural. He was libido driven, not family driven.

But he wanted to be part of a family, too. He wanted the time. It just came second. He was who he was.

And Luke was who he was, too.

Mark, her relationship just prior to Luke, had simply been a self-centered, egotistical smooth talker.

And Josh, before that, had sucked her in with how much he'd needed her. Only problem was, he couldn't be there when she needed him back. He knew how to drain her emotions but didn't get that, in a healthy relationship, he also had to do his share of filling up the well.

"I can't speak to what I did to you." Luke's voice broke into her thoughts—the tone, the sincerity shining from his gaze, hooking her. "But I have to believe that I can make amends."

Luke didn't lie. The memory came to her. When he was being rude, he did it right to your face, just as when he'd been talking about saving lives.

Telling her about his mother's death.

And letting her know how drawn to her he'd been. Her body, yes, but her thoughts, too. They'd spent an afternoon on a couch just talking, about all kinds of things, and neither of them had wanted the time to end...

"I can promise you, as the man who sits before you right now, that I will do everything in my power to make it up to you."

Those blue eyes, they glistened with the power of his message.

Reminding her of Carter's big blue eyes filled with tears as he asked her why he didn't have a daddy.

"There are some things that aren't that simple," she said. She wasn't the only one his callousness had hurt.

Question was, even if he couldn't make it up to her, could he be there for Carter?

In some capacity?

She made the mistake of meeting his gaze, and Luke, hands together on the table, leaned forward as though reaching out to her, but he stopped before actually touching her.

"I don't care how high the mountain I might be facing turns out to be," he said. "I will climb it."

Oh, God, was the man trying to break her heart?

Was she wrong to hold a grudge against him? Was she letting her own feelings get in the way of a relationship her son desperately needed?

Luke was close with his team. They all admired him. He was there for them. So many examples from past conversations came to mind. The way he'd been there for a guy who'd come home to find his wife in bed with someone else. The time he'd helped build a memorial after a female team member's father had died.

And, extremely telling—his closeness with his own father.

She'd known about that five years before.

Had the knowledge been what had kept Luke on her mind, and in her investigations, ever since? Subconsciously, had she known this day had to come? Assuming Luke matured and was interested in being a father...

Would she trade having known her own father if it meant she hadn't had to be the rope in her parents' tug-of-war?

Did it matter if Luke remembered what he'd done to her before she told him about Carter? Would it ever matter?

What had happened between her parents...they'd brought it to her—or rather, her mother had used her as a sounding board for her own very real and understandable pain—but Shelby had grown up knowing that both of her parents loved her.

"I don't have much of a past right now to shape my present," he told her, not sounding at all needy, just plain factual. "All I know is the bottom line of who I'm sitting here with, inside me. All I've got is who I'm left with. And I have memories of you...of being drawn to you... And I know, down to my core, that I don't want to go through the rest of my life without making this right."

He had to stop.

There was nowhere for her to run, to get away from him.

And while he couldn't help not knowing his less-than-likable side, she did know that guy. Far too well.

"Haven't I already done enough for you?" her broken heart cried out. To him and to the others who'd wanted her to keep giving, over and over, to keep understanding. And forgiving.

And then she froze. Was she turning into her mother? Putting her own pain above that of her son? Her own peace of mind over his emotional wealth?

She wasn't here for herself—well, other than staying alive, of course. But she'd been following Luke Dennison's life for Carter's sake. After identifying him, she'd made the choice to pursue the possibility of Luke being in his son's life.

With all the DNA options available—and she'd have to assume they'd be even more prevalent as Carter got older—her son would likely discover his father on his own at some point...

Luke had pulled back from the table. Was sitting there, nodding, his gaze open. As though he was about to tell her that she was right. That he'd respect her wishes and leave her alone.

That she'd never hear from him again once their lives were out of danger.

She was afraid that that was what he was about to tell her.

And before she could form another thought, the words ripped out of her.

"Carter is your son."

Chapter Ten

He didn't believe her. Of all the horrible things he'd imagined he'd done to harden her against him…

"I told you about him…"

"I would never turn my back on my own child." Point-blank.

There was no arguing that one. Didn't matter how much memory he did or did not have. No way anyone would ever convince him that he'd do such a thing.

She'd said that she'd gotten pregnant a few months after knowing him. Because of him. That she'd done so knowingly, wanting a child, but not a man in her life.

She was the liar.

He stared her down. Didn't care if he was coming off like a high-handed moron. She didn't flinch.

He admired that about her. The ability to stand her ground.

But not when she was trespassing on his.

"You can get as strong and fierce and determined and adamant as you want," she said then, her chin jutting. "Biology doesn't lie. I'll provide Carter's DNA, you provide your own."

"Well, we're damned well going to do that," he said, fire

burning through every inch of him. Inside and out. "I'll get Sierra's Web on it right now."

He stood up and strode over to the door, knocked once to let Bruce know they were okay. He waited for the knock back and then pulled open the door. Stepped outside.

He explained to his bodyguard what he needed, went back inside and shut the door.

If she thought she was going to...

He'd just call her bluff...

If he had a four-year-old boy in the world, he'd have been coaching T-ball or soccer or dance or swimming or...just sitting and watching cartoons. Just as his father had done with him.

He'd hated them all—except the swimming. Then his dad had taken him rock climbing...

Oh. Another memory. One that would have to wait.

Still on his mission to walk forcefully, to stand for himself, he made it back to the table. Sat. Ready to find out why the woman he'd thought he'd felt such a pull for would try to mess with his head in such a despicable way...

He didn't look at her. But as he sat, another thought hit him. Hard.

Had he pulled something similar on her? Lied to her in a way that had changed her whole life? And she was trying to show him why he couldn't just waltz in here and tell her he'd make it up to her?

Giving him a taste of his own medicine because he didn't remember having dished it out to her?

Taking a deep breath, calming for a second, he looked over, expecting to see her watching him, waiting for him to get it.

She wasn't even looking at him.

She had paper in front of her. And a pen. Obviously taken from the open drawer of the single cupboard in the place.

With a flourish, she appeared to be signing her name at the bottom of whatever she'd written. And then, after turning the paper toward him, she slid it across the table. "You'll need my permission to get Carter's DNA," she told him. "It's on file with his pediatrician. Most hospitals are required to take newborn DNA at birth for certain screenings, and I requested that Carter's be kept. I'd read having DNA on file can actually save a child's life in certain circumstances..."

Stop talking.

Was she ever going to stop talking?

He wouldn't touch the paper. As if doing so would give any credibility at all to what she was saying. But he wasn't blind. He could see the words.

She'd just given him legal access to her son's DNA.

Why would she do that? Just to keep him going? To take her little game to the last possible play?

Okay, then, he had to keep up with her. "If you had my child, then you did so without my knowledge."

And he was the aggrieved party.

Though he couldn't be sure if he'd have been as adamantly gung ho about wanting to be a father five years ago...

He might have had misgivings.

Serious ones.

He still would have done the right thing—by her and for the child. He'd never have turned his back. He knew that as well as he knew that he would give his life to save another.

Again and again.

No matter what.

But if she hadn't told him... If the kid was his...

Holy hell. He jumped up from the table and went to the

door. Knocked once, barely waiting for the response before yanking it open. "You'll need this," he told Bruce, handing the man the signed piece of paper through the wide-open door.

And then, closing out the world, he returned to the table.

Ready for Shelby to come clean. To let them both off their hooks.

"Two months after...what happened *happened* between us, I drove to your cabin in Payson. I told you I was pregnant. You called me a liar and shut the door in my face."

No way. She was lying. There was just no way he'd do such a thing.

He was not that guy. He never could have been.

He was ready to blurt out his disgust for her charade, but he stopped short of calling her a liar out loud.

That was his immediate reaction to her telling him that Carter was his: *he didn't believe her.* She was lying.

Was it so far inconceivable that he'd had the same reaction five years before?

A string of silent expletives filled his brain long enough for him to breathe.

How in the hell did he know what he'd thought? Or done?

She'd given him access to her son's DNA.

Would she really do that just to prove a point to him? That people could be cruel in how they played with each other's emotions?

He shook his head.

She wouldn't.

But the alternative...

He just couldn't take it on. Couldn't even fathom...

She was sitting there calmly. More calmly than he'd seen her since she'd shown up in his hospital room the morning before.

God, a lifetime had passed since then.

In less than forty-eight hours he'd...

When he met her gaze, she didn't look away. "Can we talk about this?"

She shrugged. "I'm not going to get into it with you, if that's what you mean."

He didn't know what he'd meant.

And then it dawned on him...

Horror sluiced through his pores. His veins. "My memory... The Marnell fire..."

She'd had a very definite reaction to the mention of his earlier injury...

"I told you the baby wasn't mine because I didn't remember us together..." Yes. It was the only thing that made sense. She had to see that.

Had to... He didn't know what.

They'd lost four years because he'd had a slight head injury?

Could life be that simple?

And that cruel?

"Maybe if you'd tried again..." He knew as soon as he said the words that they were wrong. Putting the blame on her was absolutely not what he'd intended.

But how could he have tried again when he had no memory of...

"You made it very clear there'd be no discussion, Luke. You shut the door in my face. It was clear to me at the time that you were entertaining. I heard a woman calling out to you from inside."

A woman? In his cabin?

That didn't feel right, either.

Tense, hot and tired—and so completely out of his element he wasn't sure of his next step—he put his hands to the back of his head. Held on.

What the hell did he know?

Really know?

He could see her hating him...if things played out as she was saying...

And no, they most definitely were not simple. This wasn't going to be fixed. Ever.

Carter.

He had a four-year-old son? His name was Carter?

And he'd missed...everything?

He'd been feeling such an incredible attachment to her. Had been hoping that when the would-be killer was caught, he could talk Shelby into continuing a relationship with him.

By whatever definition she'd allow.

He'd just wanted her in his life.

And now, was she playing some kind of sick game with him to teach him a lesson?

It was just... To believe what she was saying...

How could he, when he didn't believe? When he'd have to turn his back on his own sense of self to do so?

"I know you don't want to discuss what actually happened between us until I remember it all," he said then, weary beyond the hours he'd gone without sleep. "But can you tell me this? You said two months passed between when we were last together and you came to my door."

"That's right."

"So how did things end between us?"

From what he sensed, supported by what Bruce had told them during his report, he had women in his past, but he didn't leave them angry with him.

She shook her head.

He stared at her. "It ended badly."

"That's an understatement."

"Did we argue?"

"No."

"I just did whatever I did and that was it."

"Yes."

And yet, when she'd known she was pregnant, she'd done the decent thing—put the past aside and had gone to find him. Had told him about the baby.

And he, either knowingly or possibly not, had told her she was lying and shut the door on any possibility of conversation about it.

He just didn't get it.

Was pretty sure he never would.

Even if he remembered every single intimate detail from his past.

HE'D PAID HER off before the injury. Shelby could not get by that one conscious choice that spoke to what he thought of her and their time together...

"Wait..." Luke slumped farther in his chair, looking over at her with a seriously grim expression. "Even if I didn't remember our...encounter...when you came to see me in Payson, I'd have known that I had memory issues... Would have known that there was a possibility I didn't remember..."

The man just didn't stop grabbing at her.

Which was exactly what had happened the week she spent interviewing him. And why she'd ended up in bed with him.

She knew how that had turned out. There was just no getting away from that fact.

And then there was Carter.

"And of course you already know all of that," Luke said as she sat there, saying nothing.

She was lost. Stuck in one room with him for the night.

Missing her son. Afraid for her life. Scared of the things she was feeling for a man who'd already proven he wasn't good for her.

Being guarded by trained strangers.

And she'd never felt more alone.

Or unsure.

"Holy hell!" Luke sat up straight. Jumped up. "Carter... If he's mine...his life could be in..." He'd gone so pale she thought he might pass out. He'd just been released from the hospital. Could be...

"Luke." She stood, too. Reached for his hand, just to be there to steady him if he swayed, assessing distance to be able to lower him to his chair were he to lose consciousness. "It's okay," she said.

Surprised at the strength of his pull against her, his attempt to get to the door, she held on tighter. "No one knows he's yours," she said quickly. "No one."

Except now probably Bruce. And any Sierra's Web expert the man might already have contacted.

What had she done?

Luke shook his head, his look urgent, but he was no longer pulling away from her. "What about your mother?" He threw the question at her, his frown intense.

With a head shake right back at him, she said, "Not even my doctor knew. You and I. That's it. Ever."

It was like all life drained out of him as he glanced at her and then off toward a corner of the room. His jaw tight, she could see the muscles in his throat working. She could feel his struggle, like a physical weight beneath her ribs, and hated the fight she had to wage inside herself.

Wasn't it enough to have to defend herself from the rest of the world?

But from her own self?

How did she even have a chance at succeeding?

"I need to sit down." Luke moved toward the couch. He didn't really pull away from her that time, but she dropped his hand.

And then, like a lamb to slaughter, followed him to sit on the opposite end of the one piece of living room furniture.

"I can't believe this is real," he said, shaking his head. "Can I see pictures of him?"

She held up the unconnected electronic device she'd been given.

His chin hit his chest as though her inability to give him even that much was his last straw. And then he straightened, meeting her gaze head-on, no distress evident.

"I intend to be a part of his life."

Just like that, her world turned onto an axis she'd been avoiding—yet barreling toward. She couldn't accept his words. Not carte blanche.

Not until she knew more.

"You just gave me what I need to fight for the legal right," he said, reminding her of the man who'd shut the door in her face.

The one who did exactly what he wanted to do in spite of how it might affect anyone else around him.

"As soon as the DNA comes back as a match, I'm established as his father and—"

"Yeah, yeah, yeah," she said, cutting him off. Panicking.

Sierra's Web had expert attorneys, too. She had to hire one for herself before Luke bought them away from her...

"I have no intention of usurping your right to determine what's best for him." The voice came softly, reaching through her fog.

She glanced over at him. Saw the man she'd thought she'd known. Aware. Concerned. And not just for himself.

Throwing up his hands, he said, "I'll definitely provide back child support, as soon as we are physically able to make it happen," he told her, looking her straight in the eye. "And the rest... I leave it up to you to determine where and how I fit..."

The guy was killing her, one heartstring at a time. And before she could take a breath, she said, "He's been unhappy more lately because he doesn't have a father." She let the damning words fall out of that remote hiding place. "His best friend's dad takes him fishing and...you know, other things. I don't think the things matter, really, he just doesn't understand why he can't have a father, too."

Carter was his son. He deserved to know the little guy's state of mind. Didn't he?

"But... I can't give you access to him right now, Luke. Not until..."

What? Her feelings from the past were assuaged? Channeling her mom, again?

"I can't let you close the door in his face." The truth became clear to her.

She settled back into the corner of the couch. Stared him down without a flinch.

And found her peace again.

Chapter Eleven

Bare feet pushing against his own woke Luke. He wasn't sure of the time or how long he'd been asleep. The bare feet, though… He'd tangled with them before. In a hotel-room bed. Silky sheets. Bare breasts.

Eyes still closed, he lay there with the moment.

Skin to skin, from toes to head. Sliding, teasing…then not.

Wet with sweat.

With her.

Held captive by such explicit pleasure.

Knew he'd been changed.

And…

He moved his heel. Against rough tweed. Not cool, smooth softness.

And he opened his eyes to the dim light left on over by the small sink. In the tiny cabin, the past days came rolling back over him, flattening him.

The other foot—just one, not both—had barely touched him. A heel to his arch. Enough to wake him up. His pull-back barely perceptible, he disconnected the contact.

He lay there on the end of the couch that had held him for much of the night. Aware that the mother of his child, still in the shorts and tank top from the morning before, had fallen asleep on the other end.

His child.

He had a son.

Carter.

He couldn't wrap his mind around this state of affairs. Didn't feel the truth of her words. But he no longer doubted her.

She'd been keeping track of him, had come to identify him, for Carter. He'd figured out that much.

Just as he knew she still wasn't sure if she'd dare let him around her little boy.

They'd fallen asleep talking. Him first? Her? He couldn't be sure. He'd had a million questions. The pregnancy, delivery, who'd been with her, had it been hard?

She'd been alone, other than medical personnel, for the twenty-seven hours it took their son to show his face to the world. Her choice.

She'd wanted the time for just her and Carter.

The family of two that they were going to be.

His son had rolled over at three months, pulled himself up on the side netting of a playpen at five months, had been walking by ten months. And hadn't spoken a legible word until he was almost eighteen months old. Then he'd talked in sentences.

A man after Luke's heart. Or rather, a son taking after his father. Luke had always been a guy who listened more than he spoke.

Who had no talent for small talk.

Lying there with a mind filled with the facts he was certain meant more to him than any he'd remember, he flashed back to seconds before when he'd woken up.

He'd been in a hotel-room bed with Shelby.

Remembered undressing her, the leggings and long button-down blouse she'd had on. No underwire on the lightly padded bra. Black.

The matching bikini panties... He grew hard as the memory slammed into him.

Took a deep breath. Pushed forward...forward...forward...

The call. He'd pushed to answer before the first beep finished, not wanting to wake her. Had slid into his pants as he listened. There'd been a fire. A small desert community surrounded by flames.

He'd had to get out of the room so he could ask the questions burning on his tongue, give the orders he had to give. Had made his way out of the afterglow of a night of incredible physical pleasure as he entered his own room down the hall.

And had been on his way to the fire less than five minutes later.

It had been four thirty in the morning.

And he'd just left her there.

He had intended to call the first chance he got. Knew she'd understand. His career, his life of firefighting had been what had drawn her to him to begin with.

She of all people had seemed to understand how he rolled.

Had he called?

He didn't remember calling.

And...heard a gunshot.

There'd been a shot at the fire?

No. Senses sharpening, he lay perfectly still, listening.

He heard another pop.

Felt a small movement against his foot. Pushing on him and not letting up.

Shelby.

She'd heard it, too.

Acting purely on instinct, when a third shot rang out, he tangled his half-bare legs with hers. Gently but determinedly, he rolled them both off the couch to the floor, and then, crawling up over her, holding his body above hers as a shield, gave a quick nudge toward the bathroom door. His legs moving against hers only enough to get her crawling, he kept pace with her. Across the floor.

Keeping her covered the entire time as a fourth shot sounded. If she noticed the residual hardness left from his thoughts just seconds before, he'd deal with it later.

Welcomed the possible distraction for her.

Neither Bruce nor Lorraine had come to the door or given any signal. He had to assume he and Shelby were alone.

Whether she'd figured that out or not, he didn't know. Couldn't worry on that one.

Lives needed saving.

The four-year-old son he'd never met would not be an orphan.

SHAKING, PRAYING, VISIONS of Carter flashing before her eyes, Shelby sat crunched in the fetal position in a corner of the small bathroom.

Where were Bruce and Lorraine?

Had the shots come from their guns?

What was Luke doing?

He was supposed to have stayed in the bathroom with her. The protocols they'd been given were very clear.

He didn't have a gun.

No amount of determination and smarts was going to win against flying bullets. Or get him close enough to the shooter to stop him without a weapon.

Afraid for him, panicked she'd never get a chance to tell

him that she wanted him in Carter's life, needing him to know that...

A minute passed. Then five.

The knob turned, and her heart leapt to her throat. Blocking air. Butterflies the size of birds attacked her from the inside as she watched the door open.

"Shelby, let's go." Luke's voice, coming from the man's shadow she could see at the entrance to the unlit room.

She did as he told her, without consideration. Keeping her gaze on him, his knees visible beneath his shorts, she unfolded herself and moved toward him.

"We have to move fast," he said, his tone different than any she'd heard before. Commanding. And confident enough to offer hope.

As soon as she was in the room, she made out two other shapes.

Bruce and Lorraine, standing tall—seemingly uninjured—both by the door.

"Firebombs were shot into the brush on all four sides of us," Luke told her, taking her hand as he turned to include the other two. "Fire department's on its way. Smoke and flames are eating up the entire area, preventing any possible sighting of the perp for now, and that's our only chance for undetected escape. We have to act before this guy realizes that the cabin isn't going to burn. There's a fire block set up around this place, including a path to the creek that we can walk. An emergency vehicle will meet us somewhere upstream, with uniforms. We'll dress in them, complete with shields over our faces, and be positioned out on a perimeter of the fire. Stretchers will be carried out from the fire, looking like they came from here, and be taken up to the house to be loaded into ambulances. All four will have bodies posed on them, with sheets up over the heads. A news crew will be there and told specifically to film the sheet-covered bodies. The home's owner will be interviewed, and he'll identify me, two women and another man as the four people staying on his property. When we can be reasonably sure that the killer will be caught up in the drama, we'll be loaded into a fire truck and driven to safety."

The bodyguards nodded. Shelby didn't question how Luke knew who was coming.

"Take this and put it over your face. Hold it there while you walk," Luke said, handing her a cold wet piece of sheet before passing one to Lorraine, saying, "Signal when you see the creek."

Taking the wet cloth, Shelby slapped it up to her face and hurried through the open door as Luke motioned her forward behind Lorraine but in front of Bruce and Luke. A wave of Arizona-summer heat hit her before the acrid scent of smoke did. In her shorts, tank top and rubber-soled sandals, she moved through the night at a near run, without stumbling, just following Lorraine and focusing on what Luke needed her to do. The path was wide—raw soil kept clear of vegetation—and she realized the perimeter of the cabin had been landscaped in exactly the same way.

Something Luke would have recognized, she knew, as snippets from the past flashed in her brain: Luke telling her about fire blocks, digging perimeters around fires to prevent their spread. Raw soil didn't burn. The memories helped distract her from the process of breathing while engulfed in heavy smoke.

"In. Out. Deep enough but no deeper than absolutely necessary," Luke's voice sounded from over her shoulder, just before she felt his body graze the right side of hers. He took her arm then, guiding her, almost as though they were in a choreographed dance—one of his legs between hers, the other on the outside of her right.

"You and the others are only being identified in the news by gender," he said, as he hurried her along yet seemed to be holding her steady, too.

In case smoke overtook her?

His next sentence came several seconds later. "Your families won't have any idea you'd even be in the area."

She nodded. Didn't dare take the second she'd need to turn for him to hear any verbal response.

"He knows where I am, which means he knows who I'm with. He hears that I'm one of the four dead, the gender IDs will make sense to him. Be enough for him."

And… Luke didn't have any family who would be devastated to hear about his death on the news.

No one who knew about him.

She couldn't see him, not really—just peripheral flashes when his head moved. He was clearly keeping watch—seeing things, she surmised, that she wouldn't catch had she been staring straight at them. Watching flame height, assessing spread speed… She didn't remember everything he'd taught her about hotshot firefighting, but she remembered a lot of it.

Mostly, she remembered being impressed by his mastery of the field. And of himself in times of crisis.

The wet cloth against her face was getting pasty, starting to itch. Her hand slipped, and she inhaled a puff of smoke. She coughed. But didn't miss a step.

"In and out." Luke leaned in closer. "Just keep it simple."

His tone, more than his words, put her in a different place. A stronger, calmer moment. Lorraine moved in front of her without a hitch. She couldn't hear Bruce behind him, his big frame silent in the soil, but she assumed he was there.

She told herself the smoke was getting thinner as they moved away from its source, but she had no idea if the wish was fact. Didn't much matter. She needed it in that second, and so she went with it. Hurried along, determined to help in any way she could.

When Lorraine slowed and raised a hand, Shelby remembered hearing Luke tell the woman to signal when she reached the creek. And seconds later, Shelby was eagerly stepping into calf-high water that she couldn't see. Didn't matter what was in it.

Leeches, even snakes, were better than death.

Rattlers didn't live in the water.

No other poisonous snakes in Arizona.

Facts presented. And calmed her.

Water flowing through sandals wasn't pleasant or easily manageable. Most particularly when sliding atop loose rock. Each step was harder than the last as she slid, both her footwear against the rocks and her feet in the sandals. But she couldn't let it slow her down. Wouldn't be cause for any of them to be caught.

Or worse.

Putting her foot down quickly, she landed on a bigger-than-normal rock, slid down it, and her big toe hit something sharp. Drawing back was instinctual. And she fell sharply against Luke's torso.

Before she could right herself, he swung her up against him, all within one step of strong, steady wading.

"You don't have to—"

"It's faster this way," he said, cutting off her words, not missing a beat as he closed the distance between them and Lorraine. She could see Bruce behind them. The bodyguard didn't seem at all concerned with Luke carrying his other charge. His head kept moving from side to side, clearly keeping watch.

As was Lorraine.

Someone had just tried to kill them. Had they not been in a cabin purposely built to withstand attack, they'd have all been dead.

Tremors started within her as fear rose up. Luke's arms tightened.

As though he knew. Could feel her fright.

She didn't want that. Didn't want him to see any weakness in her.

To think that he had more of what it takes than she did.

She heard a bit of a splash ahead, like Lorraine was stepping over something. And in the next second, she felt Luke's thigh against her hip as his leg rose.

Another splash sounded, just beneath her this time, but she was too busy focusing on the pressure of his body against her butt to care. That touch... It sent her back to the cabin, to Luke an inch or two above her on the floor, keeping her covered as they slid to the bathroom door.

So close that she'd bumped into him. More than once. Had felt the unmistakable firmness in his groin grazing her body...

He'd been hard.

Because of the danger?

It would be safer to think so.

The steady rhythm of Luke's jostling lulled her, even as she pressed her cloth, grown warm, into her face.

They'd been lying on the couch, feet touching.

Had he remembered the love game they'd played? Did it matter?

Breathing, while labored, became easier as his chest rose

and fell against her. Her body became part of his rhythm, inhaling air as he did. Slowly, steadily. Taking time to exhale.

He'd remembered her breasts.

Did it mean something that he couldn't remember a single detail of his life, but he remembered having sex with her?

It had to mean something, didn't it?

Their sex had meant more to him than anything else. Including his disgusting actions afterward...

She tensed. Felt his arms tighten again.

No.

She wasn't going to give him any reason to doubt her strength. She forced herself to think smaller. Be in the second. His chest. Rising and falling.

His chest.

Covered with hair that tickled her nipples...

Inappropriate. They could die at any second and...

Wouldn't it be better to go out with pleasure on her mind? Better to enjoy the last breaths she took?

What was the matter with her? Thinking about sex with the man who'd abandoned her rather than going out with only Carter on her mind?

A flash of her son's sweet, smiling face nearly did her in. She couldn't die. Couldn't desert him.

Oh, God, she couldn't...

Think like that. Carter was safe. Sleeping securely, well loved, in his room at her mother's house.

Her mother...

Shelby was all Sylvia had...

And she'd make it back to her. To both of them.

After all, she was in the arms of the world's most accomplished danger fighter...

Another pressure of hard thigh against her butt, a slight

bump, and the arms holding Shelby changed, loosening her from Luke's chest, lowering her.

They'd left the creek.

And just as reality—the smoke, the darkness, the hot air—smacked her in the face again, Shelby's feet touched solid ground.

Barely waiting until she had her balance, Luke strode toward a big shape in the distance.

Leaving her without a word.

Again.

Chapter Twelve

With his mind drowning in a sudden blinding onslaught of memories, Luke didn't slow down. Pushing aside the mental breakthrough, he did what he always did. The only thing he knew how to do. Put the personal stuff in a box so he could get the job done.

Instinct drove him. He let it.

And didn't stop letting it until the door closed, locking him in the captain's living quarters with Bruce, Lorraine and Shelby at a Phoenix fire station. There were two rooms. One with a couch, television, mini kitchenette and a small table. The other, a bedroom with two twin beds. The bath was small, accessible only off the bedroom.

More close quarters.

It was what it was.

Captain McDonald had worked with Luke. Had been instantly agreeable to bunking with the crew for however long it took…

"Friday is shopping day," he announced to the room in general, avoiding all eye contact, as he'd been doing since setting up the fire rescue for the four of them. "Essentials and clothing changes will be brought in for us with the groceries."

The idea was for the four of them to remain hidden—no

sign of coming or going, no sign of anything out of the ordinary—until the police found the would-be killer/arsonist who had it in for Luke. The guy wanted Luke dead for a reason.

"I appreciate you all going along with me here," he said, again to the air around him. Yeah, he was paying Sierra's Web. Didn't mean Bruce or Lorraine had to stay on the job.

And Shelby...

He couldn't go there. Not even a little bit.

Or venture beyond her to the little guy...

Not yet.

"Hopefully, he'll think he's succeeded and show his hand." Most likely by accessing Luke's money. Or his seventy-thousand-dollar truck. With the cabin in Payson burned, there were no other assets.

Something else he wasn't focusing on.

"In the meantime, as long as we're dead, we're safe." That was the thought, anyway.

As soon as he'd opened the door of the cabin to discover the fire burning and heard that the four shots had been fire-bombs, he'd taken control of Bruce's radio. Talking with Hudson from Sierra's Web, he had come up with the plan. On the spot.

It's what he did: assess and command.

The fire department had already been on the way. Luke's earlier assessment of the fire barriers around the cabin had filled in the blanks. The rest had been a no-brainer for him.

Who'd suspect firefighters at a fire?

Or follow the engines as they came and went?

Ambulances were what you'd watch for.

And his plan had delivered.

Four stretchers with dead bodies. Loaded into four buses.

They just had to stay dead long enough for the guy to show himself.

And that's where his wind tapered to less than a breeze.

Leaving the other three in the living area, Luke strode into the bedroom as though he had a plan. Something to do.

Standing in the small room, looking at McDonald's digital clock plugged into the wall, he fought to maintain homeostasis. Taking action was the only way he knew to do that.

Even a need to pee would be better than just…stagnating.

But the bodily function wasn't going to keep his brain at bay. Already, memories were swamping him. Peeing outside in the woods…

Hiking—the tougher the climb, the better—was how he coped.

His mother's funeral. And his father's.

The fiend had killed his father!

Shelby…

He'd just bought new living room furniture for the cabin.

Randy's wedding next month… He was his second-in-command's best man. And knew the man who was more brother to him than anything wouldn't give a rat's ass about Luke letting him down on his big day. He'd just need to know that Luke was okay.

He couldn't let Hudson get in touch with him. If anyone knew he was alive, acted in any way counterproductive to his death, the whole plan could be blown.

And Shelby would once again be in danger.

If there hadn't been a perimeter around that damned cabin, they'd all be dead. Another fire attempt.

A good one.

Made him think the guy after him knew fires. And had reason to want him to die in one.

Which gave him a plan. Silently apologizing to Captain McDonald for the intrusion, he pulled open drawers until he found paper and a pencil, and then, starting at the beginning of his career—his first training course—he started a list of anyone he'd encountered whom he might have pissed off.

And kept his mind off the woman he'd walked out on to go fight a fire. The woman he'd planned to see again. The first woman who'd ever given him the sense that, with her, he could have more than a career.

The woman who'd lied to him about coming to tell him about their son.

DROPPING TO THE couch while the bodyguards, leaning on the counters on either side of the small kitchenette, conversed quietly, Shelby flipped on the television.

More as a distraction for them—a sound barrier to give them privacy for whatever it was they had to discuss—than because she had any hope of actually being able to pay attention to some show that she didn't give two hoots about.

In the ride back to Phoenix in the fire truck, she'd been able to speak to Hudson on a private radio channel to record a message to Carter.

And was more grateful than ever that Luke had already arranged to have a Sierra's Web bodyguard stay with her mother and son until they apprehended whoever was trying to kill her and Luke. Her mother was now being told that the danger was over, that the guard was a formality required due to the story she was covering.

Hudson had told her. Not Luke.

The man who'd fathered her child, who'd crawled—with a hard-on—to the bathroom with her, who'd carried her in the stream, hadn't looked directly at her since he'd put her down on dry land.

Or spoken to her, personally, either.

He'd walked away.

And come back a changed man.

Albeit one who was still providing for the safety of her son and mother.

His son. And his son's caregiver.

The past was repeating itself with one huge difference.

Luke Dennison was no longer denying his son's existence. He was ensuring the boy's safety.

Because he'd ordered the DNA test and now believed that she'd told the truth?

His questions the night before, wanting to know every little thing about Carter—they'd been so sincere. So heart-rending.

She'd babbled like a lovesick kid.

Maybe she'd gotten through to him.

As far as Carter was concerned.

And where Luke was involved, Carter was her only concern.

But...

The change in him...

From a man swearing he'd do anything to take accountability for what he'd done to her...to the stranger who'd set her on the ground outside the creek...

And it hit her... He'd been hard after their feet had touched... She wondered if he'd had another memory of them. Like his breast one.

But what if...it made sense that the traumatic events of the night before had triggered his brain?

He'd remembered.

And he wasn't...

Jumping up off the sofa, she left the television running,

no idea what show was even on, and stormed into the bedroom, uncaring that the door had been closed.

Uncaring if the man happened to be just out of the shower, butt naked. He was not going to...

Luke sat on the floor, still in the tan shorts he'd had on two days before, writing in a wire-bound notebook.

Where he'd gotten it, she didn't know. But the man managed to make fire trucks with extra uniforms appear at will, so why not paper? And a pen, too, just because he could.

"You remembered," she proposed when, after a brief glance at the door, he returned to what he was doing.

How dare he think he was going to ignore her?

Everything she'd been through for him in the past couple of days—being in danger because of him, doing the right thing and telling him about his son, the promise he'd made to atone for the past...

And he was just going to sit there?

She'd exposed Carter to him!

And Luke was providing protection for him. Even after the danger was most likely gone and no one knew that Carter was his son.

Although...some Sierra's Web team members were privy to the test being conducted.

There hadn't been time yet to get results. Even Sierra's Web wasn't that good.

As her thoughts flew, she stood there, boring holes into him with her gaze. Not that he felt them. Clearly.

The man's pen hadn't faltered even for a second.

If he thought he was going to freeze her out, get her to turn around and leave him to his privacy, he'd underestimated her. She had all day, maybe even two, with nothing better to do but stand her ground.

Or lean into it, she decided, when five minutes had passed

and the hotshot firefighter still hadn't said a word. Shoulder to the wall, she faced him.

"You were great last night." Apparently, her silence was too easy on him. She kept it nice, though. "Or rather, pre-dawn this morning." They'd had a few hours' sleep on the couch prior to being forced to vacate.

The pen might have paused, briefly. She was pretty sure it did. Otherwise, her words garnered no response.

Which was just plain making her mad.

Had the man forgotten she was a reporter? Someone trained and with a real talent for getting information out of people?

Was he going to sit there and insult her further?

"Am I to assume that your desire to make up for the past vanished when you remembered what you did?"

He'd apparently thought paying her off served his purpose. She'd figured, as smart as he was, that once he'd remembered, he'd found his choice to be a good one.

And...maybe he hadn't remembered.

Could be that leaving and coming back a changed man was just who he was. Memory or not.

But he wasn't turning his back on his son.

That mattered.

And frustrated the hell out of her, too, as she had no way of knowing if, once he spent time with Carter—once Carter grew to love him, to need him—he'd turn his back on the boy.

She'd made the choice to sleep with the man. Had paid the price.

Carter didn't deserve to pay, too. That wasn't how it was supposed to work. The kid paying for the parents' choices. Her mother's decisions had shown her that firsthand.

Eventually, Shelby slid down the wall to sit on the floor. Eye level with him. Facing him across the small space.

She could stay there all night. She had no place else to be. Except in one of the two beds mere feet away from them, and that wasn't a choice she intended to make.

The bodyguards were going to take turns with watch and using the couch.

Of course, they hadn't even had lunch yet. There was dinner to get through after that, before it would be time for sleeping.

"Setting up a breakfast station for the entire crew was a nice touch," she said, remembering the semi-hot meal they'd had in the truck on the way back to Phoenix.

The pen didn't slow at all that time.

"Has anyone ever told you you're rude?"

"Many times."

Startled, she jerked when she heard his response. Stared at him. Waiting...

And got nothing but more silence.

So...if she criticized him, he'd respond? Because he didn't care what she or anyone else thought of him?

Leaning her head back against the wall, she thought back to the interviews she'd done with him five years before. Drawing not so much on the information he'd given her but on the impressions she'd had.

Remembering for the sake of gaining real, honest insight into him, not to analyze or conclude. Not to hurt or hate.

But with a true need to reach the man. Whoever he was.

Because whatever he turned out to be, he was still her son's father.

He'd been hesitant about the interview at first, until he found out that she'd chosen him as a source to shed light on the dangerous and mostly underpaid teams of hotshots who risked their lives every day they went to work. Members of a crew had been lost in a fire, and not only had Luke prevented a much bigger loss but he'd also been trying to raise money for the families left behind.

Which showed compassion, caring, justice, brotherhood.

He'd been honest in his assessments, hadn't tried to sell her on anything or convince her that his beliefs were right. He'd only told his story from his point of view. As he saw it.

And he'd seen so much. Could look at people and see deeper than the surface.

"Last night…you knew what to do. It's because you see what others don't see…" Like she did.

That's what had drawn them into a personal sphere. The pain that came from seeing and sometimes being unable to help.

Like her mother. Try as she might, she'd never been able to get through to Sylvia.

And subjects whose stories she only got to tell after the fact—it had been too late for them. And their stories would never have been told if she hadn't gone with her instincts and dug deeper.

"I'm not looking for you to be someone you aren't, Luke," she said then, softly, though she could still hear the drone of the television on the other side of the wall. "All I want is honesty."

She needed to know why. Not to judge. Or condemn. Nothing was going to change the past. Or undo the mistakes either of them had made. She wanted to move on. To make the right choices for her son's future.

She'd been playing with a string on her shorts, but at his continued silence, she glanced up at him, wishing she could take off her stream-ruined sandal and throw it at him.

His pen wasn't moving.

He was staring right at her.

"Honestly," he said, "this isn't the time to do this."

Seriously? That's what he was giving her? What he thought she deserved?

There'd be a better time when they were free from captivity, off living their own lives? With him wanting to see his son?

If he even still did.

The right time was right then. Where they could talk it all out, figure out where they went from this point.

When they had nothing and no one else pulling at them, nothing else they even *could* do.

"When is the time, Luke? What's more important than figuring out where we go from here?" He'd said he was going to be in his son's life. That her DNA test would give him legal rights.

"More important is trying to figure out who's out to kill us."

Oh. She glanced at his pad. The entire page was filled with notes.

"You've got your memory back," she said again.

He didn't look away. Just slowly nodded, then held up his pad. "I'm making lists, with notes."

Potential stalkers or attempted killers. Because he could remember who might have a grudge against him.

He'd been sitting there, living through every bad moment he'd just remembered, cataloguing them, in order to help set her—and himself—free.

Without another word, she stood and slipped silently out of the room.

Wishing there was some way she could help him.

Chapter Thirteen

The room went stale the second the door closed behind Shelby. Luke noticed, pushed the sensation away and went back to work. He finished his list. Took it out to Bruce, who used interstation-landline paging to signal Captain McDonald to his quarters. None of the crew on shift knew the four of them were in the station. The firefighters had been told there was a clogged air-conditioning duct that had pushed McDonald down with them.

Shelby was in the small kitchenette, cleaning—walls, countertops, cupboards. In her same black shorts, she had to feel as desperate for a shower as he did, especially after being in the creek, but she didn't complain.

She cleaned.

He got it.

Keeping busy. Making something good out of tension-fueled adrenaline.

He didn't want to be aware of her. Couldn't not notice her. That long, wavy blond hair; the deep brown eyes that spoke without words; the curves in all the right places—they were captivating. But not nearly as much as the energy she exuded.

She'd lied to him.

And he couldn't walk away. She was the mother of his child.

Fully remembering their time together, he didn't doubt that they could have made a baby. He'd used condoms but had gone more than once without pulling out. Spillage was believable.

The lovemaking was what had been unbelievable.

"I'd like a word with you." He leaned over the counter to deliver his edict while Bruce was at the door of the quarters, conversing softly with McDonald. Lorraine was asleep on the couch, obviously used to catching sleep when and wherever she could.

Shelby held up a soapy rag. "I'm kind of in the middle of something."

He wasn't used to being argued with.

"Please."

Luke had no idea if his plea fell on deaf ears—if Shelby still had any desire to speak to him. She'd realized he'd regained his memory, that he knew she'd lied to him about coming to tell him about the baby, about his shutting the door in her face.

As soon as she'd figured it out, she'd come to him to talk it out and—being his usual blunt, focused self—he'd shunned her.

He'd been right to get the list made first; catching whoever was after him was paramount.

He could have been kinder in his delivery. Shelby wasn't someone who worked for him, part of his crew who knew him and understood the way he got right to the point to save lives. Including, on more than one occasion, their own.

And...her being able to deal with him mattered.

She finished wiping the shelves she'd been leaning on. Loaded goods stacked neatly in three piles on the counter back onto them. Rinsed the rag in the sink. Washed her hands.

And without even looking his way, walked back into the bedroom the two of them would be sharing. While still affording each other complete privacy.

A tall order, to be sure, but he didn't doubt either of their abilities to manage that one.

His confidence on the matter faltered as he walked into the room, saw how small it was with her standing there between the two beds, arms crossed and somehow looking... professional in spite of the two-day lack of grooming.

Or maybe the stance was pure defense. "You lied to me."

Dropping her arms, she pushed past him. Headed for the door.

His bluntness really paid off on that one.

"Shelby, wait," he said as she reached for the knob he'd just secured behind him in the latch. "I don't blame you." The words stuck in his throat. He'd lost the first four years of his son's life.

"Well..." He shrugged, facing her as she stood with her fist wrapped around the door handle. "I do, but... I understand, too."

Her stony expression remained right there, glaring at him. Not even a hint of softening.

Or caring.

But she was still there.

"I walked out on you after sex without a word," he allowed. "You grew up with a philandering father. Your mother constantly tried to force you to choose sides." He shrugged again. "I get it."

Who'd want to risk doing the same to their own kid?

Those soft, so-incredibly-kissable lips remained two thin

lines. And her eyes—they were more like sharp points rather than the resting pools he'd found them to be in the past.

"You thought you were protecting your son."

His son. God have mercy, he had a son.

The idea just kept hitting him over the head. Seemingly brand new each time he thought about it.

Him being a father just wasn't taking shape. He had to see the boy, to listen to him, in order to believe having a son was real.

He had to make things right with the boy's mother first.

Even if he had some beef with how it had all gone down.

A full minute passed without words. Shelby was still there, more combative looking than not.

Unnerving him some, truth be told. He'd said his bit. Either she was going to meet him halfway or not.

Make peace or leave the room.

"That's it?" Her tone, much softer than he'd expected, fell into the silence. The words seemed to be laced with disappointment, not battle.

Maybe his good judgment wasn't in full force yet, still stifled by the blow to his head.

What more did she want?

All he had for her was another shrug.

"You sure you want to do this?" she asked next, still holding the doorknob.

"Yes." No doubt there. It was the first step toward his son.

And…toward maybe finding a place where he could talk to her again. As he had five years ago. Where they could be…friends. Or something.

"And you honestly think all you did was walk out after sex without saying a word?"

If possible, the slits in her eyes had narrowed further.

"Yes." He'd regained his memory; they'd established that.

He was willing to get beyond her having lied to him about visiting him in Payson to tell him she was pregnant. Didn't that earn him some slack in the disappearing-without-a-word fiasco?

It wasn't like he'd just sauntered out to breakfast and then meandered through an easy day. He'd been called to a fire. And had suffered a minor injury on the job, too, resulting in brief memory loss. All of which she currently knew.

"So the money…" She shook her head. Her entire expression filled with disgust. Except that brief flash of hurt in her eyes before they sharpened right up again.

Money? "Did I leave you with a room service bill?" They'd had champagne. Chocolate. Filet mignon. He thought he'd charged it to his room, but maybe it had gone on hers since that was where they'd been…

"You left me with a thousand dollars…"

"I did not." Absolutely not.

Her expression flattened. It was as though all fight had gone out of her. But none of the warmth he'd found in her returned.

And he had to wonder…had she confused him with some other man?

Did that mean the boy wasn't his after all?

"You signed the thank-you card, Luke."

"What thank-you card?"

"The one that was sent up with the breakfast charged to your room."

The unmistakable accusation in her tone slowed him up. Concerned him.

Had he sent breakfast? He didn't remember much after getting the call to report to Marnell. Lives had been at stake. He'd already been mentally assessing…

But…there'd been a huge flash of regret that he'd left

Shelby to wake up alone in bed. Sending up breakfast sounded like something he'd have wanted to do, if he'd had the wherewithal to think of it.

But a card?

And a thousand bucks?

Shaken, he stared at her, needing to read her mind. Wishing she could see that the scene she described wasn't in his.

What possible reason could she have for lying to him?

If the boy wasn't his, she'd never have offered him access to her son's DNA. And he'd already let her off the hook over not having told him she was pregnant.

Money wouldn't have been an issue.

Well, not exactly accurate. Money was *part* of the issue.

The fact that he'd given it to her, not that she'd wanted to get it from him.

But even if she'd been after money, even if he'd done what she'd said—denied that the child was his—all she'd have had to do was sue him for child support.

And...another thought came tumbling on the top of the rest, a memory from the past couple of days, sitting there with his past. And not fitting.

When she'd told him that he'd denied that the baby was his, she hadn't yet known about the memory loss he'd suffered in Marnell. She'd have been working under the assumption that when his memory returned, he would know she was lying.

Unless...were there still pieces missing? Had he never completely recovered memories after the Marnell injury? His doctor had said there could be blanks from the current injury. Ones that might never be filled.

How could he possibly trust himself if he didn't know what he knew was all there was?

While his thoughts stumbled along—tripping over each

other, leaving him feeling weaker than he could ever remember feeling—Shelby just stood there.

Giving him time? Refusing to leave until he'd given her... some kind of closure? An apology?

And explanation.

He knew what she needed.

"I remember our night together," he told her, voice low because it was all he had in his current situation with her. "I remember the week of interviews. I remember feeling a connection to you like none other... Even considering for the first time in my life that there might be someone with whom I could partner and make a family..."

Nope. Wrong thing. She pursed her lips. Closed her eyes. And when those expressive brown orbs reopened, they were blank.

"I remember waking in your room to my phone beeping on your nightstand." He felt more like himself as he got back to his normal way of sticking to facts. "I didn't want to wake you. Left the room. Found out about the fire. And never went back."

And after the fire...had he not remembered their time together even after his memory returned the first time? He'd gotten the memories back. But how did he know if they'd just arrived back the night before with the rest of his past?

Could they have been missing during the entirety of the ensuing nearly five years?

"I don't remember breakfast, Shelby." He wasn't a liar. "It sounds like something I'd have liked to have done, but truthfully, being on a run to a fire, I'm finding it highly unlikely that I'd have done it. Except...you were so different..." He shrugged yet again. Then said, "But a card? Money?" He had nothing. Fell short of offering her...anything. Just shook his head.

Then, as she continued to stare at him, her silence like a nail in his coffin, he said, "It's just not something I'd do."

How did you convince someone that you didn't do something when you couldn't remember what you had done?

He knew he didn't.

"You slammed the door in my face when I drove up to Payson to tell you about the baby."

He just wouldn't have.

Ever.

"I have no memory of it."

A sense of acceptance seemed to come over her. Not in a joyful way.

"I can still remember the sound of the dead bolt as you slid it in place," she said. "It slid, seemed to catch. And then, as if to shoo me off, it squeaked as it fully locked."

No.

But, God, yes.

He remembered the catch, had chiseled at it—which caused the squeak—but didn't fix the original problem. He'd replaced the whole thing...

Everything inside him stilled. Hardened.

She'd been to his home.

A hard ball of nausea sat in his gut. Sick of not remembering, not knowing his own thought process, he felt equally undone at the thought of remembering that man. Of being him.

"I have no memory of ever paying anyone off for anything. Or of ever shirking my responsibilities or deliberately being an ass to anyone just to suit myself." He had nothing else to give her.

"What about the girls in the threesome?"

He'd forgotten that detail. Tried to bring up any pictures to go with what he'd been told.

Nothing.

Was it possible that he'd just chosen to lose that part of himself? Could the brain arbitrarily do that to a guy?

"So maybe your memory hasn't returned as completely as you thought."

Maybe.

He'd remembered himself pretty thoroughly.

It felt done.

As proven by the list he'd just turned over.

And none of it changed a very key fact. "I want to know my son."

He wanted to have the boy's mother in his life, too, as more than just a baby mama. But reaching for the stars was beyond him at the moment.

I WANT TO know my son.

Standing with her back to the bedroom door, Shelby faced Luke and let go of her death grip on the handle of her escape to freedom.

She was never going to be free of the man.

Carter made that feat an impossibility.

"He needs to know you, too," she said, practically choking the words out. Knowing, even as much as she hated letting them fly, that they were the right ones.

Regardless of why he'd refused to take accountability for what he'd done to her, whether he really didn't remember or just didn't want to own what he'd done, what mattered was whether he could fill the gaping void in Carter's life before her son started having issues she couldn't fix with a hug, a tickle or a bedtime story.

Her father had lied to her. So smoothly she'd believed him for a long time. But only about the affairs, the women who meant nothing to him.

Because he'd wanted them to mean nothing to her and Sylvia, too.

And he'd lied when he put sex with the current flavor over getting to a birthday party or dance recital on time. Or at all.

But he'd always shown up. With birthday presents, recital flowers, praise and support...whatever she'd needed. Just in his own time.

His love had given her confidence in herself.

His existence had given her identity...

Luke dropped to the edge of the bed. Sat there staring up at her, eyes wide, brow raised high. She could almost hear the questions racing through him. Felt as though some of the fear she was experiencing belonged to him, too.

But the elation she also read in his expression...took her breath away.

"There will be strict guidelines," she blurted out, panicking at the sudden impulse she had to hug him.

To hold on as they twirled together in a circle-dance of excitement. Or just stand together, body to body, absorbing life's goodness.

"I agree to them."

Nodding, she swallowed. Then said, "You haven't heard them yet."

"Doesn't matter. I agree."

For a second, she was transported back to the afternoon before they'd spent the night in bed together. Luke had been talking about disclaimers he had to sign for a side job he'd taken during the off-season. He'd agreed to help rescue all of the people from a small endangered community who were trapped in a valley built beneath a mountain ledge that had been compromised. And if anything happened to him, he'd be on his own. If the job went over budget, he was on his own.

It wasn't that he'd refused to consider the possible cost to himself. He'd been fully aware of his own potential inconvenience, discomfort or loss. He'd simply been willing to deal with them if he was called upon to do so. The job had meant that much to him.

Did that mean being in Carter's life meant that much to him as well?

Meeting his gaze, she had her answer as silently as she'd had her understanding. He'd do what it took.

At least until she pushed him too far, and then he could always get a lawyer and sue for shared custody. The thought came with a dose of reality.

But even then, she couldn't...

A sharp knock on the door right behind her interrupted all thought. Swinging around, she was barely out of the way before the wood swung open.

"Did either of you order pizza?" Bruce's question, though seemingly bland, was issued in a harsh, urgent tone.

"Of course not," she said, her voice colliding with Luke's "No."

"We need to get you out of here," Bruce said, motioning them forward and then pushing behind them.

Lorraine waited by the outer door, holding two sets of fire gear, one over each arm, with a pair of boots on either side of her and head gear on the TV table to her right.

Shelby had no time to think. One quick look at Luke, his nod, was all it took for her to step back into the gear she'd recently vacated, listening as the fire sirens went off.

Figuring they were going out as they'd come in, as firefighters, she was surprised to reach the truck garage a quick staircase later and find an entire wall of uniformed men and women—dressed exactly like she, Luke, Bruce and Lorraine were—all lined up.

An engine roared out of the station, followed by an ambulance.

Three minutes later, another engine left, minus the sirens, with some of the firefighters inside. She and Luke and their bodyguards were crammed together in the back of the fifth ambulance to pull out of the station. And from what she'd seen, there'd be a sixth following right behind them out into the street.

All going in different directions.

All outfitted with cameras that would record anyone who was following them.

Because of a random pizza delivery to the fire station.

She caught the gist of what was happening through observation and a few hurried comments along the way. Luke's plan hadn't worked, was the assumption.

Not long-term.

He'd gotten them to safety.

But their killer knew he was alive.

And had already found him.

She understood what was going on and why.

What she didn't get was the way her hand found its way under Luke's bulkily outfitted thigh as she sat next to him on a gurney.

Or the way her panic calmed when she felt his fingers slide beneath hers.

They were two ships caught in a debilitating storm, she told herself. Banding together to fight the disaster attacking them.

They were an error in judgment she'd made years before. A soulmate mirage she'd created in her own mind.

They were the mother and father of the same child.

They were not a couple.

And they never would be.

Chapter Fourteen

How in the hell had the killer found them?

If he'd found them.

Pizza-delivery mistakes happened.

He had to hope that was all they were dealing with.

But he wasn't taking any chances. Not with Shelby.

Luke owed her. She'd had his son alone. Raised him for four years.

Made sense that he couldn't stop feeling her.

Resolution reached, he allowed himself to stay connected with her as much as possible as they drove from one fire station to another, loaded into different vehicles and drove around the city. When Sierra's Web deemed it safe, they had quick showers at the last station, dressed in clothes that had been delivered to them as they'd been leaving the first one, and were driven in a firefighter's personal truck to a fancy hotel, where they climbed into the back of a swanky limousine.

They'd look conspicuous arriving at their destination—a six-thousand-square-foot home built into the bottom of a mountain on the beach of a popular lake dividing the Arizona and California borders—in anything less.

He'd been thoroughly briefed while Shelby had been

in the shower. Had been given choices and made on-the-spot decisions.

The activities were overkill. So many people, so much effort to keep one man and woman alive. But he had the money to pay for it all. And nothing else he cared to spend it on.

More than ever, he was driven only to keep Shelby and himself alive to get them back to their son. Thoughts of meeting that small boy were more compelling than any he'd had while putting out flames. All assessment and planning went to that end.

The fire vehicle game of tag had come from him—as an escape route, if necessary—prior to occupying McDonald's quarters.

The rest—the limo, the house on the beach—were all Sierra's Web's doing. The firm had former clients in high places who were only too happy to help out.

While Bruce kept watch, moving from one side of the long car to the other in various seats, Lorraine drove the nearly two hundred miles across the desert.

And Luke, in his clean black shorts and gray short-sleeved shirt, sat beside Shelby on the couch along the back of the vehicle. They'd each had three outfits from which to choose. She'd put on denim shorts and a white sleeveless blouse.

An outfit making it harder for him to not notice her as a woman. The shorts were no shorter than the ones she'd been wearing the past couple of days.

But his newly recalled memories filled in all the blanks.

Not that she seemed to notice.

Other than nodding where appropriate and thanking those helping them, Shelby had been quiet. He'd heard that she'd made another recorded call to Carter while he was in the shower.

"I apologize that I'm taking you farther from Carter," he said when Bruce answered a call from Hudson on his new burner phone.

"I travel all over for work. Distance isn't the issue. The time away is."

A sentiment he'd heard from various hotshot team members when they'd put in notice to take local jobs. One he fully understood for the first time. Although his brain had comprehended them before, his heart just now felt the emotion that had driven those choices.

He had nothing to say to that.

Bruce, hanging up the phone right then, turned toward Luke. Seeing the grim expression on the man's face, Luke braced himself.

"Sierra's Web, with the help of law enforcement, traced the pizza delivery to an online order from an internet café, one with no camera coverage…"

Of course. Tracing the order placer wasn't going to be easy. They'd probably need a warrant for payment information.

Which meant more time before they'd know for sure if the latest threat had just been a mistake…

"The order was paid for with a card connected to a Cayman Islands account."

As soon as he heard those last words, he tensed. Felt like Bruce and Shelby were staring straight at him.

"I wasn't at an internet café," Luke blurted out. So unlike him. To blurt. And to jump to his own defense.

He protected himself slowly. Methodically.

And why in hell would he order pizza and then lie about doing so?

"Of course not." Bruce nodded, holding Luke's gaze for a telling second.

The payment method made the chances of the delivery address being a mistake a bit less likely. Which meant Luke's overall plan had failed.

His killer knew he was still alive.

Luke didn't look at Shelby. He felt her move. Not away. Or closer. Just…move.

"That's proof that someone else is accessing the account, right?" she asked, still obviously on the Cayman thing. The anticipation in her voice… That's what he heard most.

"They don't know that it's Luke's account, just that the account originates there."

"But it's a pretty big coincidence, don't you think?" she asked.

And Luke wanted to preen like a little kid with a double-decker ice-cream cone. Dipped in chocolate. Shelby was coming to his defense.

Even if it was just a desperate attempt to convince herself that her son's father, the man who'd soon be meeting the boy, was not a complete creep—he liked hearing it.

For a second, until he remembered that they were likely still being hunted like animals.

"It's not my place to say." Bruce's response was job appropriate, until the man added, "But I agree—there's a whole lot going on here that's not fitting right."

With what sounded like a second man on board his sinking boat, Luke needed a beer. "Are we getting a daily report sometime soon?"

"Later today. They're waiting on the pizza toxicology report. And Hudson said that the warrant for Gerard Michaels's financials came through. Winchester's on standby to go through them himself as soon as they arrive." Bruce named the financial expert.

So-so news, now that he had some of his memory back. Michaels was a good guy. Luke had trusted him implicitly.

As he would have if they'd been in cahoots together? Had Michaels helped him live a double life? Did the man know the side of Luke he couldn't seem to remember?

Or had Michaels been playing him for a fool? The man knew every time Luke was out of contact. Could the financial manager have orchestrated his own exploits on Luke's dime, making it appear as though Luke had done it all?

Paying off Shelby... She'd said she got cash in a card sent up at breakfast.

Anyone could have ordered that breakfast, signed his name to the card. But Michaels had Luke's electronic signature on file...

Didn't explain Luke slamming the door in her face when she'd visited him in Payson...

He didn't slam doors.

But that dead bolt—she'd described it spot-on.

Maybe he'd misunderstood who she was. If he hadn't remembered her...he could have assumed she was someone else. His phone could have rung, signaling an emergency, and he'd shut the door hard out of urgency, not rudeness...

"It could have just been a mistake." He hadn't meant to say the words aloud. Not when he couldn't have the private conversation with Shelby they warranted.

"The pizza delivery?" she asked. "You think there's still a chance that someone just put in the wrong address? Or maybe a grateful homeowner was sending it to the station as a thank-you for helping remove a snake from the yard or something..."

Some local Phoenix-area fire departments went on rattler duty if they were available; he'd been on one such run himself.

"But who pays for pizza with a Cayman Islands account?"

Shelby continued, and Luke knew she was reaching the same conclusion he had.

No one bothered to answer that one. They rode silently across acrid desert. But the tips of Shelby's fingers found the underneath of this thigh again.

No pressure.

Just…there.

Luke didn't move. Didn't reciprocate. But he wanted to hug her.

Just that. Hug her tight.

For as long as she'd let him hang on.

SHELBY HADN'T KNOWN until they were pulling into the circular drive of the lovely stucco home that she and Luke weren't going to be staying anywhere in the plethora of rooms.

He'd apparently known, though, based on his steady, sure movements.

Their destination was an underground shelter just to the left of the back door, a few feet along the tree line that bordered the beach.

They went through the house to get there—in case anyone had drone eyes on them somehow, she surmised by the way Bruce even had them under a big umbrella as they moved quickly from the car to the door. She caught a brief glimpse of the lake—gorgeous blue. Peaceful along that stretch of private beach. Felt the sun's warmth.

And the next thing she knew, she was climbing down a ladder just behind Bruce, with Luke following her.

Funny how the hotshot firefighter made her feel safer than a trained and proven bodyguard did. But there it was.

When it came to men…she was off-key.

A fact that hit her square in the face the second Bruce

climbed back upstairs to relieve Lorraine of guard duty so she could rest from the drive and be prepared for a long night.

With both of their personal Sierra's Web experts gone, there was just her and Luke. Alone.

In a fully decorated—rather elegant—dungeon. It was all one long, skinny room. She figured a partition down at the far end marked off a toilet area but didn't ask.

And there was a sink set in a countertop at that end. She'd seen, coming in, that there were two other partitions with beds behind them. The rest was a living area, complete with bar, mounted flat-screen and some electronics.

"There's a generator in that cupboard," Luke told her, pointing toward where she'd been looking. "We won't have any reception down here—which is the point—but I'm told there's an ample selection of DVDs and a player. The refrigerator, also on generator, is kept fully stocked. And the toilet has a pump that runs along plumbing in the ground and empties into a cesspit."

So there she had it. The basics.

She was going to be sharing very intimate quarters with the only man she'd never been able to forget. The man who'd turned her on like no other.

And had hurt her like no other, too.

A man who was going to be in her life, part of her son's family, for the rest of her days.

And one with whom she'd wanted to lose herself in lovemaking in the early hours of that very morning, when the touch of his foot against hers had woken her from dreams of him.

The same guy who still claimed he hadn't paid her off and shut his door in her face.

It was all so messed up.

They'd had lunch on the way to the lake. A casserole had been prepared and left in the refrigerator for dinner.

If they were still there the next day, they'd be on their own.

Other than an electronic device that would be dropped in a little cage in the ceiling for message-passing, there'd be no more contact with the outside world until someone could prove that the pizza delivery had been a simple mistake.

That their cover of Luke's death hadn't been blown.

"All we need is the tox screen to come back clean," she said to the room at large, standing there with her hands clasping each other. Trying to keep a lid on the myriad of emotions roiling inside her. She wasn't claustrophobic... but she'd never been trapped underground before, either.

"And for the account to check out," Luke added. He was hunched down in front of a door he'd opened on the entertainment center that took up one whole wall. "If it's my account that paid for that pizza—and it was sent to the quarters in which we were staying—even if it's not poisoned, the warning is still clear. He knows I'm alive and where we were staying."

She'd already figured that out, of course. Just hadn't wanted to think about it. Keeping panic at bay was key to a clear head.

Which was paramount to preventing her from contemplating the one thing she could think of that would momentarily wipe everything else from her mind. Every worry. Every fear. Every doubt. Gone.

For however many minutes the man would do to her body the things he'd done five years before.

"H-how could he have found us?" she blurted out. A question she didn't want answers to. Not while she was busy trying to maintain total control.

"Johnson. Maybe in league with Michaels at this point. Sierra's Web. The dozen or so firefighters involved in our escape from the fire this morning."

Not just the ones who'd given up their truck but the ones who'd posed as cadavers under sheets on stretchers. The ones who'd stood beside them in the line for the brief time they appeared to be working...

There was so much... Too much...

Fear engulfed her for a second, and she wanted nothing more than to walk over to Luke and beg him to hold her. Just until she got her grip back.

"National Lampoon's Christmas Vacation," Luke said, pulling out the case. "You want to watch it?"

"It's a Christmas movie." In the heat of summer.

The heat of him.

"It's a comedy," he pointed out, but he hadn't moved from in front of the collection or taken the disc out of the case.

She could demur.

She thought of a few scenes from the classic film and nodded. The movie was entertaining no matter how many times you watched it. It was filled with slapstick. Family ridiculousness.

And most importantly, there wasn't one sexy, tender moment in the entire reel.

Chapter Fifteen

He sat on one end of the plush sectional sofa set after Shelby took the other. Far enough away that he could hardly see her in his peripheral vision. Couldn't feel the cushion move when she laughed out loud.

Not so far that he lost the feel of her. Even for a second.

Nor did he stop thinking about the news they were awaiting. The movie was only a third over when a clink sounded up in the ceiling.

Shelby's laugh cut off mid-guffaw. He stopped the movie as he stood, dropped the remote behind him on the sofa and raced to the ladder, taking the rungs two at a time.

The device was a phone with no SIM card. There were recorded videos to watch from Hudson and Winchester.

And one from Carter and then Sylvia, too. Luke had scrolled down the list by the time he reached the couch, reading aloud.

"Can we please save that one for last?" Shelby asked as he sat down. Busy casting the videos from the device to the television, he was ready to argue with her.

Was she kidding?

He was finally going to get to see and hear his son.

But she was right. They had much more urgent business than his emotional needs.

He could hardly believe *he'd* needed the reminder—the blunt guy whose job was giving out orders to handle life-threatening emergencies. That he hadn't been immediately keyed into the facts he had to assess to save his own life. Or Shelby's.

Sitting a full cushion's length away from her as the phone's contents came up on the flat-screen taking up the wall, he adjusted the volume up, and—leaning forward, arms resting on top of his knees—focused completely.

Winchester Holmes, the finance partner, was first. He'd found nothing unusual on a preliminary check through Gerard Michaels's financials, but he hadn't yet looked at tax reporting. He was going to spend the evening doing a much deeper dive to look for hidden accounts or expenditures that didn't fit. For instance, a car-maintenance bill on a vehicle for which there was no purchase record.

"Because he could have paid cash for an expensive car?" Shelby asked. "Spending money with no trail to its origin?"

Luke nodded. He'd assumed the same.

Winchester's last note was that the Cayman Islands account used to pay for the pizza was tied to the one owned by Luke. Either he had more than one account or someone was draining his account into another.

Most likely Gerard?

Either way, whoever was after him knew he was still alive. That was the reason for the pizza delivery. To let him know his plan hadn't worked.

He wasn't surprised. He'd seen it coming since their forced evacuation earlier that day.

And sitting with a frustration that was becoming way too familiar, he clicked to the next video.

Hudson. The video was brief.

Toxicology had come back on the pizza. No poison.

Not in the food.

But it had definitely been there in the message that pizza had delivered.

His killer not only knew he was alive—he'd found him in a matter of hours. Maybe he hadn't found a way to murder Luke at the fire station, but unless Luke intended to stay hidden forever, the man was going to get him eventually.

When he could have just laid low until everyone thought Luke was dead long enough to come back to life.

Whoever was after him didn't just want him dead. He wanted him to suffer. It was like with every failed murder attempt, the guy was finding some kind of fuel, more cruelty.

Making Luke doubt everything he knew about himself.

"Obviously, the guy isn't going to be accessing any of your assets, so that part of the plan is probably done," Hudson continued. "Johnson and his team are looking into every one of the firefighters, and both teams—Johnson's and ours—are scouring the list you gave us. I've got one investigator, Stan Busby—a man I trust with my family's lives—looking into the entire Sierra's Web team and into Johnson's team as well." Hudson paused, then added, "Johnson is also actively trying to trap any mole he might have in his department. We'll find this guy. But until we do—until we know where the leak is, how he's finding you—the two of you are going to have to stay underground."

"What about Bruce or Lorraine?" Shelby's tone held a hint of panic. "They were the only two who knew, at all times, where we were."

"If they wanted us dead, we would be," Luke said.

And without his hotshot training, they'd all have likely died in the bomb fire. If he hadn't recognized the slim control line perimeter leading to the creek, they'd have probably all hidden out in the steel building and been consumed by smoke inhalation.

There wasn't much else on Hudson's video. The team would be working through the night.

And he and Shelby would be spending it alone, together.

In an elegant underground prison where he couldn't be in charge of fixing any situations at all. Couldn't give orders or throw his body into danger, taxing it to the limit, to save lives.

He had to rely on others to save lives while he was forced to sit with a woman he knew he'd been drawn to, whom he'd apparently hurt and insulted beyond repair. A woman who was making him feel things he'd never known he could feel.

A woman who was the mother of the son he'd never met.

And he had to do it without a single screwup.

Lord help me.

SHE DIDN'T WANT Carter's face plastered on the big screen, consuming the room. Or rather, out in the open in such a huge way for his father to consume.

She'd set the whole mess in motion by going to identify the man in the first place. And then going back a second time...

Part of her knew she'd done the right thing for her son.

But damn...

Were they ever going to find the guy who wanted Luke dead? Who'd tried to kill her, too?

Would Luke ever fully regain his memory and at least tell her why he'd done what he'd done to her?

Like the reasons could somehow help her prevent Luke from hurting her son in the future?

Or...hurt her again?

"I'm sorry."

Her head jerked up at his apology. Were they so connected that the man could read her mind?

"I know you were hoping that the pizza was just a mistaken address…"

Right.

And maybe she should have been thinking on those lines, worrying about a fiend wanting them dead.

Maybe thinking about Luke, the past, her son's future, put life on the front burner instead of death.

"I don't blame you for any of this, Luke." How could she? The man didn't want to be dead any more than she wanted to be in danger.

"You just blame me for the past."

She wasn't going to feel bad about that. "You would, too, if you'd been in my shoes." He was a fact guy, and she had the facts.

"I'd like to watch the last two videos."

She understood. He needed to see what Carter looked like. Without her phone, she hadn't been able to show him.

Or comfort herself with the thousand or more photos she kept on the card in her phone. Images she scrolled through frequently when she was away.

"They were meant for me, personally," she told him. "I'd like to see them first."

His expression hardly changed. Just went blank.

She'd hurt him. Hadn't meant to. Or even wanted to.

But…her family trusted that their messages were in her care.

Luke handed her the phone, got up and walked to the far end of the long room, disappearing behind the partition. She watched him the whole way with a hurting heart, but she didn't call him back.

Instead, with shaking fingers, she turned off casting from

the device she held, turned down the volume low enough for just her to hear and hit Play on her mother's video first.

It was short. Just letting her know that everything was great and not to worry. It ended with the "Love you" that had been their standard goodbye forever. Always.

She watched the short clip a second time, feeling better. It wasn't the content of her mother's words that calmed her but the unlined expression on her face, the easy tone.

Her mom wasn't worried.

She figured that Sierra's Web, whoever they'd sent to her mother's home, had played a huge part in that situation.

And owed that one to Luke.

The video from Carter made her so lonely for her boy she teared up for a moment. And then, playing it a second and third time, she smiled.

And felt...a little less alone, too, for the first time since his birth. Because there was another person on Earth who shared the responsibility of being her precious boy's parent. Who wanted to take him on.

A man who would share the wonder of knowing they'd made such an incredible little human being.

Because, everything else aside, she knew in her deepest heart that if Luke said he'd be there for Carter—that he *wanted* to be there—he would be.

He'd done some things to her that were hard to accept, but he'd never lied to her. That week they'd spent together, the personal questions she'd asked, he made it very clear that he'd given his life to hotshot firefighting. In lieu of any kind of committed partner relationship. He'd made a clear, purposeful choice.

And in all the years she'd kept track of him since, she'd never once caught him out in any kind of lie. Not ever.

So while he was most definitely not a candidate for her

heart, he did fit Carter's needs. Recasting the phone to the screen, she dropped it on the sectional and called out toward the kitchen portion of their odd-as-hell lodging.

"Luke?"

If he was…occupied in there with personal business, she didn't need to know. Or want to interrupt. But if he was waiting…

"Yeah?" Still fully dressed, hands in the pockets of his shorts, he stepped out to face her.

"You ready to meet your son?" She tried to sound excited. Like the moments ahead were going to be filled with all fun and happiness.

But, like Carter's birth—the first time *she'd* seen her son—there was a lot of pain and anguish mixed in with that happiness, too.

Moving slowly, hands still buried in fabric, Luke approached, holding her gaze the whole time. "You're sure?" he asked, that way he had of assessing—and determining— out in full force.

"I am." She didn't hesitate. The choice had already been made.

Right or wrong. Good or bad. Better or worse.

He studied her a moment longer but didn't ask again if she was sure. He must have seen what he was seeking. He seemed satisfied as he nodded.

And then walked right by her and off to the sectional as though she didn't exist.

HE HAD A TASK. A job. Something he had to do.

A moment in life to experience that he knew, going in, he would never forget.

Knew, too, that it was going to change him forever.

She'd asked if he was ready.

How in the hell did he know? He had no answers for anything to do with parenting—or much about childhood, either.

His own had been cut short.

The glance she sent in his direction as he sat down seemed questioning. "Were you ready when you found out you were pregnant?" he asked.

"No."

Nodding, he felt a bit of vindication. And waited for her to pick up the phone and change his life.

He might not know what was ahead or have any solutions to problems that would present themselves, but there was not a single doubt that he was already on the Carter road for life.

She didn't turn on the video. He glanced her way. Noting that she'd chosen a seat a little closer to him on the couch than he'd chosen earlier.

Didn't matter.

Didn't mean anything.

He wanted it to.

"If you'd rather wait…" she started, turning those brown eyes he couldn't afford to get lost in his way.

He nodded toward the phone between them. "You're the one making the introduction." It was up to her to share her boy with him.

Not his right to take Carter from the mother who'd been there for him.

"Right." She picked up the phone. He tried not to notice that her hand was shaking. The moment ahead wasn't about her. Or him, either.

"So," she continued with a trembling smile. "Luke, meet Carter."

Just Carter. Not, *meet your son.*

Words didn't change facts.

It took two pushes for her to get the video up on the screen. A mostly black background, with some red and a white Play arrow.

Another bunch of unending seconds passed before she hit Play.

The black dissipated as the camera moved, and a small tennis shoe came into view with a blotch of red on the top. "I spilled paint, Mom, and it's alweady dwy," the voice came out loud and clear. And, as only the shoe was in view, the voice continued, "I hope yow coming home soon, and I miss you and guess what? We had macawoni and cheese for dinnaw!" The screen became a dizzying blur—or maybe it was his eyes, filling with moisture—and then, before he could do anything other than feel, the camera stopped moving. He saw a brown couch spread out before them, as though the phone was leaning against an armrest. And then a little body lay down. And…

There. Chubby cheeks. Light-colored hair, a little long. And…big blue eyes, filling the screen. "I ate a doughnut." Hands came up to cup the little boy's chin, and the top half of his body, up on his elbows, came into view. "And when awe you coming to get me? Jason's dad took him fishing again. I love you, bye." And just like that, he was gone.

Seconds. He'd had mere seconds. Not enough for…

Not nearly enough.

Luke couldn't move. Couldn't assess or determine.

Frozen, he stared at the screen. Mostly black again, with the white arrow. The cover of the video.

His son. Carter. He had eyes that blinked, five fingers on each chubby little hand. He knew how to hold himself up on his elbows. He liked doughnuts and macaroni. Wasn't afraid to tell his mother he'd ruined his tennis shoe, but the fact was important enough that it was the first thing he'd told her.

And his friend had a dad who took him fishing...

The image on the screen changed, the camera moving out from the black to show a small tennis shoe...

She'd started the video over.

He absorbed...everything.

Again and again.

Hiding underground from someone who wanted him dead, he sat on a stranger's couch next to the mother of his child and watched the boy over and over again.

And then some more.

He had no words.

She didn't speak, either.

He had no plan. Just had to sit there. Getting to know every little thing he could about his son.

Carter struggled with his *r*'s. He licked his lips when he talked about food.

He loved his mother.

Who'd moved closer to Luke. Handing him the phone so he could watch and rewatch under his own control.

She didn't leave, though. Didn't move away.

They'd entered into a brand-new world together, and maybe neither of them knew what to do next.

Chapter Sixteen

A need to pee finally forced Shelby off the couch. And a glance at her watch told her they'd missed dinner. Sitting underground, one kind of lost sense of time of day.

Or, maybe, watching a man gain a son did that to you.

Luke was still sitting with the video playing when she came back to the kitchen. Opened the refrigerator, found an unopened bottle of wine, along with the casserole—some kind of pasta—and heating instructions.

They had a convection oven. She'd never used one but got dinner going easily. Opened the wine and poured a glass for each of them.

He was more of a beer guy. But he'd had wine with dinner a time or two the week they'd been together. And the refrigerator had no beer.

If he didn't want the wine, he didn't have to drink it. She was making an executive order, pouring it and walking it over to him. They had nowhere to be. Most definitely wouldn't be driving. And the man looked like he needed a little nudge to help him chill.

"He's incredible." Luke looked straight at her as he took the wine. "Confident, secure and transparent with you. He trusts you." The long sip he took from the glass she'd handed him bore its own testimony.

"He has your biology." Carter needed his father. She had to share him.

But she didn't have to *want* to. So…why was she starting to?

A distant rumble sounded. Like thunder? They'd left blue skies and sunshine to descend underground.

Setting his glass down, Luke moved to a cupboard by the ladder, one she hadn't paid attention to. Set up at eye level and small, the thing was mostly inconspicuous. Luke's tight expression, the urgency in his deliberate movement were not.

Opening the cupboard, he reached his hand up and then stared. She had to go see what he was doing.

And why he suddenly looked not at all like a new dad. He'd completely transformed into the supervisor of a hotshot-firefighting team. He was the man who'd led them out of the fire before dawn that morning.

The CCTV screen behind the cupboard doors, reflecting the camera of the outside, was black and white. More black than white due to the darkness, but the moon's glow on the water was clear. Not so much the body she was pretty sure she was looking at on the sand directly behind the house.

"Is that Lorraine?" It looked too small to be Bruce.

"No idea."

Heart pounding, her throat so tight she could hardly swallow, Shelby moved closer to Luke. Made herself breathe. "He's found us *again*, hasn't he?"

Luke's gaze never left the screen. "The bunker isn't registered anywhere. Only our bodyguards, Hudson, the homeowner and the two of us know about it."

And if Lorraine was down, that left Bruce or their team leader at Sierra's Web as the possible moles?

"Who wants you gone so badly they'd pay off someone

like Sierra's Web?" she asked, struck with chills, feeling the wobbles in her knees. "That wouldn't be cheap."

Someone would have to be paying more than Luke was…

He didn't speak. Just continued to study, as though he could see movement, change, on the mostly black screen.

Her question had been rhetorical, anyway. If he knew who was after him, they wouldn't be locked underground.

"The people who built it…"

"It was ten years ago, and again, not on record…"

She'd seen him in deep conversation with Bruce when she came out of the shower. Had assumed he'd be a part of determining whatever plan came next. He was footing the bill, after all.

Made sense, knowing Luke, that he'd be privy to every little detail.

About the bunker.

The camera hooked up to the screen in the cupboard.

He was the guy people called in extreme emergencies. For the worst fires, in season, and for any other life-threatening situation that came up when he *wasn't* fighting fires. The man had a reputation.

As she knew better than most people.

The intense concentration with which he was staring at the screen scared her. She hadn't even seen him blink.

And it hit her…

Oh, God. "Are we sitting ducks?" she blurted out.

"That's what I'm trying to find out."

She moved closer to him. She couldn't help it. Didn't touch him. She wasn't going to turn into some needy clinger. But she drew strength from his body warmth.

"We're safe down here," he said then. "From any kind of blast, flood or fire."

Relief coursed through her.

"But if he knows we're here, that the bunker is here—if he knows the codes to release the locks…"

Like if he was holding Bruce hostage and threatening to kill his family if…

She'd read too many suspense novels. Watched too many police shows.

"Does Bruce have a family?" she asked him, pretending she was just making conversation to try to keep a sense of calm between them.

"No idea."

Studying the live feed, growing more used to the grayish images, she pointed to the left corner of the screen. "That looks like the tree line just outside of here…"

"It is. There's vegetation over the door."

With their entrance and the small cage for supplies up in their ceiling both being flat in the ground, that made sense to her.

"So we'll know if anyone approaches."

He didn't answer that time, but she knew then why he wasn't taking his gaze off the screen. He was ready to take action if anyone got close to them.

Which gave Shelby hope. There was no one else she'd rather have down there with her.

ADRENALINE RACING THROUGH HIM, Luke fought against the frustration mounting alongside it. Fires didn't sit around and wait, and death didn't do surveillance; those were the entities he was used to doing battle with.

The ones he knew how to fight.

And he was no longer saving someone else's loved ones. He was saving his son's mother.

And…the boy's father.

Someone who could take him fishing and to ride in a

fire truck. Or just…give him a dad, too, like Jason had. He'd felt, deep in his gut, the sorrow in the little guy's voice when he'd mentioned his friend going fishing with his dad.

It was one of those things he was never going to forget.

Shelby's warmth beside him was another. The woman unhinged parts of him that had been hanging on a hook, with chains around it, since his teens.

A good thing—or a very bad one, depending on the moment. Either way, it was a fact.

He wasn't going to be able to change it.

Eyes dry, he blinked quickly and then refocused. No movement yet. Didn't mean there wouldn't be. While he'd never heard a shot while encased underground in cement and steel, he'd bet his bank accounts that there'd been gunshots at the house.

There was a body on the beach.

And no one standing outside the bunker.

The plan had been to have Lorraine and Bruce taking turns patrolling the beach with their little bit of tree line in sight at all times. And for one or the other of them to be continuously visible via camera to Luke as well.

Failing that, he was to assume there was serious trouble unless he got an all clear through their message cage. Until he saw one of them approach and heard that rattle, he was standing guard.

Bruce and Lorraine could both be gone. Sierra's Web would know soon enough, when the bodyguards didn't signal their predetermined all-is-well. The firm would deploy law enforcement.

Who wouldn't know about the underground quarters.

A flash on the screen nearly blinded him.

"What's that?"

Shelby's question was like fog in the background as he

moved in closer, staring intently. Powerful lights lit up the entire beach within his view. Uniforms moved in, all wearing guns, followed by two bodies in suits.

"Law enforcement," he said, mostly to distill the tension that could get in the way of him doing his best work. "Dealing with the body."

Not Lorraine. Or any name. Just a body. The time to grieve came when the work was done.

While he couldn't identify any of the living, either, he'd have been able to pick out Bruce. The man was taller than most.

Shelby moved to another part of the shelter. He didn't welcome the immediate chill that followed her departure, but he figured it was for the best that she not see whatever else might happen up above them.

Still: "Stay close," he said. He might need to grab and go. Already knew the direction through the trees he'd take before circling around to get her back to the beach. To a cove he'd seen off in the distance when they were heading in.

A cove offered protection, and the beach wouldn't burn.

From there, he'd figure it out as they went. His forte.

Officers had spread out. They were canvassing the perimeter of the beach as far as he could see, guns in hands stretched out in front of them. Ready to shoot.

Bruce had told him there was a loaded pistol in the small drawer beneath the cupboard he now stood before.

He had a carry license.

Wasn't going to worry about that, either way.

The body, covered with a sheet and on a stretcher, disappeared from view.

Shelby was back; he heard her before he caught a peripheral glimpse. "You need to eat," she said, holding a plate to him at chin level. Close enough that he could smell the onions, tomato sauce and cheese.

He took the plate, shoveled in food with his attention never leaving the screen. And when she lifted the empty plate from his hand, he nodded his thanks.

While the beach remained boldly lit, there were fewer bodies combing it. One group at the edge of his screen, standing closest to the house, had been in consultation for several minutes, with one member on the phone.

He'd still seen no sign of Bruce.

And not a clear-enough view to tell if Lorraine was among those walking around. She'd been wearing long black cotton pants and a dark short-sleeved shirt the last time he saw her. He wasn't seeing that attire on anyone, but she could have changed.

Without the bodyguards, it was unlikely anyone knew Luke and Shelby were on the premises.

Except their would-be killer.

Was he out there? Among those scouring the beach for clues?

A team with individual flashlights had entered the beach and were bent over, studying the sand. Forensics, he figured, by the way they appeared to pick up things and then put them in bags.

Shelby was back, standing just to his left and half a step behind him.

"Assuming we remain undetected, I'm planning to stay right here until morning," he told her.

"I'd have thought it would be best to move in the dark..." She didn't sound like she minded staying put. More like she was trying to be part of whatever was happening to her.

He got that.

"Ordinarily, yes, but because we don't have any idea

what's happened, who's out there—even who the bad guys are—it would serve us best to be able to see."

"To assess our adversaries."

Luke almost glanced her way when she made the comment. "Yes," he confirmed. Proud of her for no reason whatsoever.

Because he didn't have any relationship with her that would give him the right to take pride in her accomplishments.

Except when it came to motherhood.

And he was damned proud of her there...

No.

Screen movement. The scene unfolding. That was all he could know until the coast was clear.

Pulling himself back wasn't easy. But he did it.

"If no one knows about us—most particularly, if the guy after us doesn't know where we are—we're safest right here. We've got more than a week's provisions. And with daylight, I'll have a much better view of our surroundings through here." He pointed to the camera.

She wasn't his crew. Didn't have to just do what he said without question. Her life was in danger, and she deserved to know everything he could tell her.

Unfortunately, he'd given her everything he had.

Another half hour passed as he stood there. And then an hour. Other than brief stints away, Shelby stood right there with him. Mostly silent. She asked a question or two, procedural things about the group, including the two suits, that crowded around the area where the body had been.

And then: "There he is!" she screamed, just as Luke saw a man who had to be Bruce come into view.

The bodyguard was alive.

And if Bruce wasn't the mole, Luke's chances of getting

Shelby back home to Carter alive had just gotten better. The man knew where they were and hadn't pointed anyone in their direction.

The danger wasn't done. Not by a long shot. Clearly, their general location had been breached.

But not their exact one.

They still had a fighting chance.

As he stood there next to her in the small space, relief flooded him—and, acting completely like a guy he didn't even know, he reached down and took her hand.

Chapter Seventeen

Shelby almost wept when she saw Bruce's face take over the screen. She'd been standing for more than half an hour, holding Luke's hand.

Not speaking about the connection.

Or questioning, either.

But she missed his touch, felt the cool air on her hand when, a few seconds later, he left her to climb up to the message cage.

They'd heard the thunk together.

She watched alone as Bruce stepped back out to the beach.

Luke came back with a memory card. She followed him to the couch and waited as he inserted the small plastic piece into the phone and then scrolled to find whatever was on it.

"It's a video," he said, coming over to her, standing close, huddling over the small screen with her.

"There was an intruder at the house," Bruce's voice started when his face appeared on screen. "He briefly had Lorraine captive with a gun to her head, told her he'd let her go as soon as she told him where he could find Luke Dennison. She was able to throw him but not immediately contain him. He fled to the beach, where he saw me, pointed his gun—at which point, we both shot our weapons. After which, we immediately called the police. The intruder's prints came up. He's a known hit man working almost exclusively out of California. Unfortunately, he did not survive to be questioned. Law enforcement, with Sierra's Web's help, are combing through financials and phone records to determine who hired him. Lorraine and I have been interviewed, said that we were staying on the premises as guests of the owner, and have been let go. Sierra's Web cleared us to remain on duty.

"Local law enforcement do not know that the two of you, or the shelter, are here," Bruce's voice continued. "It's been determined that the two of you are safest right where you are, at least until morning. Sierra's Web has assigned a couple more bodyguards to the detail. The four of us will be taking turns throughout the night, resting and patrolling.

"Other members of the team will be working throughout the night to figure out how you're being tracked. There's been no evidence of any kind as to who a mole might be. Everyone is checking out with provable alibis. Our current burners weren't traced, and the car's tracking software had been physically removed before the car was put in service with us this morning. It's been gone over a second time, and there was no device found.

"If you have anything to report, send it up. Otherwise, get some rest."

Not likely, Shelby thought, glancing around their surroundings before Bruce's voice called her attention back to the phone.

"Oh…and Hudson said to tell you the DNA test came back as a match."

Her mind blanked for a second as the screen went black. She'd known, of course. There'd been absolutely no doubt.

But now there was official medical record… Carter was no longer just *her* son.

Legally, she was going to have to share him.

The thought scared her to death for the second it took her to glance up at Luke. Or rather, for her gaze to follow him as he took a few steps and fell to the couch.

"He's really my son."

She didn't think an *I told you so* was appropriate. But she moved over to sit beside him.

"I just…"

His gaze as intent as it had been on the screen for the past couple of hours, he studied her. Her eyes, her face, back to her eyes. "I have no idea why I'd ever have called you a liar and shut my door in your face," he said. "It's not me. I can't accept that I'd do such a thing. I'm many things, but I would never turn my back on my own child."

"If you didn't remember having sex with me…" She couldn't believe she was helping him make excuses.

But how did you hold someone accountable to something they couldn't remember—and therefore, couldn't explain or defend?

She'd never forget… Would always be on guard… But…

He shook his head without breaking eye contact. "I'd have asked for proof…"

"It's water under the bridge, Luke," she heard herself say. There were so many more important things to figure out between them.

At the moment, they had to get through spending the night alone together in the small space. She was about to crawl out of her skin.

With fear.

Claustrophobia. Not so much of the closed space but of

being trapped underground, with a killer believing they were in the area.

With wanting him.

The look in his eyes when'd found out he had a son…

The moisture she saw in them right then as he looked to her for answers neither of them had…as he slowly comprehended that he was really and truly a father…

She was sitting with the man she'd fallen head over heels for in one week's time.

Five years before.

The man whose child she'd borne.

Alone.

They were fighting for their lives.

The reality was too surreal to grasp.

"I lost the first four years of his life."

And there was nothing anyone could do about that. But: "Most of it, he's not even going to remember. Can you—" She broke off abruptly and then said, "I have very few memories from when I was that young."

"I don't have many, either," he said then, and she realized that he knew what she'd been about to say. Asking a man with memory issues to take comfort from what he couldn't remember—as though if he couldn't recall, no one else would be able to—wouldn't have been her best argument. "I do remember the first time my dad took me to play T-ball, though. I know I was four because that's how old you had to be to start the league, and I'm told I kept asking how many more days until my birthday so I could go play. I guess I was crushed that, with my actual birthday being out of season, I had to wait another two months for the league to start."

If she hadn't already figured out just how far Luke was

from his normal self, his uncharacteristically long speech would have shown her. She ate up every word.

Smiled at him.

Grabbed his hand, squeezed and held on.

"I have videos from day one forward and thousands of pictures, too," she told him. "You'll know about every moment, will be able to picture them, to hear him say one of his first words—not as he's saying it but later that same day…"

And most importantly, Carter was going to have what he needed most.

A man in his life.

And her?

She dropped Luke's hand, under guise of reaching for the glass of wine she'd left on the table hours before, uncaring that it was warm.

Could memory have enhanced the lovemaking she'd shared with this guy? Had she built it into more than it had been to justify getting pregnant by a man she hardly knew? One who'd paid her off?

Had it been her way of not feeling…cheap? Pretending that she'd thought they'd had something out-of-this-world special?

She remembered his touch so clearly—when she let herself think about it at all. Remembered the couple of days before it had happened, how she couldn't stop thinking about going to bed with her interviewee. That had been a first for her, and she'd struggled with the ethics of it.

But was her mind playing tricks on her? Had she reframed it all to suit what her life had become?

How did she know?

Memory was a tenuous thing. Clouded by time and differing perspectives.

She'd never have slept with the man if she hadn't believed them to be mutually connecting on some deeper level.

Not *be a couple* or *get married* connected. Just…two people who were meant to meet and share something more.

Never in her life had she had sex with a man who didn't mean something to her.

And only knowing him a week? She'd known every other man she'd slept with more than a year before going to bed with him.

She was just weird that way.

Except when it came to Luke Dennison.

He'd been sitting there, watching the video again with the volume off. When he flipped it off, she tensed.

Told herself to relax. She wasn't going to do anything stupid.

Until the man reached for her hand again, taking it between both of his. "I need you to understand that I'm not a guy who uses women or takes sex lightly," he said, meeting her gaze. "You're letting me into your son's life. You have to know that I will teach him to respect and honor people, not take advantage of them."

She had to look away. Couldn't look away. Those vivid blue eyes—their look touched her.

Just as they had in the past. She hadn't imagined that part. Or enhanced it, either.

Had everything else been real, too, then? The lovemaking part?

The rest… Who knew? Maybe he'd left the money to cover her week's expenses? Because she'd expressed concern about mixing business with pleasure? He hadn't said, but he was a guy of few words…

She had to know.

Before they moved forward, she needed answers…

He couldn't tell her why he'd left the money, and only he knew. Same with shutting the door on her.

But the rest...

She leaned forward. Didn't think. Just did it.

When he didn't pull back, she leaned in more and...a little more.

Until her lips touched his.

And recognized him.

OH, GOD.

Have mercy.

Those lips. Her scent. Her softness.

Just as he'd remembered. And then some.

Had to stop.

Couldn't take pleasure from her.

He owed her.

Had wronged her.

Was already hard with just their lips pressed together.

And couldn't reject her. Not ever again.

He waited for her to finish. Focused on maintaining control.

It was just mouths touching.

Her tongue slid between his lips. Torture.

Sweet, exquisite torture.

He had to respond. To ignore her would be like shutting a door in her face.

His tongue, his mouth, his arms—they knew what to do without his direction. Free to not reject, they moved of their own accord.

Giving, and taking, too...

For her.

And—God help him—for him, too.

The woman was hungry and delicious. He kissed her, danced his tongue with hers, until he couldn't breathe.

And when he broke to gasp for air he couldn't draw in quickly enough, he planted his lips on her neck.

Moaning, she tilted her head back.

Moaned a second time.

A sound he remembered with more blood flow rushing straight to his penis, as he kissed his way down her neck.

She lay back, giving him easier access to more flesh, and his chin pushed the neckline of her shirt down as far as it would stretch.

He'd never known sex like it had been with her. As though his body knew exactly how to help her reach paradise.

He was a fire extinguisher, not a fire starter. Hadn't ever been particularly hot with women. But with Shelby…

"Don't stop," she half gasped when he raised his head.

"We should…"

Her hands up his shirt, she stopped moving them all over his chest. He missed them. They were still there, and he missed them. Their passion. On him.

"You don't want to?" she asked, looking him straight in the eye.

He couldn't lie to her.

"I want to more than just about anything I've ever wanted." Stupid, trite words. To show her what he meant, he lay back, pulling her down on top of him, and, holding both hands at her butt, ground his penis into her pelvis.

"I want to, too," she said, a Madonna-like smile spreading over the lips pink and moist from his kisses. "We're here, locked in alone, no outside world for the entire night…"

The way her words drifted took him on a trail to what they could do with an entire night alone. Together.

He wasn't going to shut the door on her. Not ever again.

And he knew just how to please her. With his hands, his lips. Even his feet tangling with hers, holding them while he slid her legs apart.

Fully clothed, right then, and later, he spread them again, naked on the first partitioned bed they'd fallen onto.

He had a condom in his wallet. She carried a couple in her purse, too.

When the thought hit that her unexpected pregnancy had caused her to be more careful that way, he pushed it firmly away.

She wanted him to pleasure her, and he could do it.

As well as he fought fires.

So he did.

Over and over.

Until they finally fell asleep wrapped around each other.

Chapter Eighteen

She wasn't sorry.

Waking up from what seemed like a long, deep, restful sleep, Shelby was immediately aware of the body snuggled up to hers. She knew who he was and that he was every bit as naked as she was. But in the partitioned space lit dimly by the small light they'd failed to turn off in the living area, she had no idea of the time.

She saw Luke's old-fashioned wristwatch on the arm wrapped around her. Was pretty sure it said it was just after seven.

She had to pee.

And to walk away from that bed and finally be able to leave the past behind. Reframed.

The lovemaking had been as incredible as she'd remembered. She hadn't fooled herself. Or been a fool.

The parts of Luke's personality, his spirit, that had drawn her were real. They connected in a deep unique way.

She'd found peace.

And this time, he wasn't leaving.

She was.

Not leaving him. She couldn't. Like it or not, the man was going to be in her life forever. Even if, after Carter was grown, she never saw Luke again, he'd still be there. The father of her child.

But she was leaving their bed.

And that was for good.

Sliding out from under the arm slung over her waist, she moved her leg slowly from beneath Luke's heavier weight, rolled over and off the edge of the bed, and quickly scooted around the partition closing them in. The bag of clothes and essentials that had been delivered was hanging from a hook behind the toilet partition right where she'd left it.

At some point, Luke had left his own there on the hook next to hers.

A practical necessity—not a sign. They weren't a couple. They were going to raise a child, not hang out together. Luke was... Luke.

Parts of him fit her. Parts did not.

Maybe if he could remember the way he'd treated her after the last time they'd had sex, if he could explain and there really had been different inferences, other circumstances and intentions...

No.

He'd called her a liar and then shut the door in her face. For a second there, she'd even thought he smiled as he did so, but she'd never been sure about that one.

And beyond the past, which she'd now put behind her, Luke Dennison would feel trapped by the needs of a woman, of a partner relationship. As a noncustodial father, he could come and go.

As a spouse, or even a monogamous long-term boyfriend, he'd feel obligations that warred with the man he needed to be.

She'd understood that from the beginning.

He'd even told her so during his interview, but only because she'd seen the battle inside him, had been fascinated and moved by his incredible commitment to what he did, and had wanted to be able to somehow express that part of him in her story. Luke was married to hotshot firefighting—a commitment that required him to drop everything at a moment's notice to rush off and put his life in danger. He'd said he couldn't, in good conscience, ask someone to be a life partner and then ditch the partnership on a constant basis.

And in the off-season, he was committed to overcoming other dangerous physical feats to save lives.

She'd gone to bed with him years ago, knowing that it wouldn't lead to any kind of coupling outside that hotel room. She'd made a conscious decision because she hadn't wanted to miss the experience of making love with him. Hadn't wanted to live the rest of her life never feeling him as intimately as she possibly could.

She'd wanted to know the real thing rather than risk carrying around a mirage of what she imagined being with Luke would be like, forever comparing every other man she met to the fantasy.

Instead, for once in her life, reality had been better than fantasy.

Until breakfast had arrived the next morning.

But no matter. She'd moved beyond all that. Doing her business, dressing quickly once she'd climbed out of her mental monologue, Shelby grabbed the travel toothbrush and paste she'd found in her bag. She went to the kitchen for some water and saw Luke standing, fully dressed in yesterday's clothes, in front of the open cupboard by their ladder up to the world.

"All's good," he said, smiling at her. "Lorraine's on duty right now. The beach is quiet. And I made coffee."

The look in his eye as he came toward her made her duck

her head into the sink and shove a glob of toothpaste on her brush from down there, which was incredibly awkward. Then, with no water running yet, she started brushing.

No kissing.

The night was over.

Absolutely no kissing.

Resolve firmly strengthened, she turned the water on to rinse and spit. Didn't even attempt to be elegant about it.

He was Carter's father—period. And their son... There was nothing even halfway classy about his spitting toothpaste at the mirror to see if he could make it stick.

Luke was gone by the time she'd finished brushing and had rinsed out the sink. From behind the back partition, she heard him bang what sounded like an elbow against the wood. She poured herself a cup of the coffee he'd made, deliberately leaving him to pour his own.

Not to be rude. At all.

But because she couldn't let herself pretend, even for a second, that they were...well...more than they were.

Pouring his wine the night before...that had been before.

She heard the clank of a message dropping into the cage upstairs before she'd even had her first sip of the strong black brew.

"Luke? A message dropped," she called out. Two seconds later, he appeared from behind the partition, still getting dressed. His dark cargo shorts were on but unfastened, the orange T-shirt still in his hand.

Someone had picked green boxer briefs for him.

They...um...molded to his... Yeah, he was hard.

But when she lifted her gaze—filled with intimate knowing—to meet his, Luke's eyes were not trained on her. He was focused on the ladder ahead of him, his head tilted up toward the cage she knew was there but, from her angle, couldn't see.

Had she been his girlfriend or even a woman who'd spent the night with him hoping they were starting a relationship, she'd have been hurt by his complete lack of awareness of her.

Of course he needed to get to the message. They needed to get out of the shelter and back to life. But he'd already said that everything up on the surface was peaceful.

The message in the cage was the briefing they'd known would be coming after all hands had been on deck during the night. A little eye contact could wait.

Maybe just a hint of regret that the night was through?

And, bing! Right there. Her hurt feelings. That was why she could never be in a relationship with Luke Dennison. Not that he was open to one. But even if he was, she couldn't be because of their son. It would be a recipe for disaster.

She knew that as clearly as she knew she'd give up her life for Carter's.

She couldn't give her heart to a man who would break it, making her defensive against him. Making others around her choose sides to keep her safe. Forcing people to feel horrible about loving the man who'd hurt her. She would not be her mother.

Because Carter didn't just need her in his life; he needed his father, too.

Just watching him glom on to the one video of Carter the night before, sitting through all his questions about the boy... Luke loved their son already.

Which thrilled her. More than she'd realized could happen. Made her teary-eyed with joy.

Her son came first, always.

So why, when her heart tried to tell her that having Luke in Carter's life would be enough, couldn't she believe it?

NOT THE LEAST bit concerned about Shelby seeing his hard-on, actually thinking about his own personal future for the first time in a long while, Luke was eager to retrieve the electronic device—to find out who was after him, deal with the guy and go meet his son.

With his son's mother right by his side.

Where it all led, he had no idea. He was still him. Dedicated to firefighting. But most of his team members were married. Had families.

If they could do it, he could learn how, too.

Right?

With the right motivation, he could learn anything.

Shelby knew what he was. She'd come on to him with the same hunger she'd given him in the past—even knowing that, as a partner, he'd give her challenges and bumps in the road.

Not that they were going to be partners...other than in raising Carter. But they could at least look into the possibilities.

After climbing back down into the shelter, with thoughts of the work ahead shrinking his penis, Luke fastened his pants as he approached the sink, where Shelby still stood.

It had to be business first. For both of them.

Something they'd had in common in the past. An understanding that had made him lower his defenses around her from almost the beginning.

Wishing he could take charge, get the job done, just to wipe the concern off her face, he saw the video on the front screen and moved in close, needing to be there for her as much as they needed to huddle to see the screen at the same time, and tapped the Play arrow.

Hudson's face, needing a shave, filled the screen. The IT expert had obvious shadows under his eyes as he said, "The guy on the beach last night… He's suspected in several professional hits, but there's no sign of him getting paid for last night. No money connection at all between any of your possible enemies—or Michaels. But we did find an odd connection between the two of you, just not what we expected. You pulled his mother out of a fire a few years ago…"

Shelby's shocked indrawn breath echoed his own "What the hell?" He was being stalked by someone he'd helped?

What kind of world had he woken up in?

His expression grim, he stared at the screen.

"It's possible that he heard there was a price on your head, heard the job offer come through channels, knew where you were, and was there to warn you or get you to safety, but why threaten your bodyguard with a gun to her throat…and then pull that gun a second time on those keeping you safe? Surely, if he's at all connected, he'd know, as your killer does, that you've hired protection…and would find a way to warn us…"

So… Luke saves a life, and the woman's son thanks him by trying to kill him? It didn't make sense.

But then, so much about Luke's actions and activities didn't add up.

He could feel Shelby tense next to him. Could only imagine what doubts were raining down upon her.

Regrets from the night before?

"Moving on," Hudson continued, still staring straight at the camera, "nothing about Gerard Michaels looks fishy. Not anyplace. His books are meticulous. His bills are paid on the same date every month. Nothing at all unusual or noteworthy about his spending. There's no sign of any assets unaccounted for anywhere in his life. No numbers he calls, even, to people who might have such unaccounted-for assets..."

He was relieved about Michaels. For the time being.

Would be good to know that his trust in the guy wasn't misplaced. That he had the wherewithal he felt like he needed to judge people, situations, and get it right.

Still, while Sierra's Web was impressively thorough, if they'd found whoever wanted Luke dead, wouldn't Hudson have said so by then?

Which meant...

"We've been through the names on your list," Hudson went on. "Nothing suspicious stands out—no new gun license requests, nothing on social media that directs us anywhere in the direction of any of the locations where fires have been set..."

How much longer could the whole thing go on?

And if they couldn't find the guy, would it end only when he succeeded? Luke couldn't let that happen. Not to Shelby. And not to himself, either. He had a son who needed a father.

"With teams working together, side by side—comparing notes, dates, phone records, expenditures—we've discovered what we think is the key to solving the case." Hudson's voice dropped the news as though the guy were discussing dinner plans.

Stiffening, Luke felt Shelby's arm wrap through his, like he needed her to hold him up. And while he could stand perfectly fine on his own, it was...different, having someone stand with him. In a personal sense.

At the same time, he braced himself for her withdrawal, depending on what came next.

"Johnson's on his way over now, but our working theory

is that you're a victim of identity theft," Hudson continued after a pause to take a sip from a water bottle. "A few time-lines, phone calls to Michaels logged as you calling, but there's no record of you making the call from your phone... It's stuff no one would notice..."

Except Luke was paying for teams of experts in many fields...

"There's nothing linking Michaels to the Cayman accounts other than the deposits he made from the fake charity, but there was a call to the Caymans from a phone that called Michaels, at a time he'd logged a call from you. The other phone has been off since before you were found nearly dead in the desert."

And they weren't assuming it was Luke?

That didn't make sense, either. Not feeling Shelby's departure from him yet, he said, "I could have had a separate phone." He'd have said the words to Hudson, if the man could hear him. Instead, he just put them out there.

And got an arm squeeze for his effort.

"Which got us looking into that number and yours again," Hudson went on. "You were up in the mountains, having just finished a job, and made a call to Payson at the exact same time the other number made a call *from* Payson to Michaels. A few minutes' difference between beginning and end of calls, but you were both making calls during some of the same time."

Luke's entire body went limp for a second. And then stood tall. They were getting somewhere. They just weren't there yet.

And still didn't know their destination.

Then, more than ever, he had to keep his mind on the immediate challenge in front of him. Shelby's presence, the knowledge of his son were constant pressures at his back to get them all safely through whatever demons his life had brought upon them.

"It's not the only call made from Payson from that phone, but there were only a few. Many more from Phoenix—and California, too—so not likely that this guy resides in Payson. And that's the bad news. We still have no idea who this guy is. We've checked his call locations against every single name on our list of people who've been privy to this case and on the list you gave us, and every single one of them has an alibi putting them someplace different than where the calls came from."

Seriously.

They had theories and no solid leads? Except a dead guy whose mother he'd helped?

How could anyone be that good? To know everything but leave behind only dead ends?

It was like he had a ghost out to kill him.

Luke had never believed in ghosts.

"Lastly, we believe we have a motive for wanting you dead."

The bombshell fell out, kind of pissing Luke off. Couldn't the man have led with that?

His gaze bore holes into the small screen as Hudson's image continued. "Say this guy started out using you as his mark for identity theft because you're absent for long periods of time and don't handle your own money. A simple hack into Michaels's business could have told him that."

He shared a glance with Shelby and felt his tension ease a small bit. Just because she was there.

"It's possible that this guy got so fully entrenched in your life, your assets, he believes they belong to him. Or, at the very least, is determined to have them all for himself."

Pulling himself away from Shelby at that, Luke focused

fully on the screen. On the words he was hearing. Someone who was mentally ill was trying to kill him and Shelby? Not just someone with hatred for him or someone who was stealing from him…but someone who was so out of touch he believed he could *be* him?

"Right now we're combing through years of your records and whereabouts, comparing them to all withdrawals and hits on the Cayman accounts and this phone number. It's a burner phone, but we can see the calls and locations until a week or so ago, so that's a start. And anything you can give us, any memories of anything odd you might remember, send it up. We're going to pin this guy to the wall."

He'd possibly had someone stealing his identity for years? Without his total memory, how in the hell did he fill in the blanks to help the team? His whole life…this guy hadn't just wanted to rob him of property, money and belongings—he'd wanted to live his life? To take over and leave Luke for dead?

He didn't know what to do with that. How to take it down.

But he'd damn well figure it out. He had to.

"One last thing," Hudson was saying. "If either you or Shelby have anything on you that has been in your possession since the hospital, we need you to send it up. Every other avenue for figuring out how he's finding you is a dead end. Lorraine said something about Shelby's purse. Johnson's team ran a wand over it, but we've got to see it another time."

Hudson then told Luke and Shelby just to hang tight, assuring them that all agreed they were safest right where they were, and said he'd be in touch later in the morning. The video ended, returning to the start screen with the little white arrow.

He set the phone on the counter, frowning, but looked at

her then, his gaze connecting with hers as it had done the night before when they'd been talking about Carter.

And later...

"Wait," she said, sounding tense, as the expression on her face hardened.

"The theory about this guy wanting me dead was because I identified you, right? Because he just wanted you gone, then he assumes your identity, empties your accounts and moves away, right? Maybe he sends a letter to the forestry division, resigning your position. Even saying that after your memory loss, a second one, you've determined to focus your life in another direction..."

"I can't imagine anyone there, higher-ups included, believing that one."

Everyone knew his career sustained him in ways nothing else could.

"Right, but say he doesn't know that part. Just go with me here a second. If I'm dead and can't identify you, assuming he doesn't know you've regained your memory, what's to stop a member of your team from coming forward now? I mean, if he kills us now, wouldn't he then need everyone who knew you dead? Anyone who could identify him as a fraud?"

She was right. He had to get a response to Hudson. Had to focus fully on the news he'd just heard.

His feelings for Shelby—what they'd done, who they'd been or could be—didn't matter if they didn't have lives to live...

Shelby's gaze dropped. She turned away from him. Picked up her coffee cup as though that was what she'd been after but then put it back down again.

"What?"

She shook her head but didn't meet his gaze.

"Shelby."

Nothing. Had she remembered something else? Something he'd done that was no longer on his radar? No matter how hard he tried to bring everything back?

"Tell me what you were just thinking," he said in his supervisory voice. Then, hearing the tone, softened it with "Please."

Reaching out, he touched her shoulder, nudging her back around. The night they'd spent...they'd become something more. "Please."

Her glance met his, was gone and then back again. "It's nothing," she told him. "Just... I know how you work. You take the information you're given, and you do what you need to do with it to solve whatever problem is in front of you."

Yeah, but that didn't make sense because, "That was what made you turn away?"

Her chin lifted, she looked him straight in the eye and said, "It makes sense that someone who is planning to deal with you for the foreseeable future would need to find a way to communicate with you. You don't sit down and discuss things or have some heart-to-heart talk. You just state your facts, or hear others' facts, and move on. Meaning that those communicating with you need to move on also, out of the way, so you can solve the problems in the way you see fit."

He saw it. Clearly. Saw himself. Exactly as she described.

And, for the first time, he saw how his blunt, abrupt ways could make others feel...superfluous. He'd gotten so used to knowing what had to be done and getting it done in the most urgent ways possible...

He'd saved more lives than any other hotshot firefighter. But...

"I'll be more aware," he told her.

For her—for Carter—he'd do better.

Or die trying.

Chapter Nineteen

"We need to gather up our stuff," Shelby said, breaking eye contact with Luke before she drowned in what seemed like promises she'd love to have. She couldn't afford to hold on to them.

He wanted to be more aware. But Luke was Luke. You didn't get to change a person into being who you needed them to be just because you cared about them.

Her father—case in point.

She had to love him in spite of his flaws, not expect her love to fix him up into the package she wanted.

Her dad, she had to love.

Not Luke.

Her purse wasn't big. She'd given up the key fob, her phone, everything but the little bit of makeup she carried, the package of cleaning wipes she always had on her and her wallet, but she handed the whole thing over to Luke.

"It's never been out of my possession," she said. "Even when they wanded it, I was right there. No way anyone could have bugged it."

But she didn't want it anywhere near her, either.

"If someone we're working with is a mole, it's possible they were close enough to your purse to inject something into the bottom of it."

They could do that with tracking devices?

"If someone we're working with is a mole, they wouldn't need a tracking device," she pointed out. "They'd know where we are."

"Not if it was someone at the hospital."

People had been in and out of his room. Had their killer posed as a doctor? A nurse? Or hired someone else to do so?

Was there no end to the possibilities?

Luke added his wallet to her purse.

"Your watch," she reminded him. It was ancient. Battery operated. Non-digital, and always on Luke's arm, but Hudson had said everything. Adding the time piece to the pile, Luke carried their meager items over to the ladder. He'd drop the things in the basket and push a button to have the conveyer belt move them through a pipe to a place farther down the beach, where Bruce or Lorraine would get them.

You didn't give up the location of your entryway by receiving goods through it.

Apparently, people in the bunker business thought of everything.

Something she was going to research when she got out of there. How many people in the country had places like this? Was there a whole society of them that people like her knew nothing about?

Or was their host just a guy who feared some huge threat might catch up to him?

Watching her only physical ties to the life that was currently not safe for her to live rise up that ladder, Shelby tried to keep her spirits in a healthy place.

They'd get past their days of running and hiding. Life would return to normal—a new normal with Carter having a father around sometimes—and she'd be home with her son, and all would be good again.

They were planning a trip to California's most famous amusement park later in the summer. It would be Carter's first, because she'd wanted to wait until he was old enough to know where he was. To maybe remember, as he got older, that initial feeling of magic and unending possibility...

So he could grow up and realize that it had all been make believe?

This intrusive thought was so unlike her that Shelby knew she was in trouble. And had to take back ownership of herself—the person who knew that the future always held a promise of possibility. Heartache, disappointment... If she let them, they'd rob her of that belief, just as they had her mother.

"About last night..." she said as soon as Luke descended the ladder.

His look—personal, warm. He didn't stop walking until he was standing right in front of her. He even cupped her cheek.

Surprised, unsure why he'd think he needed to make such an uncharacteristic move, she nonetheless kept her resolve but looked up at him, cupping his cheek, too, as she said, "I want to thank you. I had no right, coming on to you like I did. I just...needed... Well, it doesn't matter what I needed." How did he do it? Getting by with only facts. No feelings measured in.

He dropped his hand, so she dropped hers, too.

"Anyway, you have no worries that I'll make more into what we did than it was. And as a matter of fact, I need last night to be the only time...even if we do end up here another night."

How she'd pull that one off, she didn't know yet.

Just knew that she had to find a way.

He was watching her—listening, even—she believed. But

that personal look she'd thought she'd seen was nowhere in sight. Maybe she'd just imagined it.

Getting no reaction at all, she continued, giving him the honesty she wanted from him. "I just know me, Luke. The more we do stuff like…last night, the more my heart's going to get involved. I'm not someone who can just do the physical thing. And, frankly, I don't want to be…"

Still no response—other than apparent attentiveness.

"I'm going to need more than you can give or even want to give, which isn't fair to you at all. It would get messy, and there's too big a chance that Carter would be the one to suffer. Either from me being upset, us fighting or you not coming around as much…"

It wouldn't ever be about making Carter choose sides, though. That much she knew. Sylvia Harrington had made that mistake, and Shelby had been paying the price ever since her parents split up.

"So what was last night?" he asked her.

"Honestly?"

He nodded.

"My memories of us… I was afraid I'd embellished our time together in a subconscious attempt to explain to myself why I did what I did with you in the first place. It was so out of character for me, and ending up pregnant, my whole life was changed…" There she was, rattling on again when he'd just needed the facts. "Last night was me finding out that I hadn't been lying to myself. If I had to make the choice again, to have slept with you back then, I'd have done so." She stopped, then added, "Probably with more attention to condom care…" She stopped again. She tried to be more like him, keeping her stuff to herself, but ended up blurting, "But not really, because I don't begrudge Carter his life. Or in any way wish I hadn't had him." Her words tumbled over each other in their haste to get said. "My son is the best part of me. The happiest piece of my life."

Yeah, Carter had changed what she'd thought her life would be. But she wouldn't trade him for anything she'd thought she wanted.

"Anyway," she said, needing to get it done, "last night was me putting the past to rest."

He nodded.

Picked up the phone Hudson had sent down that morning.

He was going to walk away.

She knew it.

Knew she had to let him.

And said, "Are you mad?"

His blink, the raising of his brows, spoke surprise to her. "Of course not," he said. And then added, "I'm going to use this phone to message Hudson. I intend to keep the other until I can get a permanent copy of the video Carter made."

She figured, maybe, he intended to watch the video some more, too. Didn't want to be parted with it even long enough for the Sierra's Web team to get a permanent copy to him.

And she had to blink back tears.

Luke was going to make a great dad.

For such a skilled hotshot, he'd called that one all wrong.

During their lovemaking the night before, he'd thought they were saying hello. She'd been saying goodbye.

Wow.

And it wasn't because she wasn't drawn to him but because she knew him.

Knew, even more than he could remember, the lengths he would apparently go to in order to prevent himself from asking a woman to share his life.

And without knowing why he'd sent her a breakfast tray

with an insane amount of cash in an envelope or, most importantly, why he'd shut his door in her face when she'd come to tell him about Carter...how in the hell could he even have a conversation with her about it?

One that would ring true to her?

He'd denied their child. Refusing to even speak with her about the pregnancy.

Watching the video the night before, he'd come back to that fact over and over, until it was driving him past the edge. That one choice—one he couldn't explain, didn't feel any affinity with and couldn't understand—had robbed him of the first four years of his son's life.

And robbed him of the trust and perhaps growing love of the one woman he'd ever cared enough for to even think about having a love of his own in his life.

The money on the tray... Anyone could have done that. For any number of reasons.

But she'd been to Luke's home. Knew that his dead bolt had had the catch and the squeak, because she'd stood on his doorstep, face-to-face with him, just before he'd shut her out and turned the lock into place.

No way there could be anyone else to blame but himself for that.

No one else for her to blame.

He couldn't just sit. Had done enough of nothing to last him a lifetime.

First thing he had to do was message Hudson and the rest of the team. Pacing the small living space, he held the phone up and hit Record.

"Question. If the guy wants to be me, how does simply killing Shelby and me serve his purpose? In the beginning, she was the only one who came forward, but everyone knows who I am now. My team, my boss have been notified. They'd all be able to say this new guy isn't me."

He hadn't asked Shelby to join him. But was glad to see her come sit on the sofa. She had good insights...

Right.

Pausing the video for a second, he looked straight at her. "I might not be good at the communication thing, but I listen," he told her. "I always want to hear your opinion. You notice things other people miss..."

The way her head turned a little and her brows rose, he figured he'd surprised her. Not in a bad way.

Good.

Back to the video, he said, "I could have exposed my weakness to identity theft to this guy. I recommended money managers to my crews in classes I taught, explaining that when we're in season, we aren't going to be able to watch our accounts or pay our bills. I recommended automatic deposit on paychecks, too. This opens up a whole plethora of possible suspects."

He paused once more, thought for a second and hit Record again. "And the things that seem most odd to me— the threesome, the house party—maybe this guy did those things in my name, but it wasn't me there." So maybe he was digging deep. He'd give much of his fortune to find out that he'd at least been cleared from those activities.

There might be more, but it was all he had at the moment. He hit the button to save the video. Named it.

And looked at Shelby. She had the phone with Carter's video in her hand, was watching something on it.

Missing her son?

The little smile she wore was...transforming.

And heartrending, too.

"Hey, what do you say we make a video to send back to

Carter?" he blurted out. Selfishly, he knew, even as he heard himself, but he didn't retract the words.

What if things didn't turn out good with the investigation? What if he ended up not making it? Every single time he went to work, that possibility was right there. More for him than most. It was part of the life he'd opted to take on.

"We don't have to tell him who I am," he quickly asserted when Shelby's mouth dropped open and panic seemed to hit her eyes. "Just…say I'm an interview subject," he ad-libbed. "It wouldn't be a lie because I am. That's how you were able to identify me…"

"Interview subject is not something he'd understand," she said, but she seemed to be weighing his suggestion, as though it might have possibility, rather than outright rejecting it.

She hadn't said no. He stayed on that fact.

"He just knows I write stories about people."

So… "Can you introduce me as a person from one of your stories?"

She was looking at him, but he couldn't tell what she was thinking. Didn't want to push.

And wasn't used to waiting around to lose, either.

"I just want to tell him hello, Shelby. I want him to see my face. To hear my voice. You can always delete the video if you decide you don't want to send it."

When her gaze narrowed, he felt caught. Like a fish on a hook. And he didn't know why.

"This is in case you don't make it, isn't it?"

She saw things others didn't. Could be a problem down the road for a guy who kept his private life strictly to himself.

And yet he kind of wanted to take on the challenge.

More than kind of.

She was done with him. He got that.

Understood it.

But they'd still be talking. Be in touch...

"Luke, it's in case you don't survive, isn't it?"

"Yes," he told her, looking her right in the eye. And didn't choke to death on the revelation.

SHE WAS MAKING too big a deal of things. Luke was just a subject from an article saying hello to her son.

But...whether Carter knew it or not, she was introducing her son to his father for the first time. With a recording her son could watch for the rest of his life.

In the future—even with Luke sitting right there, watching the video with an eighteen-year-old Carter—the moment would mean something.

She wasn't going to think about the alternative.

That Luke wouldn't be around to sit with his son and do anything in the years to come.

Or that she wouldn't.

Bottom line, Luke was Carter's father. He had every right to his son, whether she wanted it that way or not. Which was why she'd gone to him when she'd found out she was pregnant—even after he'd served up that horrible breakfast—to tell him about the baby.

And why she'd stepped forward to identify him when she'd seen his picture in the news.

Apparently done with pacing, Luke sat down on the sofa, phone for Hudson still in his hand.

Ready to record one more video before sending the device back up to the surface.

It wasn't up to her to decide if Luke was good enough, if he was worthy of Carter. Unless he proved himself unhealthy for Carter's well-being, unless a court designated him as such, she had no right to keep him from his son.

And whether she brought Luke to Carter or not, her son was almost certainly going to find him on his own someday.

After Carter had been robbed of the possibility of growing up with a father's support and tutelage.

Luke bounced the phone a time or two in his hand.

She'd given up her purse. Had nothing with which to tie back her hair. "He's used to seeing me in a ponytail at home," she said inanely. Fighting back panic at how quickly life was moving forward. At how little control she seemed to have.

Even over her own body's wants. Or her wayward heart. She added the last silent lament as the man causing all the confusion in her life scooted a bit closer, revealing the video recorder up on the screen he was holding.

"I got used to putting it up when he was a baby," she said. "He was constantly grabbing at it—and I gotta tell you, that dude has a strong grip."

Luke raised a brow but otherwise just continued to watch her.

"And an even stronger pull," she went on. She swallowed, then said, "Plus, it's easier to clean the house without it falling all over my shoulders and blocking my view—you know, when I'm looking for toys under the television set. And yes, I hear myself rambling."

"Best just to do it, then, right?" Luke's calm tone stopped her.

"Why aren't you nervous?" He was the one making a first impression.

His shrug seemed to shove some of his calm over to settle upon her. "I'm me. Like it or not, it's what he gets."

Yes, but... She frowned. "Don't you want him to like

you? Or think you're cool or something?" Didn't he want to impress his own son?

"I want him to know, eventually, that he can depend on me."

Holding his gaze, she felt her eyes fill with tears. Tried to blink away the evidence but couldn't move her eyelids fast enough. Oh, God, what was the man doing to her?

"He's not going to trust me if I try to be cool and then he finds out I'm not."

His gaze sharpened, seemed to jump right into hers with a message he wanted her to get. She received one. Just wasn't sure it was the right one.

"Like I can't trust you because sometimes you're a wonderful guy and other times you slam doors in people's faces." That look compelled her to be who she was. To say what she was thinking.

It wasn't just the door. Or even the money. He'd never contacted her again. Not in almost five years' time.

And if the threesome, the house party, all the other less-than-stellar moments in his life turned out to not be the result of identity theft...

The Cayman Islands account, financed with money he'd sent through a fake charity... What was that all about?

Michaels had seen him in person on that one. They knew Luke was the one who'd mandated the entire setup...

As thoughts flew through her mind, Luke just sat there, watching her as though he was reading every single one of them.

"Do you blame me?" she asked, not even sure what the question encompassed. Just needing...words.

"No."

She needed more. Had just told him there'd be nothing

between them other than co-parenting, so had given up any right to ask more of him.

"Okay, let's do this."

Picturing her son's grin as she'd just seen it on the phone still in her hand, she scooted her head next to Luke's and smiled at the camera he held in front of them.

"Hey, buddy! I miss you so much and wanted to show you my work! This man—his name's Luke, and he fights mountain fires and stuff. I told him about you, and he wanted to say hello!"

"Hey, Carter," Luke said, jumping right in as if they had cue cards or had practiced. "I hear you like to fish, and I do, too. I wish I had a doughnut right now. I think getting a dog someday would be cool. Dogs like to ride in trucks, and I have a truck. And I just want to thank you for letting your mom be away to work, because she tells stories that help a lot of people, and helping people is the best thing…"

Shelby picked up when Luke faltered. "Okay, buddy, we have to get back to work! You be good for Grandma, and make sure you both do what Charlie tells you to do because he's really smart, and you better be practicing at frogs, because we're going to have a long contest when I get home. I love you, buddy. Most and most."

Reaching out over Luke's phone-holding arm, Shelby pushed the button to end recording. And then jumped up off the couch. Headed straight for the small partition in the back of the shelter. Sat on the stool.

And let the tears flow.

Chapter Twenty

He could hear her crying. Not that she made any sobbing sounds or moans. But the sniffles. The occasional nose-blowing.

Luke was definitely a single-focused guy—and right then, he was focused solely on Shelby. He delivered the message phone to the cage, pushed to send it along the conveyer for the slightly angled ride to the woods farther down the beach.

And then he paced until the monotony and lack of any accomplishment whatsoever drove him to the kitchen. There was fresh bread. A toaster oven. Packets of oatmeal and…a toaster oven to heat water for it. Moving without questioning decisions, he meandered around the small space, preparing nourishment. He peeled an orange, separated the sections and put them on plates, along with the toast on the outside of the bowls of oatmeal. He found some brown sugar, spooned dollops of that atop the cooked oats. And put both plates, with spoons and cups of coffee—and for her, a bottle of water—down on the small table for two along the wall at end of the counter.

He'd counted on the sounds, the obvious scents of food drawing Shelby out. It wasn't often that his plans failed. But he also didn't get deterred easily.

Standing halfway between the sink and the back partition, he called out, "Hey, Shelby, breakfast is ready. And there's water so you can rehydrate."

No response.

He stood there a second. Did he wait for her? Go eat, whether she did or not?

Communication. He'd said he'd do better.

"I'm, uh, not sure what to do here," he said then. And felt like a total ass. "You're an adult and have the right to not eat and also the right to some privacy, but if I eat without you, it seems rude, and... I don't really want to." The silence was acute. "So, in case you missed it, this was me, communicating."

With that, he turned and went to the table. Sat down. Tense. As though life and death would be determined by oatmeal and oranges.

Plan C hadn't yet formed when Shelby appeared. A bit red-eyed but otherwise seeming in complete control.

"I miss him," she said as she sat down.

He figured it was a lot more than that. From what she'd said, being away for a few days at a time wasn't uncommon, to the point that her son had his own room in her mother's home.

But welcoming a chance to be done with the whole communication thing while he ate, he let her excuse slide and asked, instead, "What's frogs?" He'd been wondering that on and off throughout breakfast preparation.

"A toddler video game," she said. She took a couple of bites of oatmeal as though she hadn't just eaten a hearty helping of pasta the night before, then continued. "Whenever I come back from a trip, I take half a day off just to be with him, and we have game marathons. I generally tell him which one I'm choosing a day or two before I get home so that he can practice. But mostly so that he has something to do to work toward me being home again. As though by playing, my being there gets closer."

He stared. "Did you read that in a book or something?" As soon as he was free, he was buying them all. Every parenting book he could find. He'd devour them multiple times if necessary.

"Read what? About the frog game?"

"No, about giving him something to work toward for your arrival, as though giving him some sense of control as he works toward the end date…"

Holding an orange piece between her lips, she pulled it back and said, "No. It just makes sense. Instead of hearing him ask me a million times when I'm coming home, give him something to distract him from the fact that I'm not there yet."

So maybe not books. Just common sense. He had a good supply of that.

And she was eating every bite of the food he'd prepared for her.

Two wins, right there together.

He was on a roll.

THEY CLEANED UP the dishes, working seamlessly, without words. And then watched a couple of movies—one her pick, one his—and discussed them both as though the fate of the world hinged on their opinions.

For a moment here and there, she forgot that their lives were at stake. Was able to ignore the fact that they were trapped in a tiny underground space and if they dared climb up to the beach above them, they'd likely be killed.

Or at least, he would.

The killer the night before had specifically asked for Luke's location. No mention of her.

If she left, now that the world knew that Luke wasn't dead, would she be safe?

Did she want to risk her life finding out?

Or tempt the fates that had allowed her to escape her own death once already that week? Had she not acted as quickly as she had, or found the exact space in which to move her vehicle, she'd have died, just like Luke's father had.

And until someone knew why the killer had taken out Luke's father over a year before attempting to kill Luke, she wasn't going to assume that she was no longer a target just because she didn't know why she would be.

They had canned chicken with crackers for lunch, watched another movie and were in the process of a half-hour workout, with Luke leading the regime, when the clang of a message arriving stopped them both. Turning down the music he'd had playing from the selection of compact discs, he took the rungs of the ladder steps two at a time while her heart thudded in her chest.

Did they have a response from Carter?

Would her son acknowledge the man she'd introduced him to? Would Luke be hurt if he didn't?

Not her business. Outside of her influence. Shouldn't be her concern.

There was only one new video.

From Hudson.

She stood with Luke at the bottom of the ladder, their shoulders touching as they watched the video together.

"Finally. A concrete answer," the man started, sending Shelby's nervous system into overdrive. Would Luke be vindicated? Or more enmeshed?

Were they getting out?

And going to be facing everything that meant in their personal lives?

"—found the—" Hudson was saying when she calmed the roaring in her ears enough to tune back in.

Lives were at stake, and she was freaking out?

"—tracker," Hudson said.

What now? They'd found the *tracker*? Which would lead to who'd been tracking them?

"It was in your watch, Luke," Hudson's voice continued, unaware that the man he'd spoken to had just stiffened against her. Every muscle and nerve was taut.

"Apparently, you weren't wearing it when Johnson's team ran the wand over you. Or the watch was somehow missed," Hudson continued, as he would since he was just a video.

Reaching over, she pushed Pause.

"In your watch?" she said, looking up at Luke. "How... When did anyone... It's not even electronic..."

"Bugs these days are so small they could be in your pocket and you wouldn't know it." Luke's response was impersonal. Cold, even. "And I have no idea how. Other than when I was unconscious in the hospital or in the shower, I've had the watch on."

She could attest to the fact that man slept with the watch on. At least, he had the previous night.

He hit Play again.

"We'll need to know every time you'd had it off," Hudson said then, as though, video or no, he'd been privy to their response. "The tracker itself isn't made or sold in the US, so it won't be as easy to trace as it might have been, though we have an expert working on it. It was too small for any hope of getting fingerprints off it, and there were none on your watch other than your own. It's being logged as evidence for now. We're looking at the Cayman Islands financials again, just in case we get lucky and find a purchase that fits, but in the meantime, we now have a solid plan."

She held on to Luke's elbow with both hands.

"We're driving the tracker, now implanted in another watch, to a cabin in a closed ski resort near Flagstaff. A fire perimeter is currently being dug around the old building and at the edge of the property, too. We'll have people all around the area, watching for anything or anyone around, and have drones set to send up as well, so we'll have eyes from all angles. Hopefully, we'll have good news for you before morning."

The screen went dead.

Not sure what to expect from Luke, Shelby stood still, looking at the white arrow on the video's starting frame.

"It was my father's watch," he said. "He gave it to me before I left for my first hotshot assignment. He told me that he hoped it would keep me on track and safe."

He walked away from her then, leaving her feeling inappropriately bereft, and she moved back to the couch. It wasn't like there were a lot of choices of places to be in the small space.

Or much to do, either.

Except try her best to ignore a cacophony of feelings for Luke.

And fight the thoughts that kept trying to run away with her.

STANDING AT THE kitchen sink, he recorded his response to Hudson, telling the man what he'd just told Shelby. He'd had the watch on since waking in the hospital and Detective Johnson returned it to him. Other than to bathe, at which time, it had been just outside the shower, which had had a glass door and had been fully visible to him.

This led him to believe that maybe Johnson had been the one out to get him all along. He paused recording when the thought struck him.

It didn't fit the team's theory.

Or make sense, when he considered how easily Johnson could have just done him in. A gunshot, claiming that Luke, in his suspended mental state, had gotten aggressive, taken his gun from him and tried to kill himself. Or any number of other scenarios.

Still, Johnson could be on the take. Apparently, Luke's life thief had no qualms about spending money in large quantities.

Tapping Record again, he sent a short message suggesting Hudson take another look at Johnson. Then hit Save and climbed up to send the recording on its way.

They were getting closer, which elated him. And bothered him a bit, too. When Shelby was safe, free, would he ever have a chance to speak one-on-one with her again?

Other than about their son?

What if he never remembered the day she'd come to tell him about her pregnancy? What if he couldn't ever explain, even to himself, why he'd done such a despicable thing to her?

Watching her as she sat on the couch—just sat there— he couldn't just let it all go without attempting to salvage some kind of friendship with her.

Saving things was his forte.

Taking a cue from her from the day before, he poured a couple of glasses of wine and carried them over to the couch, handing one to her.

She sipped and then said, "Thank you."

Reminding him of his own eagerness to consume the

beverage when she'd brought it to him. How he'd welcomed the libation that might help him chill out a bit.

He hadn't consumed enough of it the previous night to feel any effect.

Shelby had been all he'd needed.

It felt like she was all he needed, still.

Which was so unlike anything he remembered himself to be…except that week she'd interviewed him…

"We did okay, talking about the movies, yeah?" he asked, sitting not quite a cushion's width away from her, lounging back as though there were no cares in the world.

"What?"

"Discussing, giving out thoughts…the whole communication thing." He'd get it right eventually. Somehow, making a plan to save a burning mountain seemed easier.

And more likely to bring success.

She shook her head, took another sip of wine, sliding her knee up onto the couch as she turned some to face him. "This is what I'm talking about, Luke," she said, sounding to him more as if she were talking to her four-year-old than to a proven lifesaver.

The saver of a woman's life, a woman whose son later came to kill him?

He couldn't grasp it. So he let it go.

Figuring out how to make Shelby happy enough to have him in her life, not just her son's, was far more important than comprehending why a son would hunt down the guy who'd rescued his mother.

He'd been waiting for her to expand on exactly what she *was* talking about. When she didn't, he knew he was on the hot seat.

He was supposed to get it. Had missed some big emotional tell, apparently. "What?" he finally asked. All he had was honesty. And not even a full memory of that. "What are you talking about?"

"We just hear ground-shaking news, and you want to talk about a plebian conversation we had about movies?"

Relief flooded him. He grinned.

"You think this is funny?" Her tone certainly wasn't anywhere near laughter.

"No!" He got that out immediately. And with a completely open, totally sober expression, told her, "I think this is more a matter of life and death than funny," he said, and when she frowned, her lips pursing as though she didn't believe him, he added, "I was grinning because I'd thought I'd missed something big, and instead you just didn't like my way of using small talk to get the conversationing started."

Not a word, *conversationing.*

She didn't add a single syllable to it. But she was still facing him.

"So...to move on to the... Oh, hell..." He stopped. "I want my watch back." There. That was real.

Studying the shelves holding various media cases, he listened to the silence. Then started to fill it.

"After Mom died, my father and I... We just kind of became not just father and son but trusted help mates. Best friends, even."

He'd certainly never had a buddy he talked to about things. But his father had always understood, even without a lot of words.

"I think—no, I *know*—it scared him when I signed on with the hotshots. But he wanted me to do it almost as badly as I did. He took his watch off his wrist the day I left on my first call. It was like a continuation of our bond. A talisman to bring me out of the flames. And each and every time, it did."

And he didn't have it now, when he was fighting his biggest demon ever.

Shelby's fingers touched his arm. Light chills sailed through him as though on a breeze. A breath of fresh air. And when he couldn't quite look at her, he glanced down at them. Saw them moving along the white mark left in his tan by the watch's disappearance.

"You've still got it, Luke. Like a reverse tattoo, it's right here, branded into your skin. The talisman-part of it, anyway. And that's all that really mattered. By the time the tan fades, you'll have the watch back."

He'd seen the tan marks. Had viewed that white skin as a symbol of his loss.

Glancing over at her, he wanted to kiss her, to lose himself in her physically. Instead, he said, "Thank you." And acknowledged to himself that the whole *talking about stuff* thing…with Shelby…might not be as deplorable, as painful, as difficult as he'd thought it would be.

Chapter Twenty-One

She was falling for him all over again. There was no point in denying that Luke Dennison had a hold on her. The man's effect on her was different from any other guy she'd ever known. Not just sexually, though there was definitely that, but heart-to-heart...

As it turned out, she didn't need him to talk for her to feel as though she knew.

But listening to him, even the struggle he made to get words out to her... It all hit her in every single feel she had.

Right or wrong, she did herself no favors by denying the problem.

Neither of them mentioned the fact that with the trap being set for their would-be killer that very night, their time together was drawing to a close. They didn't talk about what the next day would bring or what the life ahead might look like.

They should have. Should be using the quiet alone time allotted to them to discuss what shared parenting between them might look like. She didn't bring it up.

Neither did he.

He talked about his dad some. Maybe because he'd just become one? She told him a bit more about her mother. About the promise she'd extracted from Sylvia to never,

ever bad-mouth Shelby's father in front of Carter or to ever make him feel bad for loving his grandfather.

Not that Carter saw the man all that much. Three times in his lifetime, to date.

But if Sylvia ever broke her word, if she ever tried to make Carter choose between family members, then Carter wouldn't stay with her again.

Maybe she told Luke about the promise to assure him that his son wasn't being hurt as she'd been growing up. A fact she'd told him about briefly when mentioning why, in the past, she hadn't seen herself ever marrying.

And maybe it was to let him know that no matter what he'd done to Shelby, Carter would never be privy to the information. Or asked to choose between his mother and his father.

"I just want you to know," she said as they started in on their second glasses of wine, "as far as I'm concerned, as long as you're a decent dad, you'll be a welcome part of Carter's life."

The hand raising his glass to his mouth stopped mid-air, and Shelby's stomach sank. Not because she was afraid of him or what he'd say, but because she hadn't wanted to ruin the mood between them. Just for those hours…she wanted to be able to enjoy his…friendship.

But when he put the glass down and turned to face her, knee to knee on the cushion, face-to-face, she met his gaze. Whatever he had to say, she'd handle.

"The other night, in the cabin, when I first woke up and you were still asleep on the couch…my memories from our time together came back."

Oh, God. He was about to tell her about the money. Calling her a liar. And she didn't want to hear it. Didn't want to know.

But she wasn't going to start the future trying to pretend it hadn't happened. Or that he hadn't done those things. So she took a sip of wine. And waited.

Watching his obvious struggle to come up with the words he needed.

And knowing that she needed the truth.

To hear it.

And accept it.

Including why he'd been lying to her since that night, about shutting the door in her face.

"What I remember..." He looked her straight on, his vivid blue eyes filled with emotion that yanked at her, even as she fought to hold her distance.

"I wanted to come back for more."

What? Open-mouthed, she shook her head. But he continued to watch her, his gaze searching hers, until she could do nothing but stare right back at him.

"For the first time in my career, I understood why members of hotshot teams got married even though they had to be away so much. And knowingly and willingly risked their lives every single time they answered the call. To be honest, prior to...that week... I honestly thought they were all just either being selfish or had gotten married because they'd been raised to know it was expected of them..."

He broke eye contact then, straightened in his seat to reach for his wine without finishing what he'd started.

Leaving her hanging there.

Waiting.

For too long.

Until, not without a bit of ire, she said, "And?"

Looking over at her, he shrugged. "And I'm sorry that I brought it up, especially after your honesty this morning, but I thought this was what you wanted. Mutual honesty between us. Spoken out loud."

The walls that had begun rapidly erecting themselves around Shelby's heart disintegrated, and she took a full body-regenerating breath. And a small sip of wine, too. "I meant... And why is it that you think they get married now? What did you understand differently?"

"It's because they want to spend most—if not all—of their nonworking hours with that person. That they'd rather be with the one person than anyone else. Because they want to spend the rest of their lives doing what they can do to make that person happy."

She had to swallow. Her throat was a dry lump. Got her glass shakily to her lips.

"And you feel—*felt* that way?"

He didn't meet her gaze then. But he said, "I...remembered that I felt that way...the morning after..."

But the money...

"I remember that I was planning to reach out to you when I got back."

But he'd been injured. Had lost his memory.

"But you forgot me."

He glanced back at her. Shook his head. "No, after I got back, after I recovered what I believed was my full memory, I had second thoughts..."

Oh. Well, then.

"Not about how I felt but about how unfair it would be for me to ask you to take me on, because I knew I couldn't give up fighting wildfires. I'd been pretty clear that I wasn't a guy who could ever offer, or would ever ask for, a commitment and figured it was best just to leave it at that."

So when, a few months later, she'd come to tell him she was pregnant? He'd already moved on? Was afraid of what her being pregnant meant in light of what he'd thought their chances of making it would be?

"That's why you treated me so cruelly when I came to see you in Payson? You were trying to get rid of me for my own good?"

What was he, some God wannabe? Or a hero from a medieval romance novel? Seeking anger dulled the pain.

Elbows on his knees, Luke stared at the floor, shaking his head; then, turning, his eyes direct and open, he met her own had-to-be-pain-filled gaze. "I honestly and truly have no memory of that day, Shelby. Or of having breakfast sent up to your room, either, for that matter. But the day you came to Payson…if I was doing as you said and trying to do that kind thing for the long haul—saving you from me—I still can't see turning my back on my own child. Or, for that matter, leaving the mother of my child to cope alone, you or not. And I absolutely can't see turning you away if you'd come to me. Not for any reason. So maybe that's why I can't remember. Because I just plain don't want to live with that guy…"

Her eyes filled with tears. She didn't try to hide them. Or stop them.

And didn't stop him, either, when he took the wineglass from her hand, set it on the table, and then leaned over to cup her face and kiss her tears away.

HARD AND ACHING with the need to crawl on top of her, Luke's hands shook as he pulled them from Shelby's face. Letting his thumbs trail last, he took the remaining moisture from her cheeks with him.

Being in completely new territory, he didn't immediately know what would happen next or how it would happen, but the one and only thing he could count on was his instinct. It told him not to push.

Unfortunately, from there, he was on his inept own where Shelby was concerned. And lacking in some confidence since he couldn't remember why he'd treated her the way he did in the past.

When she leaned forward, watching him with slumberous brown eyes, he stayed completely still. There for her and nothing more.

Her lips touched his, more tentatively than they had the night before. He responded, holding back the passion burning through him. He knew she wanted him. She'd shown him over and over the night before. And she'd as much as told him so that morning.

When she'd also told him why she couldn't be with him.

While her lips continued to move softly on his, he made himself think about how badly he needed her friendship.

And how friends had each other's backs.

Then her tongue slid through his lips, engaging his in a dance that was already completely familiar. Totally theirs.

Just like the night before, he couldn't reject her. And he wasn't made of stone. His penis was tormenting him for release.

But...they weren't just a man and a woman attracted to each other.

Breaking contact with her mouth, he buried his face in her neck. Kissing her lightly. And then, not. With a hand on the side of her neck, he looked at her and said, "The future."

He braced for her immediate withdrawal. Got a nod instead.

"I know."

So they were stopping, right?

That's what had to happen.

She seemed to be waiting. Again.

And it hit him. *Words, dude.*

Words.

"I don't know how it's going to look."

"Me, either."

But she was still turned toward him. When he dropped his hand from her neck, she slid her fingers through his. And his body flared to life all over again.

From a hand touch? What the hell!

Did not bode well for the picture they were trying to paint.

"I want to tell you that I'll quit the hotshots. There are a lot of other jobs I can do with the forestry division, but..."

Her shaking head stopped his words. They'd come to an end, anyway.

"You are who you are, Luke. Just as I am. You try to change for me, I try to change for you... Changing the way that's elemental to who we are...it's not right. It's not anything akin to love..."

Her expression went immediately deadpan. And she hurried on, "Not that I'm saying we're falling in love or anything..."

"Then why do I feel like I might be?" And, whoa, buddy. That was why he didn't say much. His getting-right-to-the-pointness didn't often fit well with normal human interaction.

Relief flooded him as Shelby dropped his hand and sat back against the couch. He wasn't sure how to gauge the way she leaned forward with stilted moves and grabbed her wine. Sipping before she'd even returned upright.

"I'm not asking for anything," he said. Needing to make his situation clear. "I have no confidence I'd be good at it. Can't see a way I would be."

She sipped again, nodded. Glanced his way and then back toward her wine.

"Where you and I are concerned," he said, clarifying some more. "As a dad, I'm good."

He wasn't. How could he be? He hadn't done it yet. But she'd be there to help him. Carter would help him. Memories of his own father would help him. Members of his team would help him. He'd get that one right.

"Kids grow up and away. They need their independence," he said, afraid that her silence would leave a gaping hole that would ultimately turn into another mess up on his scorecard.

But, hell, wasn't the communication thing supposed to work both ways?

"But partners... Yeah, they're independent, but they're together, too. An entity. In the same home, sharing life side by side forever..."

Now he was some kind of romance nerd?

Silence was better than this.

Even if it pissed her off.

He'd said he'd do better. He hadn't said he could become someone he wasn't.

As the thought hit, another fell right on top of it: her saying that it wasn't right for either of them to try to become someone they were not.

And she was right.

He was meant to be the person he'd been born as. He could do better. There was always room for improvement.

But he couldn't be someone he was not.

"Life would be one big lie if we kid ourselves about what we're facing."

There.

He was done talking.

"I FEEL LIKE I might be, too."

Shelby had tried hard to keep the words to herself. It wasn't her way.

Nor could she just let Luke hang out there. The man was trying. Honestly look-her-straight-in-the-eye trying.

Whatever name she gave it, she cared far too much to ignore his attempt to make things better between them.

He looked at her.

And she flooded. Down below. And in her emotional well, too.

Somehow, she had to stop getting turned on every single time his gaze met hers in that deep way it was doing.

"And I don't see a way for it to work, either." But she couldn't look away.

Wouldn't ever turn her back on him.

"Maybe there's something we can't see yet."

Always the problem solver. That was Luke.

"Maybe." She couldn't argue the point.

"Do you want to look for it?"

Her lower end was too wet, and her throat, her lips, too dry. Heart thudding, she sat at the precipice, aware that if she took a leap, she'd be changing her life all over again.

She took a sip of wine, instead, and asked, "What if we don't find it?"

"What if it's there and we don't look?" he countered back.

He'd be leaving with no notice, any time of the day or night, to rush off into out-of-control flames. Possibly to never return. Every single time.

Could she live with that?

The answer she sought wasn't in that question. Of course she could live with that. Memories of Luke were better than no Luke at all. That wasn't the problem.

"Do you see any possibility at all that you'd want to come

home to me—not just Carter but me, too, even after he is grown—every single time you put the fire out?"

"I do."

Eyes flooding with tears, she threw herself at him.

And stilled completely when he held her back. "I can't promise, once I get out there on the mountain, how I'm going to feel. I don't know how I make both lives work."

His honesty nearly broke her heart. For the years they'd lost and the future they might not have.

"I can't promise that I'm ready to take it all on," she told him.

"This morning, you didn't want to try. Do you still feel that way?"

No. She didn't. Fear had her in its grip. He'd hurt her so badly she'd almost lost her ability to live with an open heart. For months, she'd been bitter...

He'd said that he remembered wanting to try in the past. But then he'd paid her off and denied their child.

The same child he was fighting for. Just as he fought every day he went to work. The lives he'd saved...the self-lessness he engaged in...

Her head and heart battled while he sat there, close but not touching. Watching her and seeming to be ready to accept whatever answer she gave.

There was only one. The honest one.

"It's too late for me to pretend, even to myself, that I don't have to give it a shot," she told him. "Now that I know you feel something, too. That you felt it back then. That I'm not imagining our connection..."

She wasn't going to throw herself at him again. He could come for it.

Or not.

Maybe they had to figure out how it would work before...

"No matter if it works or not, I'll always be here for you," he said, melting her heart all over again. "You're the mother of my child. I'm a friend for life. One who will always have your back."

It was like their own private little ceremony—him saying his vows; her getting all weepy, listening to him giving her her heart's greatest desire. Becoming her dream come true.

With trembling lips, Shelby pressed her mouth to his, hard. Stopping him before he made more promises he didn't yet know he could keep.

Chapter Twenty-Two

The sex was better than ever. Intensely physical. Ears to toes…they explored it all. Teased and tickled. For a time, he forgot everything but the sensations exploding through him.

But he remembered, each time, to pull out before emptying his seed inside her. It wasn't like they could send out for condoms. They'd used up what they had the night before.

And he absolutely was not going to trap her with another unplanned child. There were some things a guy didn't lose track of. No matter how mind-blowing it was to enter Shelby, she mattered more.

Lying on damp sheets a few hours after he'd poured their first glass of wine—remembering how he'd been hoping to somehow convince Shelby to be friends with him—he could hardly believe how far they'd come.

"If we find a way to make the rest of it work even half as good as this part does, we'll be home free," he told her, exhausted but revved up, too. Needing to know the next step. And the one after that.

Wanting solutions, not unanswered problems.

How in the hell could he approach a wildfire encroaching a thousand acres with no fear, knowing exactly what he had to do to contain it, but couldn't see himself getting it right when it came to keeping one woman happy?

"I see you in Carter."

Not the words he'd been expecting to hear. The boy was biologically his. Of course there'd be some resemblance.

"He gets so frustrated sometimes, when he's learning something new. And, with a baby growing into a toddler, everything is new. From learning to roll over, pull himself up, walk—the boy didn't seem to care how many times he fell down, bumped his head or landed on hard things. He'd just get right back up and try again."

He couldn't help but grin at that one, but he didn't see how being determined beyond logic, and somewhat hard-headed, helped their situation any.

Her head on his shoulder, her hair splayed out around them, she looped her leg over his midsection, causing his hips to automatically rise to press against her, but he didn't have the energy to take it any further.

She didn't seem to, either, just settled that way on top of him, as though bedding down for the night.

He loved having her there. And didn't feel at all ready for sleep.

"I'll tell you what I tell our son," she said then, which was when he realized they were still talking. About?

"You take things one step at a time. You're not always going to get it right the first time. You're not always going to know how to get it right. You can't expect to master something the first time you're presented with it. Or be an expert at everything you try. You aren't going to understand every aspect of every challenge when you're first faced with it…"

His grin had grown into a full-out smile. "I get it," he said, stopping her mid-flow. And: "'Aspect?' You use words like that with a four-year-old kid?"

"No."

"I get it," he said again, completely serious, afraid his teasing had stifled her.

"So...we're trying?" she asked.

"Yes." He'd passed that point already.

Just wasn't sure what the next one was. Tried to foresee the most immediate challenges that would be facing them when they got out of the hole in the ground. Couldn't land on just one.

How did he know what lay ahead when he didn't know how his current situation was going to end? It wasn't like a wildfire that would eventually die down, the only questions there being how many acres burnt, how much property, how many lives were lost before it ended.

What if he remembered all the things that were currently a blank to him? From party girls to paying off the most incredible woman he'd ever met. From inventing fake charities to drop money in foreign accounts to denying his own child...

What if he didn't?

"I should be out there, catching my so-called killer, not lying here, waiting for someone else to do it for me." He was a doer.

And if that was the only trait he'd passed on to his son, he could live with that. As long as Carter knew to focus on doing good works, not evil ones...

"You hired the people who are doing it," Shelby said, her voice drowsy. "In the legal world, that makes you as culpable..."

Gotta love a woman who could talk law logic and fall asleep drooling on your chest at the same time.

Luke was still smiling, drifting off to sleep himself, when he heard the cage clang.

The lights were still on. They hadn't had dinner.

Raising his free arm to glance at the time, he was already out of bed when he saw the bare spot on his wrist.

"It's almost nine," Shelby said. She was out of bed, too, looking toward the digital plug-in clock among the electronics in the living area.

Back in his shorts within seconds, Luke ran barefoot up the wooden ladder rungs.

"You think it could be over already?" Shelby called out from just below him, hope filling her voice.

"Maybe." But he didn't dare hope. Couldn't lose focus on the facts by allowing his own personal wants to get in the way. Not when it came to battling death.

He pulled out what looked like the same phone he'd sent up hours before. Jumped to the ground from the third rung up and, still wearing only his shorts, joined Shelby, who was in her shorts and shirt, on the couch.

Her bra still lying on the floor in front of the right-side cushion, where he'd dropped it earlier. He liked knowing that she was still bare beneath the thin cotton shirt.

There for him to pleasure.

He liked knowing, because he wasn't sure what they were going to see on that tape. Their potential killer had apparently been stalking him for some time. Had stolen his identity and, even after a professional hit man had been killed, had still managed to escape without his identity being discovered. Didn't make sense that he'd be taken down within an hour or so of an operation getting underway. Because with the drive involved, that tracker would only have arrived at the ski resort sometime that evening.

There was only one video. From Hudson. Luke had figured that much already. With no phones being used to communicate between Sylvia Harrington and Charlie in Tucson, unless there was an emergency, all videos were being passed by Sierra's Web drivers.

Didn't mean he hadn't hoped he'd see his son again. Maybe even get a personal hello from the boy.

Shoulders touching, he and Shelby sat together while he called up the video and hit Play.

"An evening check-in to let you know that the team has arrived at the cabin near Flagstaff. Everything's in place as described. So far, all is quiet. I'll keep you posted, with as much immediacy as possible, if anything changes during the night."

Reaching over him, Shelby hit Pause.

"You feel good about that?" she asked him, sending off a surge of gratitude within him. Way more than anything he felt when his team turned to him for decisions and assignments.

She trusted him enough to want his judgment.

Who'd have thought the concept could be so heady?

"It's what I expected," he told her, pushing Play again. He wanted to kiss her in the worst way but needed to get the rest of the business out of the way first.

"Looking at specific dates and times of small purchases, fast food—that kind of thing—and comparing them against charges on the Cayman account, we've got a solid case for identity theft against this guy. He's careful to lay low when you're home but moved about pretty freely when you were off the grid with a fire, using the Cayman Islands account exclusively. We've been trying to figure out how he knew about the account when, by all traces, it should have been only you and Michaels who knew the account even existed. So we're looking into Michaels's associates but have to be aware that the guy might not be a US citizen and could have some link to the account in Cayman Islands himself. For all we know, he was a banker there who wanted to relocate in the US and is using you to do it…"

All of which just frustrated the fire out of him. He'd told Michaels to donate to charities. He remembered that part. But designating which ones? Choosing bogus ones? And the whole offshore account?

The account had been set up shortly after the Marnell injury. He had to admit that it was possible there were parts of his memory he'd never gotten back.

Which brought him right back to Shelby.

The things he'd done.

Would they always be there—unspoken, put to rest but still existing between them?

"From the phone records, we've been able to viably prove that this guy has been impersonating you for years. As smart as he appears to be, getting away with this for so long, eluding us now, he made the stupid mistake of using the same device—which lets us triangulate cell-tower locations using the International Mobile Equipment Identity number. He just updated the prepaid SIM cards."

Luke gladly took the small bit of good news. They were making progress. Not as quickly as he needed, but he had to remind himself that while it felt like it had been a lifetime since he'd woken up in the hospital, it had only been a matter of days.

"Nothing new on the hit man, Benjamin Garvey. We've talked to his mother, to friends, coworkers, and they all say that Benjamin held you in the highest esteem. To the point of letting people know that he was to be told when you were in danger. It's looking more likely that someone tipped him off to our guy, that he somehow didn't get the memo on Bruce and Lorraine and was just out to save you—"

Holy hell. Now a guy died specifically because of him?

The complete opposite of his life's purpose?

Shelby hugged his arm holding the phone, pulling it between her breasts and holding it there. Bringing him home.

Didn't make the death right. But it made him hate himself for it a little less.

She hit Pause. "You remember his mother?" she asked.

And lead hit his gut again as he shook his head. The guy died for him, and he couldn't even remember the mother's name? He told her the truth: "I don't remember any of their names. Most of the time, I don't even know them. I get them to the medics, and I move on to the next..."

Always out to save humanity, just not to get too close to it.

Was he kidding himself that he could pull off a love thing?

Since there was no way he was walking away from Shelby or their son, ever, he was just going to have to find one.

He pushed Play again, needing to get the message over with so he could carry Shelby back to bed, cuddle her close and get some rest.

"—from danger," Hudson said, finishing the sentence Shelby had cut off. "That's it, other than something Charlie shared during private radio check-in a couple of hours ago. We aren't talking about the DNA test, as you said you wanted to know results, no questions asked; but I thought you'd want to know, Carter recognized you from the tape. He was quite excited, apparently, telling his grandmother about seeing you with the cat you rescued outside his day care. He said he saw the cat run out the door and chased it, and you caught it and gave it back to him but told him that he shouldn't ever, ever talk to strangers. You made him promise not to tell anyone he'd talked to you, and you wouldn't tell, either, as long as he didn't ever do it again. He said you called it a *buy*. He thought it was quite cool that he knew you before his mom picked you for her work..."

The words might have continued. If so, he didn't hear them.

While his ears roared inside his head, Shelby snatched the phone from him and disappeared to the tiny partitioned-off toilet area. He stood. He watched her go.

And knew that it was no mistake that she'd run to the far-thest point she could get from him in what had just changed from an underground shelter to an underground prison.

TEARS POURED DOWN her cheeks. Angry tears. Really, really angry tears.

How *could* he?

Had it all been lies? The not believing that he had a son? His not remembering sending her away? His emotional acceptance that he was really a father?

The insistence he was going to be in his son's life... Yeah, that had obviously been true. He'd just lied about not knowing about Carter.

And had probably known there was no way on earth he could compel her to give up her son's DNA to a man she'd known, briefly, five years before.

She could simply have denied having sex with him.

And without that proof, he couldn't force her to let him be part of his son's life.

He'd known better than to just approach her with an apparent change of heart, almost five years later, and simply ask her if he could see Carter.

Shaking so hard she couldn't hold the tissue to her nose, she tried for a third time to get a good blow in. Took some deep breaths.

Wiped her eyes with tight, furious fists.

She wasn't going to cry another tear for the man.

Nor was she going to hide on a toilet.

He was the one who'd behaved like sewage, not her.

Face clean, she waited until she was sure all moisture had stopped flowing and stepped out into the room, expecting Luke to be on the couch.

Or in bed asleep. And it better be the bed they'd had sex in because she most certainly wasn't going to be lying down in that bed again...

He wasn't asleep. Or lying down.

He stood, arms folded, leaning back against the kitchen sink. He'd put on his shirt.

"Why?"

He shook his head.

"And this is trying to do better in the communication department?" she snapped, uncaring if she sounded irrational.

"I don't know why." He threw up his hands, met her gaze head-on. Didn't even bother to blink with shame.

She didn't get it. Didn't get *him*.

How could one man be so giving—so selfless—and so disgustingly horrid, too?

"That's your story, then? You don't know why you just happened to be outside my son's day care when he let the cat out?"

His eyes widened a bit at that, which just pissed her off more. Anything he did right then, even evaporate into thin air, would make her mad. She just couldn't...

Couldn't...

"Yeah, I know about the cat," she snapped in a nasty tone she'd never heard come out of her own mouth before. Her mother's, yes... After her father had broken Sylvia's heart for the final time.

She didn't care. Luke wasn't her father. They weren't

married and... "He didn't keep his word to you, so if you think you were something special—well, just forget it."

Luke stood up straight, surprise written all over him. "He told you about me?"

"No." She glanced away. "It wasn't about you." She wanted that part quite clear. "Carter told me he let it out. When I asked if they got it back, he said yes and then added that a man outside helped him, and he wasn't supposed to say that part because the man was a stranger."

So there. Carter had trusted his mother more than he'd feared being in trouble. For either of his wrongdoings: letting the cat out and talking to a stranger.

"You're doing a great job with him." Luke's gaze was completely serious, his tone even more so. She listened for defensiveness. For anger. For blame outside himself.

Heard none of it.

He was just doing it to confuse her. Acting like the man she'd first thought him to be.

And then thought him to be again.

"I'm warning you right now. You stay away from my son." She couldn't keep him away forever. But she could make him take her to court. And she had a whole lot to say about a man who denied his child for years and then waited outside his day care to approach him rather than contact her.

"He's my son, too."

Yeah, well, she'd see about that. No way...

Anger was getting her nowhere but sick to her stomach.

"Why?" she asked again.

"I don't know."

Another flare of anger shot through her. She let it pass. She would not become a bitter woman living with an angry heart. If for no other reason than because Carter deserved better.

She was off men, though.

Most definitely. Forever.

"How can you not know?"

"Because I don't remember any of it!" Luke didn't raise his voice. He didn't slam on the counter or do any of the things her father used to do when he'd been caught.

She heard the vehemence in his voice, though.

"I don't remember knowing I had a son. I don't remember turning my back on him, and I damned well don't remember sitting outside his day care—or ever seeing him before in my life."

For a second there, hope soared.

But sense knocked it out of the air to plop back down at her feet. Funny how the man could remember everything else about his life but just conveniently forgot the times that had to do with her and Carter. Other than an out-of-control house party, a threesome between strangers—both things which she found distasteful—the only other thing he'd apparently forgotten was the Cayman account.

And the house party, the threesome and use of the Cayman account Luke had set up could all be put down to his stolen identity.

Which left only things to do with her and Carter that he was "forgetting." And that was far too coincidental for her to just have faith that he was telling her the truth.

Nor could she put those actions down to anyone else.

She'd seen the man before he'd shut the door in her face at his home address.

And her son had recognized him from a damned video. *He'd been watching Carter at day care?* Every time the fact hit her, she lost her breath.

She couldn't keep hoping. Keep making excuses.

She couldn't do it again. Couldn't get sucked back in.

For some reason—maybe just maturity or, more likely,

his own father's death—Luke had had a change of heart about being a father himself.

And her walking into that hospital room to identify him… He'd had to think the stars had aligned for him perfectly on that one.

She'd given him an opportunity too good to be true.

She fully believed that he hadn't remembered anything yet when she first saw him earlier in the week. But when his memory had come back…

He'd seen his chance.

"I don't remember, Shelby." His gaze implored her.

And…no.

"I don't believe you." She knew how hurtful the words would be to him.

She said them anyway.

But wasn't 100 percent sure she believed them, either.

She just knew she couldn't trust him, no matter how much her heart cried out for him.

And without trust, she couldn't let him anywhere near her son, or her heart.

Chapter Twenty-Three

Luke watched her turn her back on him. The slice he felt inside… Had that been what it felt like when he'd denied their child and shut his door in her face?

Frustrated beyond endurance, he forced himself to remain completely still, to breathe, to count until the first stab of loss passed.

He didn't even consider following her as she ducked behind the partition with the second bed in it. A space neither of them had occupied during the more than twenty-four hours they'd occupied the small shelter. He didn't blame her for being done with him. Given the circumstances, he'd walk away from himself if it was possible.

Pouring the rest of the unconsumed wine in the sink, he cleaned the glasses. Tended to his own nightly ablutions. And then, leaving on only a small light over the sink—still needing to see his surroundings even after Shelby had turned off the small light shining from behind her partition—he told the mother of his child a silent good night. He grabbed a pillow off the remaining bed—the unmade, love-mussed sheets mocking him—and dropped down to the couch.

They'd made love there, too.

He needed rest. And while he was used to bunking in unfamiliar places and had no trouble catching shut-eye when and where he could, he wasn't going to put himself through a night on the hard ground.

So, determined—and with an arm up over his face—Luke willed himself to sleep. He closed his eyes.

And waited.

Turned over and waited some more.

Repositioned. Waited.

And just kept seeing Shelby's face when she'd told him she didn't believe him. It was like the image was glued to the backs of his eyelids.

He wanted to make things right. And...couldn't.

How did he remember what he couldn't remember?

And yet...why did he just not remember things that mostly had to do with her? He didn't remember setting up the Cayman account, and according to Michaels, he'd done that in person. So there was that.

Sierra's Web had determined that the partying had been done by his identity thief.

But Carter?

He'd actually been stalking his own son? Sitting outside his day care?

He didn't see it. Not ever.

Still...the things Carter said he'd said to him—not to ever talk to strangers, even one returning a runaway cat—he could hear himself having a conversation like that. Not in memory but in imagination. It resonated with the person he felt himself to be.

But the rest...

He just kept coming back to what he knew but didn't remember. He wanted to believe in the man he felt he was. The man he wanted to know.

Facts weren't pointing him in that direction.

And he was nothing if not a fact guy.

One who made life-and-death decisions based on the speed and direction of wind, watching minute-to-minute reports to adjust plans over and over as needed.

He'd spent the past few days listening to report after report. The facts were speaking.

And as much as he'd like to change what he was hearing about himself, just like with the wind, he couldn't force his will on things that were out of his control.

No matter how determined he might be to make things right.

So maybe it was time to switch gears. To figure out what to do about the situation he was stuck in. Circumstances seemed to mostly center around Shelby.

But...

He sat up.

What if it wasn't Shelby specifically, but rather the timing? She'd definitely made him uneasy, with the emotional charges she'd lit inside him. He'd had a head injury shortly after leaving her with the situation completely unresolved. Had some part of his subconscious decided to suppress that which created conflict between who he knew himself to be and the man Shelby brought out in him?

Obviously, he'd remembered at some point, though. At least during her visit to tell him about the baby. How else would he have known to look the child up?

The first-known account of him acting in a way that he couldn't now believe...other than leaving her the money, which could have been meant to pay her expenses for the week since, technically, their association had turned personal...the first-known account was him denying her pregnancy as being his responsibility. Which had come after the first memory loss. Had that head injury unrooted something in him, giving him some kind of multiple personality dysfunction?

He'd heard that emotional trauma could cause severe conditions—but how different personalities were triggered in one guy, how they presented...

Sweating profusely, he jumped up off the couch.

As soon as Shelby's life was confirmed to be out of danger, he was going to see a therapist. He'd go through shock treatment, if they still did that kind of thing. Or whatever else it took.

He had a family to provide for. Even though they weren't going to be living like one.

He had to know he was still a guy who could be trusted.

SHELBY WOKE WITH little light. She couldn't see the clock in the living area from behind her partition but felt rested.

She'd given up. Trapped underground, she'd had nowhere to go. There'd been nothing she could do, not even for her son, at the moment. Carter was safe. She was officially off duty from her entire life.

With the tracker found and nowhere near, she was physically safe.

Rest had been so turbulent during the past few days that she'd given up on trying to figure out anything and had just gone to sleep.

And then she was awake again.

Everything she'd escaped from was still there.

Including Luke Dennison.

She saw his feet propped up on the arm of the couch as she took a quick glance at the clock in the living area on her way to the back partition. Seven.

Had to be in the morning, right?

She hadn't slept through an entire day, had she?

Disoriented, lonely, she did her business, changed into clean clothes—a pair of blue shorts and a white sleeveless top—and thought about hand-washing the dirties...

No. She was not going to nest. To settle into life underground with Luke.

Her heart would never survive.

She was just finishing up at the sink in the kitchen, was putting her travel toothbrush back in its little holder, when she heard a message clang.

Luke must have sprung off the couch—leading her to believe he'd been awake, listening to her—as he was at the ladder by the time she'd turned her head in that direction.

In wrinkled beige shorts, he was up the ladder and then jumped down, barefoot, to the cement floor, already turning on the screen.

She was afraid for a second that he was going to cut her out of their briefing, but she gave him credit when he joined her by the sink, holding the phone so she could see it, too, before he pressed Play.

He didn't say a word. For once, she was glad.

Hudson's news shot at her the second the video started. "We didn't get him. There was infrared footage that showed a body in the area—six feet or so, at best guess, on foot—shortly after dark. But it looked up through what we believe were night goggles of some kind, seemed to pause on each drone we had in the air and, after a few more minutes of ground surveillance, it disappeared. Leaving no trail. Just vanished."

"How can someone just evaporate?" she cried out, so done with...everything. "This isn't a cartoon here. It's real life!"

Luke's gaze met hers, seemingly concerned, but she couldn't take him in. The man was off-limits to her.

Period.

And she should be keeping her mouth shut so as to not invite his attention.

She stared at the X shapes in the overstitching on the pockets of his shorts. *X marks the spot.* Was the same stitching on his fly?

Hudson was going on about the details of the night, the plan having continued with no activity, the bodies on the ground searching for whoever had been in the perimeter of the infrared cameras they'd set up but then just seemed to no longer be visible to them.

"We're doubling up on the evidence we do have on this guy, following every lead on his five-year trail. We'll find him. And in the meantime, if you two need anything down there, let us know."

That was it? They'd just been told they were being subjected to another day of lost life in the dungeon?

Okay, way too dramatic, but...

"The guy's prepared, probably an outdoorsman," Luke said. "All he'd need was a foil-encased fabric to wrap in to avoid infrared detection."

"But he didn't stick around and attempt anything because he knew he was being watched?" she asked.

They were still fighting for their lives together. They could talk business.

She was making up the rules as she went along.

And it was ridiculous to think that they'd exist in the small space for what could be another twenty-four hours with a cold war between them.

Unhealthy, even...

Luke's silent shrug to her comment stopped her mental concession.

"You think he knew that it was a setup?" she asked next.

"That'd be key, right? If he knows that his tracker is no longer of use to him, he'll change his method of operation..."

Luke glanced at her, almost as though he was seeing her but not. "Right," he said. Then took the phone with him as he put a few feet of distance between them.

Next thing she knew, he was speaking. To the phone. Recording.

Which was his right. He was paying for their detail...

And then, after agreeing with the teams continued attention to his identify thief's financial and phone trail—a phone that had been off since before the fire that had almost killed him—he said, "I need you to make a plan to get me up out of here without compromising the shelter's existence."

Her mouth fell open as, heart pounding, she stared at his back. Him? Not them?

"The one thing we know for sure, the guy wants me. Leaves us two choices. We can wait around for your teams to follow leads until you figure out who he is, then find him, then actually get him in custody—or, just as you were doing with the tracker, you use me as bait."

Her hissed intake of air was completely involuntary.

As was her heart's instant rejection of Luke's words.

Frozen, she listened as he continued. "It's been more than two days. I'm done letting others fight this battle for me. I'm making choice two. I'm coming out as bait. If you all want to quit me, that's your choice, but I'm coming up. I'm going to face off with this guy and get this done. I'd have a better chance of living through the experience with all of your professional assistance and connections, and am making a formal request that you stay on, while understanding completely if you determine you can't do so. I'm asking, either way, that whatever it costs, this shelter remain available to Shelby, as it's been proven safe, and that your teams continue to protect her and the boy and his grandmother in Tucson until this is done."

"No!" she cried out, every part of her aching. But he'd already turned off Record and was climbing the ladder to deliver his missive.

She couldn't believe it.

Being in the ground alone—she'd lose her mind.

Or not... she silently admitted, looking at the television set. To end this thing, to get home to Carter, to know that her son no longer needed a bodyguard—she'd sit in a much worse hole alone. For however long it took.

But... "Luke, you can't do this. No one knows who this guy is. He's already almost killed you. It's a suicide mission."

And...she cared. She heard it in her voice. Figured he did, too, when he turned to give her a long look. But all he said was, "I have to do this."

Oh, God. Please, no.

Was he doing this because of her? Because he knew, as she did, that the two of them trapped in a hole—albeit a luxurious one—was soon going to be untenable for both of them?

Or because her refusal to believe he wasn't lying had shown him the hopelessness of wanting a life where they got along and co-parented their son?

Did he figure out that she'd fight him in court and—given his rejection of his son from the outset, his lying since— likely win?

"This is who I am, Shelby," he said, standing almost directly in front of her. He held her gaze, no apology apparent, and went on, "We knew, going in, that there'd come a time when I had to take a risk that would be hard for you to accept..."

We. And *going in.*

Like they were still under the old regime.

Which…they were. Just because she couldn't sleep with him, or think about marrying him someday, they were still the two people who'd felt a connection and made a son who needed both of them.

Because, while she'd been beyond upset the night before, she knew that no court in the land was going to keep Luke Dennison from seeing his son. Most particularly not just because he'd lied to his kid's mother. Or had looked the boy up while keeping his distance. If he'd approached Carter, as opposed to just helping him save the cat the boy had inadvertently let out…

"I'm not going to try to keep you from seeing your son," she said, as though there was still hope that she'd be able to change his mind.

"I know." He was packing up his things, putting the meager pile back into the single plastic shopping bag that had been waiting in the shelter with his name on it.

Right next to the matching one bearing her name.

"And I'm not going to let either of you down," he said, but he turned his back before he'd finished the sentence.

He'd already let them both down. First with his rejection when she'd first been pregnant, and then by looking Carter up, hanging around outside Carter's day care and not contacting her.

That didn't mean she wanted him dead.

Or even out of her life. He just couldn't be the other half of her heart…

He'd moved to the couch. Put on a movie. A comedy they'd talked about watching together. Frustrating her. Scaring her.

But giving her a sense of closure, too. As he'd said, they'd reached their impasse. The one that might have broken them apart had they really tried to make a go of things when they'd gotten back to real life.

She should be thankful they'd fast-tracked to that point before Carter had gotten involved, she resolved as she made oatmeal and toast; peeled another orange; and served his up to him on the couch, while taking hers to the table.

She could see the television from there, too.

And heard loud and clear when a clang, bigger than any they'd had before, sounded in the cage at the top of the shelter.

Sierra's Web had sent a map of a tunnel system, through a hatch under the couch. And a wet suit. Luke was to follow the map and end up in the lake, not far from shore, half a mile down the beach. He'd stay in his wet suit, walk up the beach to public parking and get in a Jeep that would be waiting for him. He'd then be transported to another location, where Sierra's Web team members would go over a plan to use him to lure out his would-be killer.

The whole thing made her sick to her stomach.

Sent panic racing through every vein in her body.

"Luke…"

He didn't so much as glance her way as he immediately stripped down, dressed in the suit he'd been brought, shoved aside the couch, studied the map for a good minute and then, leaving it on the table, pulled open the hatch.

He was just going to go. Without…

"Luke!" She couldn't keep the despair out of her voice.

He glanced at her then, but he wasn't backing down.

"You let us down if you don't stay alive," she said, and watched through tear-filled eyes as he disappeared from sight.

Chapter Twenty-Four

He had his mandate.

Stay alive.

Sitting at a table inside the mansion, Luke focused but couldn't buy into anything he was hearing. The plans were television quality, with all kinds of people putting their lives on the line to protect him, and that wasn't him.

Even sitting in that room with them all, he felt responsible for every single life around the table. Because being close to him put them in danger.

As much so as if he had some deadly and contagious disease.

Hudson talked. Bruce did as well. Winchester was there and half a dozen men and women he'd never met. Everyone throwing out ideas about how to draw out his stalker, where to do it, when to do it and how best to protect Luke as they did it. Suggestions flew, were bandied about by some while others moved on to explore different ideas.

And all Luke could think about was Shelby in the shelter, alone. Wanting to be out on the beach with Lorraine and the others, making certain that the area around the shelter wasn't breached. The guards never got too close. Never blatantly even looked in the shelter's direction. They weren't giving up the location.

If it were him out there, trying to find something no one wanted found, he'd pay attention to an area that no one accessed. To all the areas they left unwalked.

After an hour passed and midmorning approached, he was about ready to go walk the beach himself. To just work off some steam and let the fiend take a shot at him.

He had no death wish.

To the contrary—his mandate was to stay alive, and so he would.

But clearly, this guy was an outdoorsman. His knowledge of drones, his ability to escape infrared—to escape, period. Everyone had agreed the guy's knowledge of safety in the wilderness surpassed many. That certainty had already been discussed. Leading some members of the team to go diving back into anyone with firefighting experience, current or past, who'd crossed lines with Luke in a negative way. Hotshots were particularly well trained in all things outdoor survival.

Including knowing how to use fabric-wrapped foil to avoid infrared detection. Because you also used the method to protect against some radiation exposure…

Setting up a dummy of him in a boat was discussed. Perhaps the attacker would be exposed trying to take out the boat. Mentally vetoing that idea, Luke came back to the infrared disappearance the night before.

If he'd known he was being watched but had been certain his target had been in the cabin he'd been sighting, he'd have used the protection to get closer. Keeping himself undercover to avoid drones. It had been dark. Some kind of umbrella, maybe…

Hell, scooting on his belly could have worked, considering they'd been dealing with northern Arizona landscaping. Trees, brush, grass…

Getting to his subject would have been a challenge but a relatively easy one...

So why hadn't the guy attacked the cabin?

Because the infrared guy hadn't been their killer. Or he'd figured out somehow that Luke wasn't in that cabin, that Luke had been separated from his tracker.

Put that together with the fact that guards were still around the house, the beach...

One could surmise that perhaps the home's owners had hired security for their own protection after the break-in two nights before.

But more likely...

He'd heard a small plane flying overhead when he walked out of the lake earlier that morning. It had been so low that he glanced up to see it pulling a bannered advertising message for beachgoers.

But that early...who'd pay for advertising outside of prime beach times?

"Planes," he said. "Has anyone been watching for planes in the area?"

"Of course. Helicopters, too." Hudson stopped in the middle of a conversation to answer him. "It's a lake. There are a couple of companies up the beach that offer aerial-view excursions. And I can assure you that nothing and no one has dropped from one anywhere near here..."

He wasn't worried about what came down—more like, what could have been captured from above.

He had to get back to the shelter.

He was doing nothing but sitting in a chair, and there was a remote possibility his stalker, if he was anywhere nearly as trained as Luke was, could know the shelter's location.

He had no proof. And without full memory, he wasn't

even sure he trusted what he knew at the moment. Not enough to stop the team of experts from doing their jobs.

They could message him when they came up with their plan.

Shelby had been alone for hours...

He had to get back to her.

The fact that the guy hadn't hit the cabin last night, just in case, wasn't sitting right with him.

After excusing himself from the table, he pulled Hudson aside, telling the team leader that someone trained in outdoor safety would likely be fully versed on satellite technology and ground-penetrating radar. A plane flying over, with the proper equipment inside and in just the right spot, could find the shelter's location.

"Even if he knows it's there," Hudson pointed out, "he doesn't know where or how to access it, and I can guarantee you that any one of our people out there on the beach will see someone—anyone—out on this property."

He didn't doubt Hudson's words. "I still need to get back down there," he said. "The guy wants me. Shelby's just an aside to him, at best. I realize the shelter's proven to be safe, and I want her where I know that she's safest, but she's not trained to... I need to be down there with her."

He sounded paranoid even to himself. But he was paying the bills.

"I get it, Luke," Hudson said then, dropping his voice even lower. "You just found out she had your son..."

He tensed. He wasn't paying anyone to get into that personal hell. But before he could speak without biting the guy's head off, Hudson continued. "I've been there, actually. A thirteen-year-old girl had been kidnapped. I didn't know she was my daughter until I'd been called to the case..."

Luke felt his eyes widen. For a second there, he thought

he was hallucinating. Did everyone have hidden nuances? Stuff going on no one else knew about?

Had Hudson's daughter been found? Safe?

Before he could ask, Bruce walked up, checking to see what was up, and Hudson explained as though Luke's desire to return to the shelter was all they'd been talking about, saying that he agreed with Luke's decision to go. The team leader assured him that they'd get a message down to Luke as soon as the team had signed off on a viable plan, and Luke hurried off beside his bodyguard.

Feeling like a lovesick fool.

And going anyway.

WHAT HAD HE DONE, really? He'd sent her away when she'd told him she was pregnant. He'd later looked her up, found out where her son went to day care and showed up there but hadn't sought Carter out. And he'd lied to Shelby about remembering both of those things.

Sending her away as he had had been hideous. She could kind of see why he'd wanted a glimpse of his son before he started the battle to be able to see him.

How long would it have been before she had legal communication from Luke if he hadn't been injured in the fire and lost his memory?

A day?

A month?

If he'd remembered her as soon as he'd seen her, would he have told her the truth from the beginning?

And…what if he *was* telling her the truth? What if he'd been so emotionally conflicted by losing his son—enough so that he'd had to find him and get a look for himself—that he really had suppressed the memory?

She'd told him she didn't believe him, leaving him no

choice but to move on. Because how would he ever be able to prove it to her?

Pacing the small shelter—television to toilet, again and again—she tried to think about other things. Recorded a message for her son, telling him all the things she loved about him, talking about his strengths and how happy she was being his mom.

She told herself the video was just to occupy her brain and keep her focused on things that would help her maintain her emotional strength.

In the back of her mind, she wondered if her fear for Luke was making her afraid for herself, too. If maybe the video was in case she didn't make it back to Carter.

Right after Luke had left, she'd finished watching the comedy he'd started during breakfast. Sitting on the couch, which was still askew. She hadn't wanted to cover the hatch in case Luke wanted to get back to her.

Video done, she left the phone on the counter, made a peanut butter sandwich and, after cleaning up the kitchen, had carried it over to the angled couch to eat.

Stupid of her to think Luke would be back.

About as ridiculous as making a final video for her son...

She'd been down in the ground too long. Was losing touch with reality.

She'd only been there two nights.

Wouldn't find a safer place to spend the night alone.

She'd only been apart from her son for three nights. It seemed like a lifetime.

Which was about as long as it seemed like since Luke had left. What was happening? The not knowing was...

What if she'd sent him out to die without telling him that she loved him?

Because of course she did, even if she didn't completely trust him. Didn't dare have him be her love.

Her lips fell open as she heard a noise at the top of the ladder, peanut butter and bread sticking to the roof of her mouth. It wasn't the cage.

The sound was louder.

A latch moved and…

The door in the ceiling at the top of the ladder was opening!

Please, God, let Luke come through it first.

Let her have conjured him back to her.

It was probably Lorraine.

She stood, swallowing her lump of soggy bread and peanut butter, tears in her eyes. *Please let Luke at least be alive…*

Legs descended, hairy. Just like Luke's…

The hem of beige shorts… He'd left in beige shorts. Holding her breath, she waited for the hem of his black shirt to appear and nearly cried out loud when it did.

Others would be waiting at the top. She knew that. It was over. They were free!

But oh, God, to have a minute with him first. To celebrate his living with the hug she'd wanted to give him when he left.

To hear him say it was over.

To tell him how sorry she was for turning her back on him.

Arms raised, ready to run to him, she got rubbery knees when she saw his face. Those blue eyes—they were intense but didn't meet her gaze.

She'd hoped, with him coming for her, that her harsh words would be forgiven. That he'd give her a chance to apologize, be open for conversation about a future for them…

"Luke?" She'd beg if she had to.

He glanced at her, as a stranger would when taking in another person, and her heart broke a little. Not just because of what she'd said, how she'd reacted to Carter knowing him already, but because of who he was.

The man who retreated.

Pulling her arms down to wrap around herself, taking back the hug she'd been about to throw at him, she watched as he quickly moved through the space, taking a long second to eye the hatch through which he'd left. His chin clenched, as though the sight didn't please him.

Because she hadn't put the couch back?

"Luke?" she asked again. "Is it over?"

He nodded. "Yeah, it's over," he said, sounding…determined more than elated. Like he was in the middle of getting the job done.

Yeah, she'd been upset, but she didn't deserve to be treated as though they were nothing to each other. If nothing else, they'd survived two days in an underground hole together.

They'd made love.

Multiple times.

Didn't that at least deserve a fond farewell?

And what about Carter? Wasn't he eager to go meet his son?

All he gave her was his back as he strode swiftly to the far end of the space, checking the back partition and then, coming back, going in the other two partitions as well. She made it over to the one closest to the couch—the bed they'd shared—in time to see him looking under it.

For what?

He was scaring her.

"Luke? Is there a tracker or something in here?"

When he didn't respond, she glanced toward the wooden ladder rungs, back at him and made her choice.

He'd do what he had to do, and if he came back to her, she'd…

At the ladder, her hands on the ropes running along both sides of the rungs, she started up. She needed to get back to her real life. To Carter.

She took the first step, still glancing toward the partition where she'd left Luke. As though giving him one last hope. And then, as she started for the second, she glanced up, ready for daylight.

Needing daylight.

There was no daylight.

The door was as closed as it had been the whole time they'd been down there. As though… She glanced at the inside latch, saw it clicked. Heart pounding, spines of fear poking her arms and legs, she lifted her leg higher—two steps' worth—and jerked when a death grip took hold of her hips.

He yanked her down so hard, so fast, her shoulders were nearly pulled from their sockets. Her hands stung with rope burn.

Luke wasn't a rough man.

He wasn't in his right mind.

Was he on something?

Or…dear God… Had his head injuries… Was he mentally ill?

He set her on the ground. Pushed her, hard, in the center of her back toward the couch. Caught her by her hair to stop her, and dragging her along with him, ripping some hair out by the roots, he used his free hand to slide the couch back over the escape hatch he'd gone down earlier.

What in the hell was going on?

"Luke, what happened?" she cried, her chin to her chest, face toward the floor due his grip on her hair.

He was beyond angry.

Letting go of her hair, he grabbed her throat. Scared out of her wits, she kneed him. Missed the groin she was going after and caught him in the stomach, just below his ribs. Winding him enough to get herself free.

Terrified, she didn't know what to do. There was nowhere to go... He'd haul her off the ladder before she could get the latch open...

Grabbing a kitchen knife, all she could think about was defending herself. For Carter.

Her son's face flashing in her brain, she blinked, could feel tears on her cheeks and sweat on her back.

If he came near her, she'd...

Staggering for a second, Luke approached, the look on his face menacing. Jeering.

He wanted her dead. She saw it on his face.

Horrified, she could hardly think...just knew she had to...

His shorts... Staring, she saw the stitching on the pockets of his shorts as he slowly came toward her.

There were no X's. *X marks the spot*, she remembered. From that morning.

And the hand raised toward her... A scar...on the forearm...

"Come any closer, and you're dead." She felt the words leave her throat, didn't recognize the voice as her own. And didn't doubt that she'd use the knife, either.

Grabbing a second one, she jabbed them both toward the figure that had stopped advancing for a second. He might win, whoever he was, but she wasn't going down without using up every ounce of fight in her.

"You aren't Luke."

He stood there, his gaze calmer, assessing…and still, not Luke.

"I will be," the man said, and the jeering look that came over his face…

She knew it.

Had seen it before.

In Payson. Outside Luke's house.

The day she'd gone to tell him she was pregnant.

Confused, disoriented, she faced the man.

Multiple personalities?

The shorts. No X's.

"Where is my dear brother?" the man asked then, as though he was suddenly, in the midst of evil, stopping to enjoy himself.

He wanted Luke. As soon as she gave him any information she had, she'd be of no use to him.

And he… Dear God, Carter!

He knew.

It had been him outside of her son's school. It had to have been.

Eyes hard with the intent to kill the man in her path, she calmed. Knowing what Luke would do. "Your brother?" she asked.

"Our darling mother… She had identical twins. Threw one away and kept the other for herself." The easy tone got lost in the sneer on his face. The content of his words.

Luke had an identical twin.

Who hated him.

For what Luke had and whoever he was had not.

"What's your name?"

She didn't want to know. Just had a sense that she had to keep him talking. As long as he stood there spitting words at her, taking heinous pleasure from their standoff, she was alive.

With time to figure out how she could knife the man before he used his greater height and far superior strength to overpower her and get the weapons out of her hands.

They'd land in her, she knew that.

"Larry," he told her. "Not by birth, of course. I grew up as Noah." The man took a step forward, as though to emphasize the name. As though it was all her fault.

Like she should have known...

"When did you become Larry?"

Keep him talking. Keep him talking. Keep him talking.

She didn't retreat. The counter was already at her back. It could help her. Steady her while she used her foot...

"Six years ago. When I got the DNA test back and found out that while I grew up in a system that didn't give a damn about me, my *identical* brother had known nothing but privilege."

Some of his spittle dropped to the floor. Shelby swallowed back bile.

"Well, now it's my turn." Larry stepped forward, his lip curled with hate.

"Wait!" she called out, completely out of thoughts. "It was you, wasn't it? Who slammed the door in my face."

"Hell yes, it was me! You think I was going to let some whore and her kid take away what was mine?"

If she died, she'd do so knowing that her son's father was a decent man. The best.

And that she'd loved him rightly.

"And that's why you need me dead," she said, seeing the writing on the wall. She wasn't getting out of there alive.

Did the man realize that Sierra's Web now knew that Luke was Carter's father?

"That's why I'm not going to fail this time."

Larry's hand came out so swiftly she almost lost her life. She slashed his hand instead. He growled, bunched his shoulders, bowed his head and came toward her.

Both knives ready, she braced for the onslaught. And heard a loud splintering sound coming from just beyond Larry.

The fiend paused, turned, and Luke came flying. Both feet off the ground, he landed on Larry, tackling him to the ground, pinning him down with a knee between his shoulders, just below the base of his neck.

Shelby stared in shock, unable to comprehend what had just happened.

Larry's expletives filled the room. He bucked, his arms swinging as far behind him as they could; he grabbed Luke's arm, twisted.

She held her knives ready. To use them, hand them over— and when Larry grunted, twisting Luke's arm again, she lunged forward.

The knife didn't penetrate. She wasn't that good. But the graze was enough for Larry's grip to loosen for the second it took Luke to free himself and grab the arm. Twisting it up Larry's back, close to Luke's knee.

She jumped when sounds came from behind Luke, but he didn't seem to budge. She stared, afraid of what else was coming, and then saw Bruce jump down from the ceiling entrance, forgoing the ladder altogether, followed by Lorraine.

Activities swirled around her. While Lorraine held a gun pointed at Larry's temple, Bruce used a belt to secure the man's arms behind him. Luke grabbed rope from a drawer in the living room and secured the man's—his brother's— feet.

Did he know? Had they all figured it out?

She had no idea what might have happened, if she and Luke would have killed his brother together, or if, God forbid, they'd have died together.

She was just glad it was over.

Chapter Twenty-Five

Luke had never killed a man. But if Bruce and Lorraine had been any later, he would have done so. He was still burning, adrenaline pouring through him, to make the bastard pay for having hurt Shelby, for what the man would surely have done if Luke hadn't gotten there in time, as he jerked the last knot tight on his would-be killer's feet.

Breathing hard, not ready to be done making the guy suffer, he sat back, hard, on the guy's tennis shoes, cramming the man's ankles toward the ground, hearing the new rash of expletives, and stood up.

As badly as he wanted the guy dead, he needed him alive long enough to get some answers. Like…what had Luke ever done to him?

And how had he breached Sierra's Web security to get to the shelter's entrance?

If Luke hadn't been in the tunnel… If he hadn't heard…

That's why you need me dead.

That's why I'm not going to fail this time.

Words he was never, ever going to forget. He'd practically come out of his skin finding the hatch closed, had probably broken a hand getting it open with the couch on top of it.

He couldn't even feel the pain.

The prisoner was swishing his body back and forth like a fish, trying to get up.

"Stay down," Bruce ordered. "The police are on their way."

The man's body went limp for a moment, but then he lifted his head, got his weight on one shoulder and turned to look right at Luke.

What the hell? Luke staggered back a step.

The man had had surgery to make himself look like... It was a mask. Had to be a mask...

Or Luke had just lost the last hold he had on his sanity.

The thief hadn't just stolen his identity. His money. He'd also stolen his looks?

"That's how he got past the guard in the yard," Bruce said. "They knew you'd come up and thought you were getting some fresh air..."

"Good to see you again, too, brother," the man said, his lips curled in a way that made Luke want to punch him in the face.

"'Brother?'" he hollered, his voice echoing off the walls in the small space. So much so that Shelby jumped, hitting her back on the edge of the counter.

Shelby.

He hadn't let himself fully look at her yet. Not while the man who'd wanted her dead was still within his reach.

Just enough to know she was fully dressed. And standing guard like a banshee...

"Yeah, *brother*," the man on the floor said. And then spit in his direction.

He would have stomped the guy's face at the lie, at the insult, except that Shelby had moved, was standing next to him.

As though she'd known what he was about to do and was there to save him from himself. She didn't touch him.

Just stood there.

He wanted to tell her how great she was. How proud he was to know her.

And that he didn't need saving.

While he hadn't been able to hear what she'd been saying until he'd reached the hatch, he'd heard her voice as he'd slithered his way through the tunnel, knew she was in trouble and had radioed his bodyguard to get to the shelter just before he'd heard the fiend tell Shelby he wasn't going to fail. That's when he'd plowed through the hatch.

If she hadn't stood up to the intruder…

The man on the floor continued to taunt him. "What, Lukey boy, you speechless now?" He didn't get it.

Reached down to pull the man's mask off.

If he was doing this, it was happening man to man.

He didn't get any further than a hand to the prisoner's throat, ready to push down into his shirt to find the edge of the mask, before Shelby screamed and Bruce grabbed Luke by the arm, pulling him back.

"Get the damned mask off!" he shouted. To the world in general. Then said, "I'm not talking to this…this…"

"There's no mask," Bruce told him.

Of course there was a mask. No amount of plastic surgery was that good.

"He's your brother, man," Bruce said, still holding on to him.

Shelby was there again, threading her arm through his free one, as he faltered back.

What he noticed was that she wasn't exclaiming any shock.

What the hell?

He had a…

Something else he'd forgotten?

Would his mind ever return his life to him?

For a second there, he flashed back to being in the tunnel. First hearing Shelby's voice and then a male one in response. He saw himself, lying there on his belly, crawling like a snake. Saw his life pass before his eyes as he filled with rage, and didn't like the image that stayed. Him—a man who lived to make his parents proud but not to ever… *ever* let himself care enough individually to hurt like he did when his mother had died.

He'd known in that moment in the tunnel, as he radioed Bruce, that it was too late for him. He'd already fallen in love. With a woman who hated him.

Didn't get much more painful than that.

Until he'd considered that woman's life being snuffed out of her.

His parents… "No way this man's my brother," he said as his vision cleared and he stood up straight.

Bruce dropped his arm but stayed close.

Shelby hung on. He didn't let himself pay attention to her arm in his. But didn't move away yet, either.

"Actually, he is," Lorraine, standing guard at the prisoner's bound feet, spoke up. "Just before you radioed up to get to the shelter, the team had heard from Dorian, one of the Sierra's Web partners. She's a doctor, and they'd run DNA on you and your father once his death had been determined to be connected to see if anything popped…turning over every rock…"

He heard the calm tone. Heard the words.

Shook his head.

"The person who was killed in that car crash wasn't your biological father, man," Bruce said.

Luke. His name was Luke.

Not *man*.

And…

He stared down at the prisoner, who was still staring up at him.

Like he was looking in a mirror.

Except not.

The eyes.

They weren't his…didn't have the same…

"What…" he started but couldn't come up with a question that would give him an answer he wanted.

"Your mother had identical twins. She kept you," Shelby said, her voice soft.

His mother had kept him. But not…not…whoever this was.

"He named himself Larry," Lorraine said. "Six years ago. He was raised as Noah Fisher."

"And my father?" He looked only at Lorraine. The calm voice in a storm that didn't end.

"Died in jail fifteen years ago," Noah-Larry said. "Yeah, you think you're so pure and privileged, but you come from the same dirt as me."

His mother was not dirt.

And his father—the man whom he'd thought was his father, his adopted father—had raised him, not with privilege but with a sense of honor. With the knowledge that he had to work his hardest every single day to be worthy of the life he'd been given.

Just as his dad—not his biological father, his *dad*—had done.

And just as Luke would teach his son.

Somehow.

LORRAINE TOOK SHELBY upstairs when the police arrived. Hudson Warner met her on the surface, and because he strongly advised that she be seen by a paramedic, in spite of her assertion that she was fine, she went along with Lorraine to a waiting ambulance.

Sitting on a stretcher inside the open vehicle, she saw a handcuffed Larry being led across the yard toward a bevy of vehicles parked in the circular drive in front of the mansion. And a few minutes later, she saw Luke and Hudson, head-to-head, as they disappeared out of sight.

Probably getting him medical attention as well.

Just in case.

It was over.

They'd both survived.

She could hardly believe it.

And yet she'd never let herself believe anything but that they'd make it back to Carter.

They.

She and Luke had to talk.

Now that the danger was gone, their future had arrived.

Minus any lies between them.

Luke Dennison had been the man her heart had known him to be from the very beginning. She could hardly believe it.

Was still wrapping her mind around the ramifications of all that Larry had put in motion.

Most particularly, the losses Luke had suffered for a choice made when he'd been a newborn baby.

As though Luke's mother keeping him had been his fault.

Why she hadn't kept both boys, they'd probably never know. Just as it was unlikely they'd ever know if Luke's adopted father had known he had a twin. Lorraine had told her that Luke's birth certificate listed his adopted father as his father.

Noah Fisher's had said *father unknown*.

Shelby's vitals were checked over the course of an hour, and her hands were treated with salve and wrapped lightly with gauze.

She hadn't seen Luke.

And just assumed that he'd appear at some point. But when Lorraine told her that she was ready to take Shelby back to Phoenix, she couldn't very well refuse to get in the car.

Luke was paying for the service, not her.

Lorraine handed her phone to her as they got in the car, and, telling herself that Luke would call, she held on to the device long after she'd hung up from a lengthy video call with her mom and Carter. Sylvia was bringing Carter home so that they'd be there when Shelby arrived.

And in spite of a heart full of tears where Luke was concerned, she was overjoyed when she climbed out of Lorraine's car just before dusk that night and saw her little guy's lit-up face as he raced toward her.

Sylvia had dinner made—Carter's favorite, macaroni and cheese—but left before they sat down to eat, saying she wanted to get back to Tucson before night set in.

And two hours later, freshly showered and in an old, short denim skirt and T-shirt, Shelby was sitting in the full dark, alone.

She'd put Carter to bed. At his request, she'd lain with him, cuddled up to his little body, until he was sound asleep.

And then, out on her own couch—in her own living room—she just sat. She wanted to call Luke.

But knew she wouldn't.

She hadn't trusted that he really didn't remember the things he'd done. Understandable, since she'd seen him, and he'd remembered pretty much everything else about his life. But still, she'd done to him what she'd accused him of doing to her.

She'd turned her back on him.

And, sitting there in the dark, she finally admitted to herself that Luke hadn't been the only one shying away from a relationship that first time they were together.

The strength of her feelings for him, the speed with which it had all happened… She'd been scared to death she'd end up like her mother.

In love with a man she didn't know well enough.

A man who, in the long run, wouldn't fit her.

Eventually, knowing she had to pick up the reins of her life, with or without Luke contacting her, she went to the kitchen for a bottle of beer.

Uncapped it. Sipped.

And felt her phone vibrate against her butt.

She had it out of her pocket in a split second, staring at the screen, and almost dropped it when she saw the newly programmed number on her screen. Lorraine had given it to her. Just in case, she'd said. Shelby had been hoping she'd done so at Luke's request.

"Hey," she said softly. Not because their son was asleep, but because…she was filled with soft places for him.

"You got a minute to talk?"

"Of course."

"In person?"

"I can't leave, Luke. Carter's in bed asleep…"

"I'm at your front door."

That's when she dropped her phone.

LUKE KEPT HIS right arm behind his back when Shelby opened the door. He held her tight, though, with his left arm as she flung herself at him, hugging him so close he was fine to just meld right in forever.

And then she let go.

As he'd known she would.

"Come in," she said, turning around as though embarrassed, and led him through a spotless, spacious entryway past a living room and into a family room and kitchen that ran the entire length of the house. Where she flipped on a light.

And he about wept at the sight of her. All gorgeous thigh and leg under denim, topped by a short white thing that was pretty much see-through. Enough so that he knew she wasn't wearing a bra.

Her hair—long, blond and silky-looking—teased against her nipples.

"You want a beer?" she asked, burying her head in the open refrigerator.

"Yeah." Thinking of the day—the week—he'd had. He'd take ten.

Or…just her.

Reappearing, she uncapped his beer and then, turning to hand it to him, saw his arm.

"A cast, Luke? What happened?" He'd break his hand all over again if it meant he got to hear that soft concern in her voice directed at him.

He shrugged. Saw a couch that looked comfortable. Made his way toward it.

"Luke?" She followed him, as he'd hoped she would. Wanted nothing more than to wrap his good arm around her, hold her close, love her slowly and then sleep for twenty-four hours.

But…he'd learned a thing or two. If you didn't communicate, others didn't know.

"I broke my hand breaking through the hatch in the floor." He brushed through that part quickly. Didn't want to spend any more time there.

Ever. He rushed on, "The hit man on the beach," he blurted out. Then, swallowing a long swig of needed sustenance, he paused.

Even her frown endeared her to him. "He's dead," she said.

Luke nodded. Then took a deep breath. He had a job to do, and his way was to get it done.

"Larry had approached him, told him he was me, asked him to kill the man staying at his house impersonating me. The guy had seen pictures of me. And owed me. He died thinking he was protecting me."

Shelby scooted closer to him. He wanted to lose himself in her.

Instead, he got lost in the things he had yet to say. Had to find the exact right words…

"I'm sorry, Luke, for not believing in you."

What? Glancing at her, frowning, he shook his head again. "You… Even when you had doubts, you were always open…" he started, and then the words rushed forward. "Don't you get it, Shelby? You reach out to me, pull me in, and I want to stay. I don't understand. I don't see how I be me and live that way, but… What I know now… I don't ever want to come home again if you and Carter aren't there waiting for me. Or…at least living there and coming home at some point, too."

He ran out of air. Out of words. She seemed to know. Ran the back of her hand against his cheek, and he took her by the wrists, turning both open palms to him.

They were raw and glistening with what he guessed was

more of the salve Lorraine had told him she'd been sent home with.

"I want to kill him for doing this to you."

"No," she said, putting her finger to his lips. "You're a lifesaver, Luke. And I don't have a complete picture of what our future looks like, either, but I know that I don't want to live anywhere but the place you call home."

"As soon as this cast comes off, I'm going to be back on duty." He had to be honest. Had to communicate.

And trust that it would be enough.

Better that than live like his twin had—a lifetime without love. His parents had taught him better than that.

"I fell in love with a hotshot firefighter once," she said. He assumed she was talking about him. Wasn't sure if she was telling him she'd try to do it again… "And I've loved him ever since," she finished.

She loved him.

Him. The guy who left home and stood up to wildfires.

"I do have a good bit of free time in the off-season I could spare," he told her. He'd always signed on with local fire departments, but nothing said he had to. And he grew completely serious. "We don't know how we're going to make this work, but…today…we kind of did, didn't we? You kept yourself alive. Safe. I knew you needed me, and I made it there. And you with your knives and me with my brute anger…we took danger down."

Her eyes filled with tears.

"I love you, Shelby." The words didn't choke him. Or scare him. Ironically, they freed him. "I…"

"Mom!" The young cry split the night, and Luke was up, heading straight for it without thought, down a hall, running into a small form that buried its head in his thighs, just above his knees, wrapping both arms around his legs.

"I'm right here, sweetie." Shelby stood beside Luke, her hand on his back and on Carter's, too.

Luke was man enough to admit he was glad she was right there. He might need her help.

"You have a bad dream?" she asked.

"No!" Carter glanced up. "I had to go pee, and I saw a spidaw!" The boy's wide-eyed look of horror turned to a frown of confusion. He'd already dropped his hands, had backed around toward his mother and was looking up at Luke. "You aren't my mom."

"No," he said. More words were there. He tried to get them out. Stood there staring at the most incredible creature he'd ever seen and had…no sound.

"He's your father, Carter." Shelby's words came softly as she kneeled down to the boy.

Carter didn't seem to react much. Luke felt poleaxed.

Afraid to fail.

And so in love he knew he could be hit over the head a thousand times and not forget either one of them.

"Huh?" Carter's nose scrunched after a few seconds, his brows almost together, as he stared up at Luke.

Taking his cue from Shelby, Luke kneeled and then said, "I didn't know about you, buddy, not until this week. I was gone, fighting wildfires a lot. But I'm here now."

"You saved the cat."

He couldn't lie to the boy. But there were some things a little guy just didn't need to know. "You need to remember always not to talk to strangers, right?" he said. Knowing that as evil as his twin was, he also had a decent bone in his body. He'd taught Carter a good lesson.

"You said you fish," Carter said next, holding on to his mom's arm as he faced Luke. Shelby had dropped to rest her butt on her calves, and Luke followed suit.

"I do. And I'm planning to teach you, too, if you want to learn."

"Okay."

The boy rubbed his eyes, and Luke remembered he'd been asleep. Standing, he reached out a hand to the boy. "How about if we go kill that spider and get you back to bed?"

He was amazing himself, as if he'd been around kids forever.

Pulling back his hand, Carter reached for Shelby's as she stood. "Mom and I will wait wight heah, huh, Mom?"

The glance Shelby sent Luke was filled with humor. And a message, too.

He'd just been given a chance to be his son's hero.

Without another word, he headed down the hall, looking for a child's room, but had to stop before he got there.

Once he became a hero, he wasn't turning back, not even for a night. "Just one question," he said, spinning around, surprised to find Shelby and Carter only a couple of steps behind him.

"What?" they said in unison.

He stood there, forgetting what he'd been about to say as he got lost in the view. The woman who took his breath, the little guy who had eyes the same color blue as his own—eyes that were looking up at him expectantly.

Eyes he would fight every day to live up to.

"Will the two of you marry me?"

He heard the words. Started to die a thousand deaths. Would he *ever* learn finesse?

"I will," Carter, said. "S'long as you take me fishing. How 'bout you, Mom?"

Carter glanced at Shelby, as did Luke. Her eyes brimming with tears, she was smiling, too.

"Yes." She said it calmly.

"Oh, and…" Carter piped in and, slightly lost in euphoria, Luke glanced at the boy. "You have to sleep in Mom's woom, not mine. Her bed's biggaw."

Luke could hardly contain himself as he looked at Shelby. "How about it, *Mom*?"

"Yes," she said again. And then, with more tears, she threw her arms around Luke's neck and whispered, "Oh, yes," right by his ear.

He held on tight.

With no idea how he was going to keep her happy but knowing he'd do better every single day they were together.

"Hey, guys, what about the spidaw?" Carter was tugging at Luke's shirt, and when he looked down, he saw the little guy had a hold of his mother's skirt, too.

And that's when he knew.

With or without all the answers, or the right words, they'd just become a family.

* * * * *

COMING SOON!

We really hope you enjoyed reading this book. If you're looking for more romance be sure to head to the shops when new books are available on

Thursday 14th September